RED
ULTRA
MARINE

Manuele Fior

FANTAGRAPHICS BOOKS

FOR ALFEO FIOR

TWO SOULS, ALAS, EXIST IN MY BREAST,
ONE SEPARATED FROM ANOTHER:
ONE, WITH ITS CRUDE LOVE OF LIFE, JUST
CLINGS TO THE WORLD, TENACIOUSLY, GRIPS TIGHT,
THE OTHER SOARS POWERFULLY ABOVE THE DUST,
INTO THE FAR ANCESTRAL HEIGHT.

J.W. GOETHE, FAUST (1112-1117)
TRANS. A.S. KLINE

1.

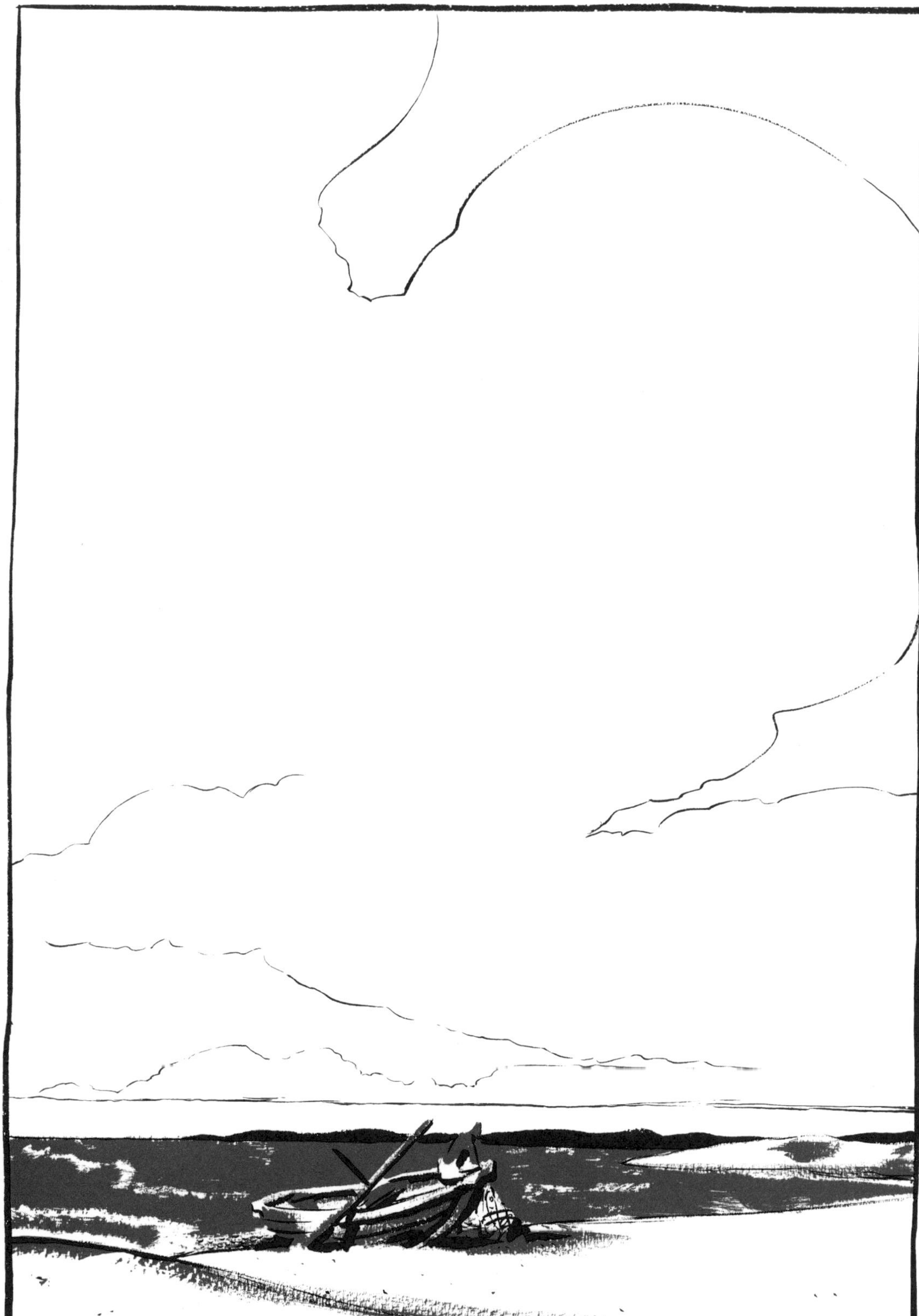

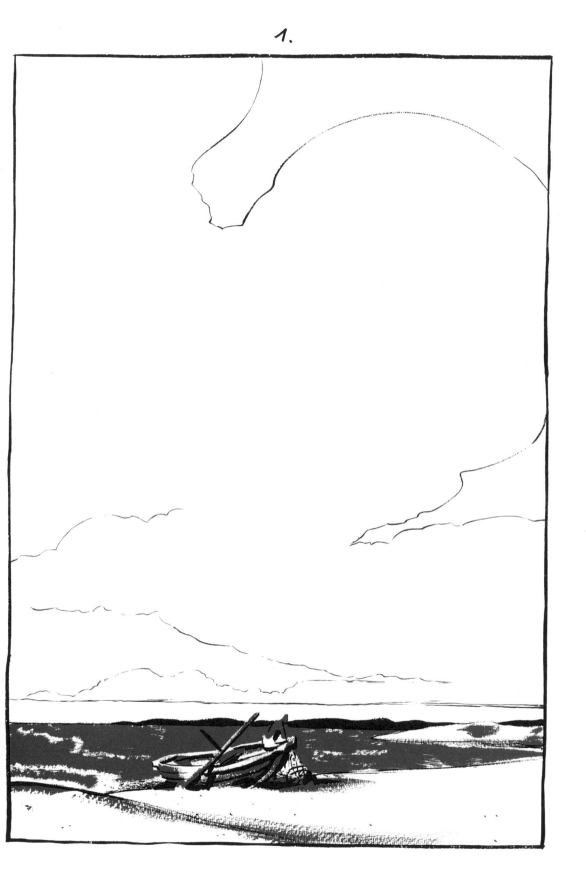

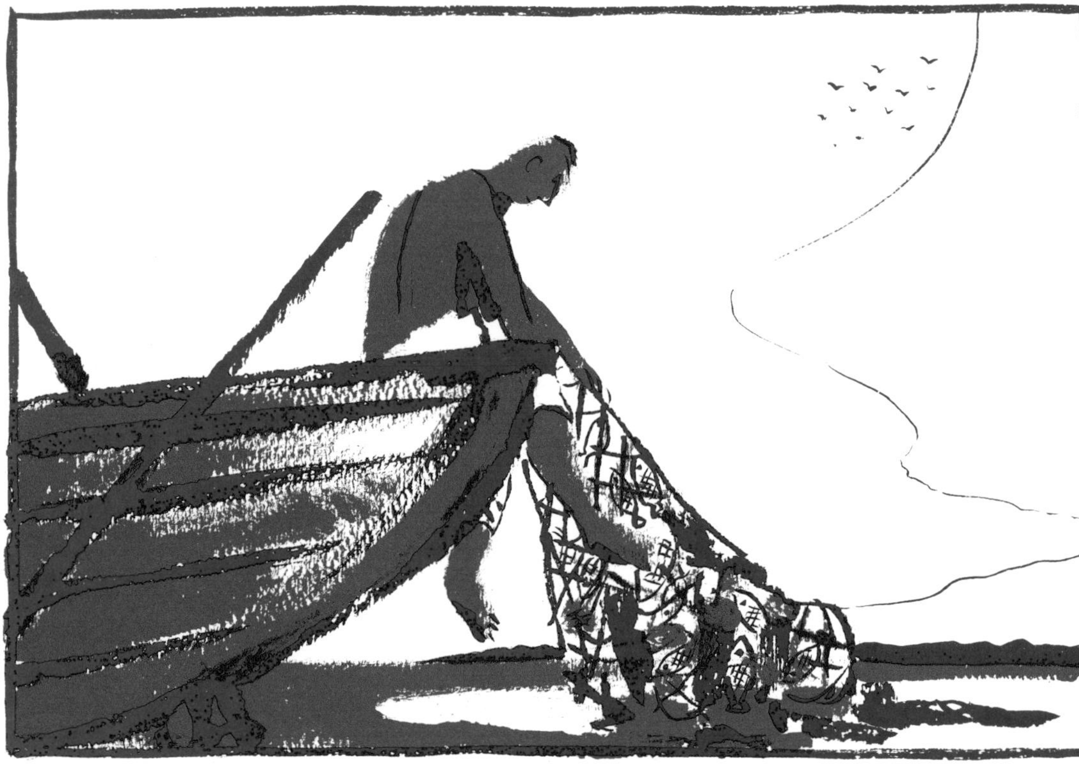

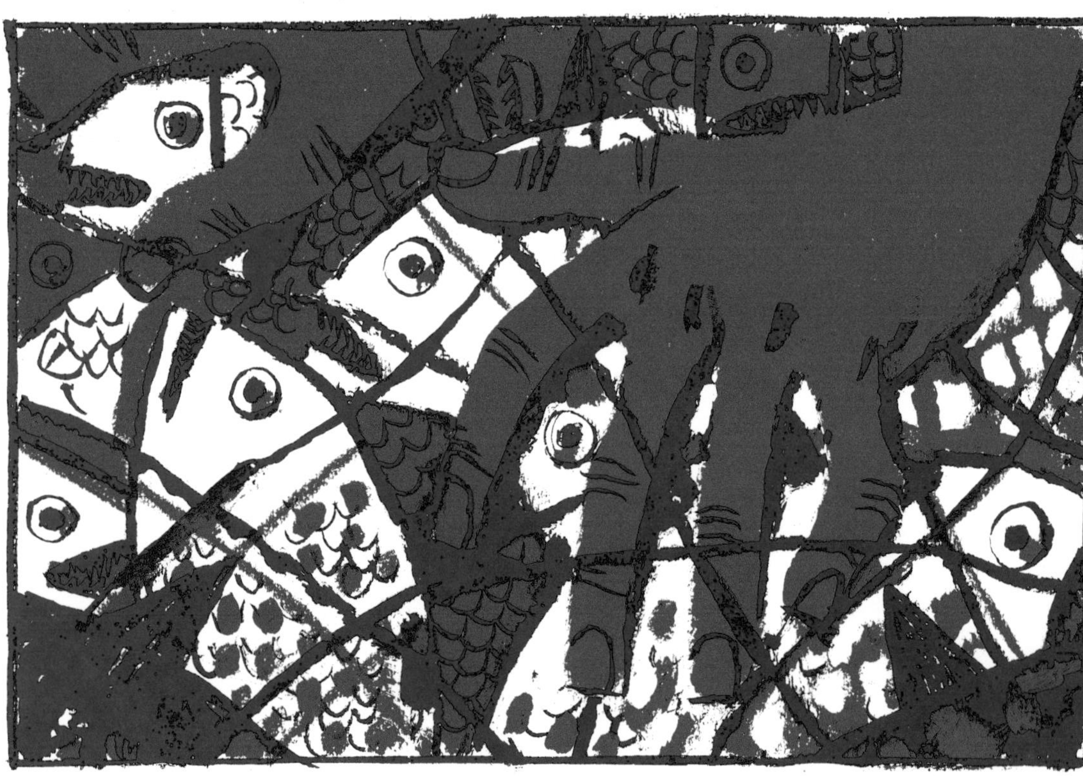

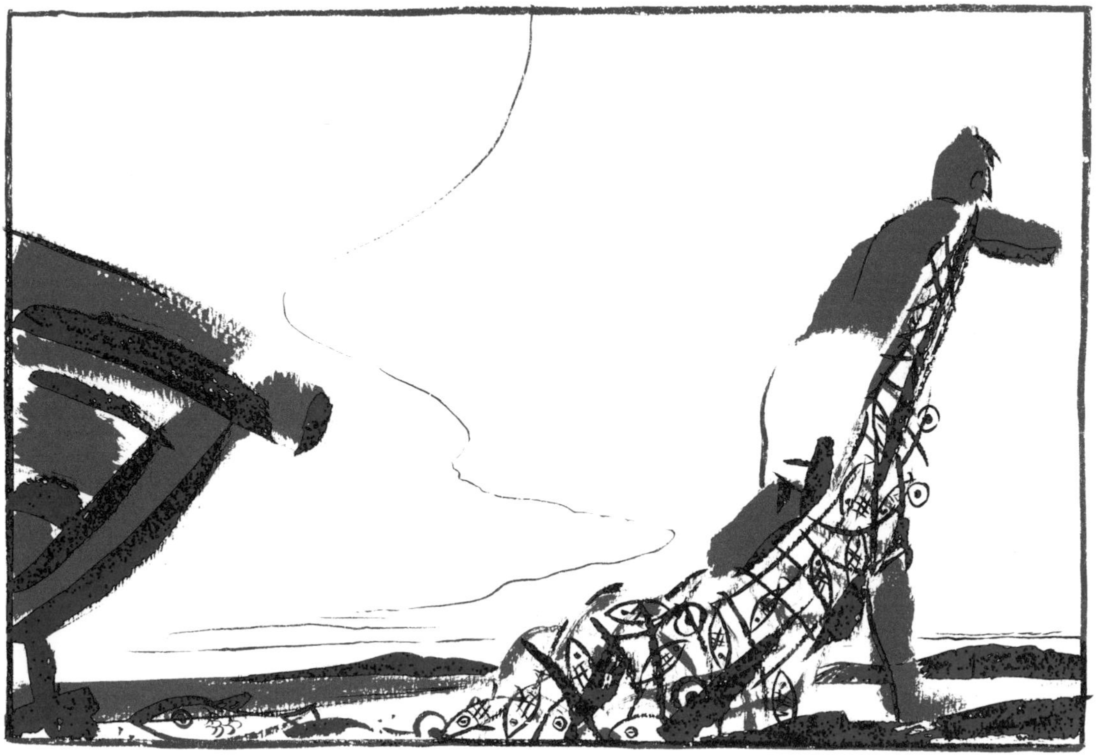

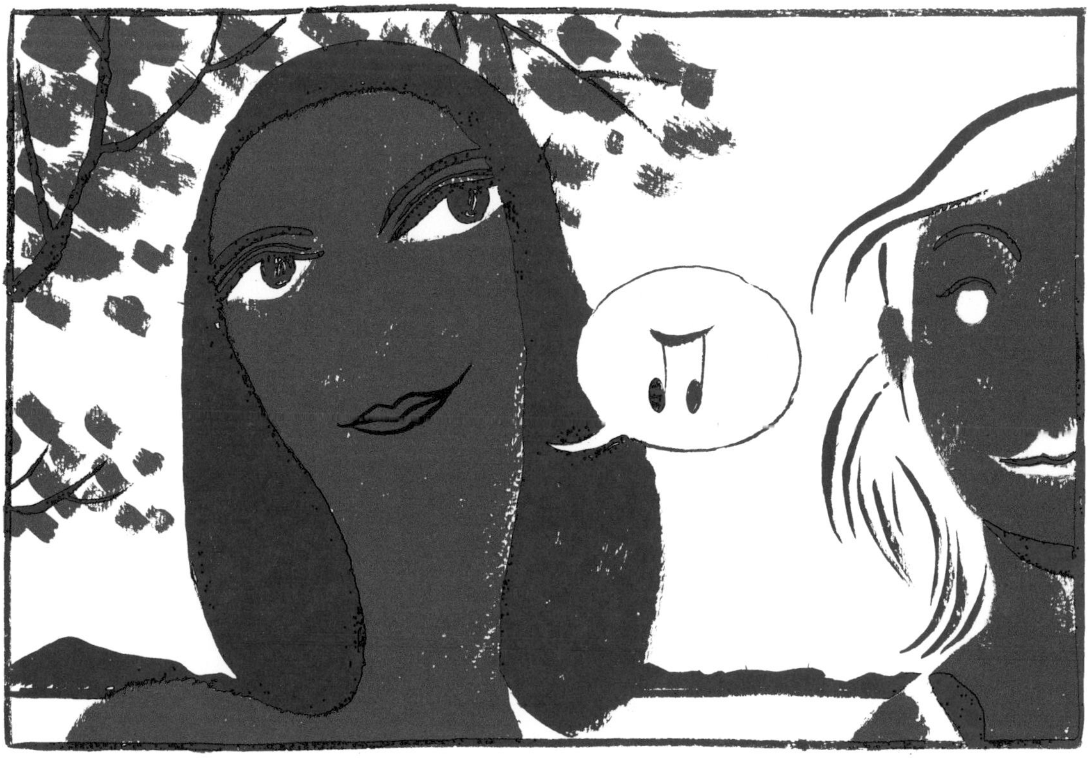

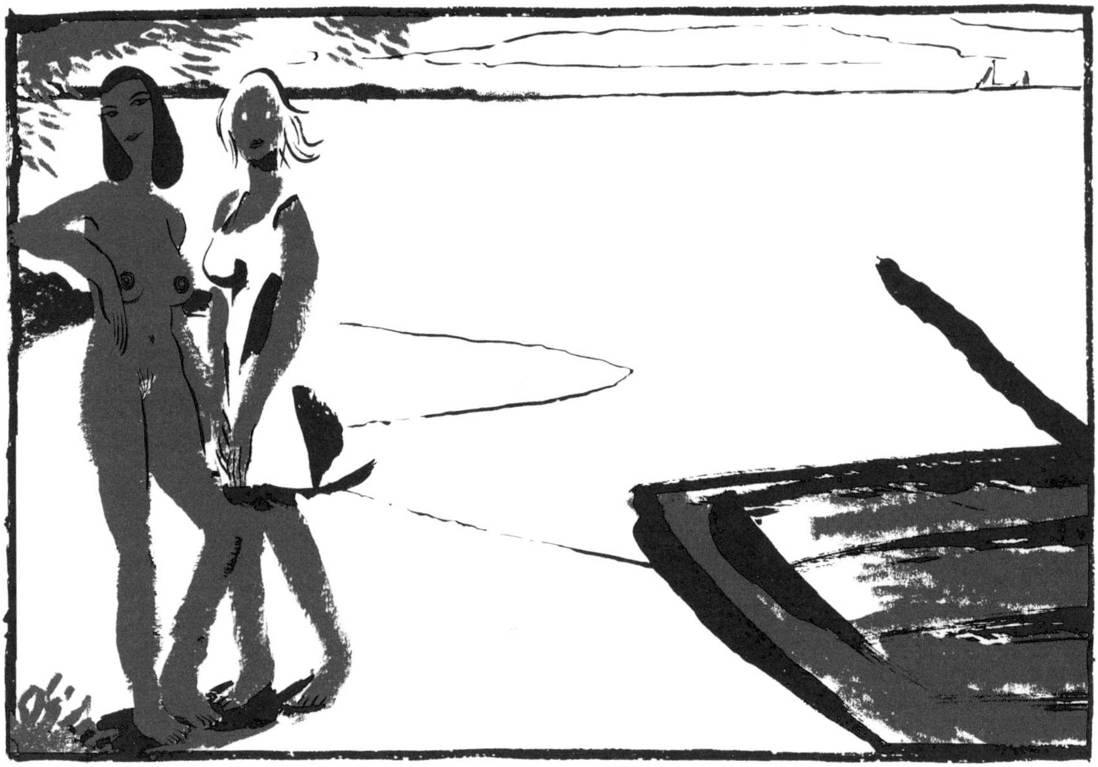

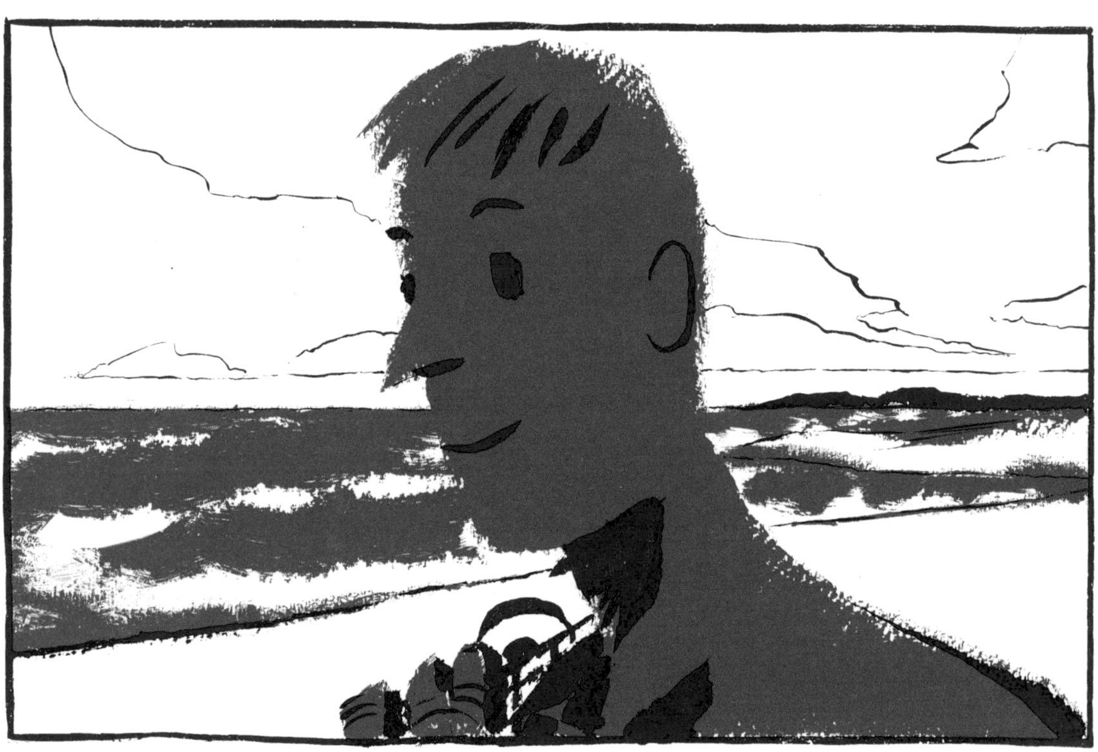

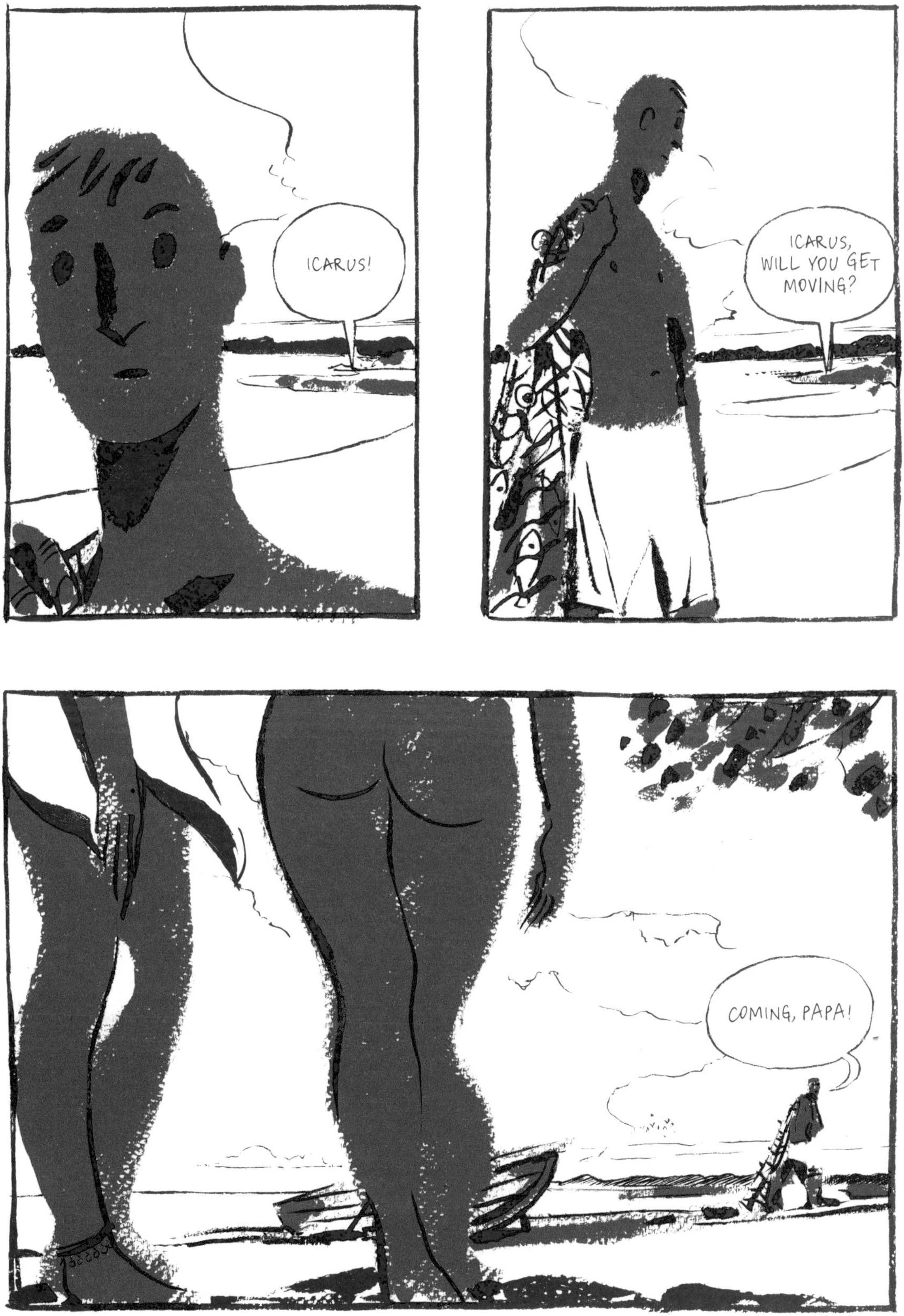
ICARUS!
ICARUS, WILL YOU GET MOVING?
COMING, PAPA!

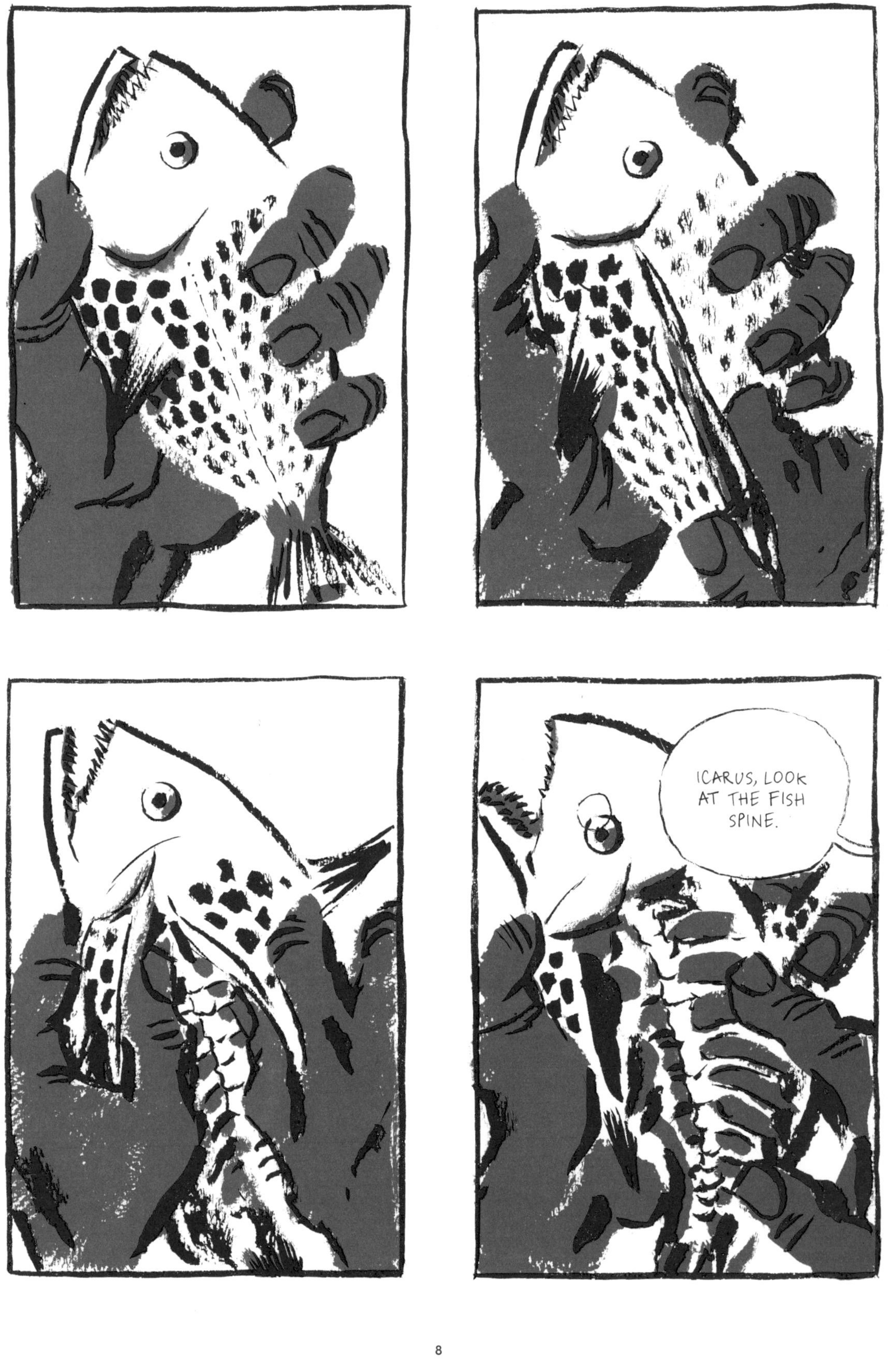
ICARUS, LOOK AT THE FISH SPINE.

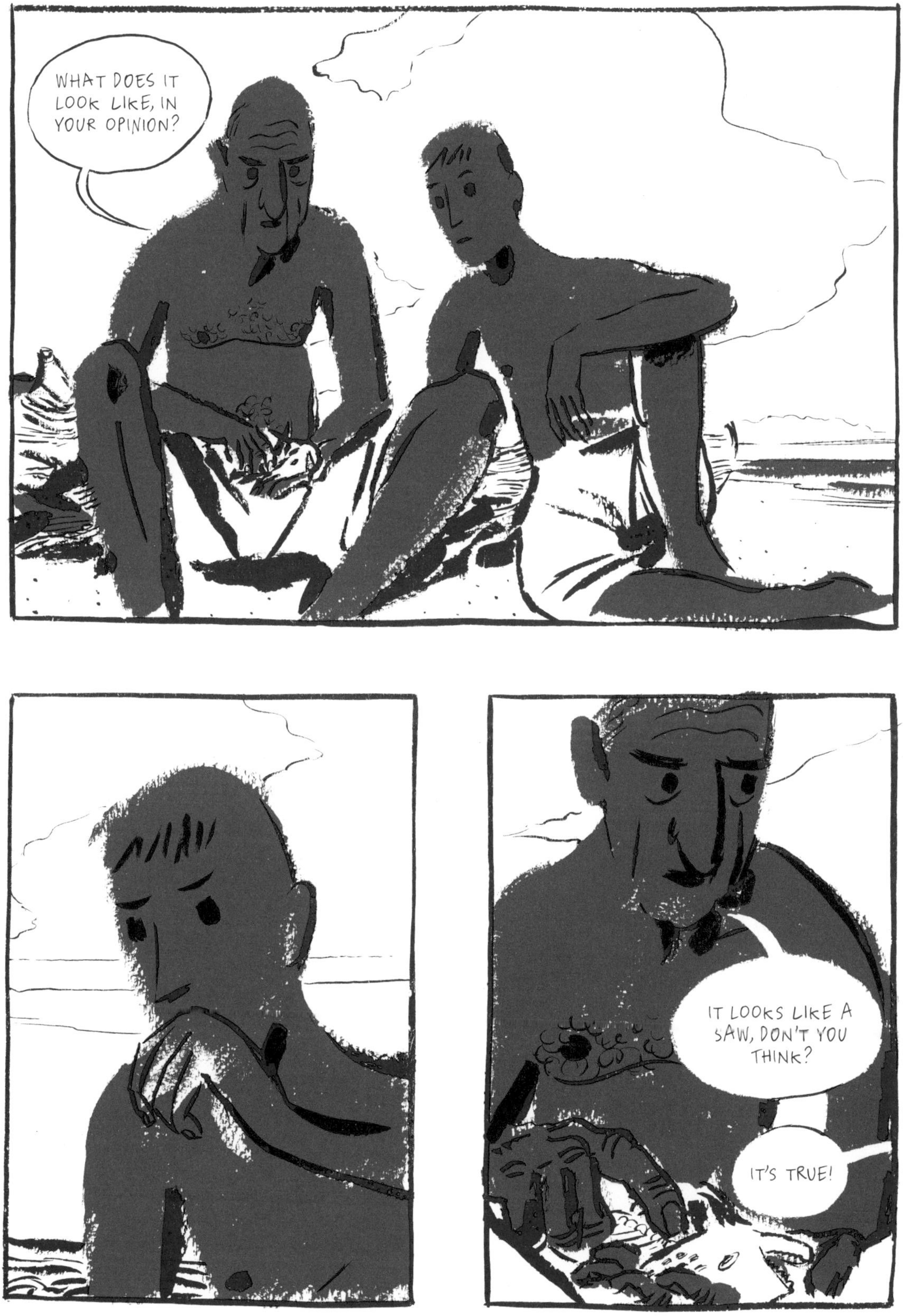
WHAT DOES IT LOOK LIKE, IN YOUR OPINION?
IT LOOKS LIKE A SAW, DON'T YOU THINK?
IT'S TRUE!

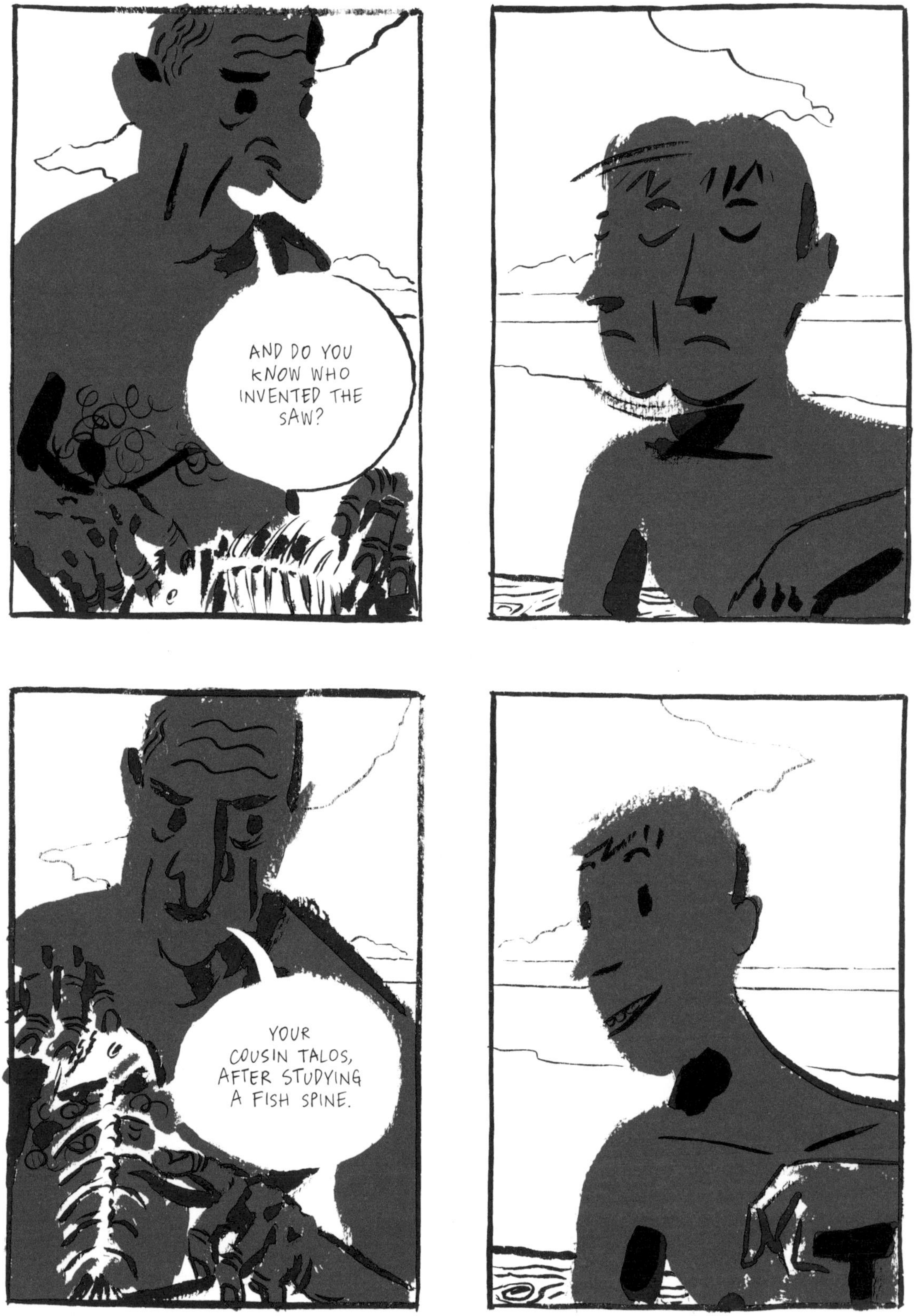
AND DO YOU KNOW WHO INVENTED THE SAW?
YOUR COUSIN TALOS, AFTER STUDYING A FISH SPINE.

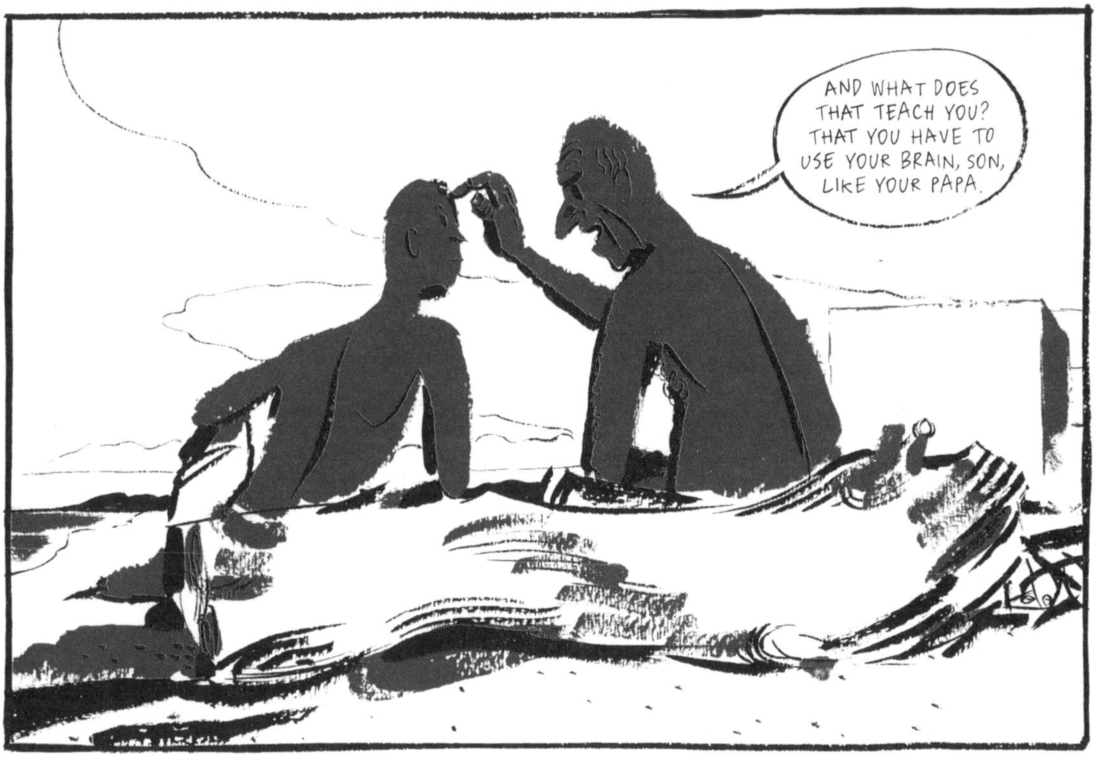
AND WHAT DOES THAT TEACH YOU? THAT YOU HAVE TO USE YOUR BRAIN, SON, LIKE YOUR PAPA.

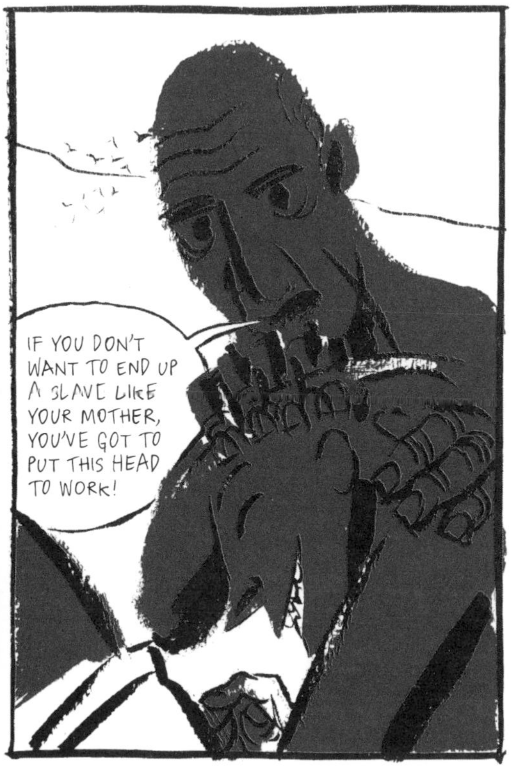
IF YOU DON'T WANT TO END UP A SLAVE LIKE YOUR MOTHER, YOU'VE GOT TO PUT THIS HEAD TO WORK!

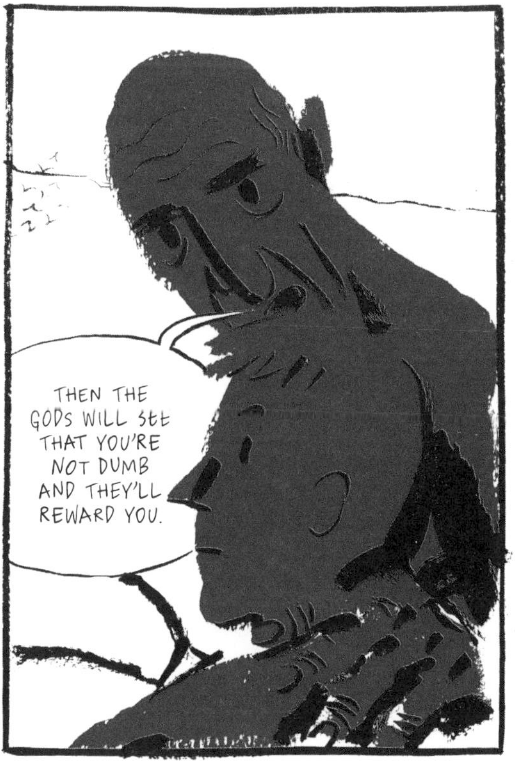
THEN THE GODS WILL SEE THAT YOU'RE NOT DUMB AND THEY'LL REWARD YOU.

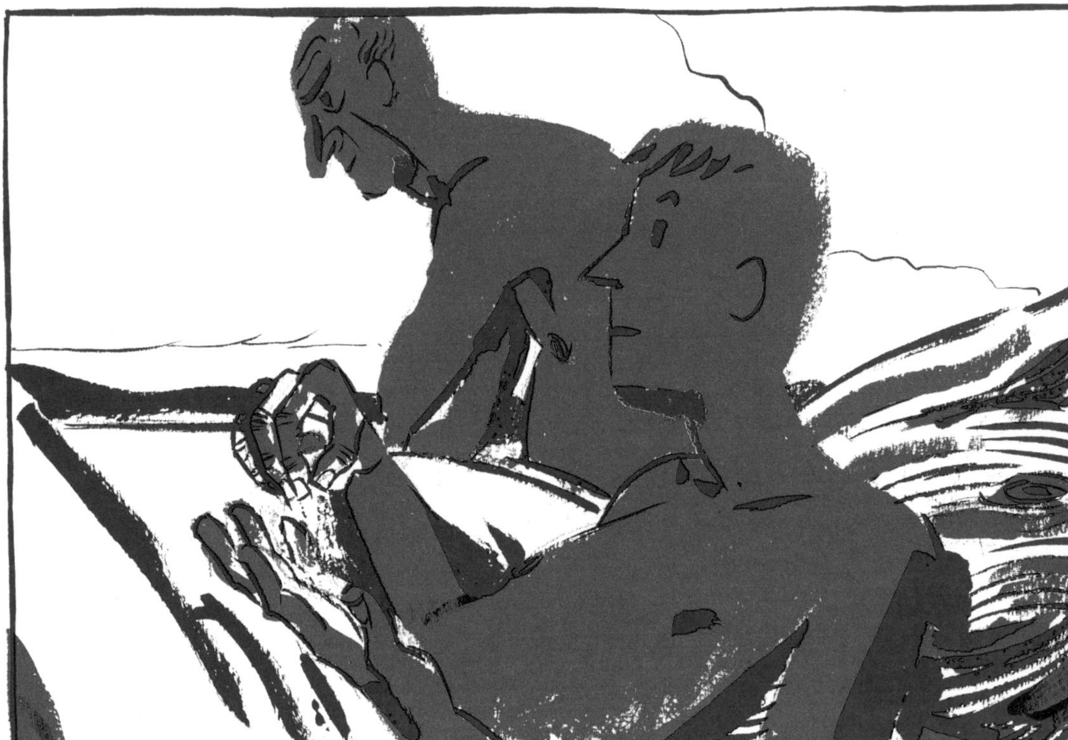

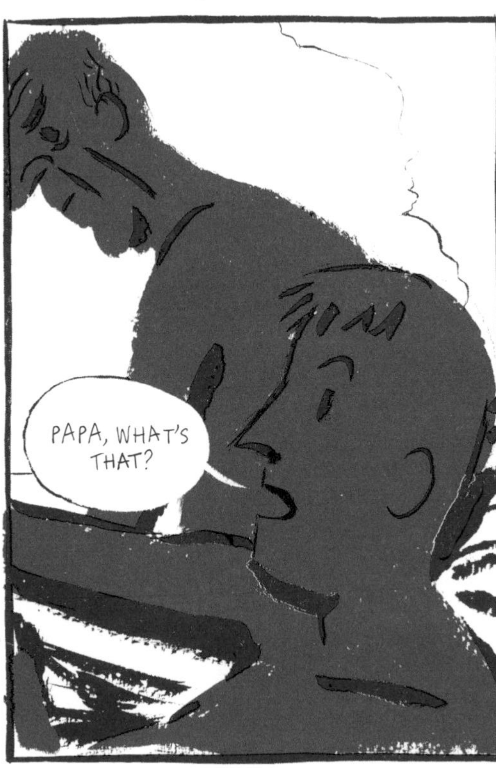
PAPA, WHAT'S THAT?

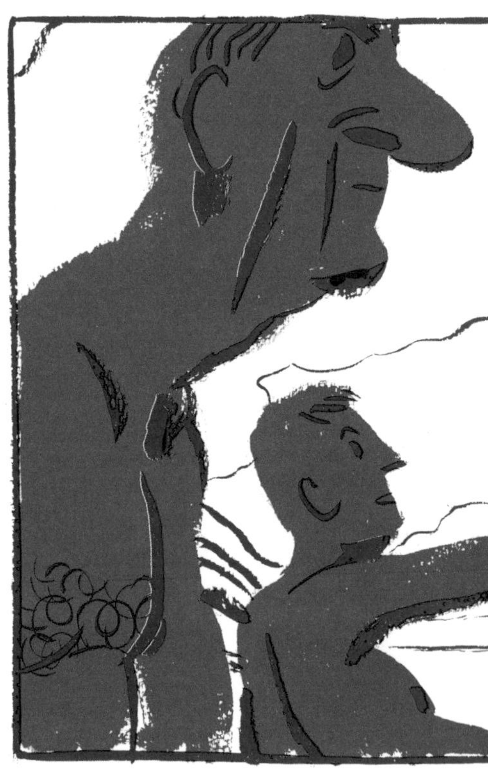

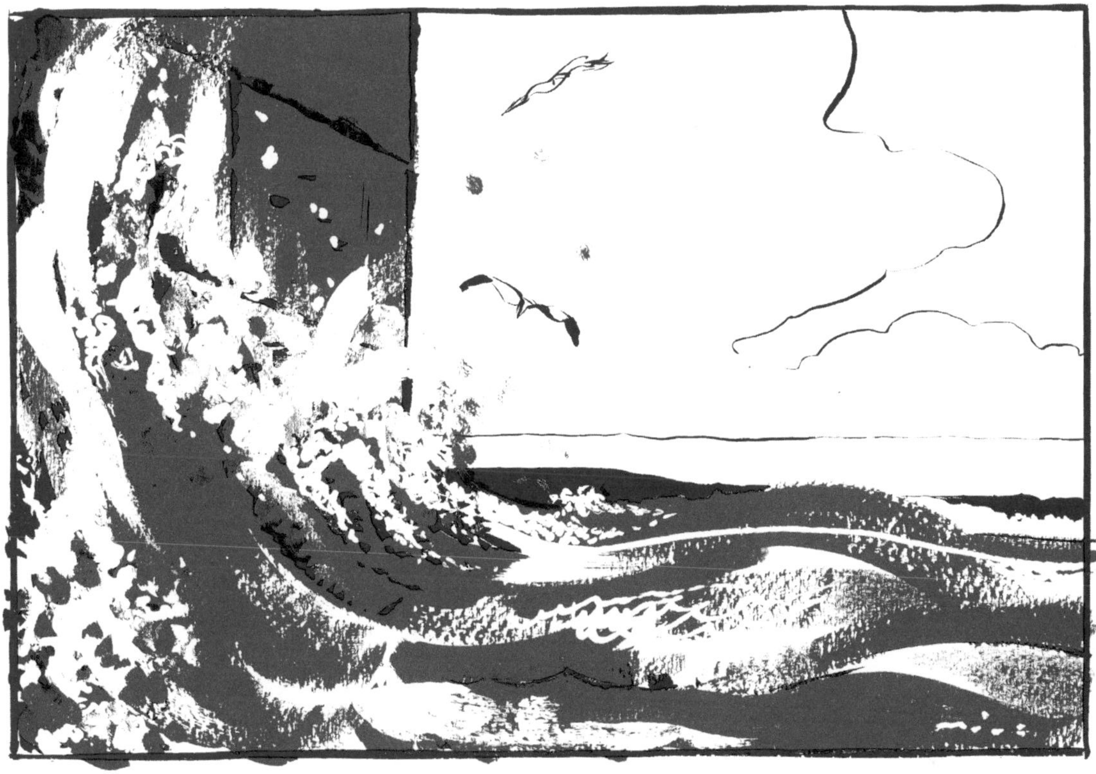

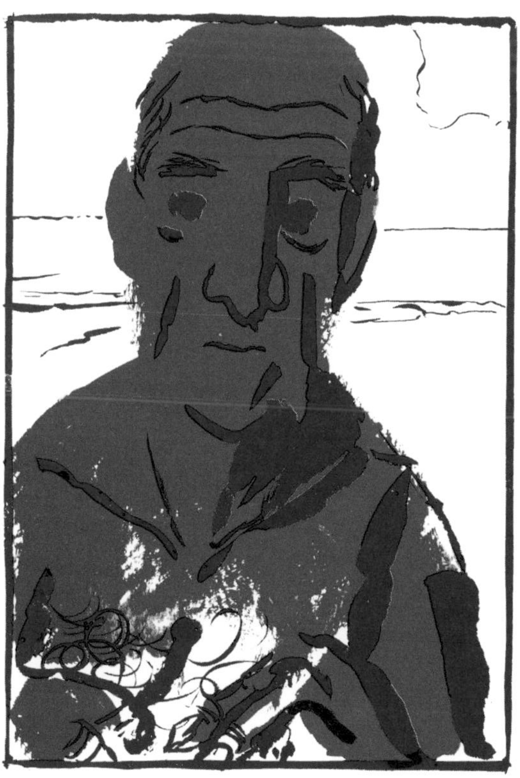

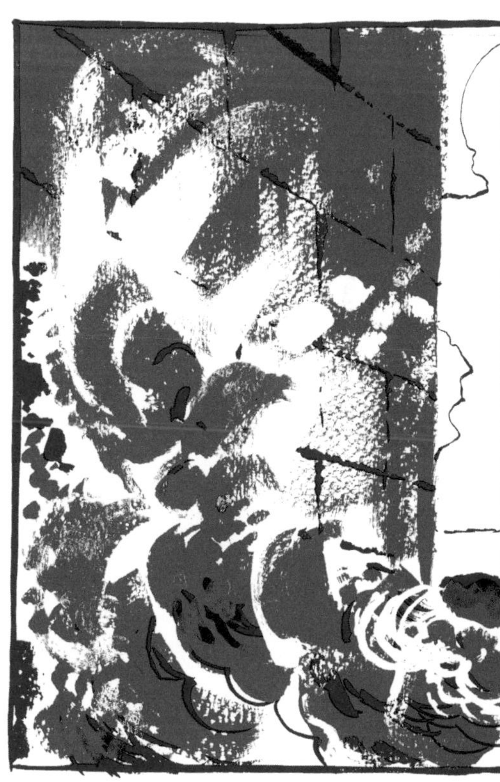

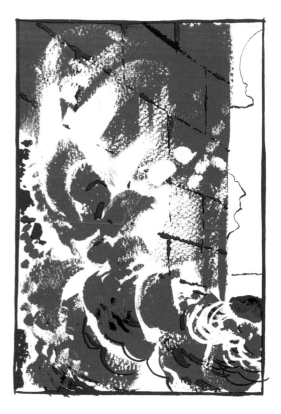

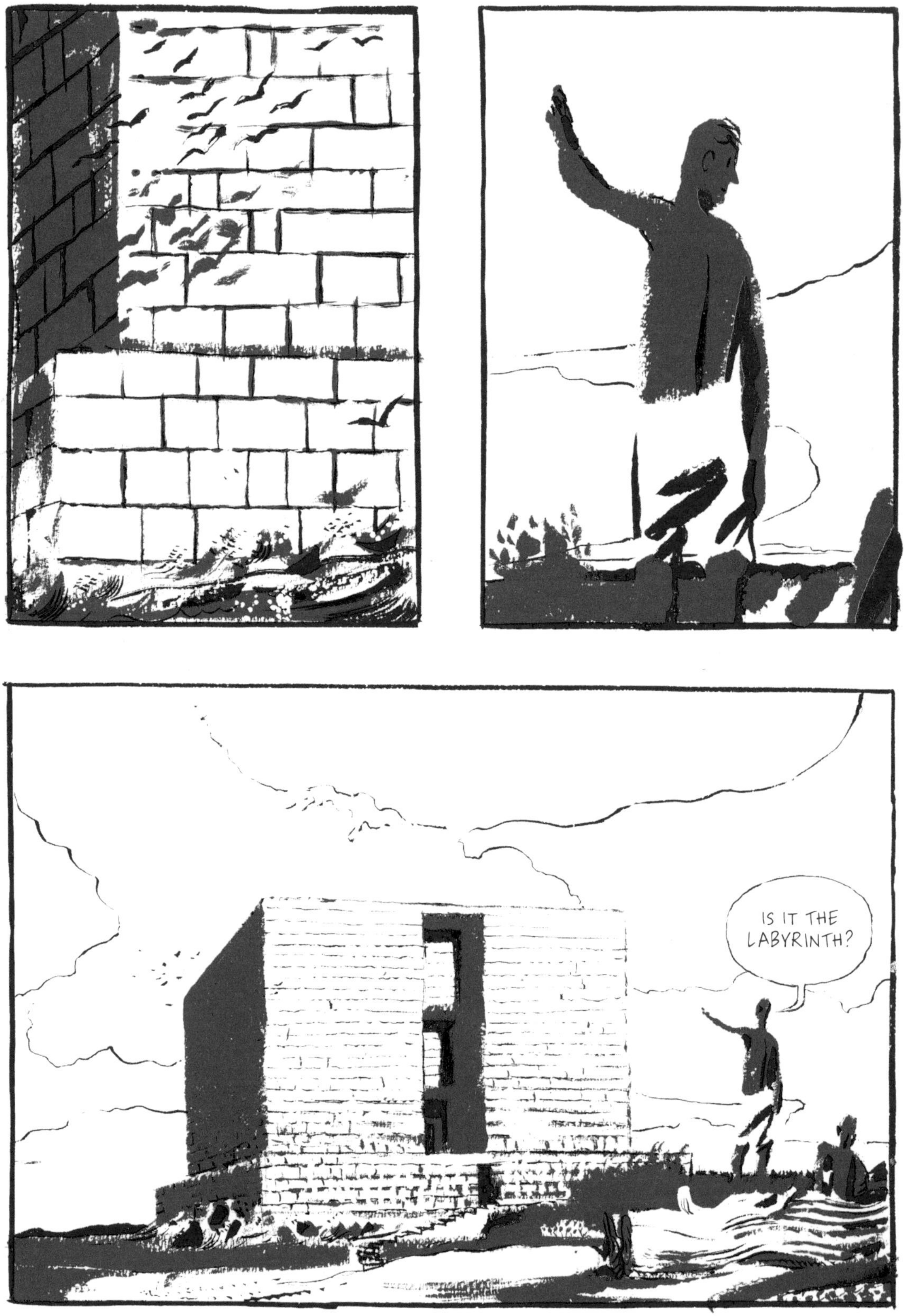
IS IT THE LABYRINTH?

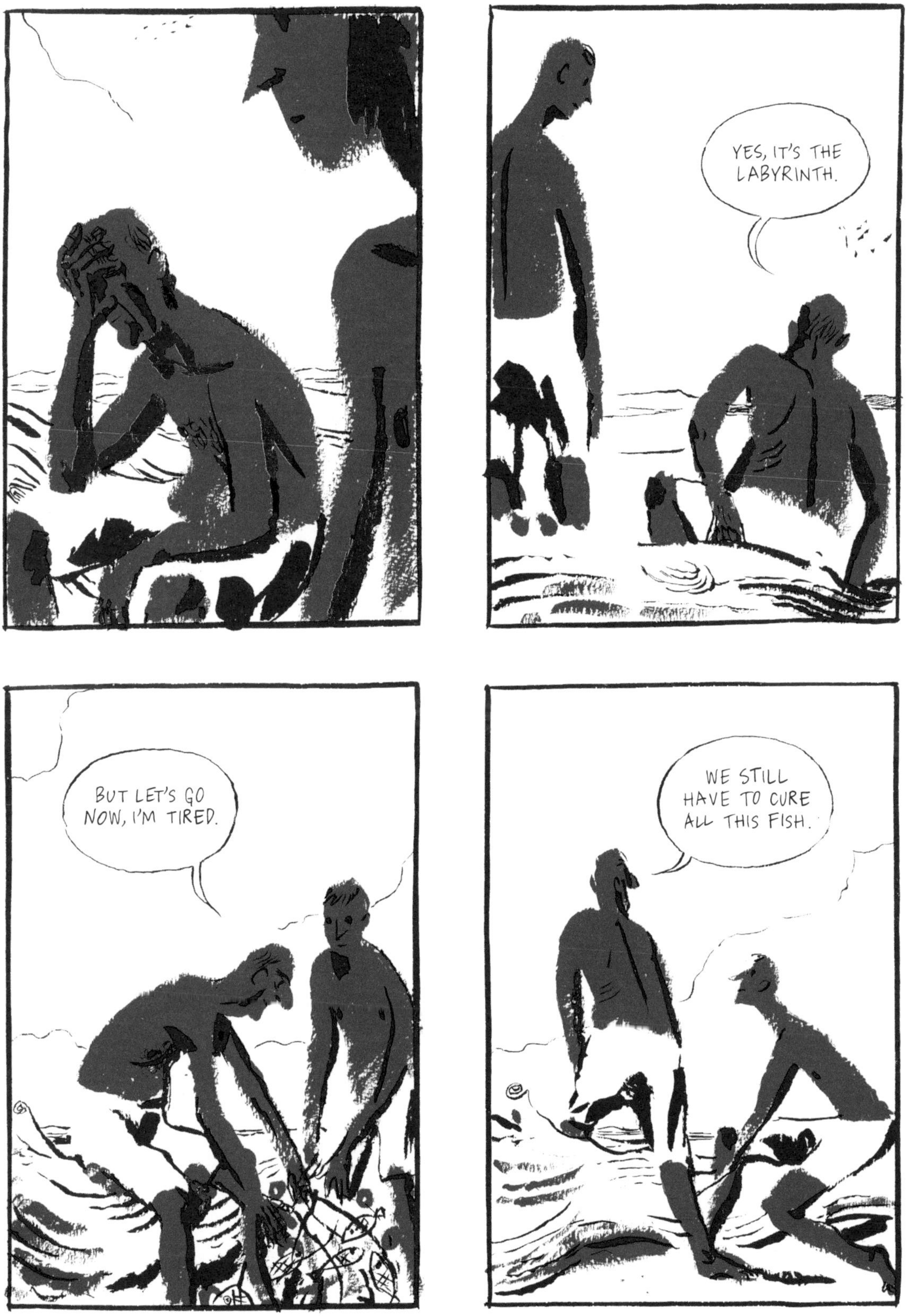
YES, IT'S THE LABYRINTH.
BUT LET'S GO NOW, I'M TIRED.
WE STILL HAVE TO CURE ALL THIS FISH.

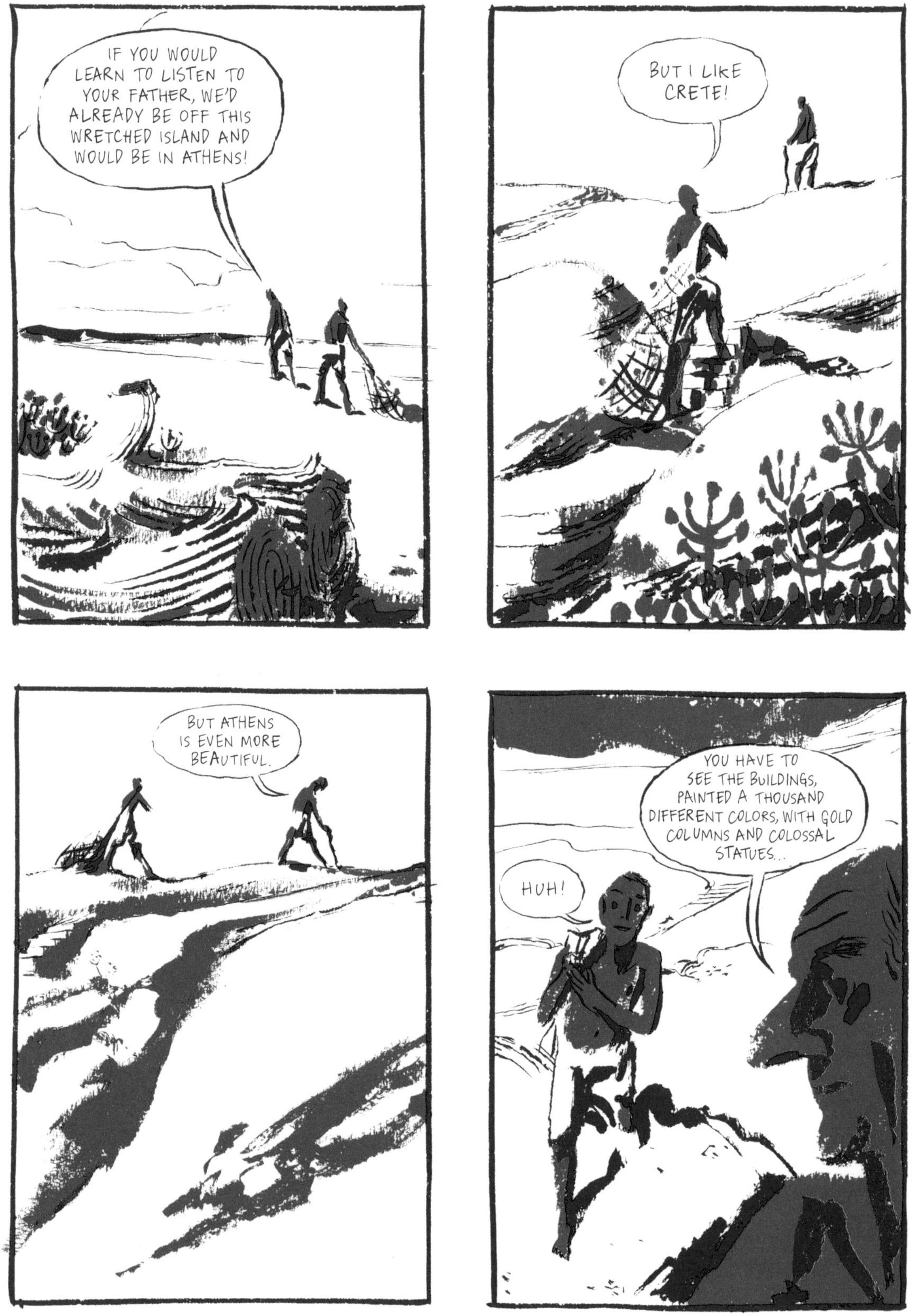
IF YOU WOULD LEARN TO LISTEN TO YOUR FATHER, WE'D ALREADY BE OFF THIS WRETCHED ISLAND AND WOULD BE IN ATHENS!
BUT I LIKE CRETE!
BUT ATHENS IS EVEN MORE BEAUTIFUL.
YOU HAVE TO SEE THE BUILDINGS, PAINTED A THOUSAND DIFFERENT COLORS, WITH GOLD COLUMNS AND COLOSSAL STATUES...
HUH!

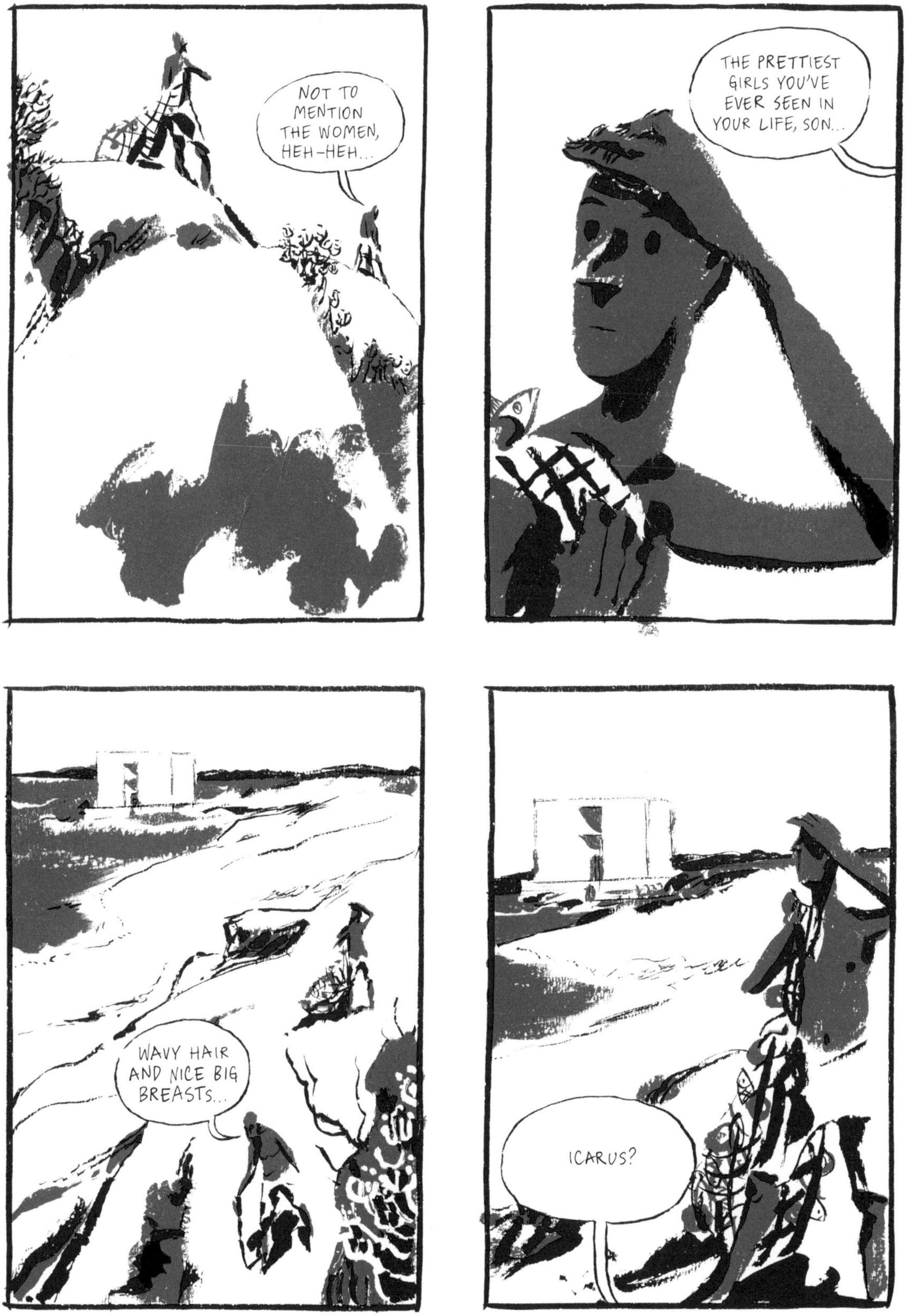
NOT TO MENTION THE WOMEN, HEH-HEH...
THE PRETTIEST GIRLS YOU'VE EVER SEEN IN YOUR LIFE, SON...
WAVY HAIR AND NICE BIG BREASTS...
ICARUS?

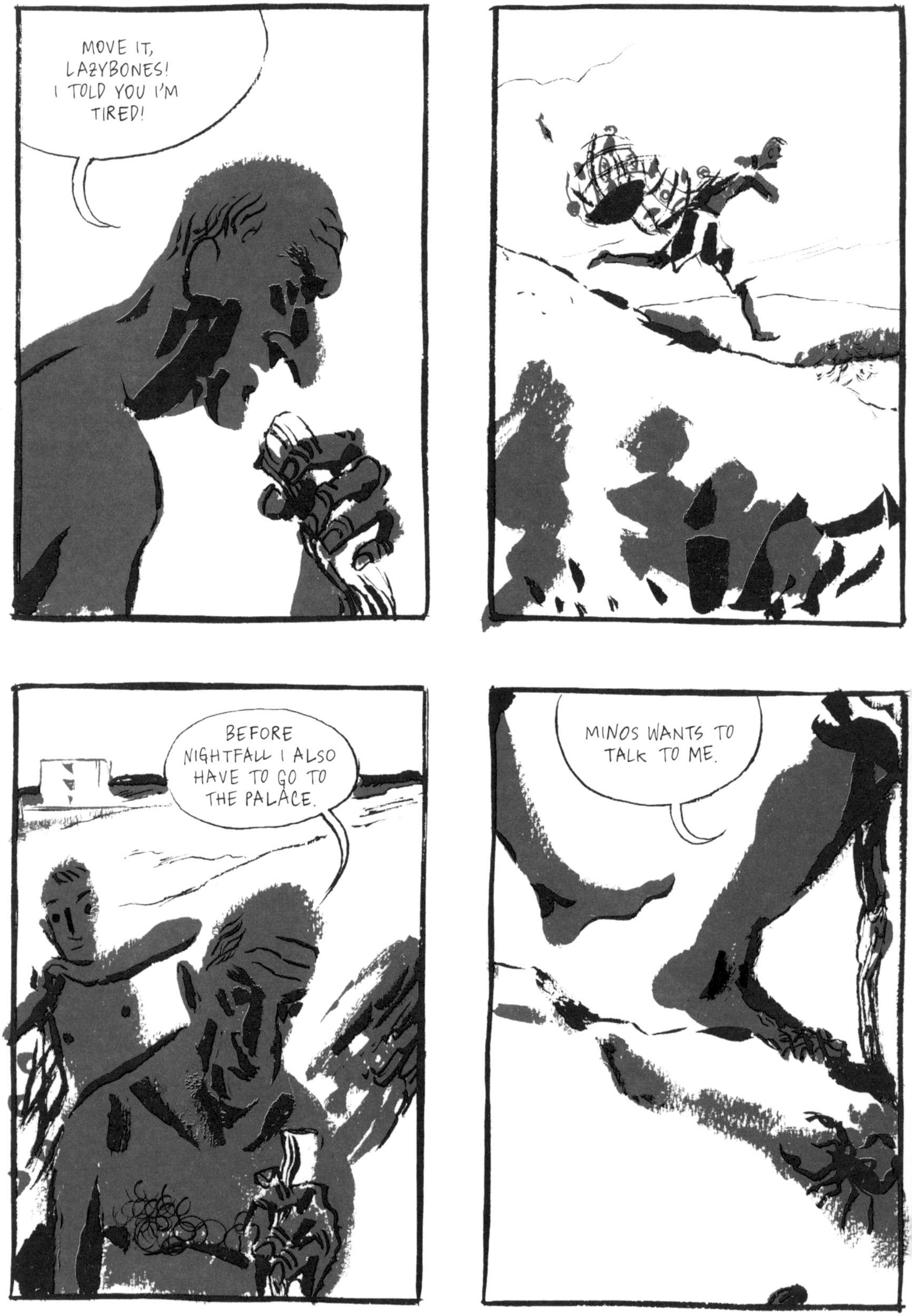
MOVE IT, LAZYBONES! I TOLD YOU I'M TIRED!
BEFORE NIGHTFALL I ALSO HAVE TO GO TO THE PALACE.
MINOS WANTS TO TALK TO ME.

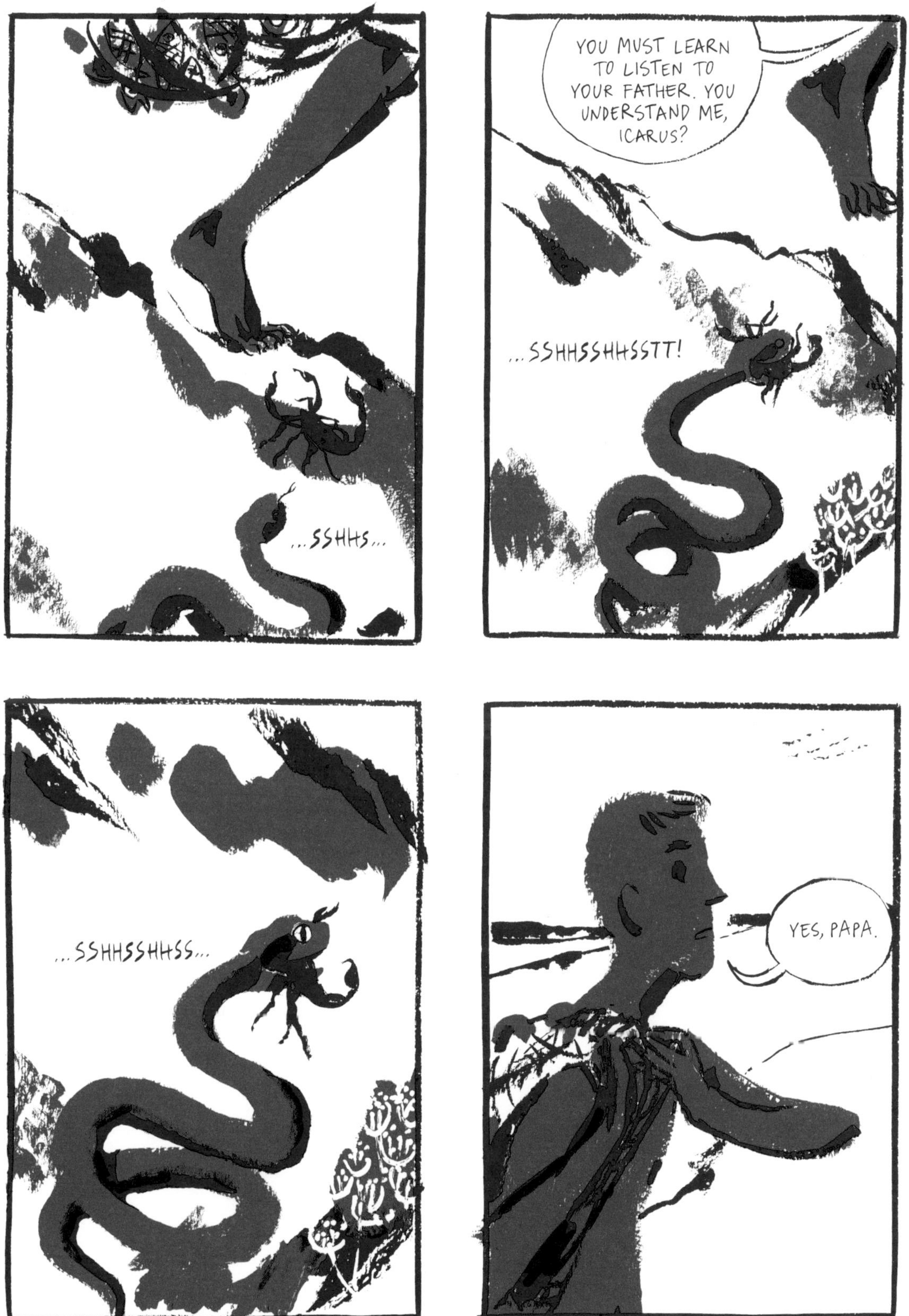
...SSHHS...
YOU MUST LEARN TO LISTEN TO YOUR FATHER. YOU UNDERSTAND ME, ICARUS?
...SSHHSSHHSSTT!
...SSHHSSHHSS...
YES, PAPA.

2.

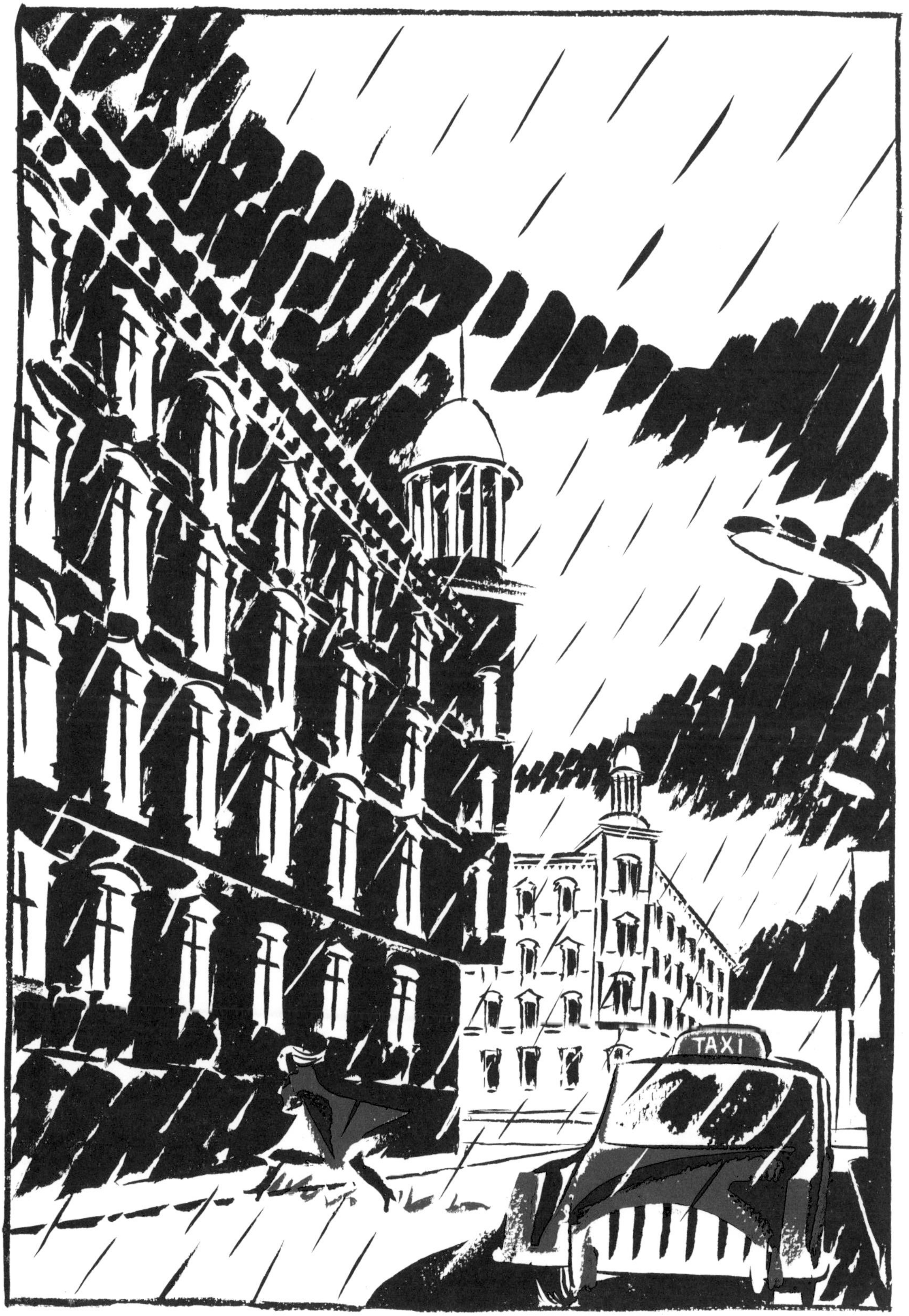
TAXI

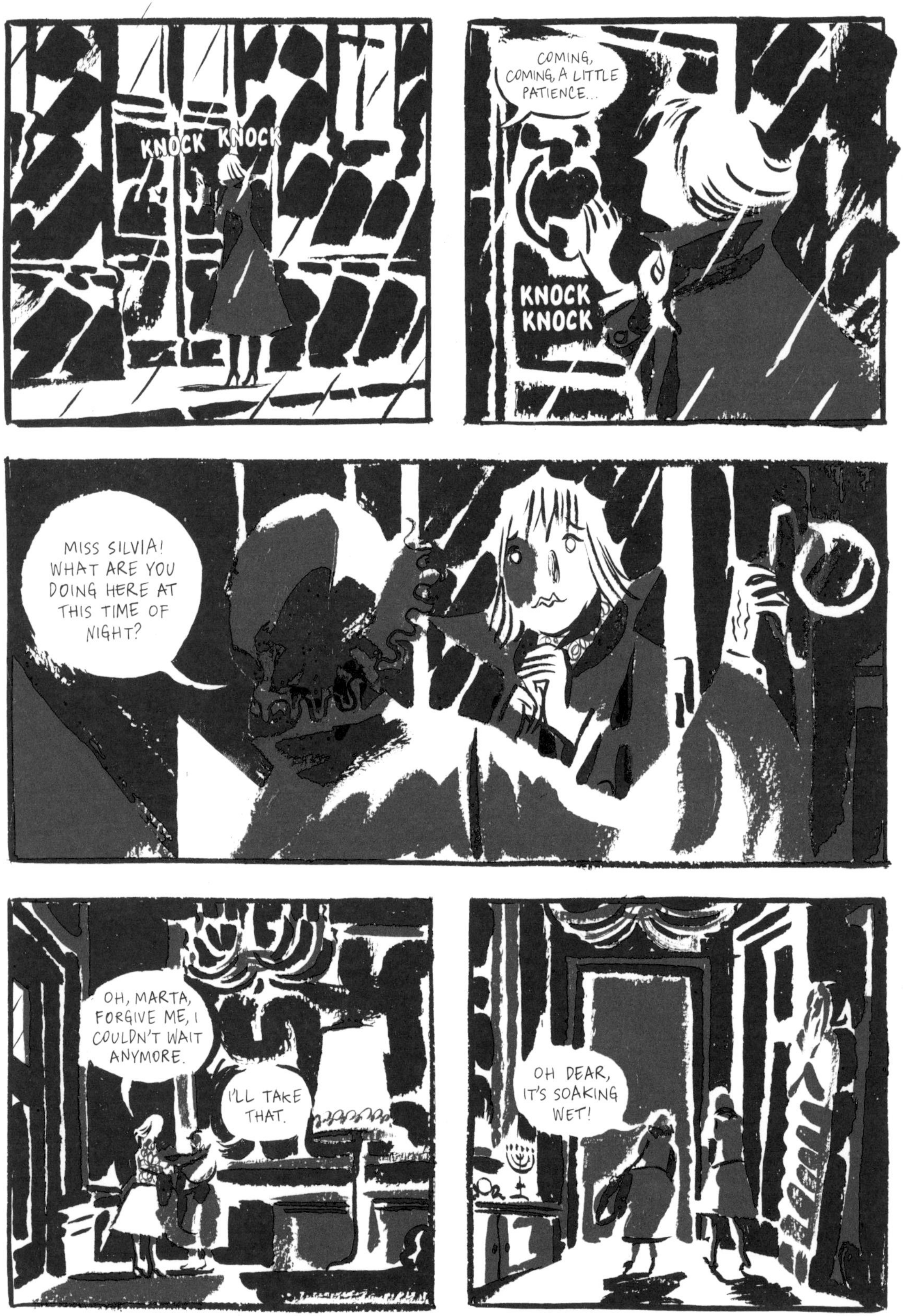
KNOCK KNOCK
COMING, COMING, A LITTLE PATIENCE...
KNOCK KNOCK
MISS SILVIA! WHAT ARE YOU DOING HERE AT THIS TIME OF NIGHT?
OH, MARTA, FORGIVE ME, I COULDN'T WAIT ANYMORE.
I'LL TAKE THAT.
OH DEAR, IT'S SOAKING WET!

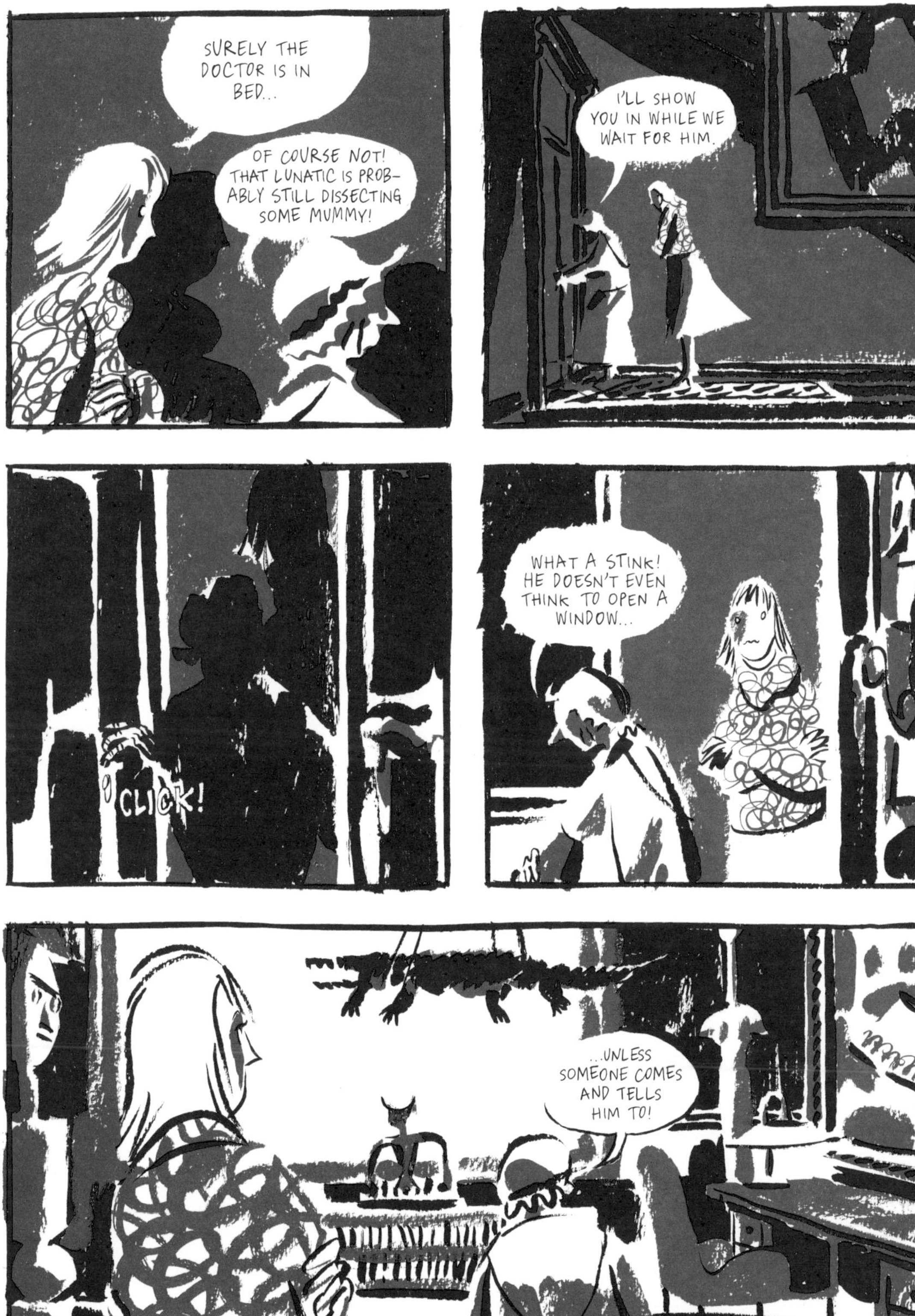
SURELY THE DOCTOR IS IN BED...
OF COURSE NOT! THAT LUNATIC IS PROBABLY STILL DISSECTING SOME MUMMY!
I'LL SHOW YOU IN WHILE WE WAIT FOR HIM.
CLICK!
WHAT A STINK! HE DOESN'T EVEN THINK TO OPEN A WINDOW...
...UNLESS SOMEONE COMES AND TELLS HIM TO!

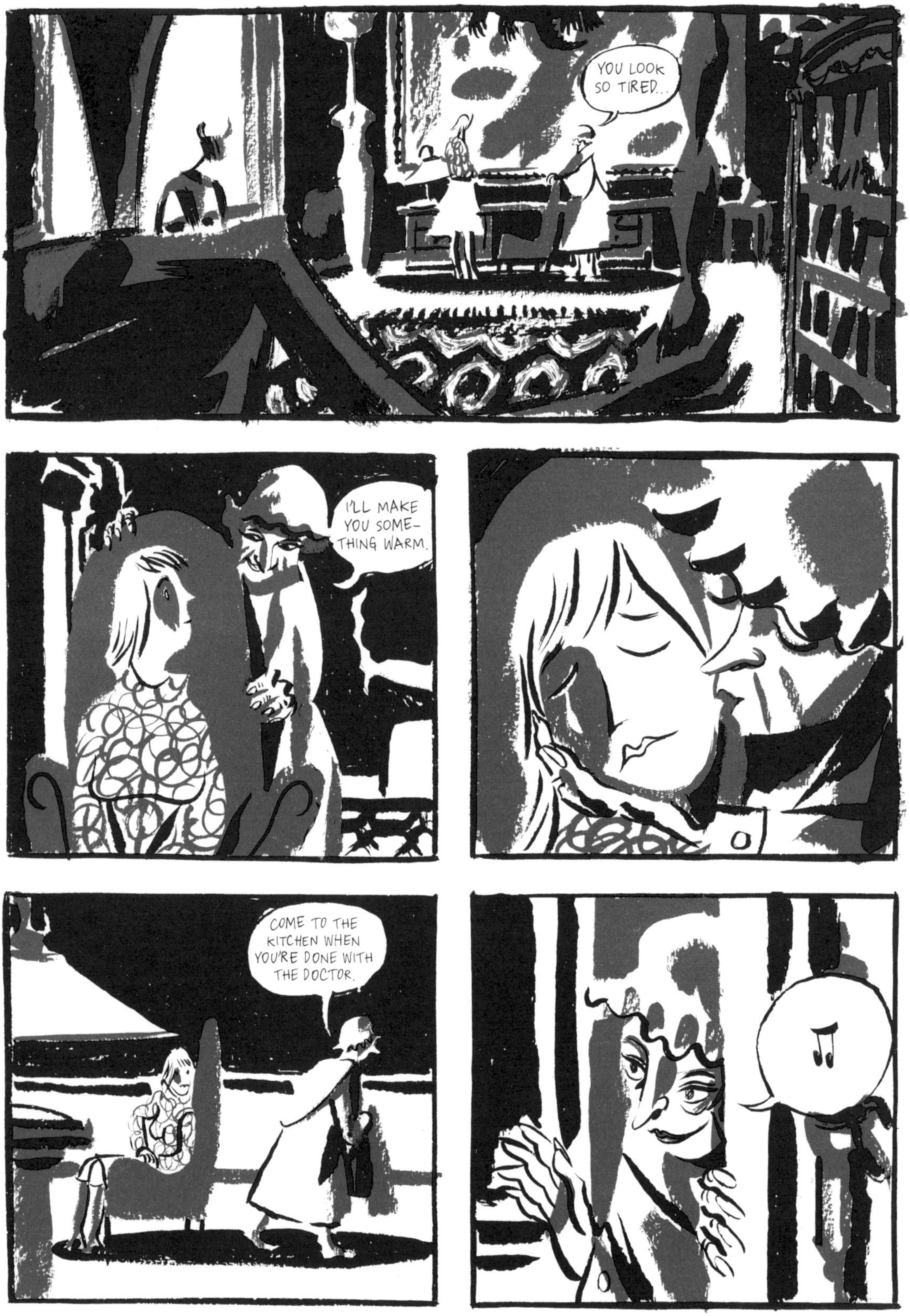
YOU LOOK SO TIRED...
I'LL MAKE YOU SOME-THING WARM.
COME TO THE KITCHEN WHEN YOU'RE DONE WITH THE DOCTOR.

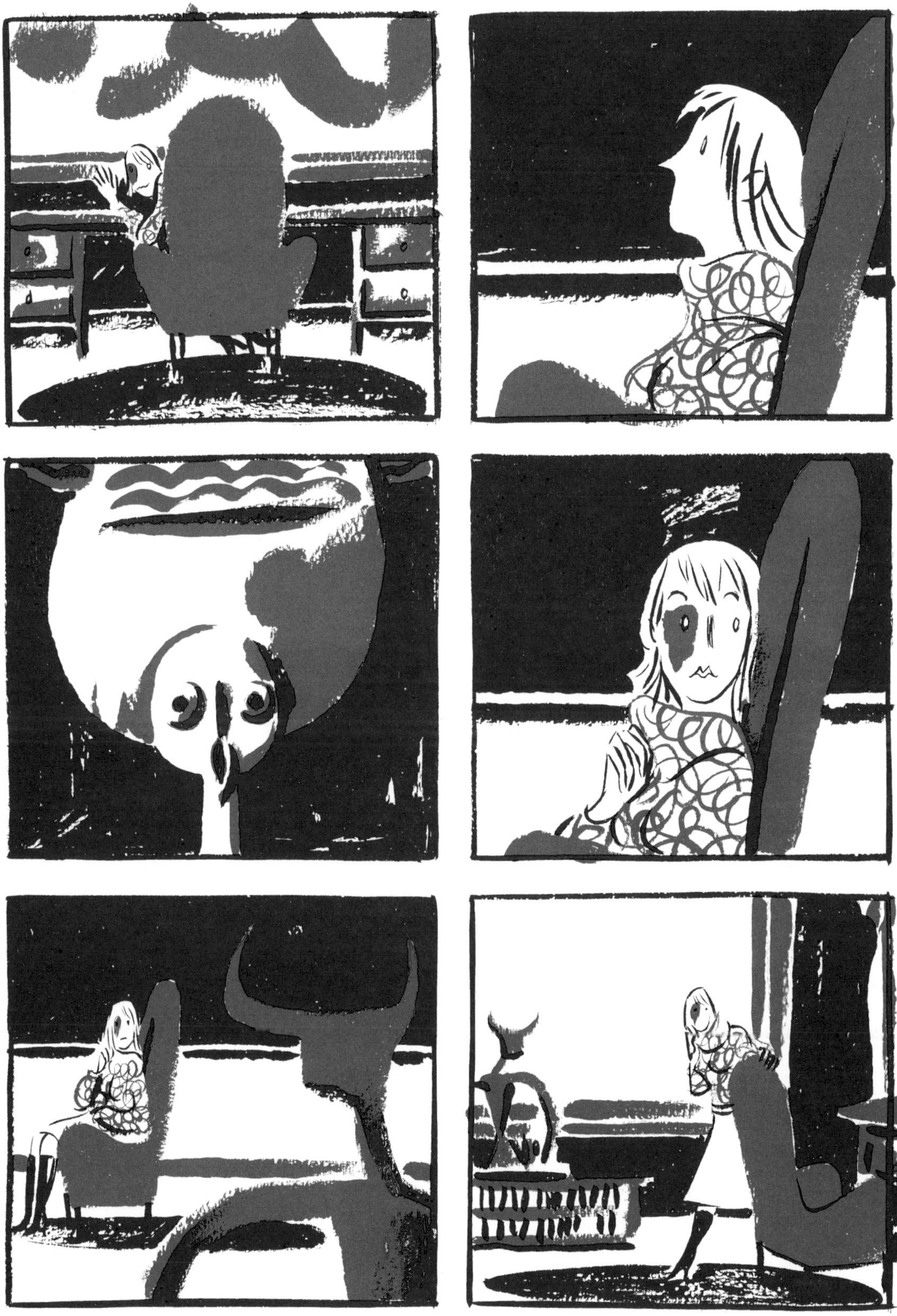

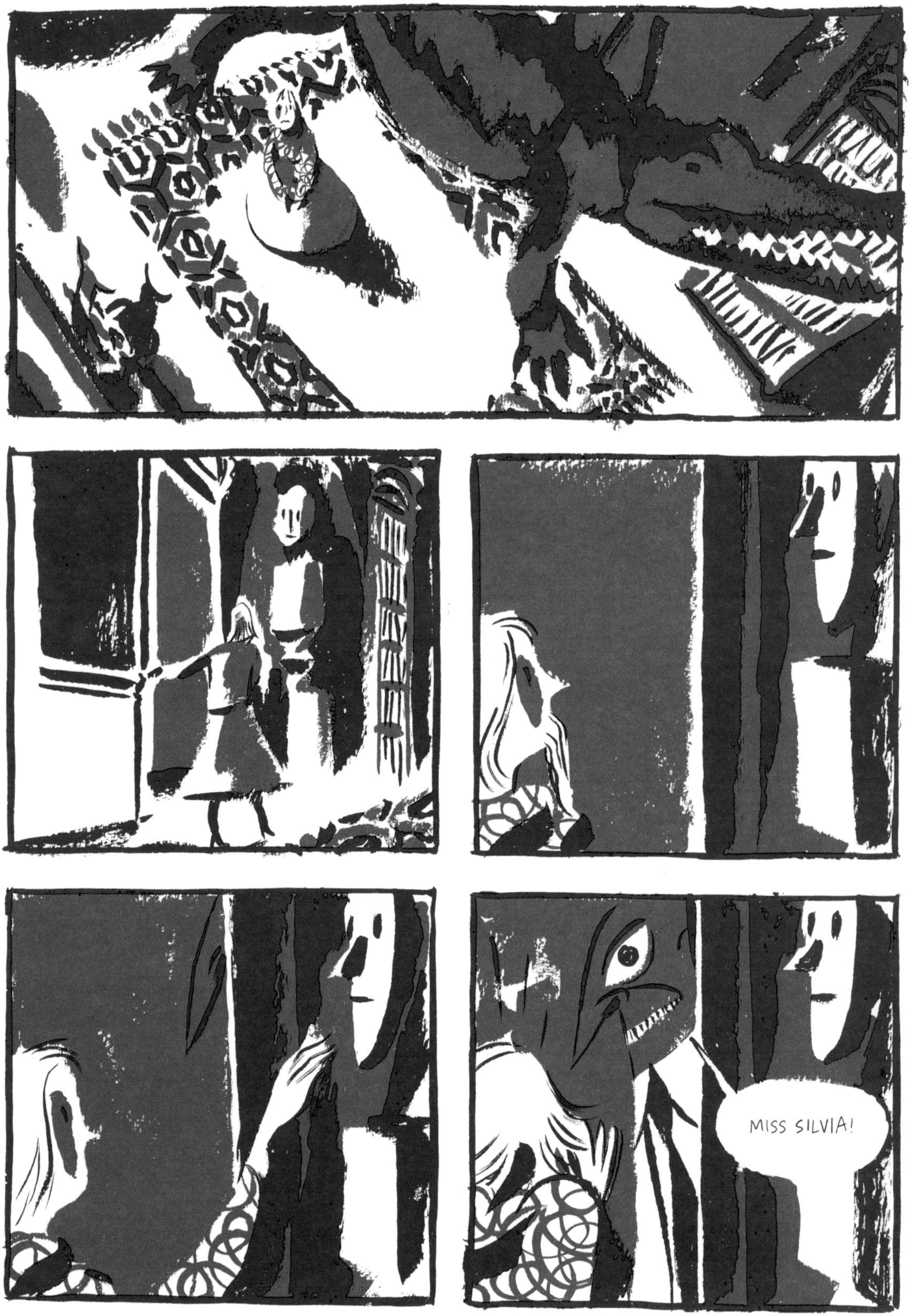
MISS SILVIA!

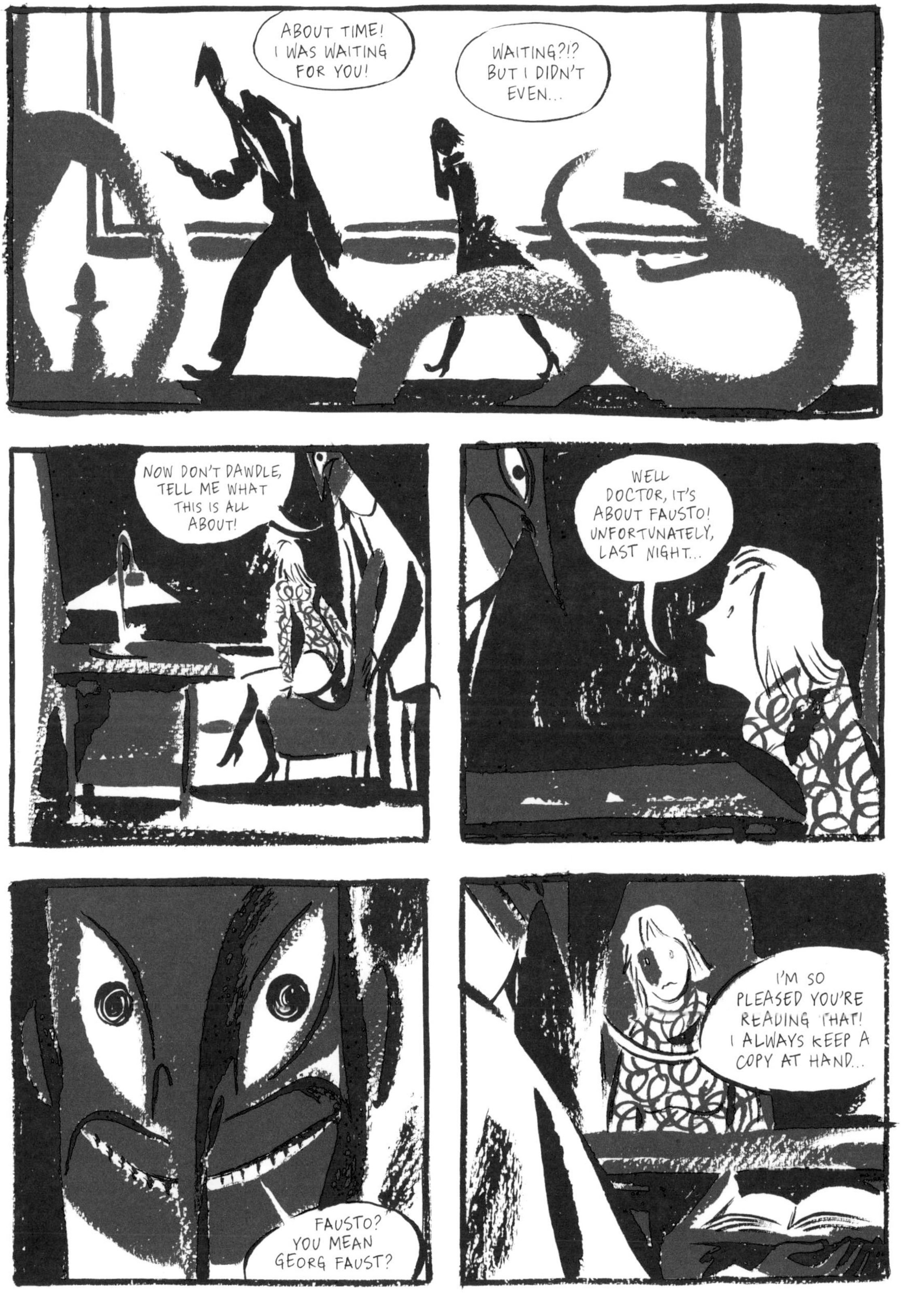
ABOUT TIME! I WAS WAITING FOR YOU!
WAITING?!? BUT I DIDN'T EVEN...
NOW DON'T DAWDLE, TELL ME WHAT THIS IS ALL ABOUT!
WELL DOCTOR, IT'S ABOUT FAUSTO! UNFORTUNATELY, LAST NIGHT...
FAUSTO? YOU MEAN GEORG FAUST?
I'M SO PLEASED YOU'RE READING THAT! I ALWAYS KEEP A COPY AT HAND...

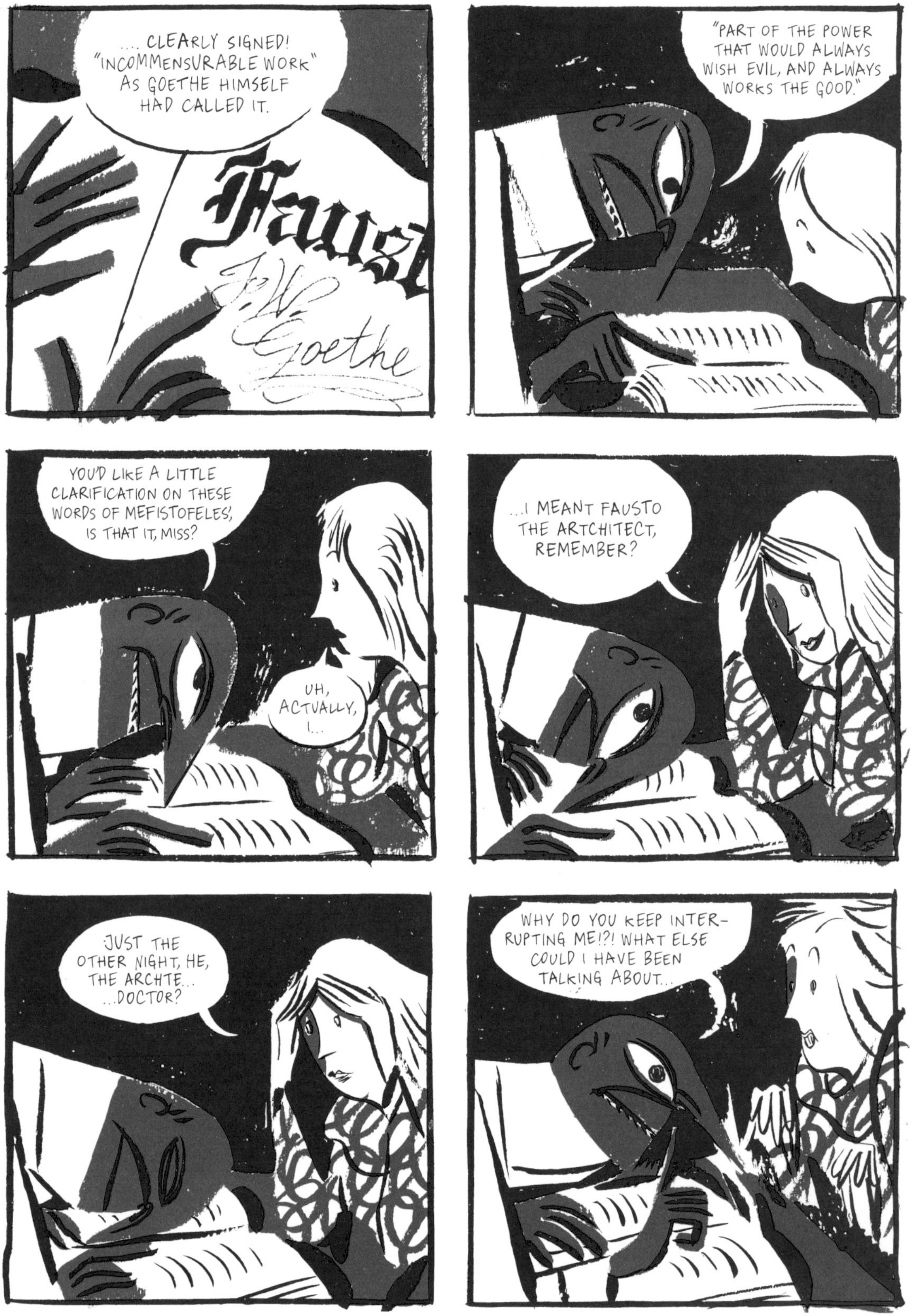
....CLEARLY SIGNED! "INCOMMENSURABLE WORK" AS GOETHE HIMSELF HAD CALLED IT.
Faust
J. W. Goethe
"PART OF THE POWER THAT WOULD ALWAYS WISH EVIL, AND ALWAYS WORKS THE GOOD."
YOU'D LIKE A LITTLE CLARIFICATION ON THESE WORDS OF MEFISTOFELES, IS THAT IT, MISS?
UH, ACTUALLY, I...
...I MEANT FAUSTO THE ARTCHITECT, REMEMBER?
JUST THE OTHER NIGHT, HE, THE ARCHTE... ...DOCTOR?
WHY DO YOU KEEP INTER-RUPTING ME!?! WHAT ELSE COULD I HAVE BEEN TALKING ABOUT...

...BESIDES THAT FANATICAL, IMPERTINENT DILETTANTE!?!

NOW HE EVEN DARES TO SEND YOU HERE TO KEEP ME APPRISED OF HIS FAILURES!!!

BUT I COULDN'T CARE LESS! DOES HE THINK HE'S SPECIAL?

I'VE SEEN ALL KINDS! ASTROLOGERS AND ALCHEMISTS, SAILORS AND SCIENTISTS! SEEKERS OF THE PHILOSOPHER'S STONE! POETS AND INVESTIGATORS OF THE OCCULT!

ALL INTENT ON SQUARING THE CIRCLE AND CIRCLING THE SQUARE...

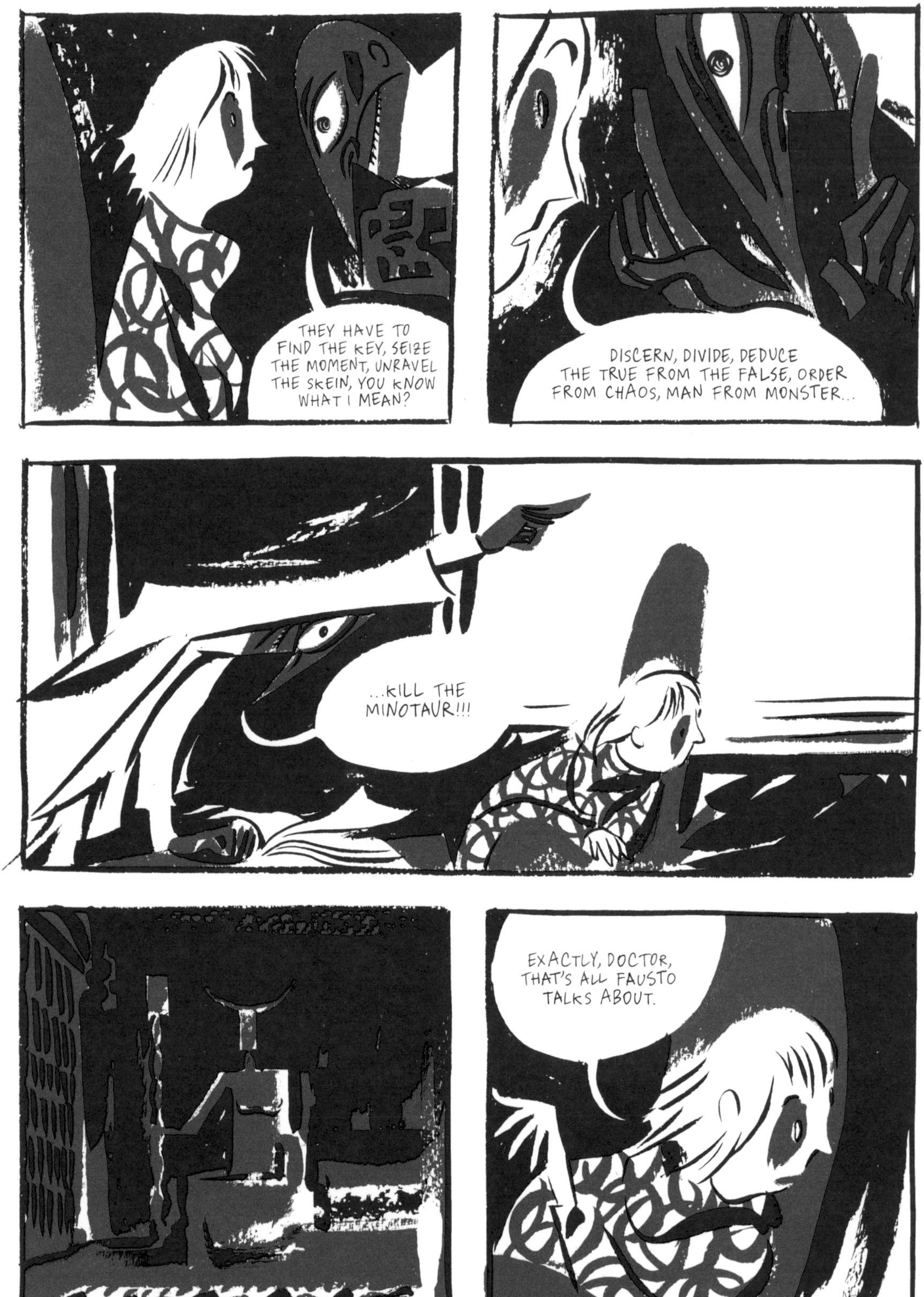
THEY HAVE TO FIND THE KEY, SEIZE THE MOMENT, UNRAVEL THE SKEIN, YOU KNOW WHAT I MEAN?
DISCERN, DIVIDE, DEDUCE THE TRUE FROM THE FALSE, ORDER FROM CHAOS, MAN FROM MONSTER...
...KILL THE MINOTAUR!!!
EXACTLY, DOCTOR, THAT'S ALL FAUSTO TALKS ABOUT.

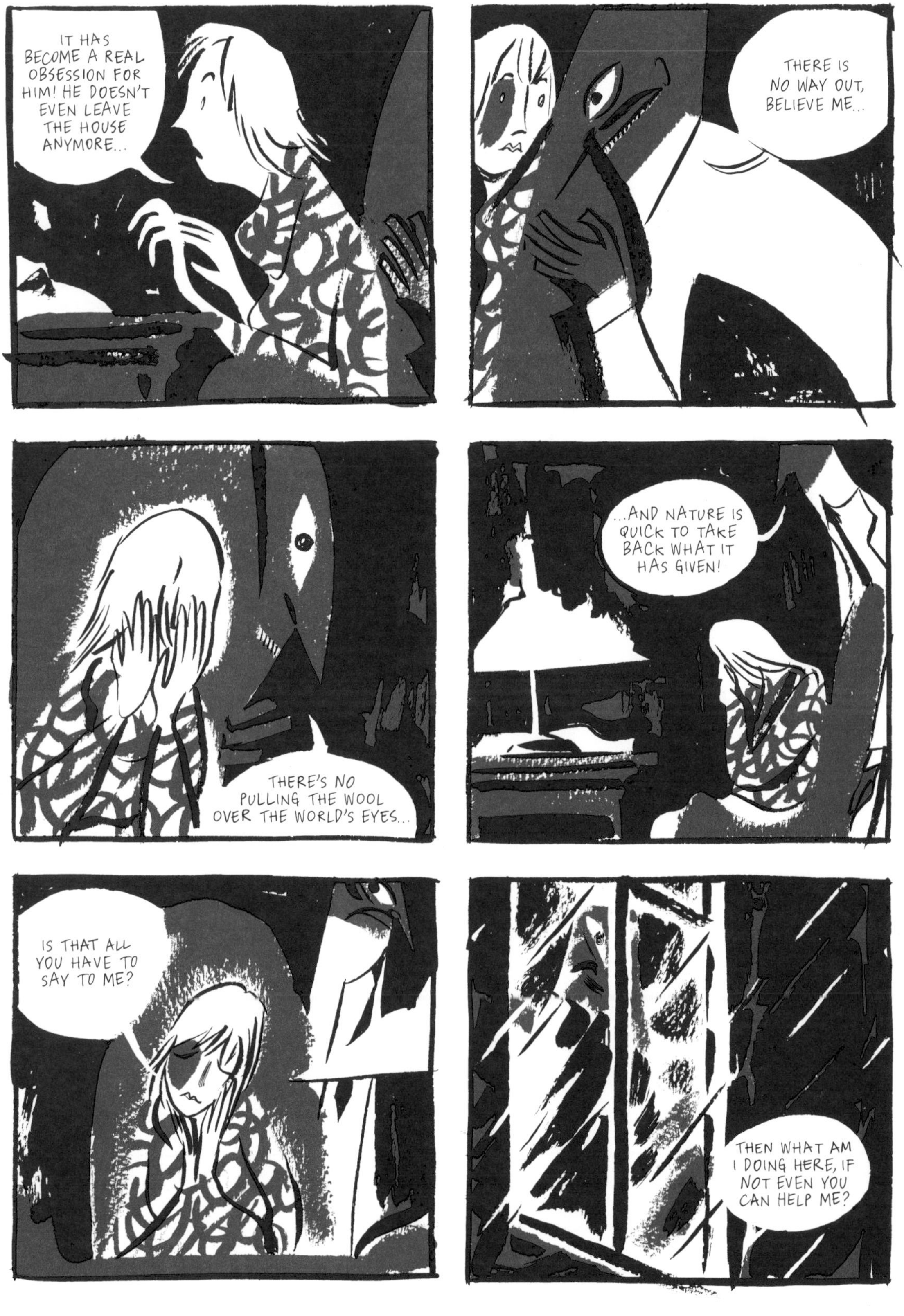
IT HAS BECOME A REAL OBSESSION FOR HIM! HE DOESN'T EVEN LEAVE THE HOUSE ANYMORE...
THERE IS NO WAY OUT, BELIEVE ME...
THERE'S NO PULLING THE WOOL OVER THE WORLD'S EYES...
...AND NATURE IS QUICK TO TAKE BACK WHAT IT HAS GIVEN!
IS THAT ALL YOU HAVE TO SAY TO ME?
THEN WHAT AM I DOING HERE, IF NOT EVEN YOU CAN HELP ME?

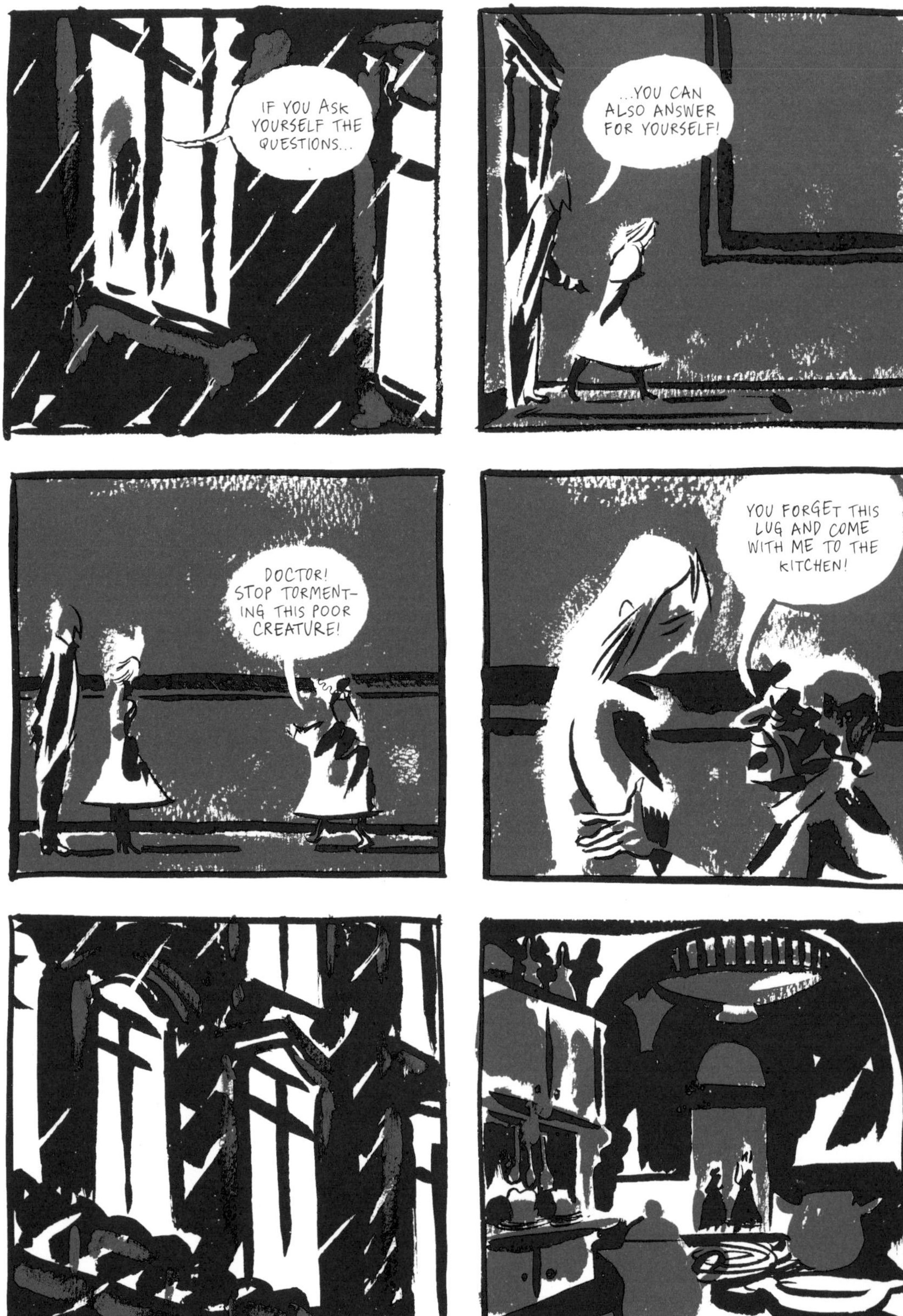
IF YOU ASK YOURSELF THE QUESTIONS...
...YOU CAN ALSO ANSWER FOR YOURSELF!
DOCTOR! STOP TORMENT-ING THIS POOR CREATURE!
YOU FORGET THIS LUG AND COME WITH ME TO THE KITCHEN!

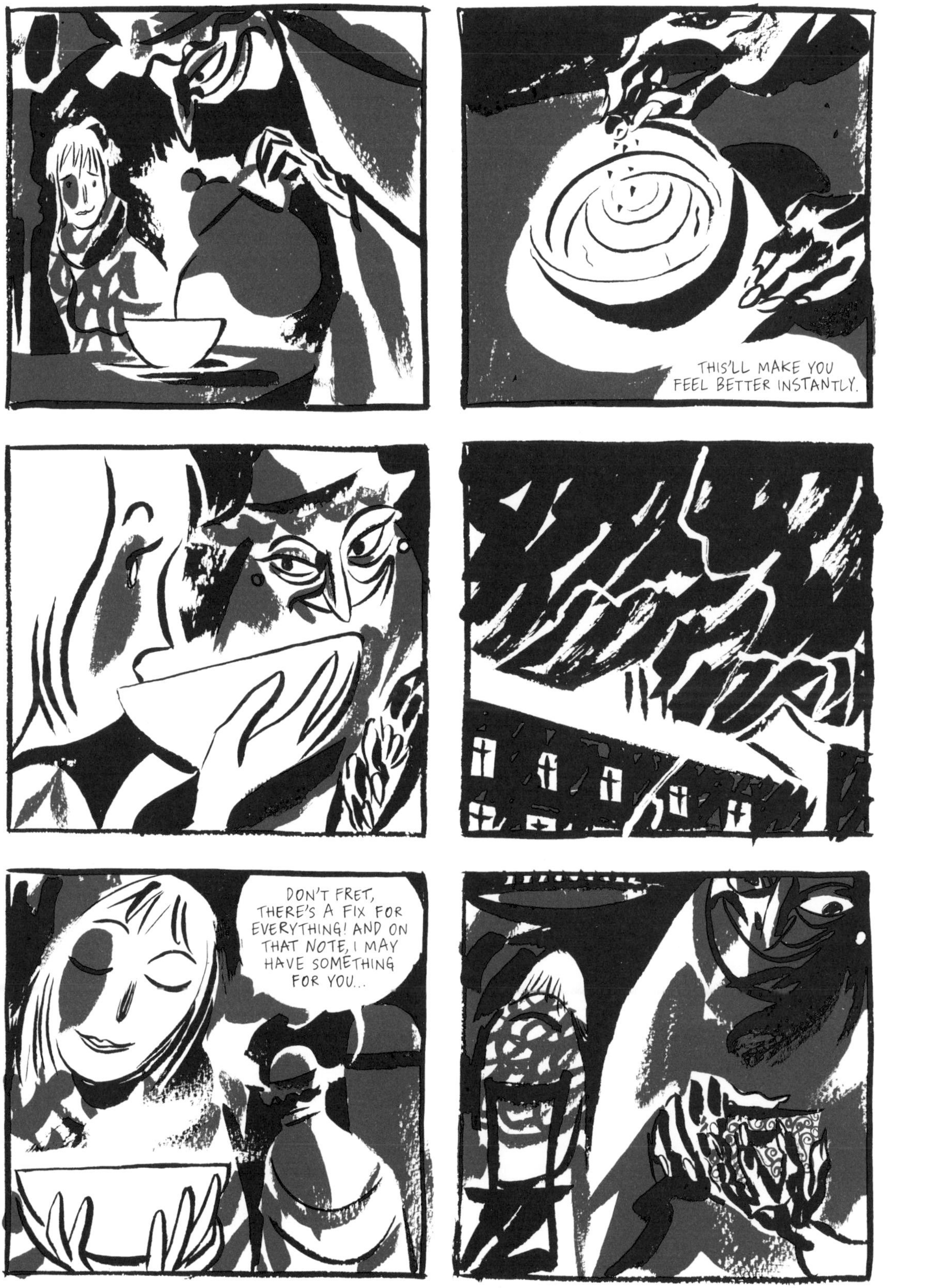
THIS'LL MAKE YOU FEEL BETTER INSTANTLY.
DON'T FRET, THERE'S A FIX FOR EVERYTHING! AND ON THAT NOTE, I MAY HAVE SOMETHING FOR YOU...

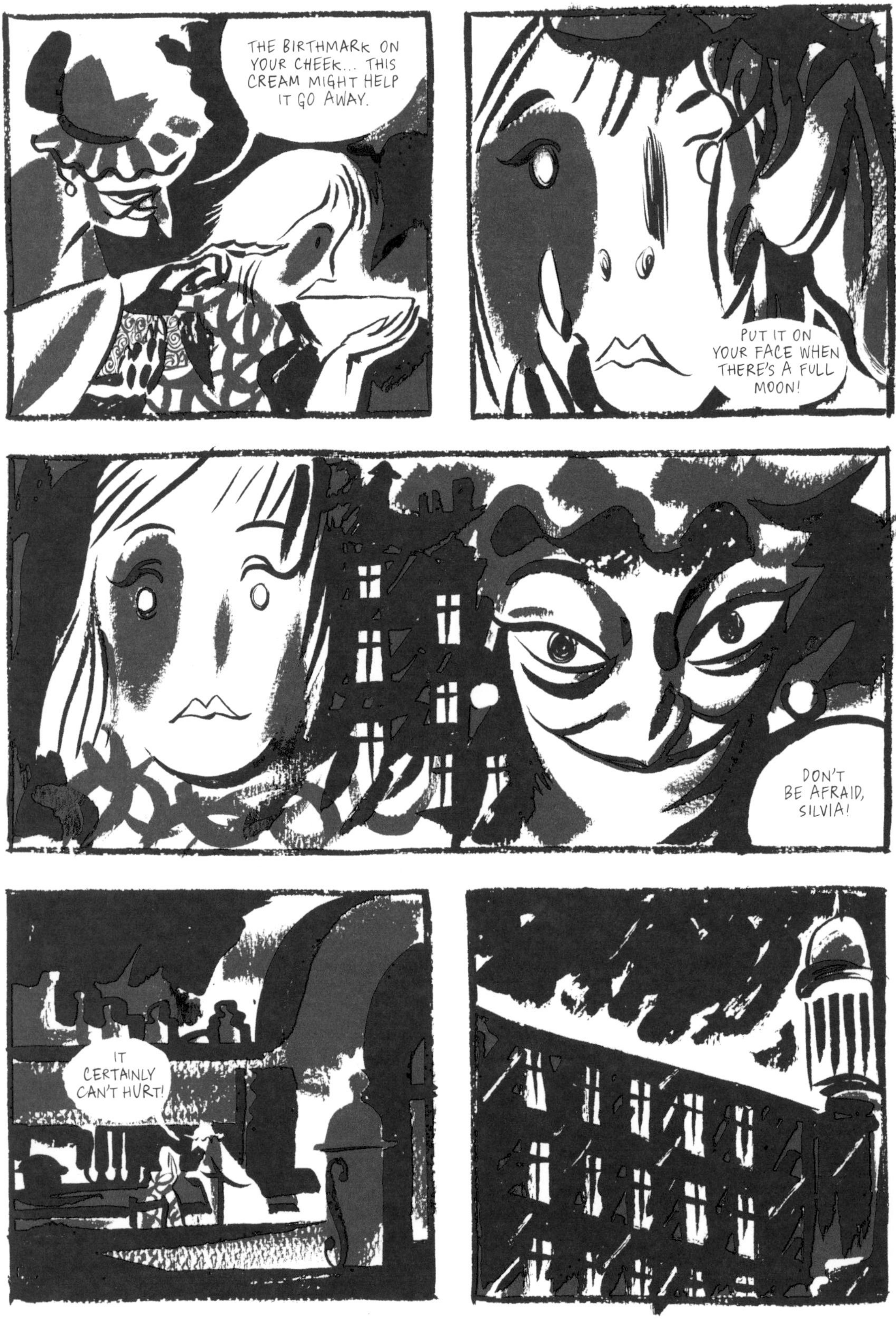
THE BIRTHMARK ON YOUR CHEEK... THIS CREAM MIGHT HELP IT GO AWAY.
PUT IT ON YOUR FACE WHEN THERE'S A FULL MOON!
DON'T BE AFRAID, SILVIA!
IT CERTAINLY CAN'T HURT!

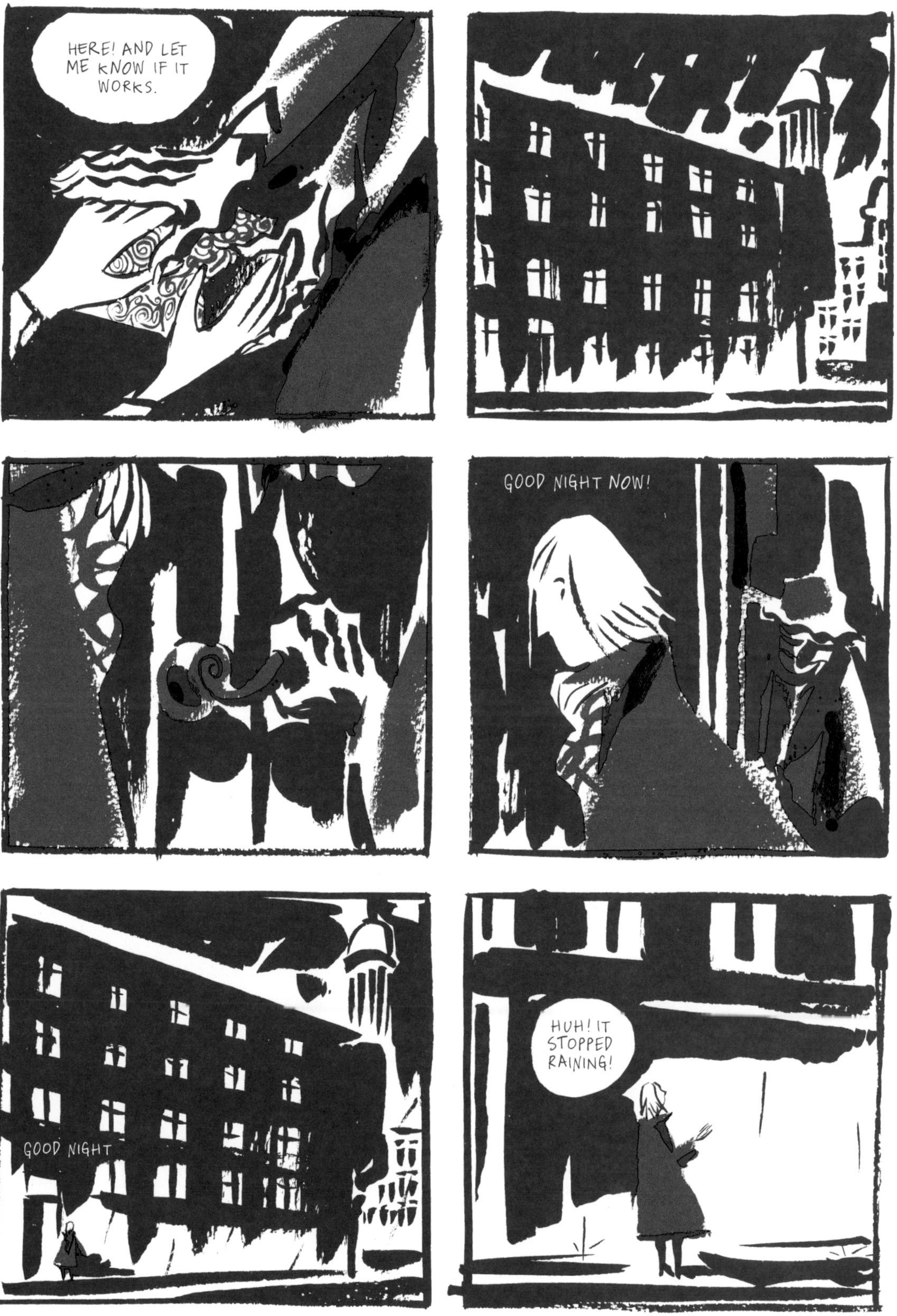
HERE! AND LET ME KNOW IF IT WORKS.
GOOD NIGHT NOW!
GOOD NIGHT
HUH! IT STOPPED RAINING!

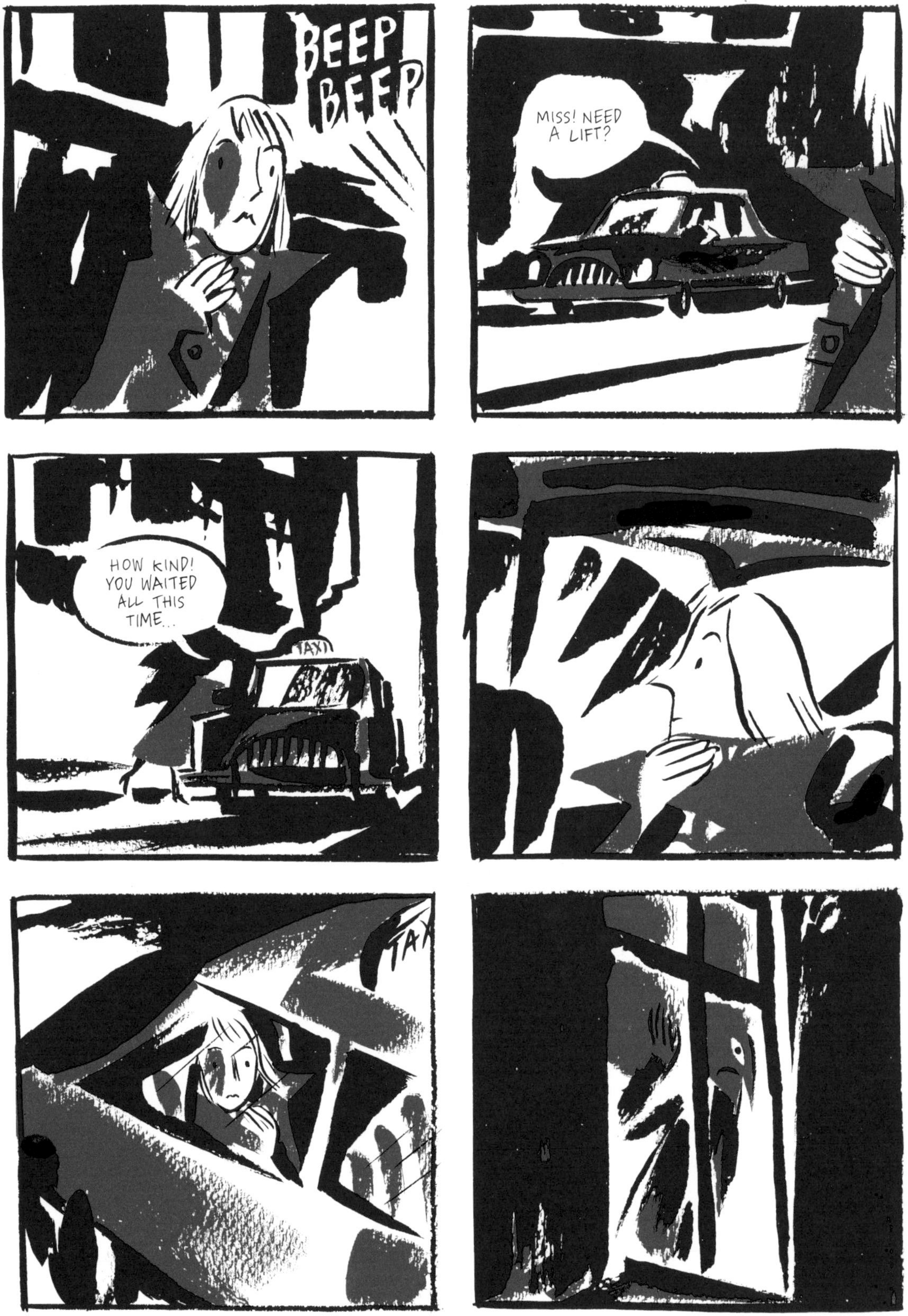
BEEP BEEP
MISS! NEED A LIFT?
HOW KIND! YOU WAITED ALL THIS TIME...
TAXI
TAX

3.

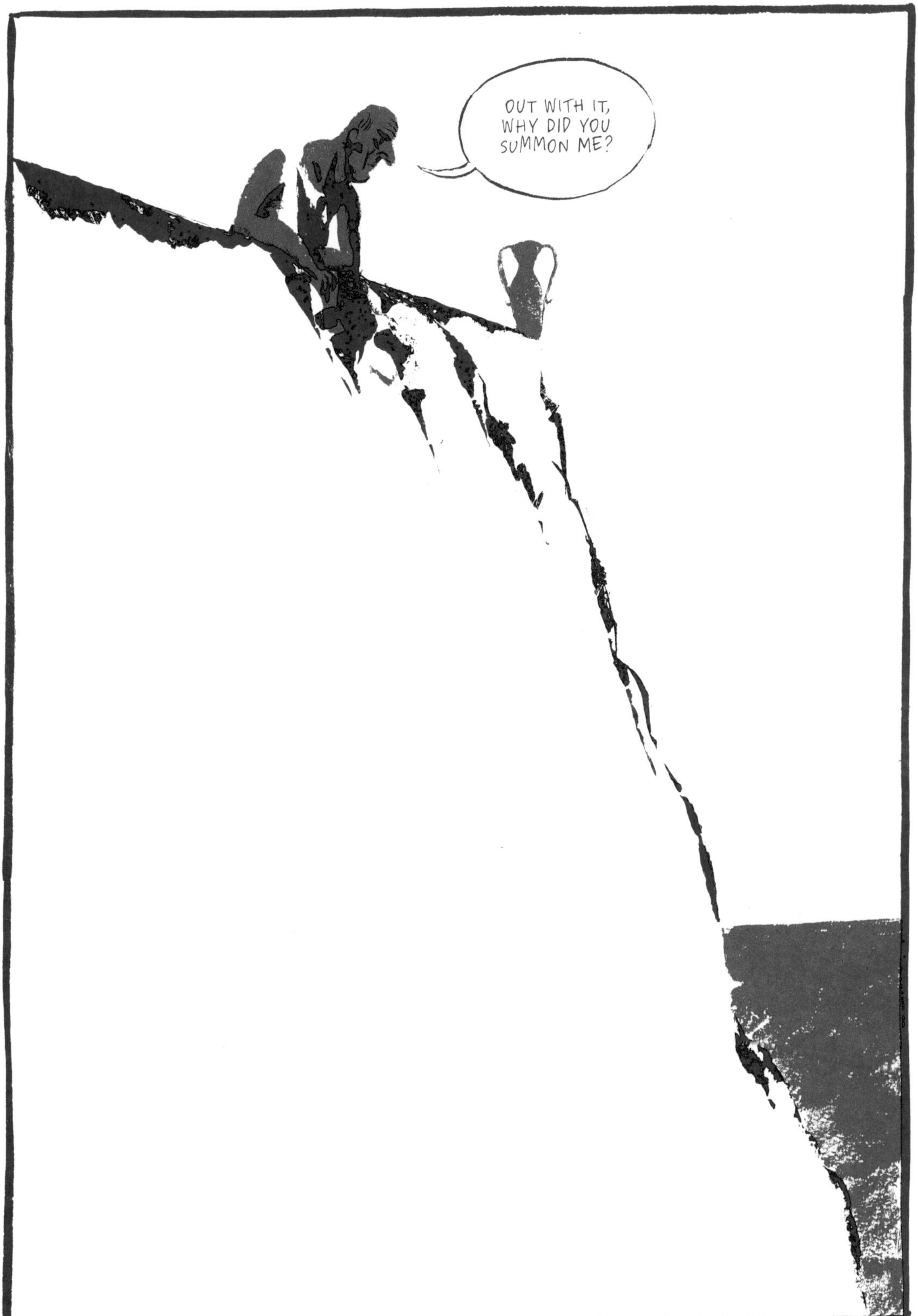
OUT WITH IT,
WHY DID YOU
SUMMON ME?

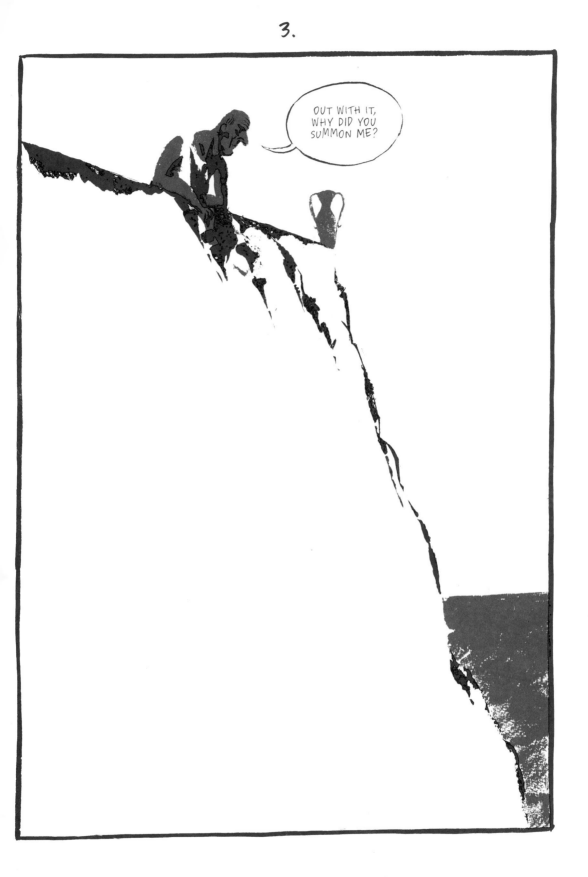

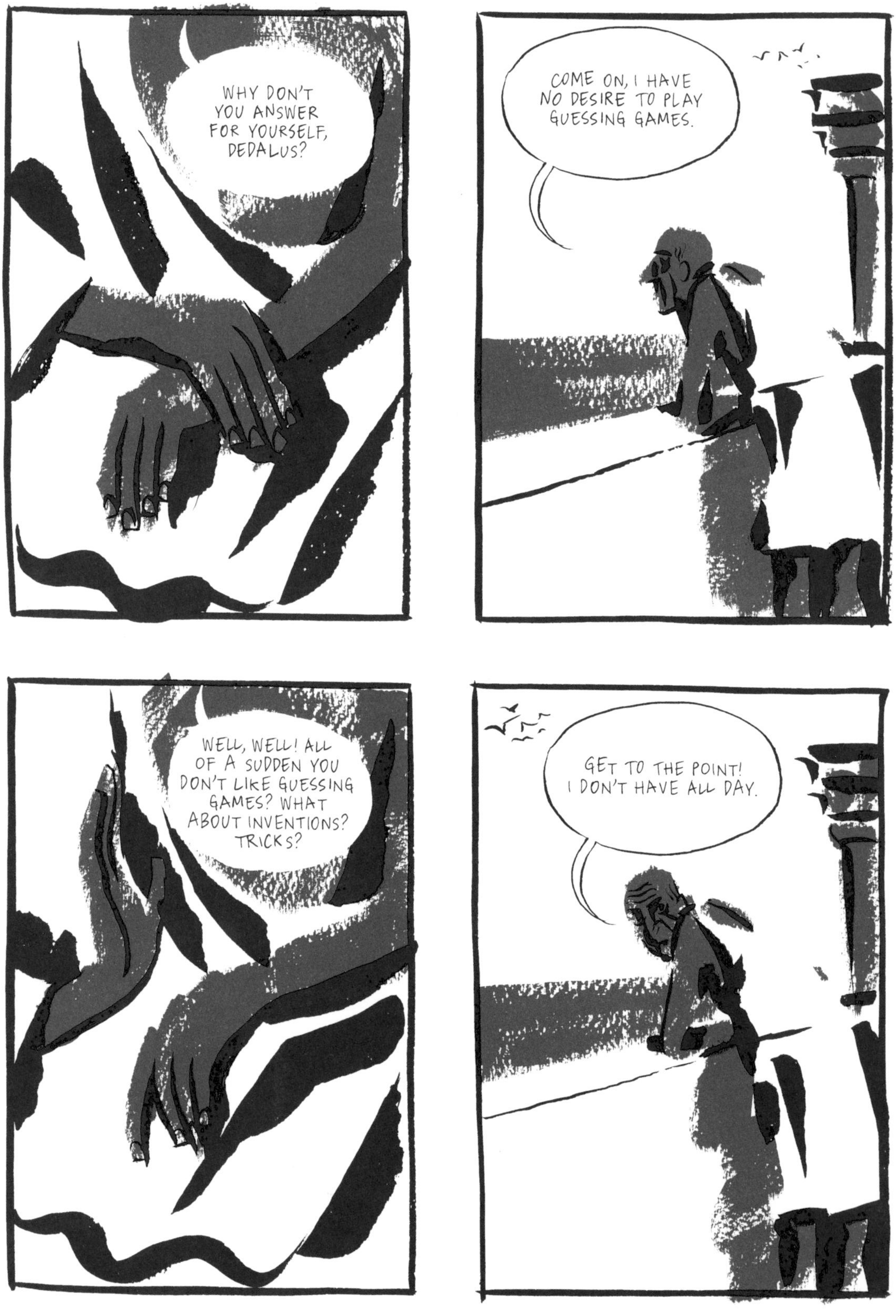
WHY DON'T YOU ANSWER FOR YOURSELF, DEDALUS?
COME ON, I HAVE NO DESIRE TO PLAY GUESSING GAMES.
WELL, WELL! ALL OF A SUDDEN YOU DON'T LIKE GUESSING GAMES? WHAT ABOUT INVENTIONS? TRICKS?
GET TO THE POINT! I DON'T HAVE ALL DAY.

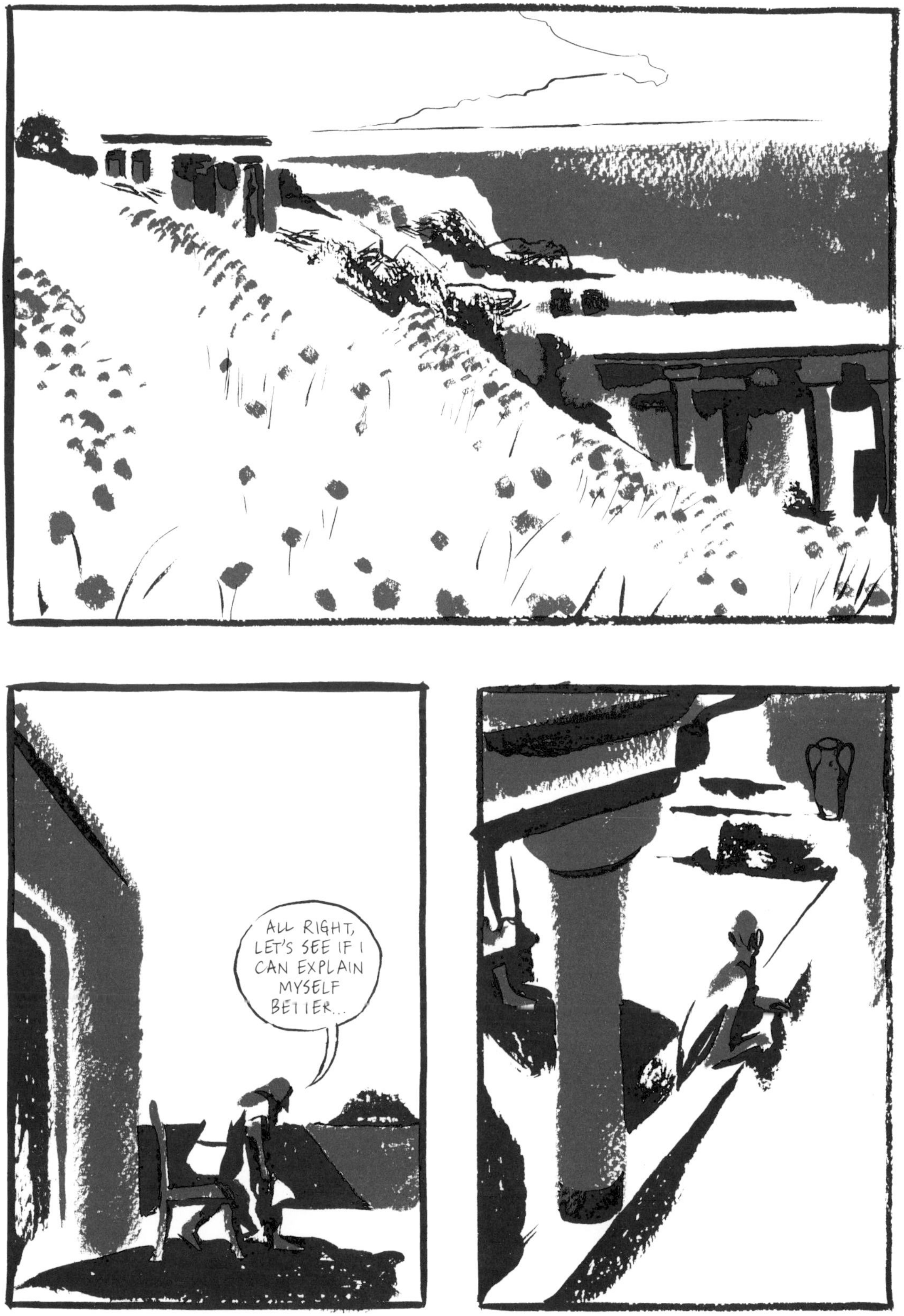
ALL RIGHT, LET'S SEE IF I CAN EXPLAIN MYSELF BETTER...

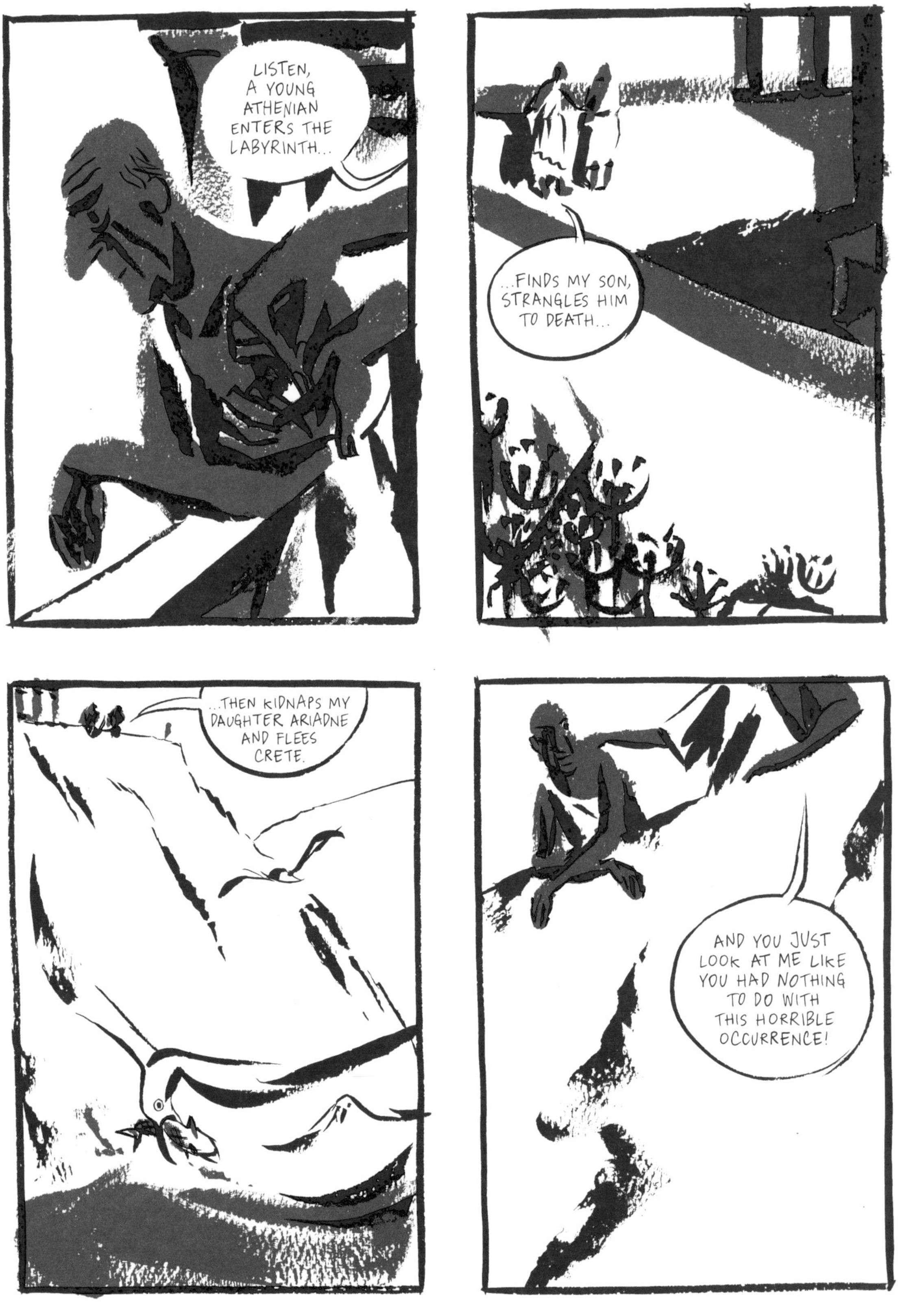
LISTEN, A YOUNG ATHENIAN ENTERS THE LABYRINTH...
...FINDS MY SON, STRANGLES HIM TO DEATH...
...THEN KIDNAPS MY DAUGHTER ARIADNE AND FLEES CRETE.
AND YOU JUST LOOK AT ME LIKE YOU HAD NOTHING TO DO WITH THIS HORRIBLE OCCURRENCE!

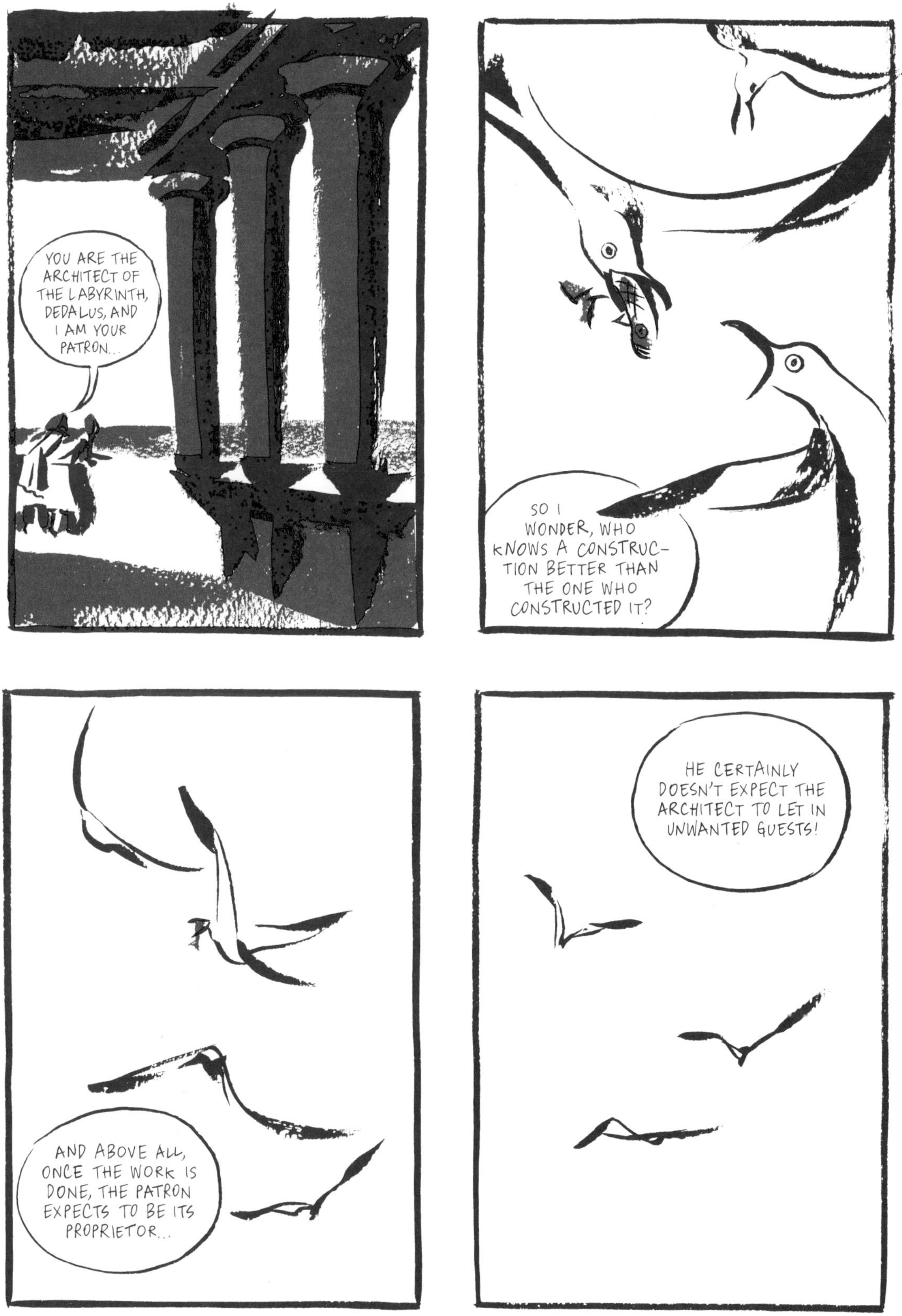
YOU ARE THE ARCHITECT OF THE LABYRINTH, DEDALUS, AND I AM YOUR PATRON...
SO I WONDER, WHO KNOWS A CONSTRUCTION BETTER THAN THE ONE WHO CONSTRUCTED IT?
AND ABOVE ALL, ONCE THE WORK IS DONE, THE PATRON EXPECTS TO BE ITS PROPRIETOR...
HE CERTAINLY DOESN'T EXPECT THE ARCHITECT TO LET IN UNWANTED GUESTS!

NOW WHO'S TO BLAME? THE KILLER, OR THE ONE WHO LEFT THE DOOR OPEN FOR HIM?

YOU'RE WRONG, MINOS. NO ONE CAN FIND THEIR WAY AROUND THE LABYRINTH. EVEN I WOULDN'T KNOW HOW TO GET OUT IF I WENT INSIDE.

YOU ASKED ME TO BUILD A DWELLING FOR THAT HALF-MAN, HALF-BULL MONSTER.

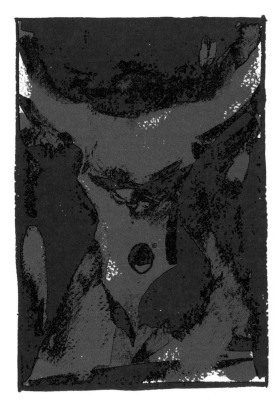

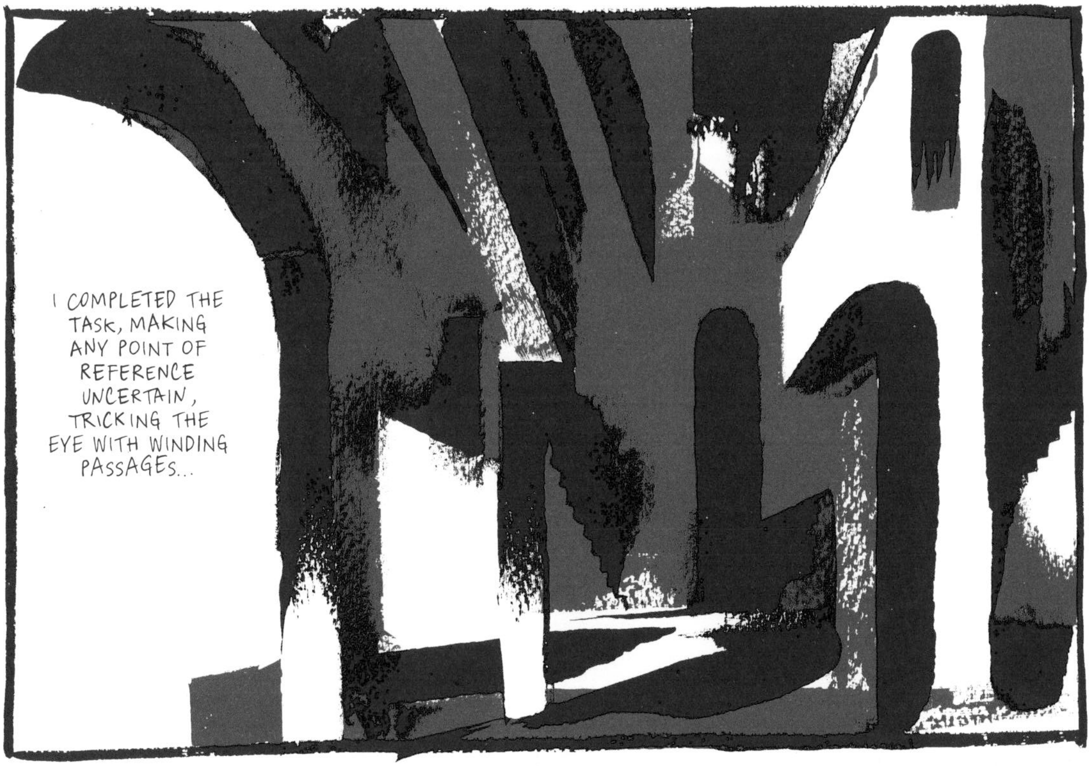
I COMPLETED THE TASK, MAKING ANY POINT OF REFERENCE UNCERTAIN, TRICKING THE EYE WITH WINDING PASSAGES...

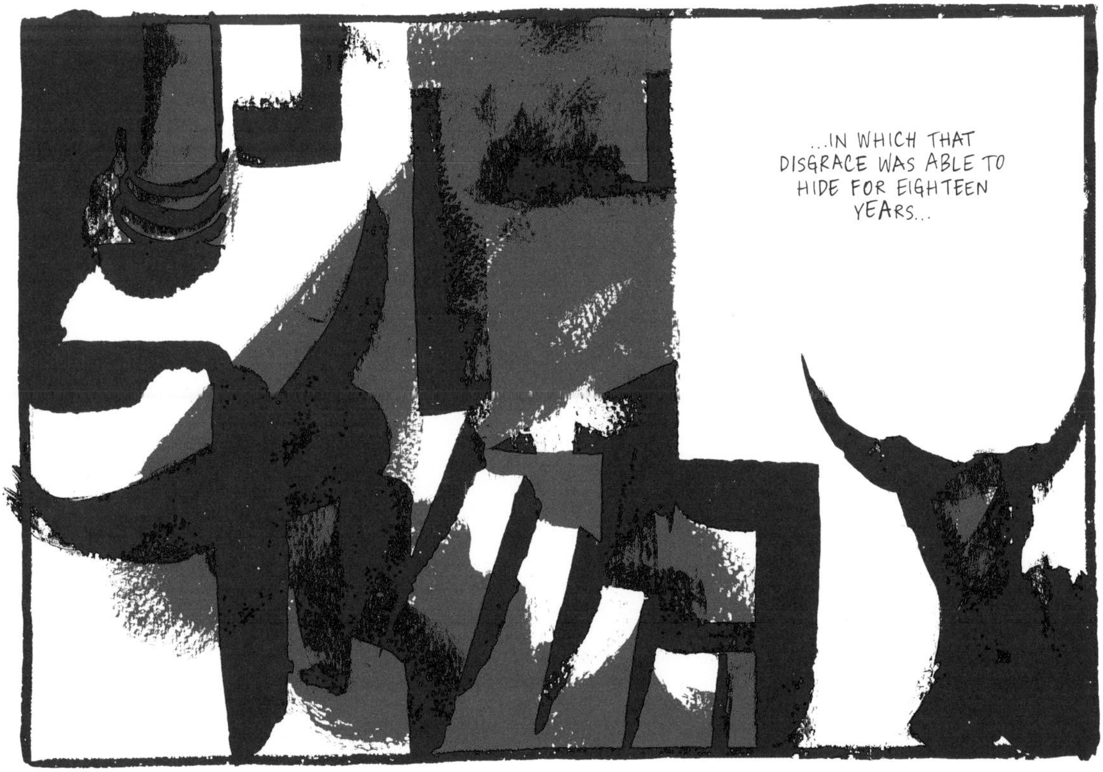
...IN WHICH THAT DISGRACE WAS ABLE TO HIDE FOR EIGHTEEN YEARS...

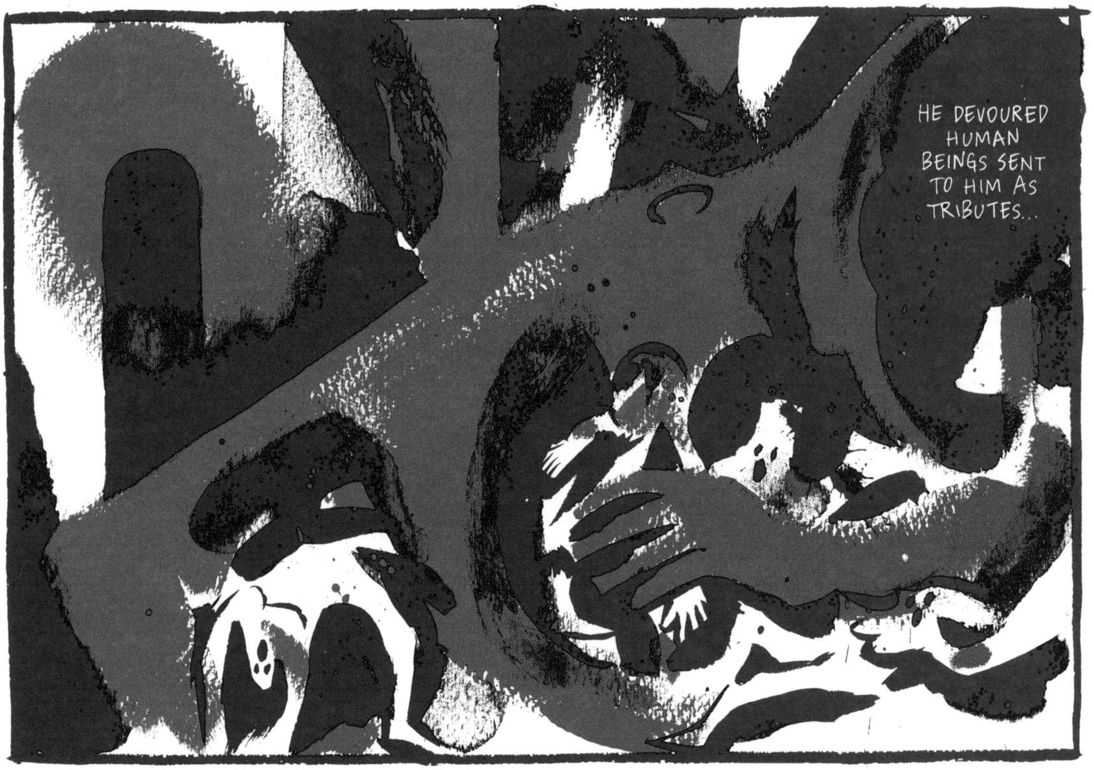
HE DEVOURED HUMAN BEINGS SENT TO HIM AS TRIBUTES...

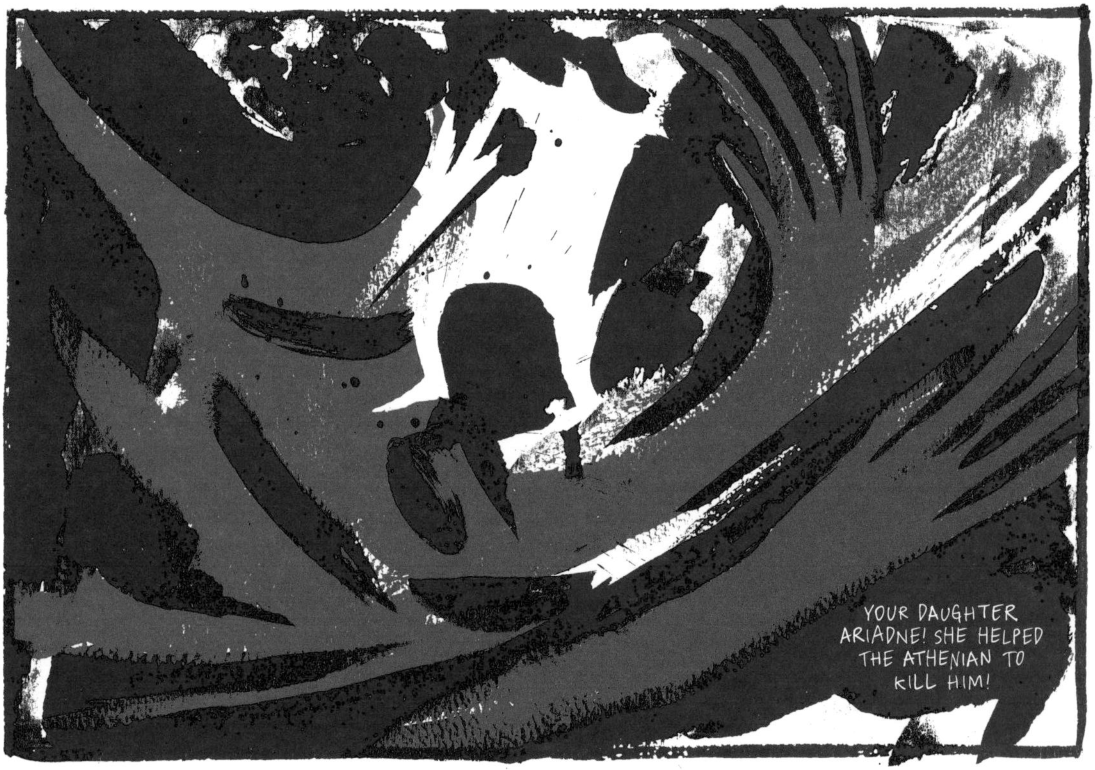
YOUR DAUGHTER ARIADNE! SHE HELPED THE ATHENIAN TO KILL HIM!

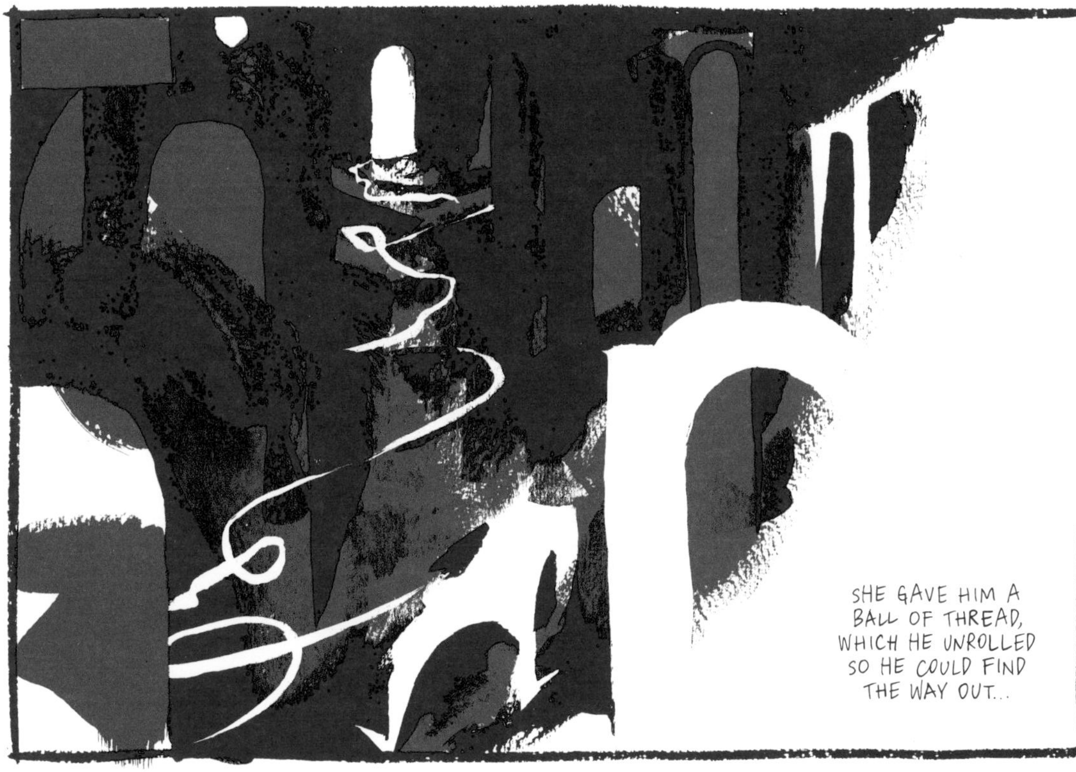
SHE GAVE HIM A
BALL OF THREAD,
WHICH HE UNROLLED
SO HE COULD FIND
THE WAY OUT...

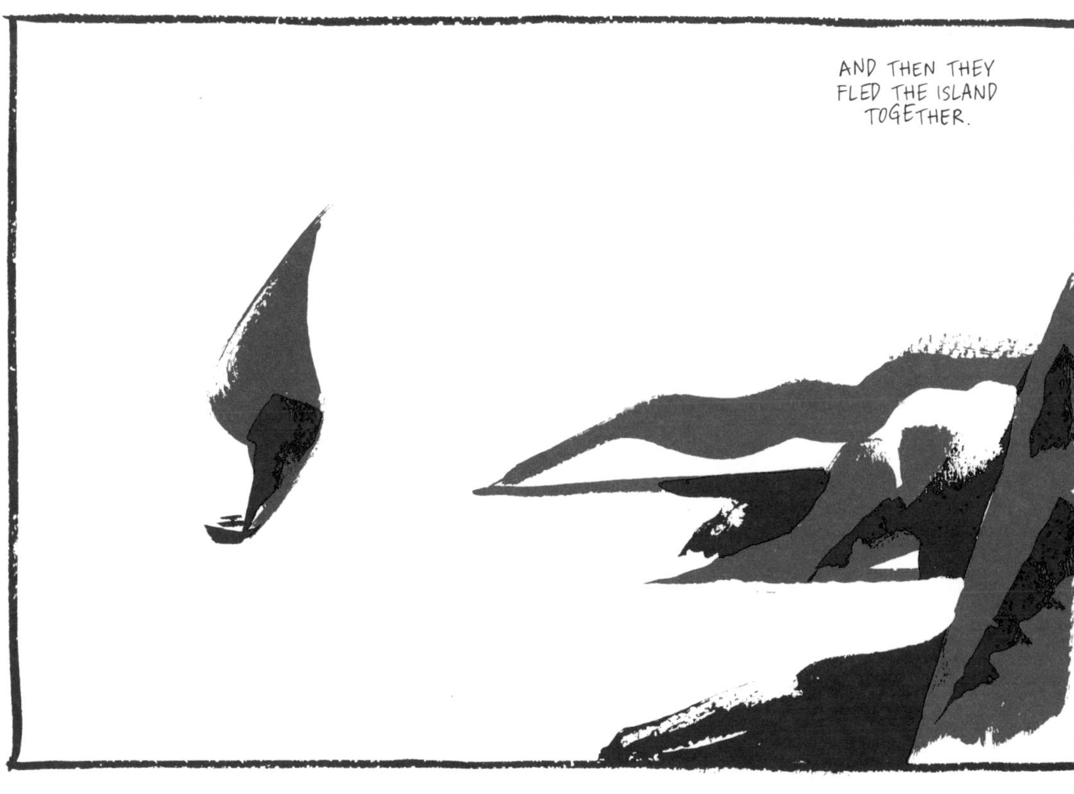
AND THEN THEY
FLED THE ISLAND
TOGETHER.

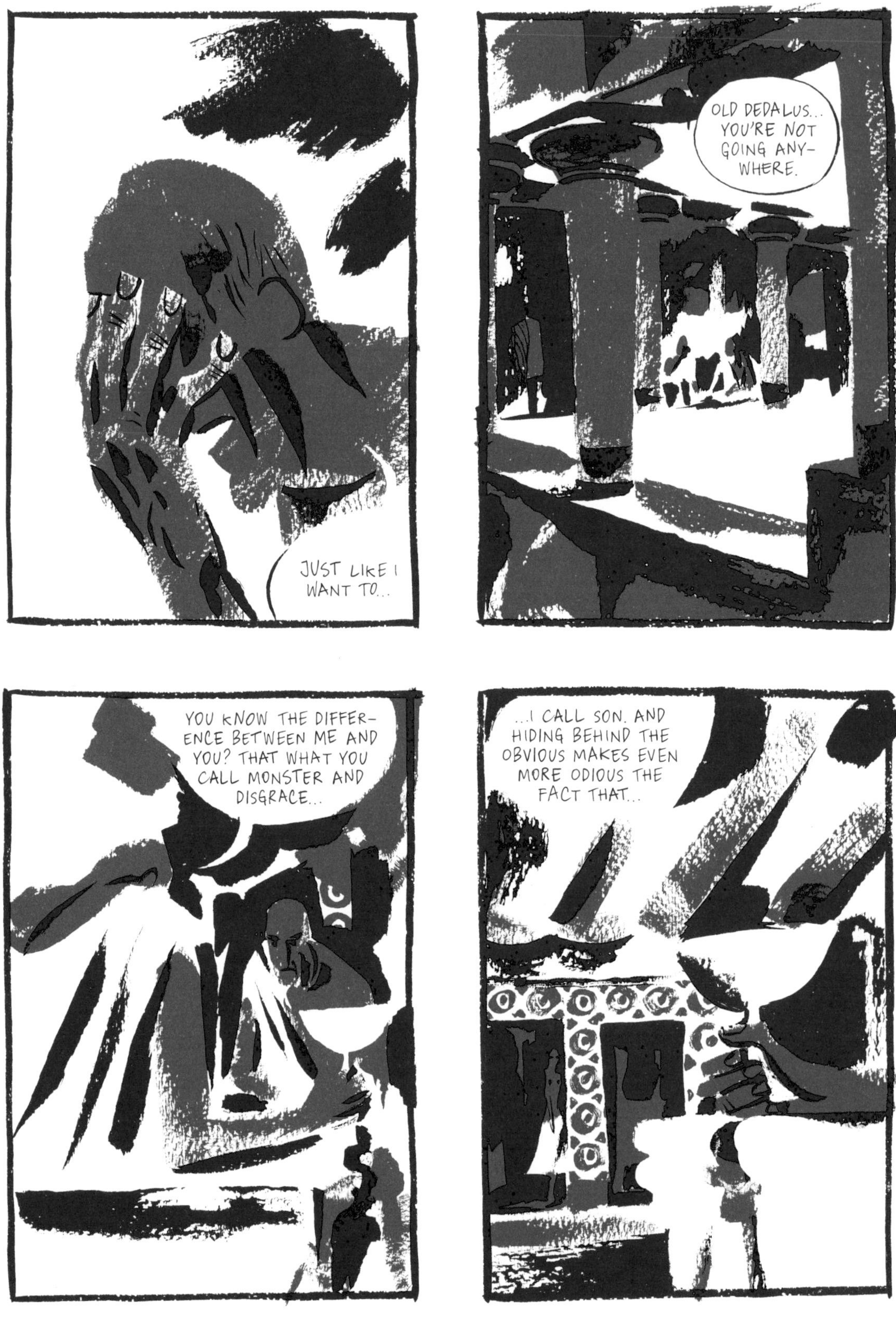
JUST LIKE I WANT TO...
OLD DEDALUS... YOU'RE NOT GOING ANY-WHERE.
YOU KNOW THE DIFFER-ENCE BETWEEN ME AND YOU? THAT WHAT YOU CALL MONSTER AND DISGRACE...
...I CALL SON. AND HIDING BEHIND THE OBVIOUS MAKES EVEN MORE ODIOUS THE FACT THAT...

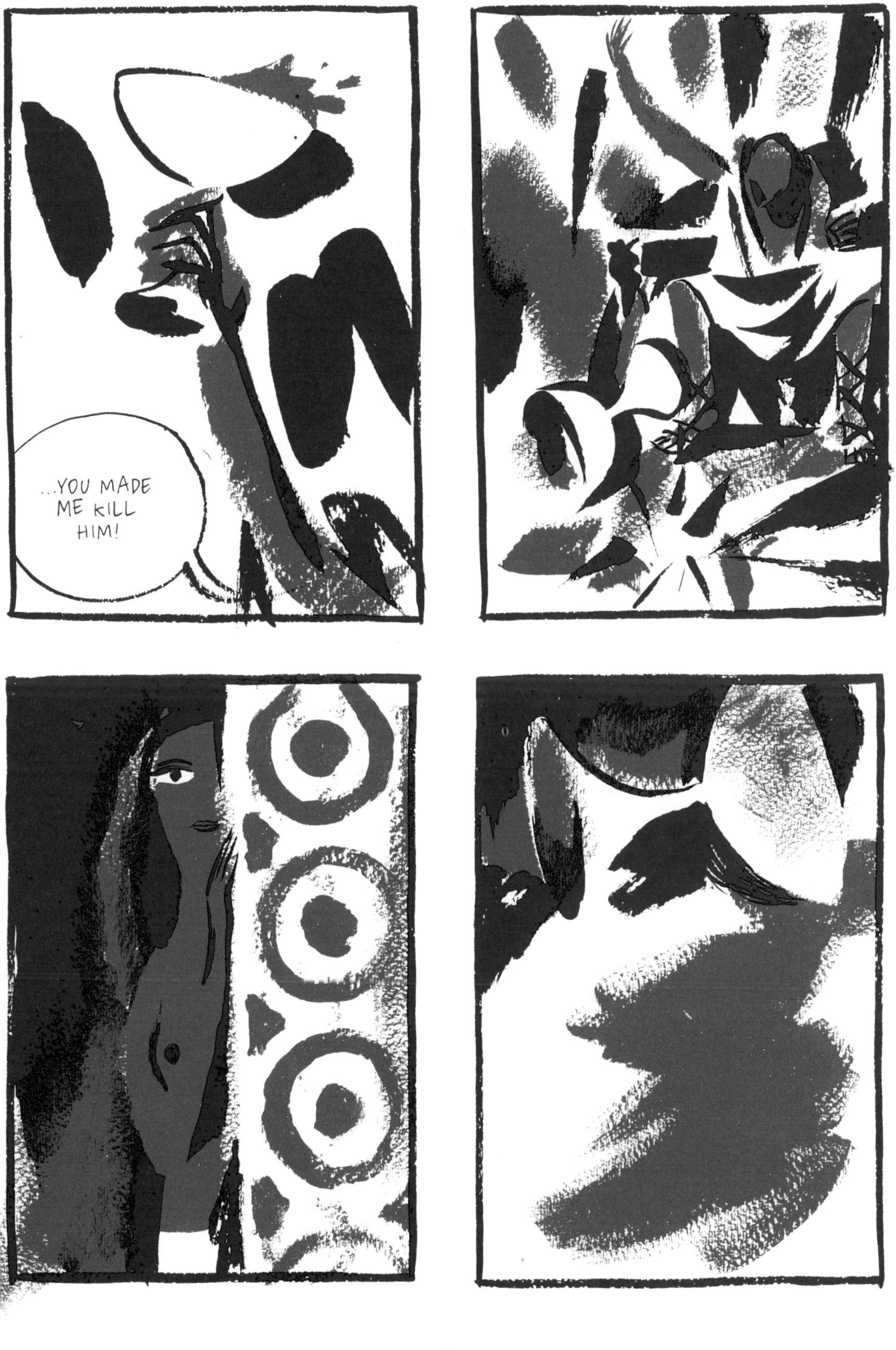
...YOU MADE ME KILL HIM!

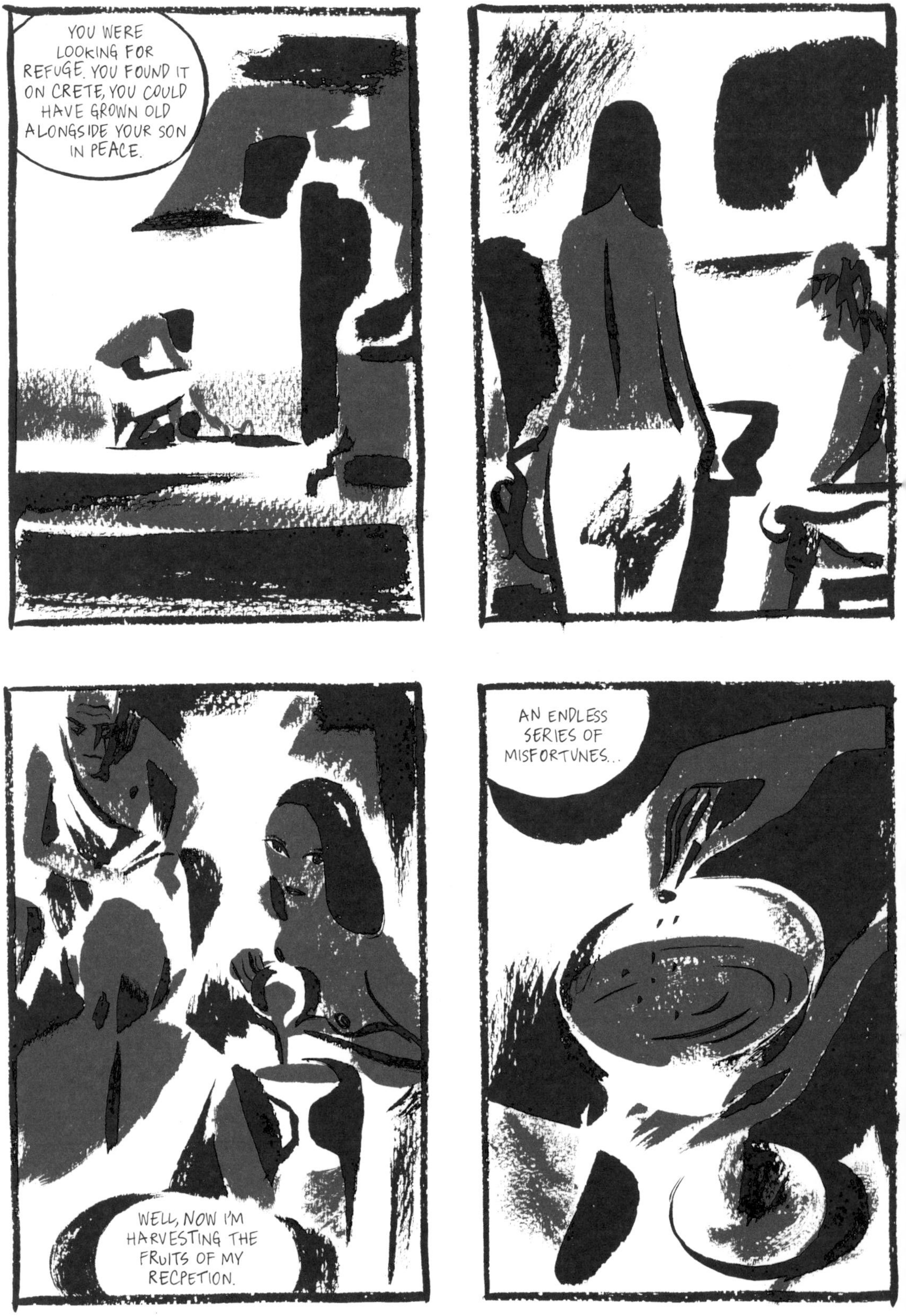
YOU WERE LOOKING FOR REFUGE. YOU FOUND IT ON CRETE, YOU COULD HAVE GROWN OLD ALONGSIDE YOUR SON IN PEACE.
WELL, NOW I'M HARVESTING THE FRUITS OF MY RECPETION.
AN ENDLESS SERIES OF MISFORTUNES...

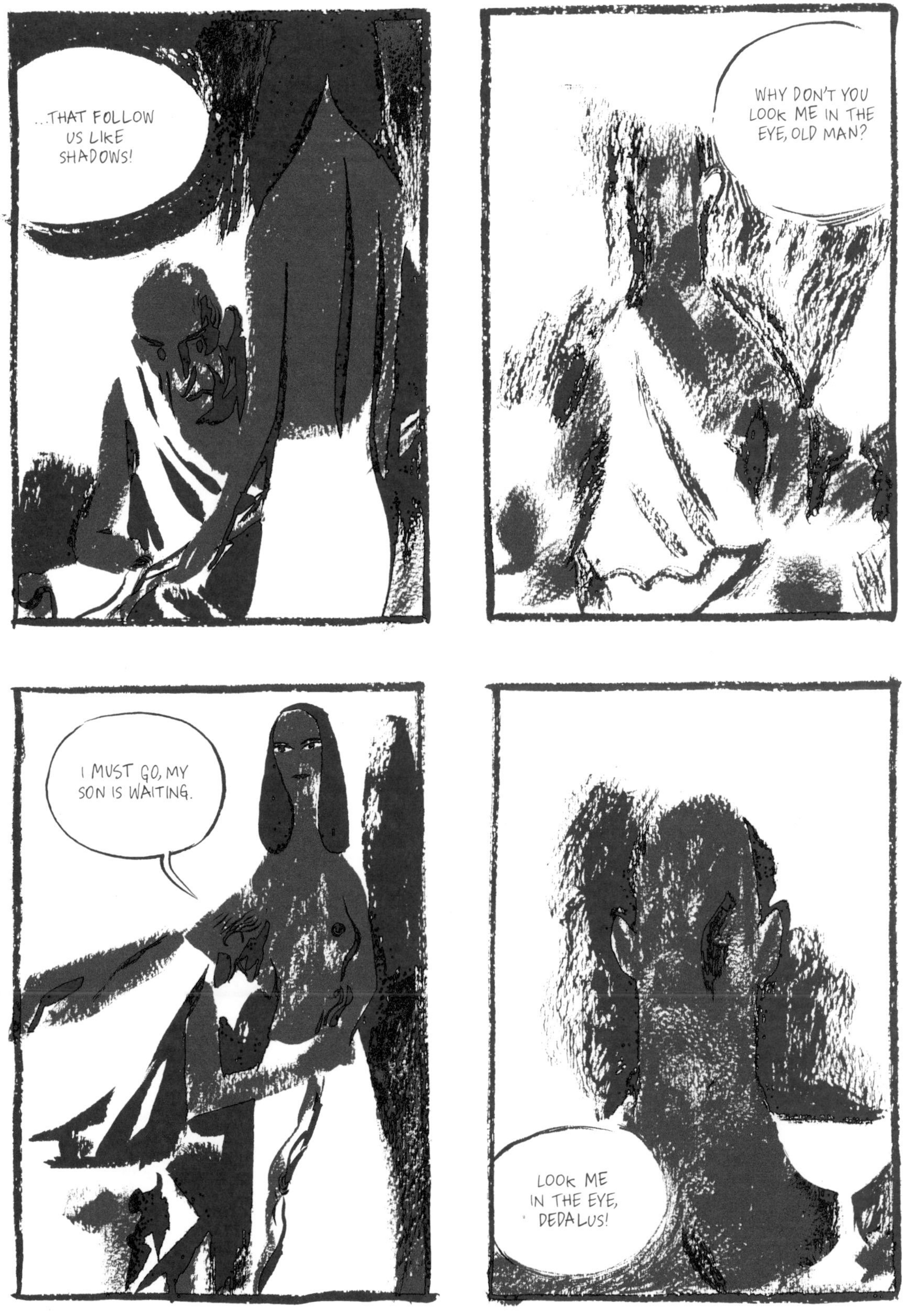
...THAT FOLLOW US LIKE SHADOWS!
WHY DON'T YOU LOOK ME IN THE EYE, OLD MAN?
I MUST GO, MY SON IS WAITING.
LOOK ME IN THE EYE, DEDALUS!

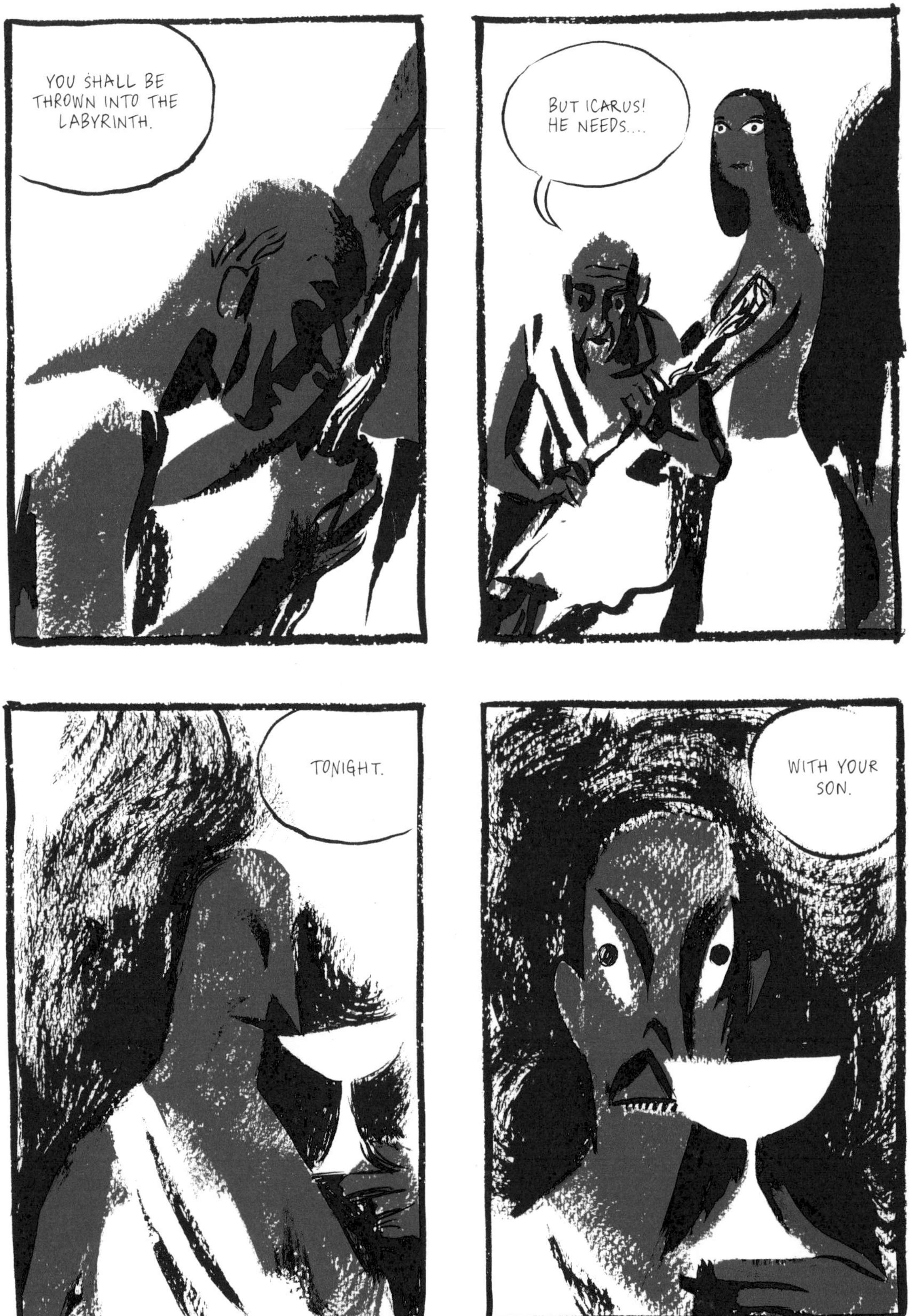
YOU SHALL BE THROWN INTO THE LABYRINTH.
BUT ICARUS! HE NEEDS...
TONIGHT.
WITH YOUR SON.

4.

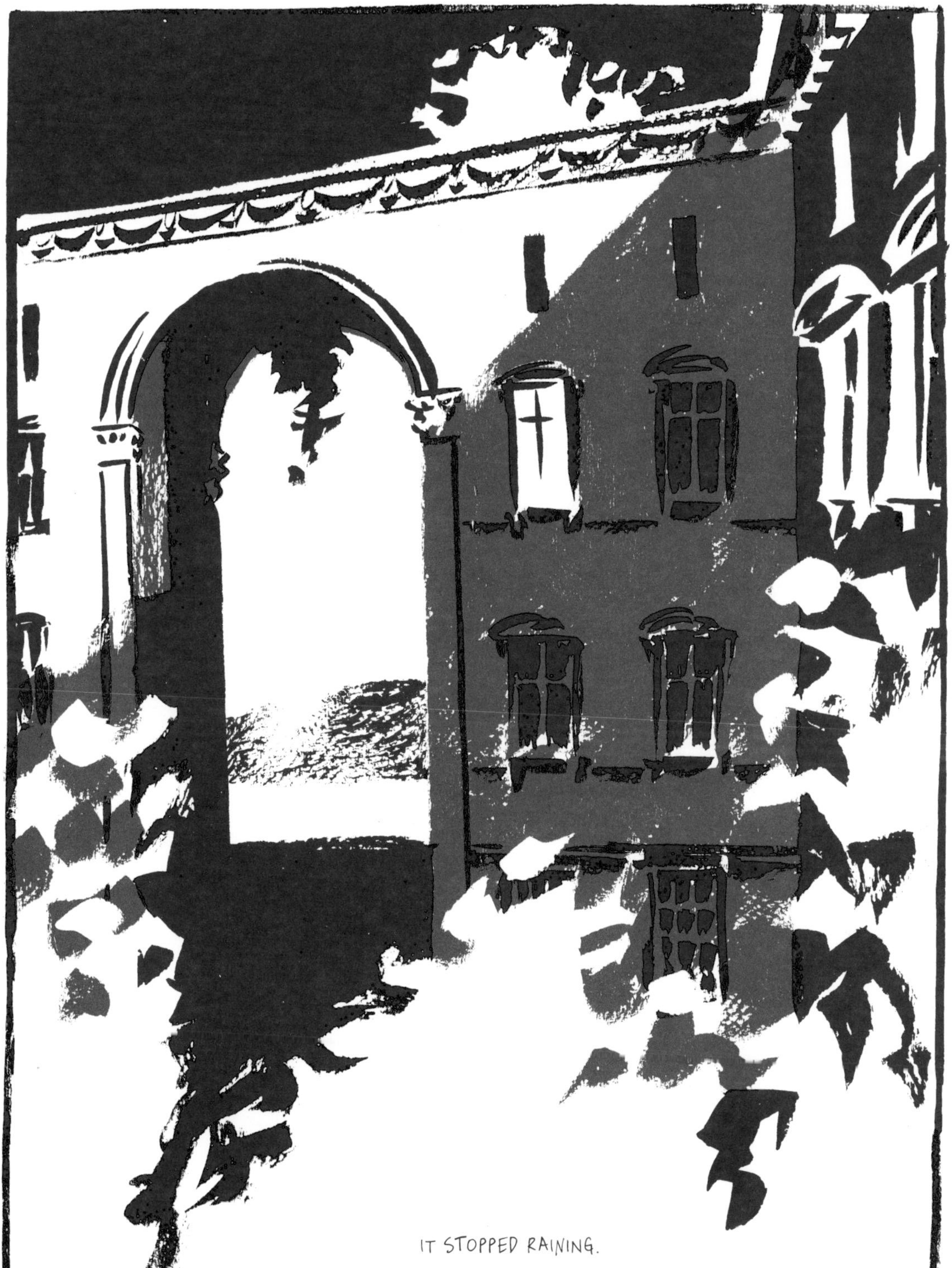
IT STOPPED RAINING.

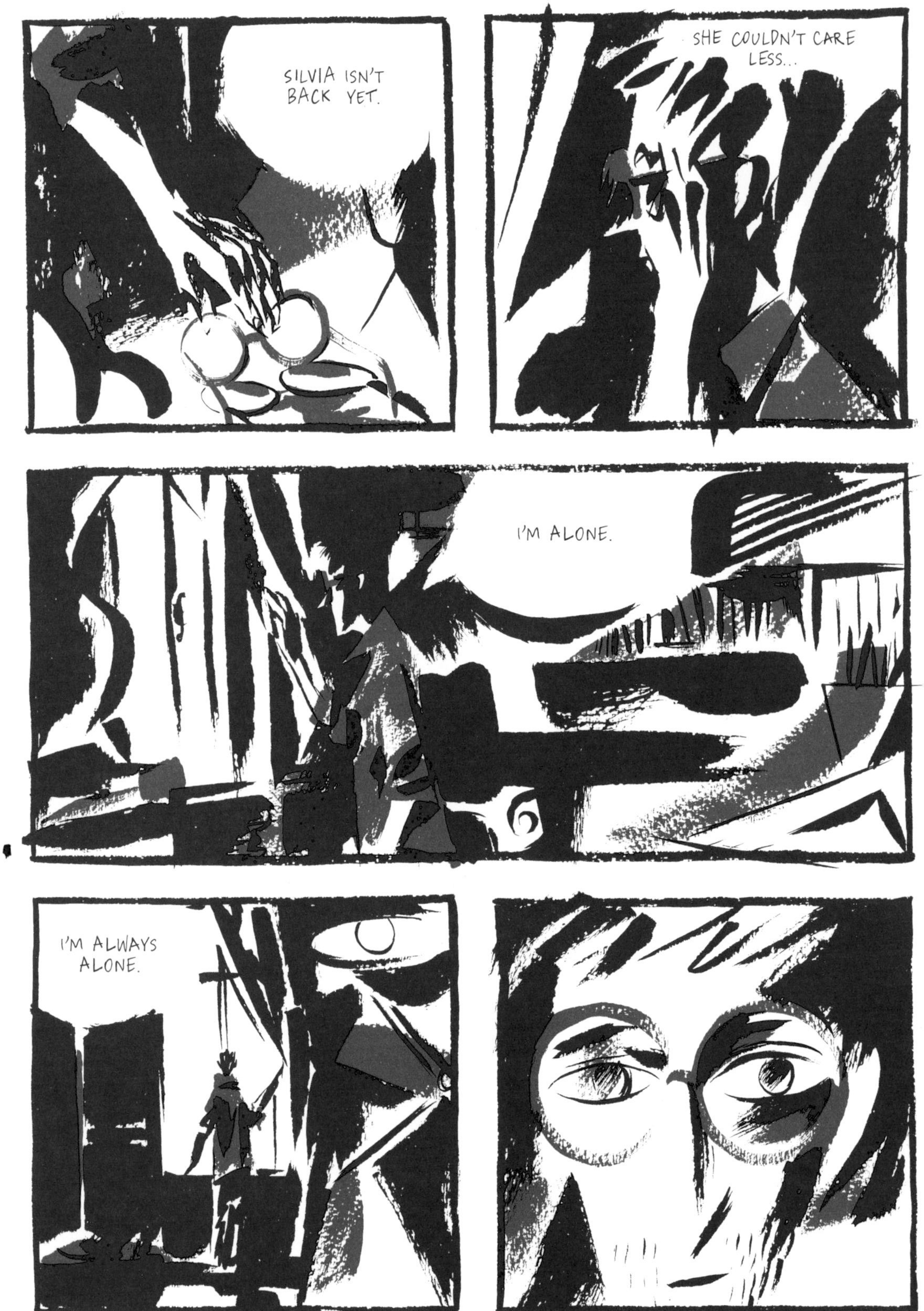
SILVIA ISN'T BACK YET.
SHE COULDN'T CARE LESS...
I'M ALONE.
I'M ALWAYS ALONE.

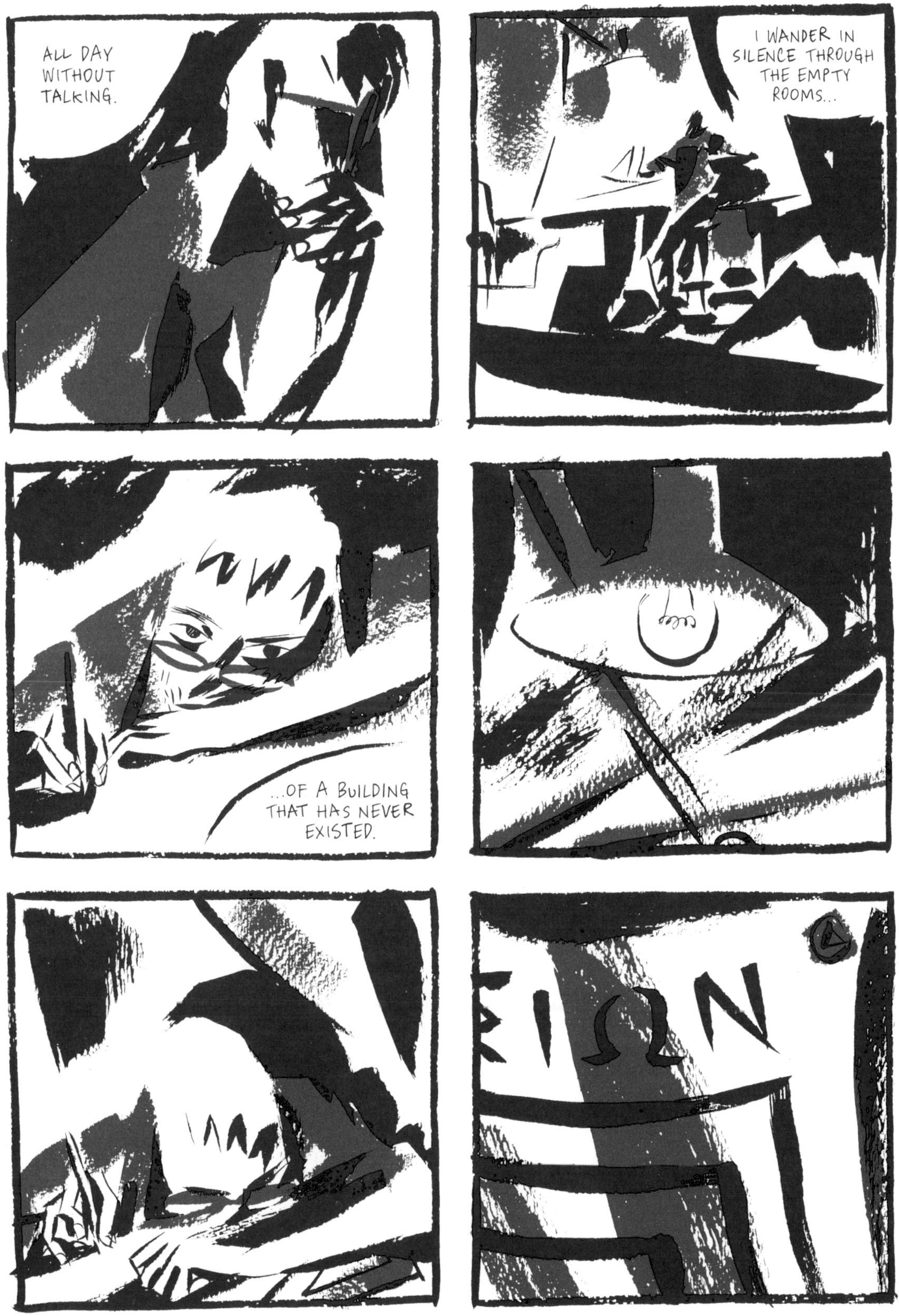
ALL DAY WITHOUT TALKING.
I WANDER IN SILENCE THROUGH THE EMPTY ROOMS...
...OF A BUILDING THAT HAS NEVER EXISTED.

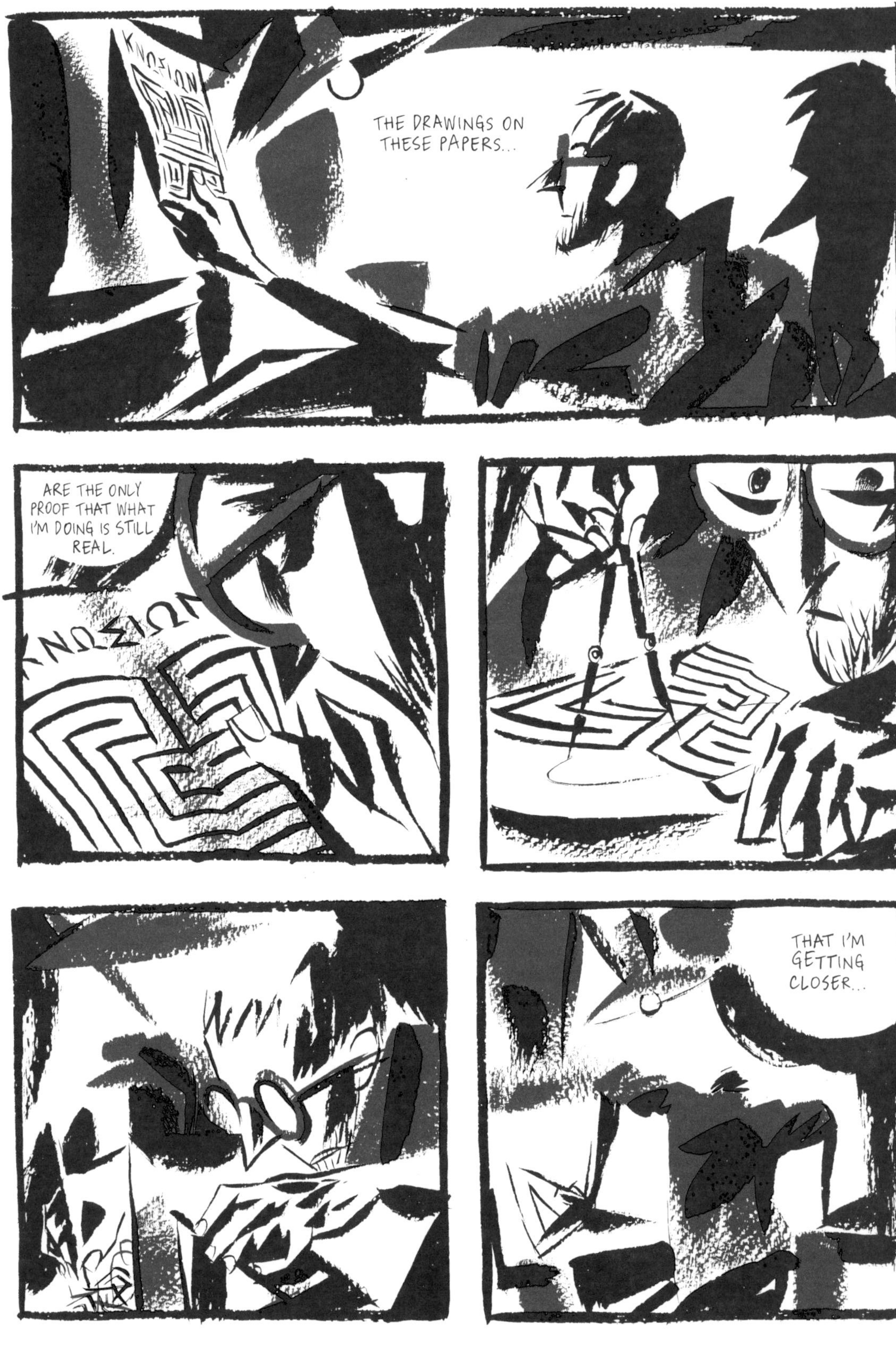
THE DRAWINGS ON THESE PAPERS...
ARE THE ONLY PROOF THAT WHAT I'M DOING IS STILL REAL.
THAT I'M GETTING CLOSER...

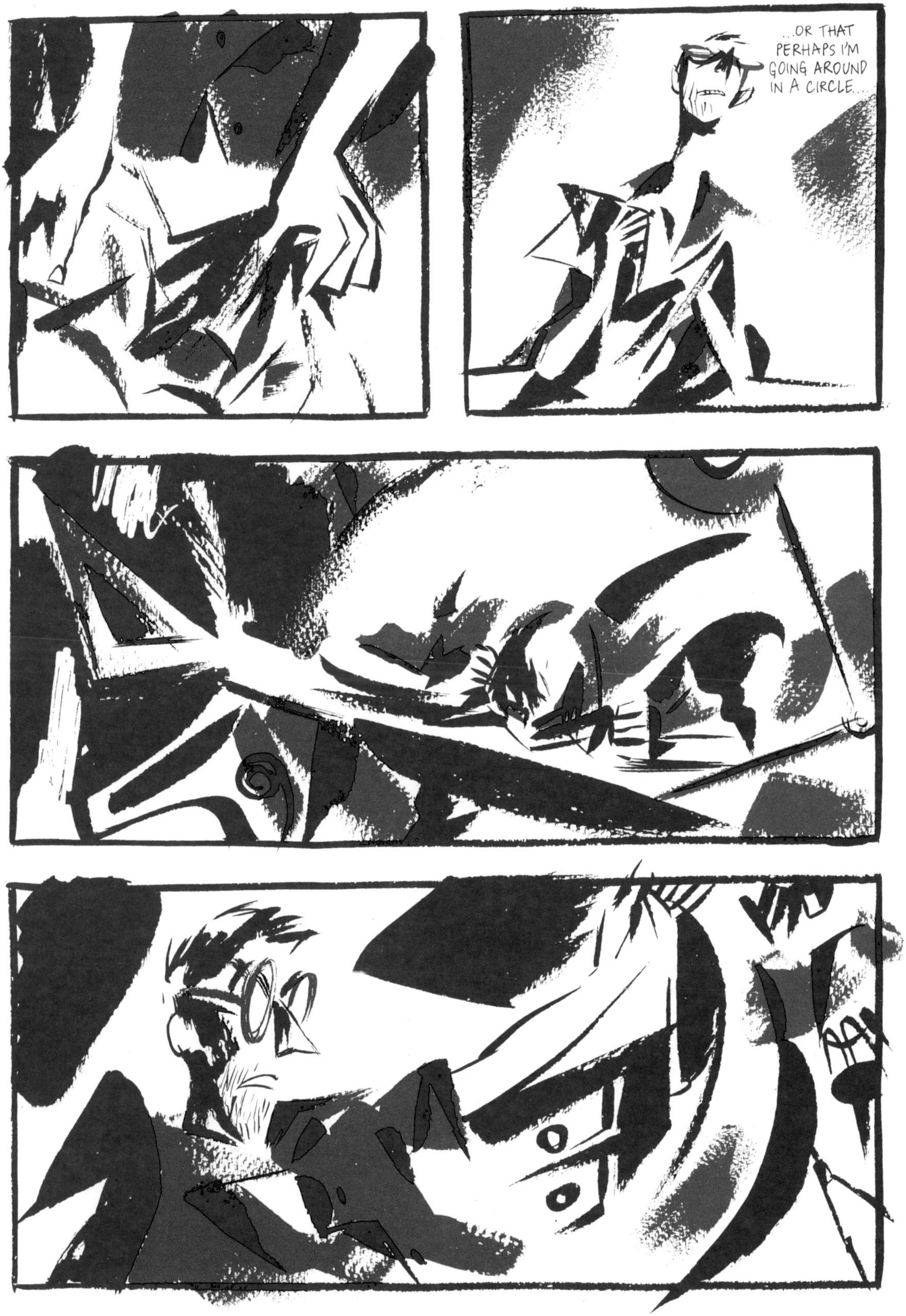
...OR THAT PERHAPS I'M GOING AROUND IN A CIRCLE...

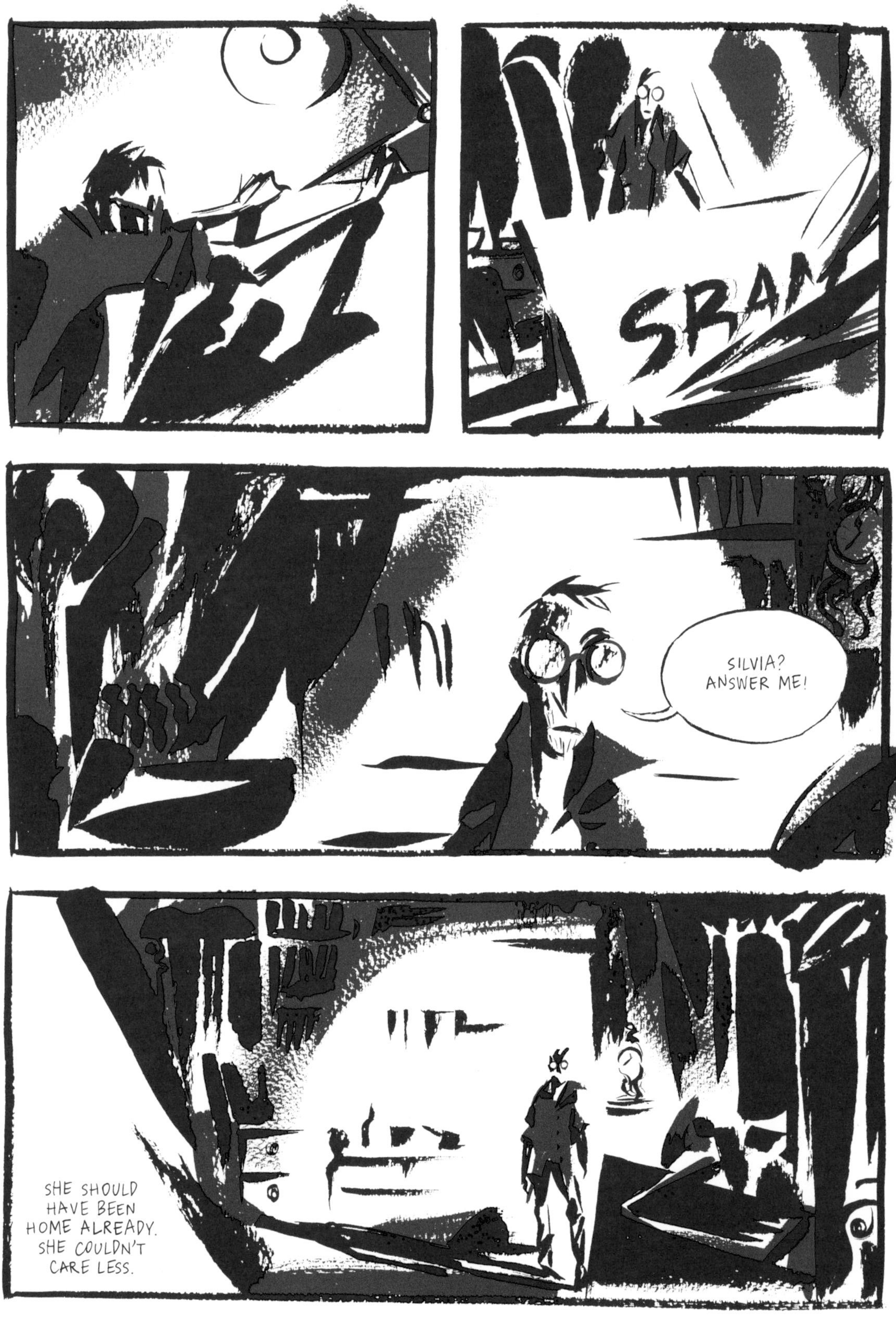
SRAM
SILVIA? ANSWER ME!
SHE SHOULD HAVE BEEN HOME ALREADY. SHE COULDN'T CARE LESS.

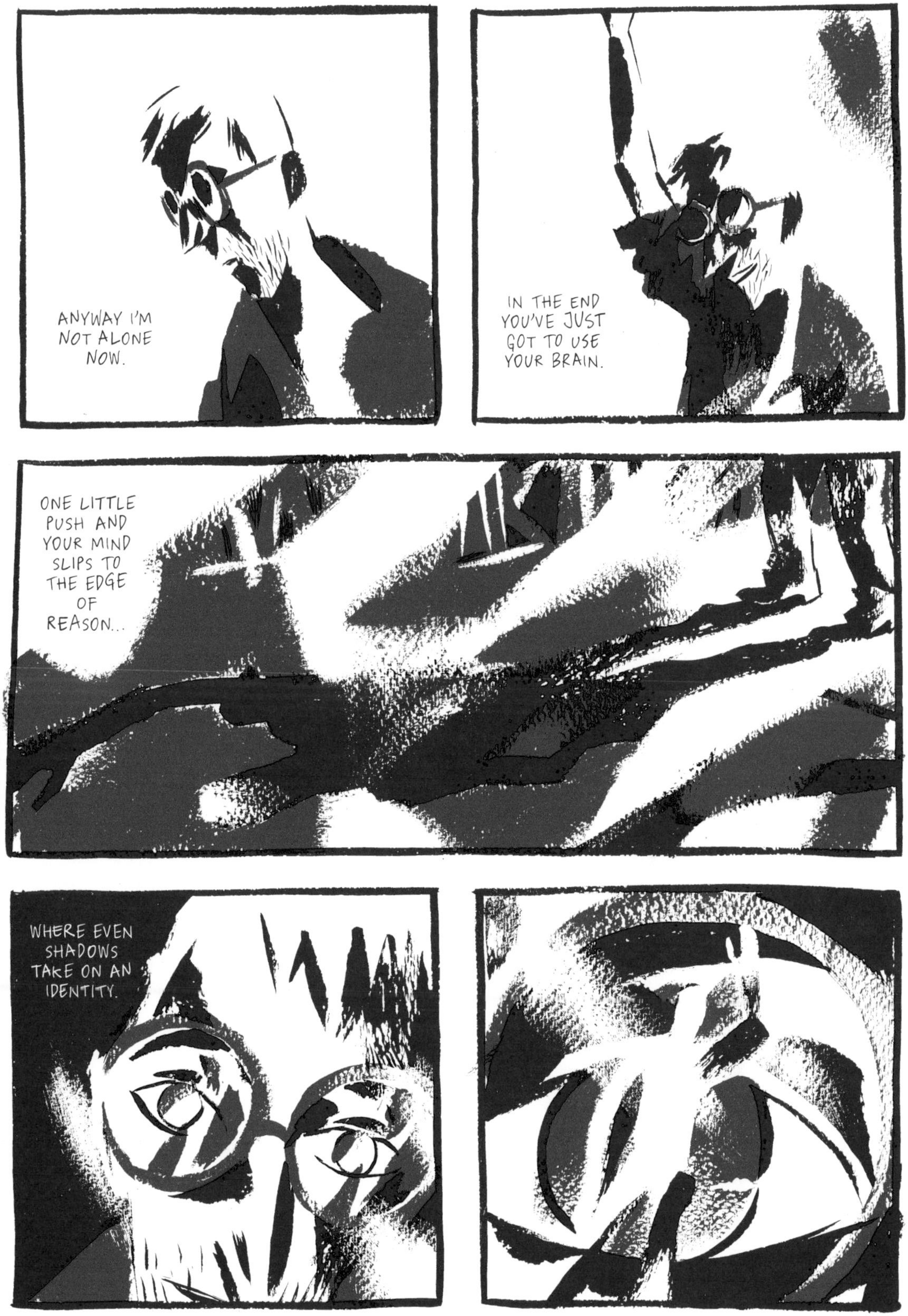
ANYWAY I'M NOT ALONE NOW.
IN THE END YOU'VE JUST GOT TO USE YOUR BRAIN.
ONE LITTLE PUSH AND YOUR MIND SLIPS TO THE EDGE OF REASON...
WHERE EVEN SHADOWS TAKE ON AN IDENTITY.

A PLACE WHERE
THE MIND INVENTS
INCREDIBLE
CORRESPONDENCES...

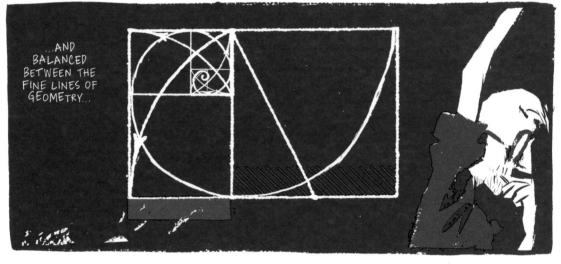

...AND
BALANCED
BETWEEN THE
FINE LINES OF
GEOMETRY...

...LIES A QUIET AND
ORDERED WORLD.

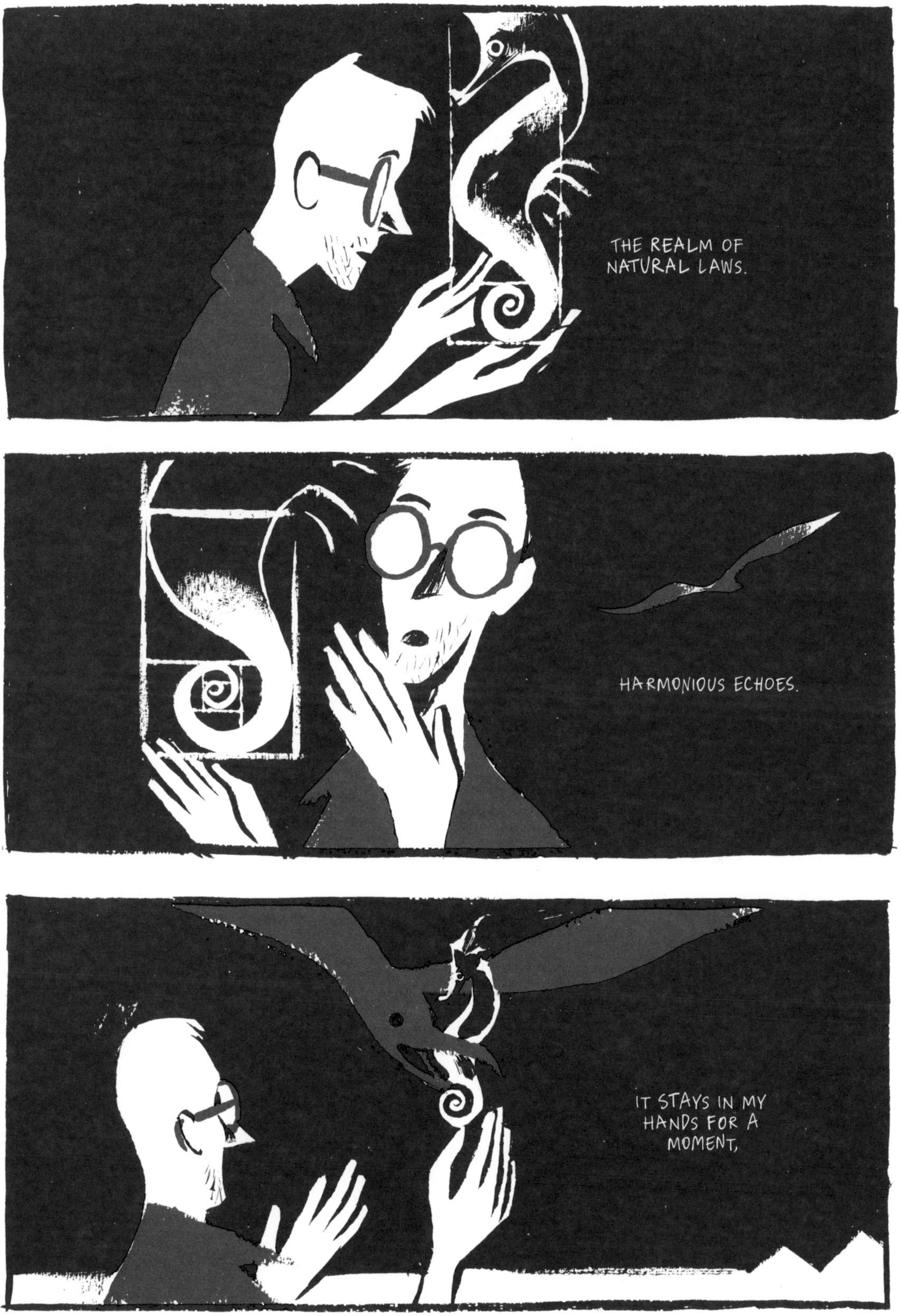
THE REALM OF NATURAL LAWS.
HARMONIOUS ECHOES.
IT STAYS IN MY HANDS FOR A MOMENT,

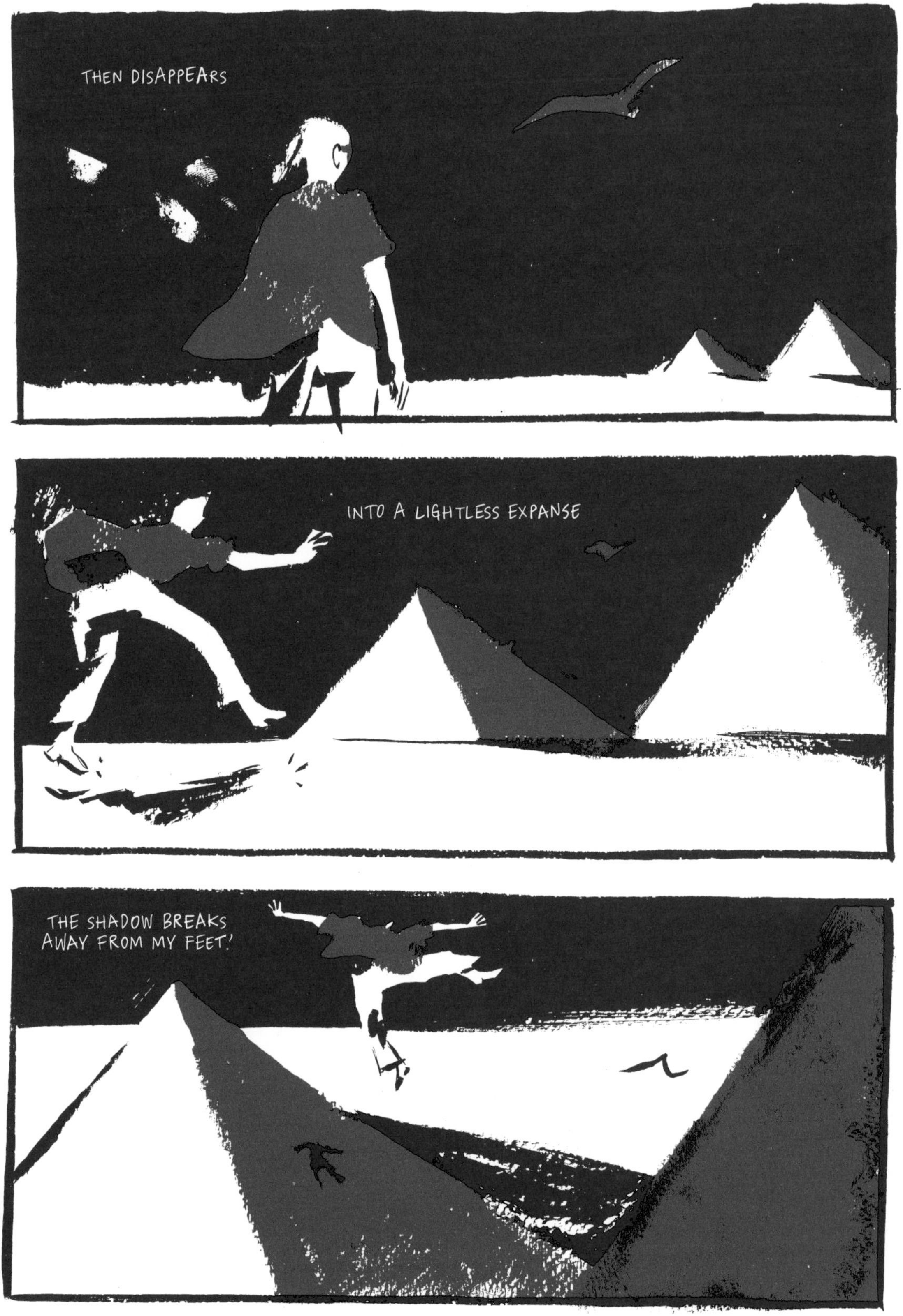
THEN DISAPPEARS
INTO A LIGHTLESS EXPANSE
THE SHADOW BREAKS AWAY FROM MY FEET!

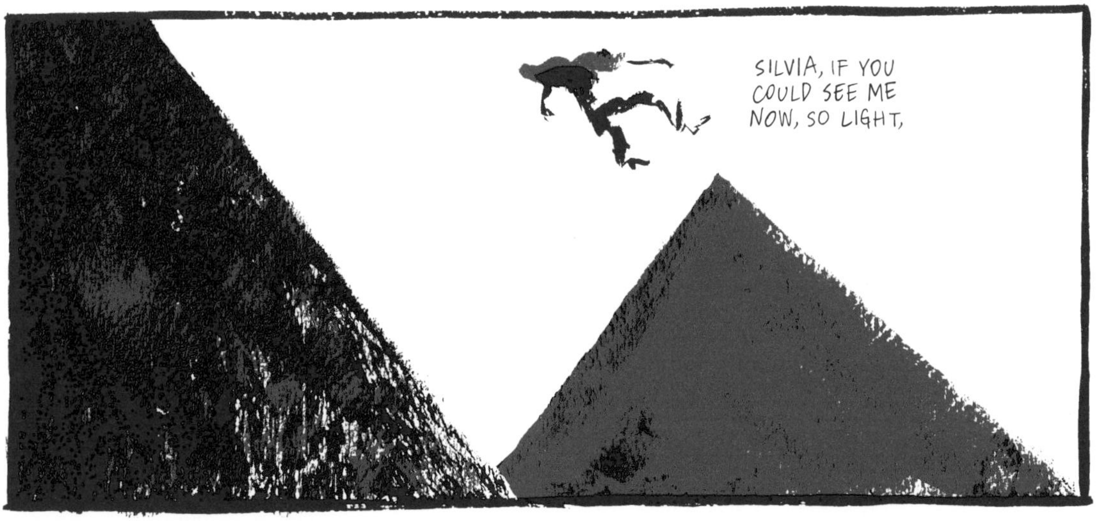
SILVIA, IF YOU COULD SEE ME NOW, SO LIGHT,

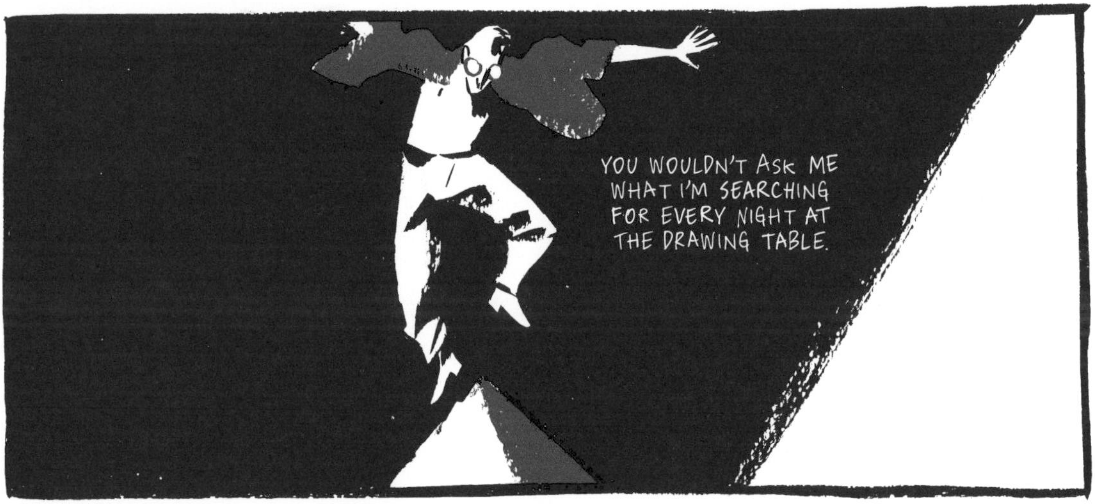
YOU WOULDN'T ASK ME WHAT I'M SEARCHING FOR EVERY NIGHT AT THE DRAWING TABLE.

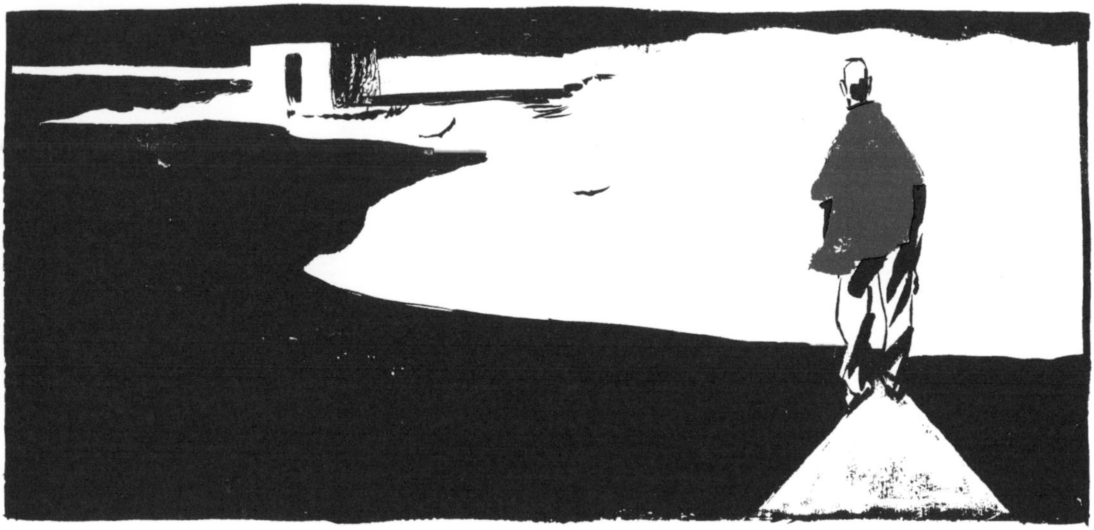

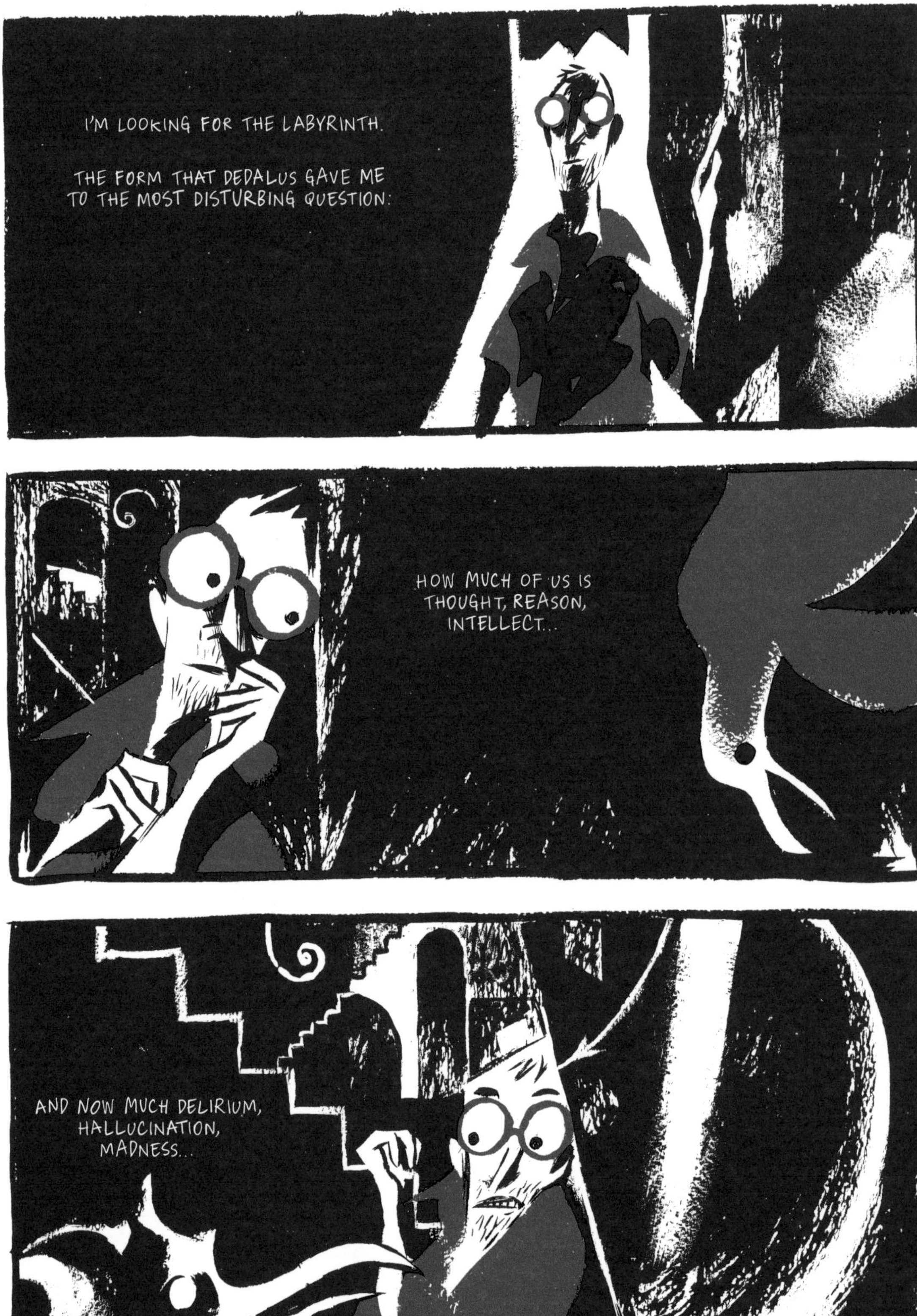
I'M LOOKING FOR THE LABYRINTH.
THE FORM THAT DEDALUS GAVE ME TO THE MOST DISTURBING QUESTION:
HOW MUCH OF US IS THOUGHT, REASON, INTELLECT...
AND NOW MUCH DELIRIUM, HALLUCINATION, MADNESS...

...AND HOW MUCH IS
A MONSTER.

THE FAILURE OF
EVERY PLAN.

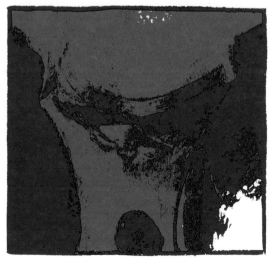

A PATH WITH NO
WAY OUT.

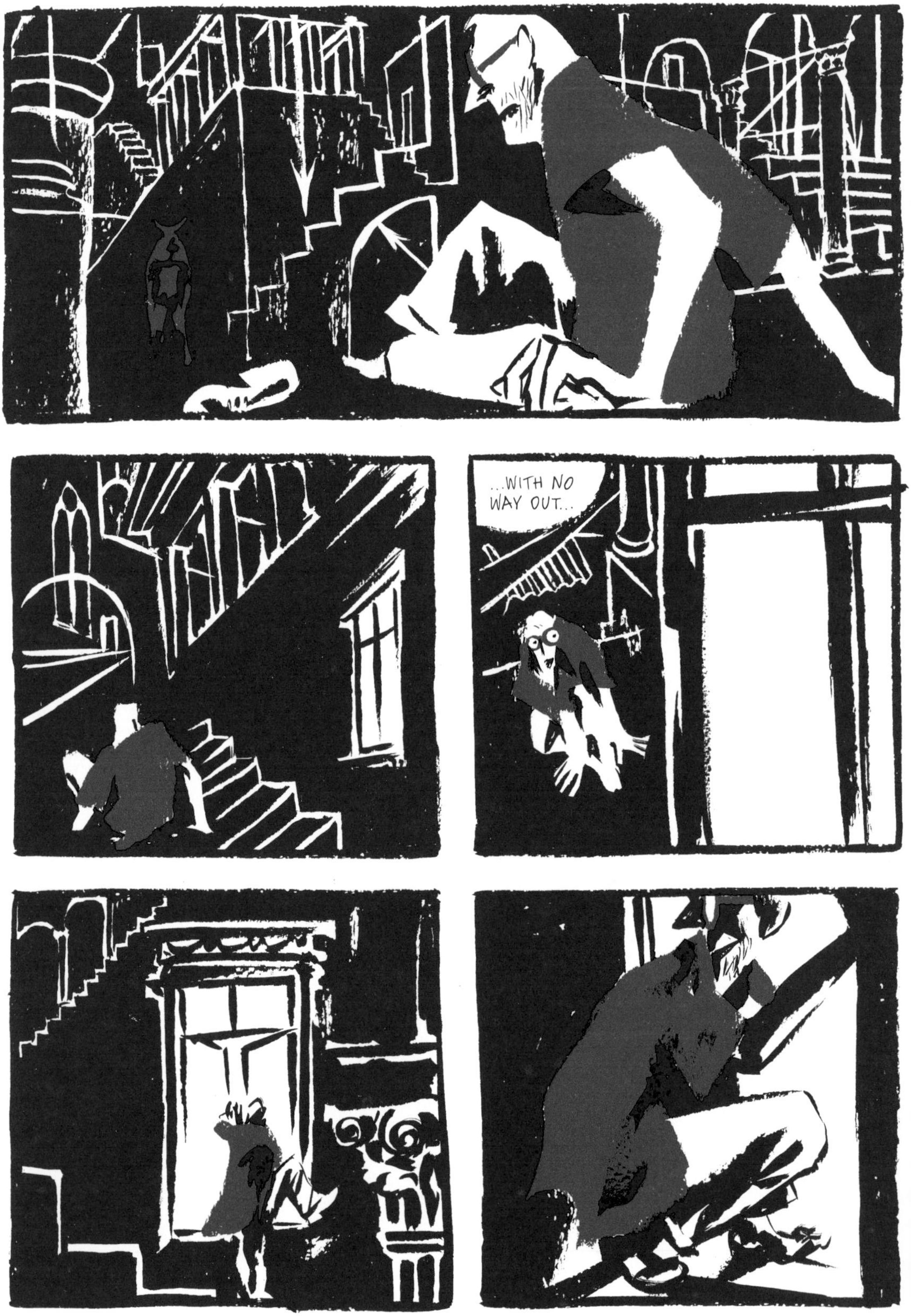
...WITH NO
WAY OUT...

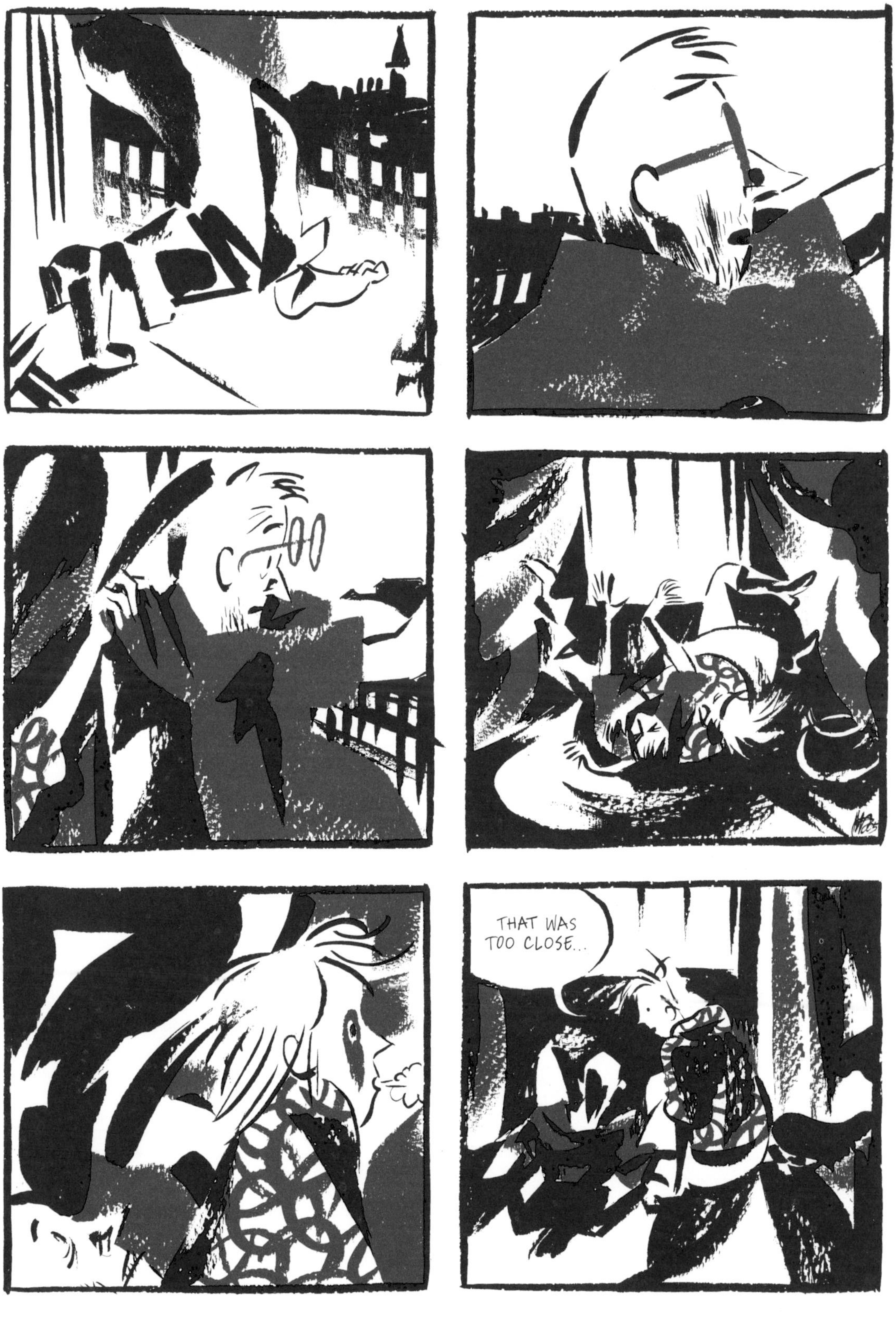
THAT WAS TOO CLOSE...

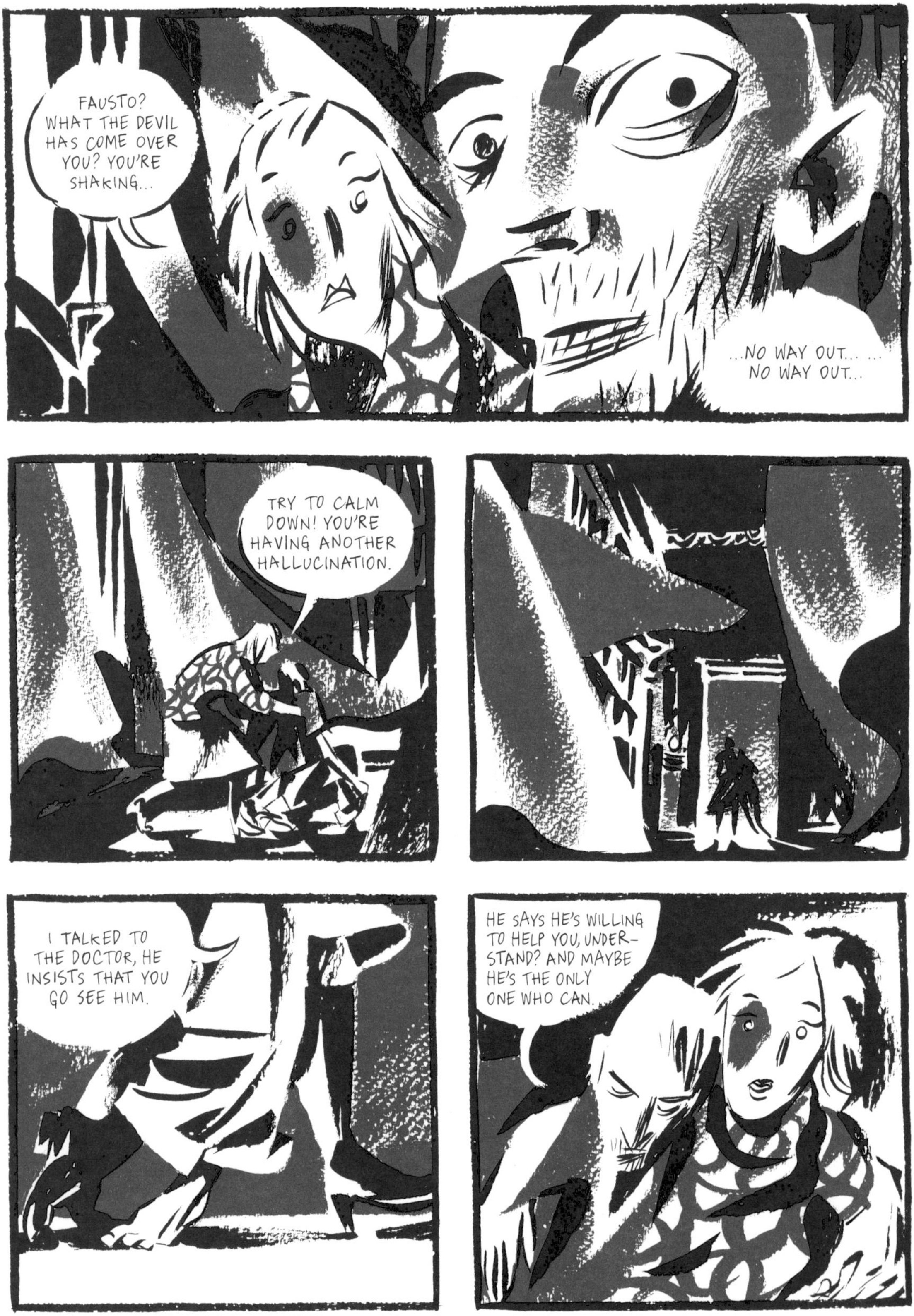
FAUSTO? WHAT THE DEVIL HAS COME OVER YOU? YOU'RE SHAKING...
...NO WAY OUT... ... NO WAY OUT...
TRY TO CALM DOWN! YOU'RE HAVING ANOTHER HALLUCINATION.
I TALKED TO THE DOCTOR, HE INSISTS THAT YOU GO SEE HIM.
HE SAYS HE'S WILLING TO HELP YOU, UNDERSTAND? AND MAYBE HE'S THE ONLY ONE WHO CAN.

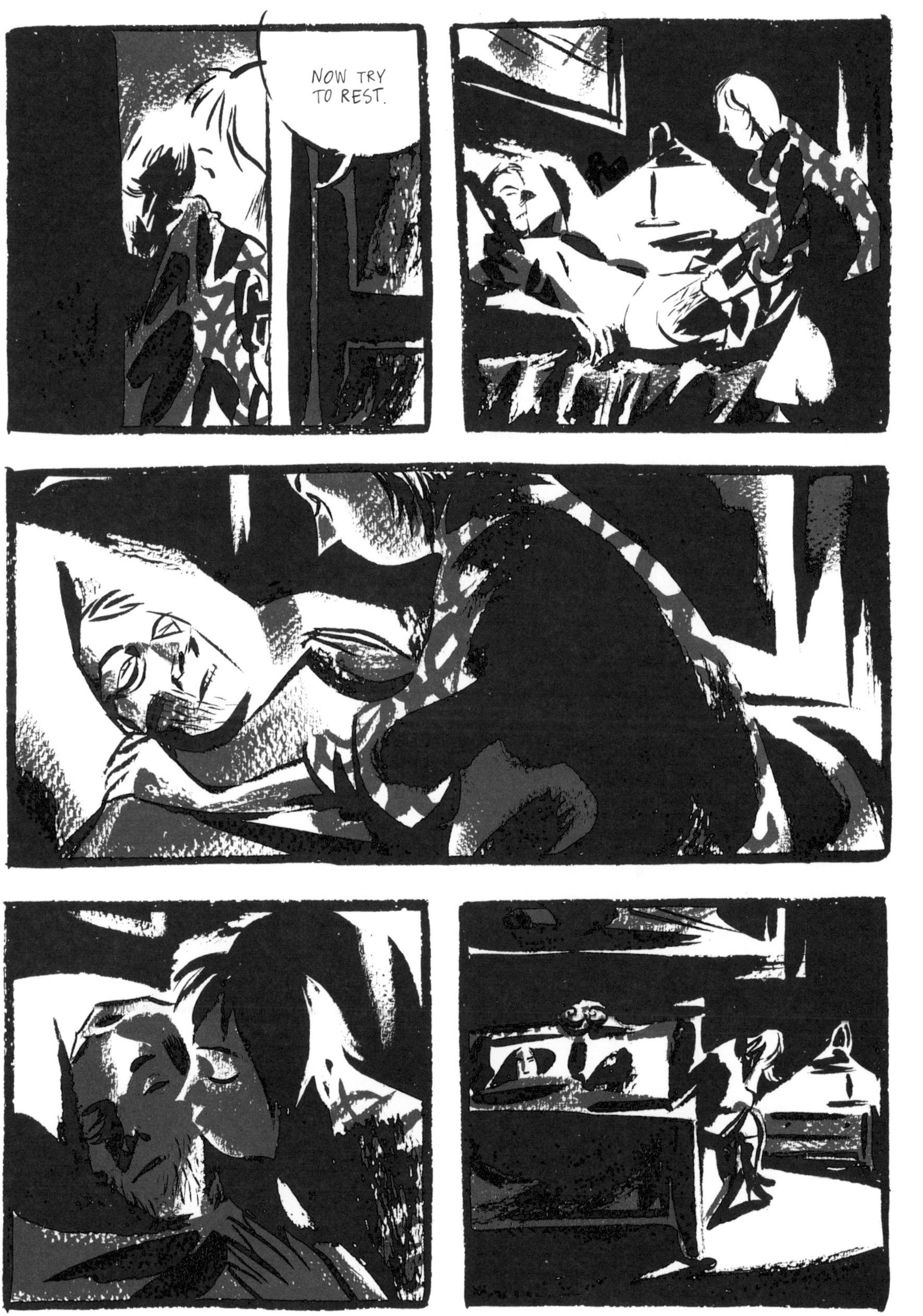
NOW TRY
TO REST.

5.

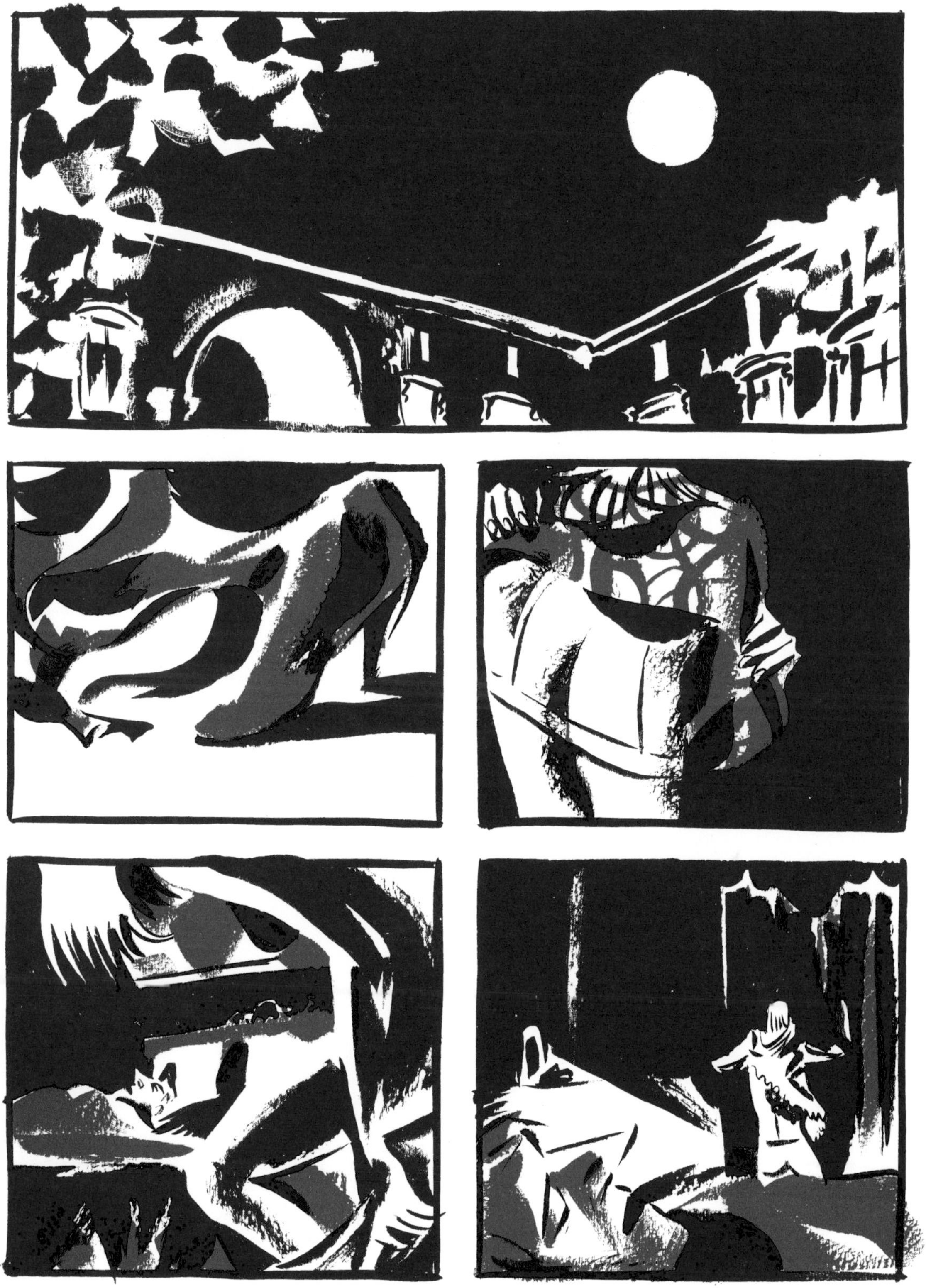

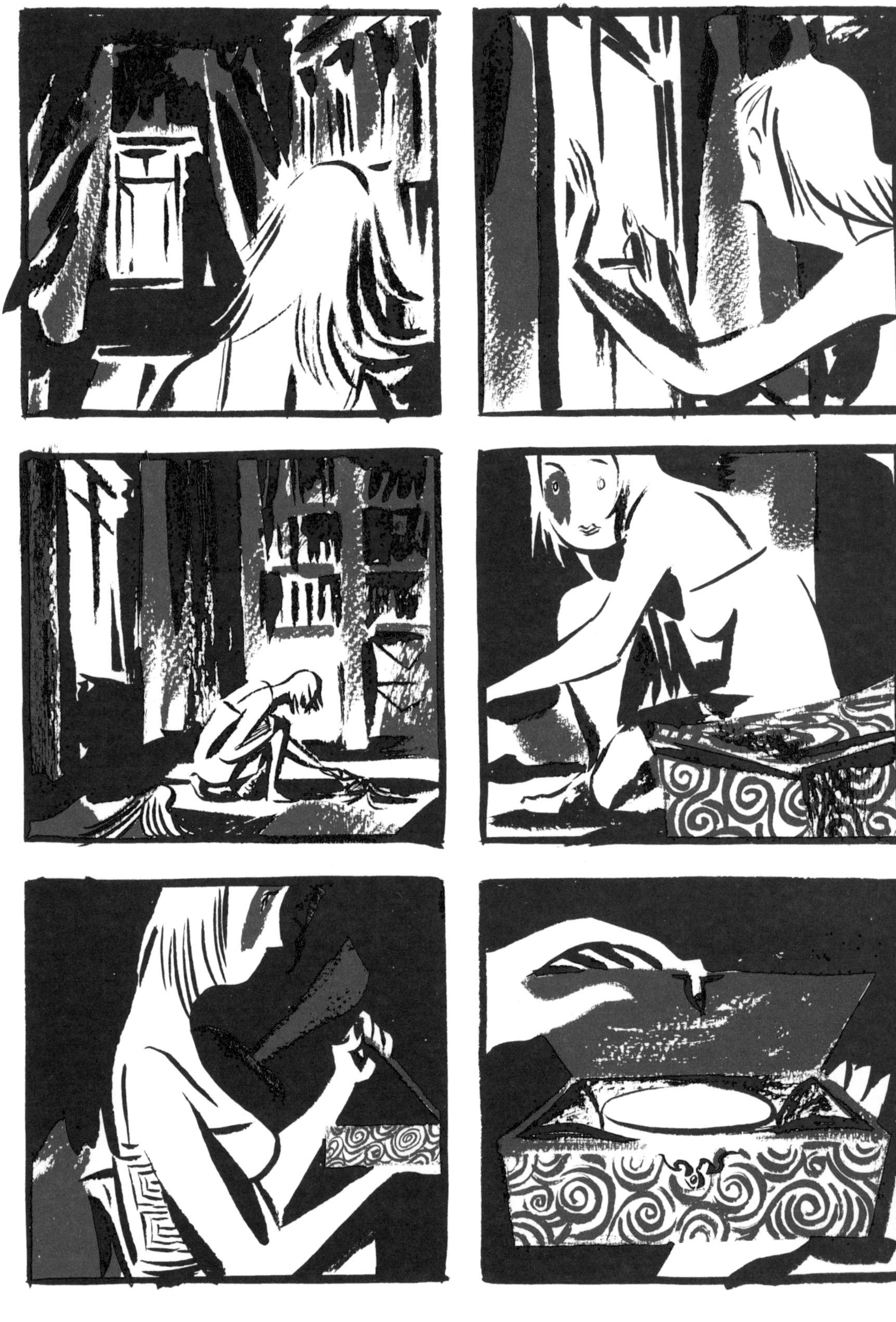

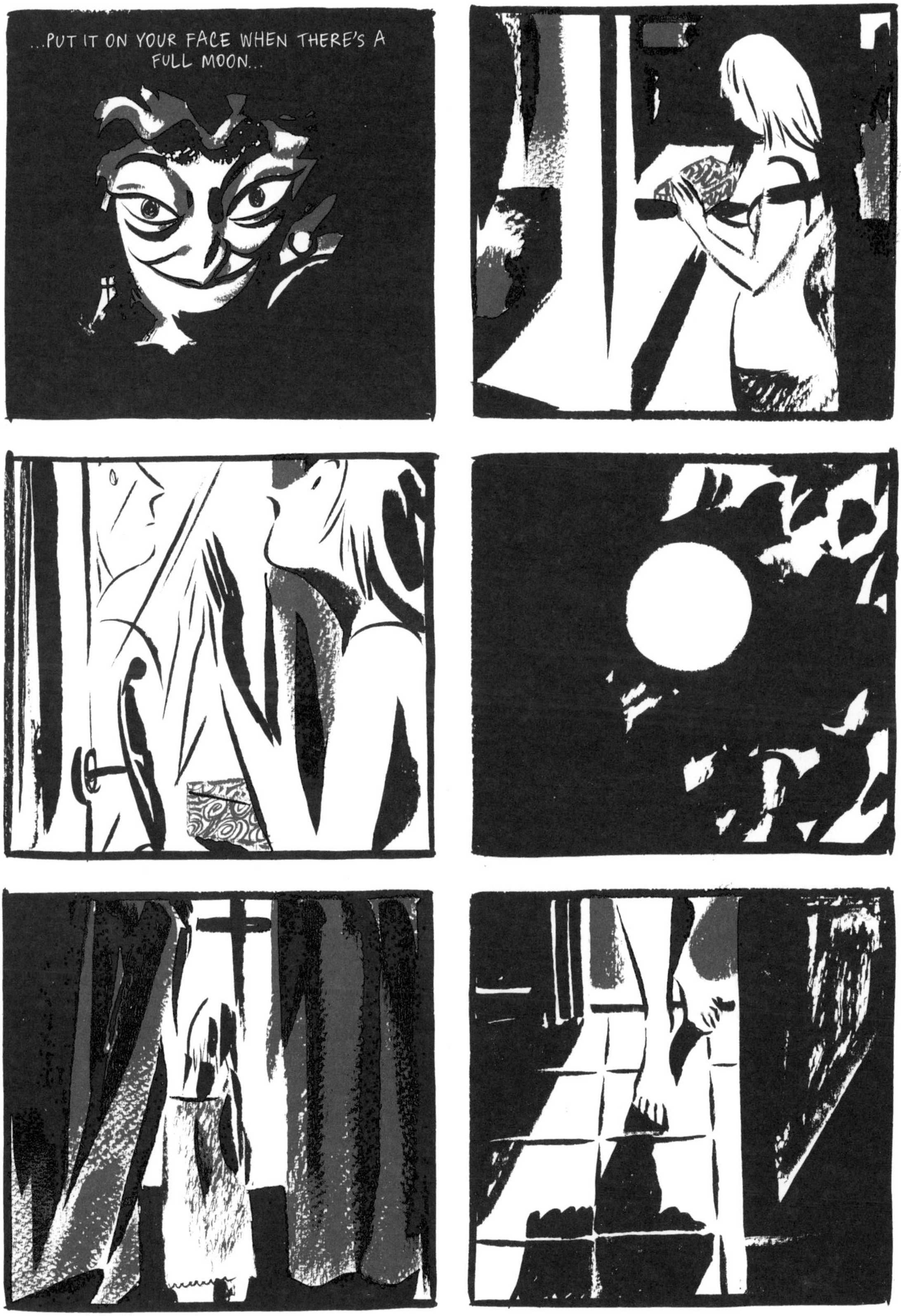
...PUT IT ON YOUR FACE WHEN THERE'S A FULL MOON...

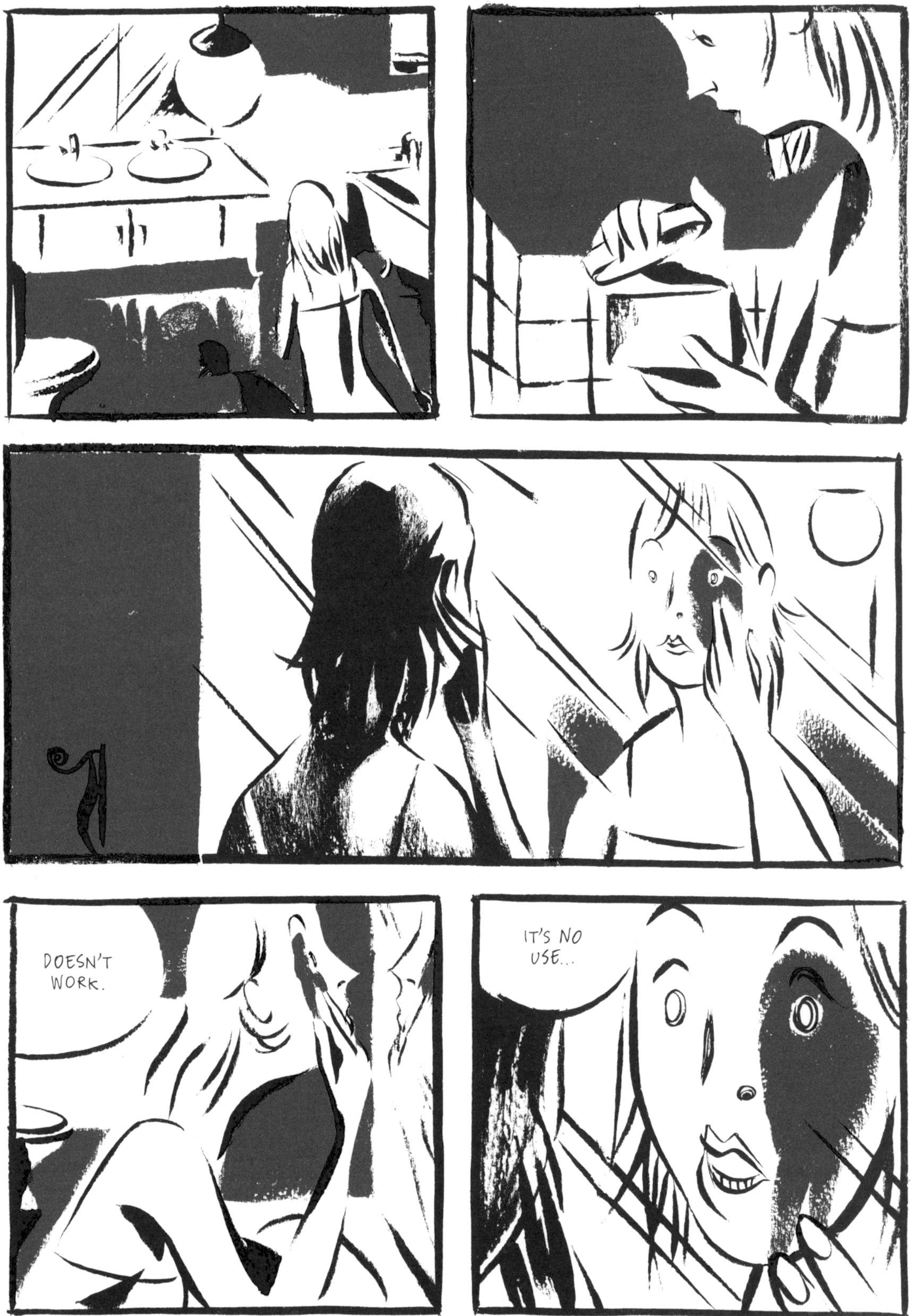
DOESN'T WORK.
IT'S NO USE...

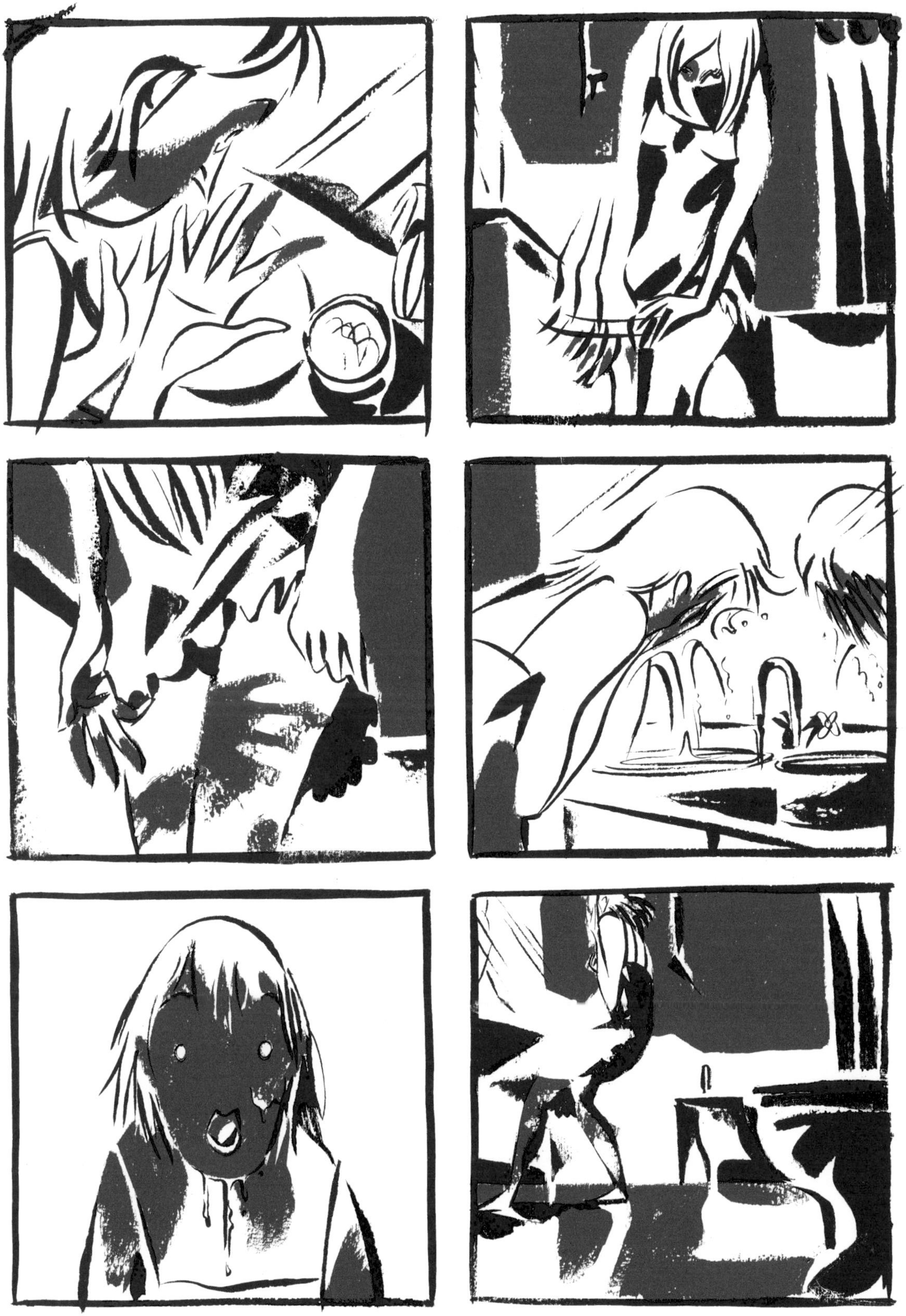

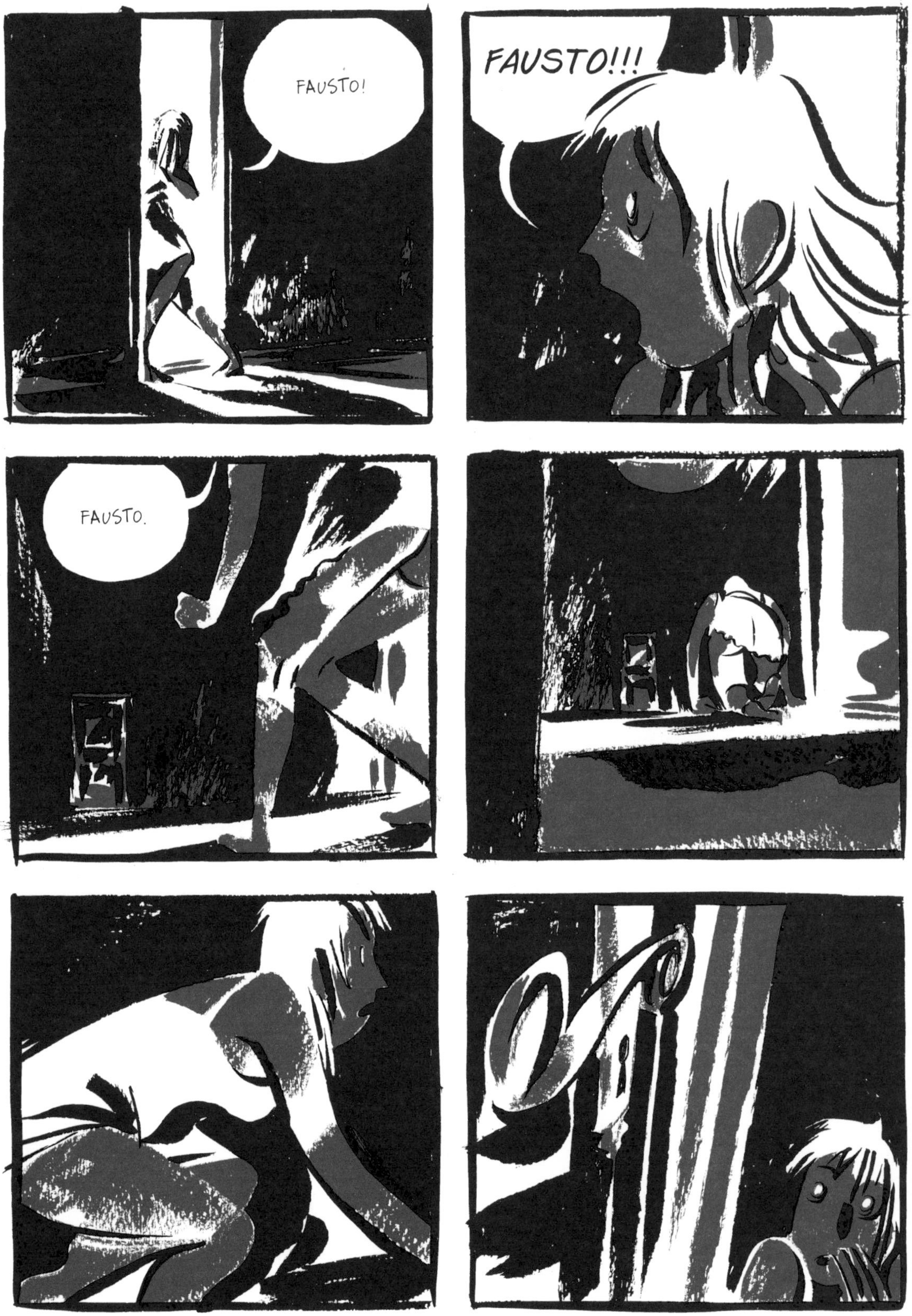
FAUSTO!
FAUSTO!!!
FAUSTO.

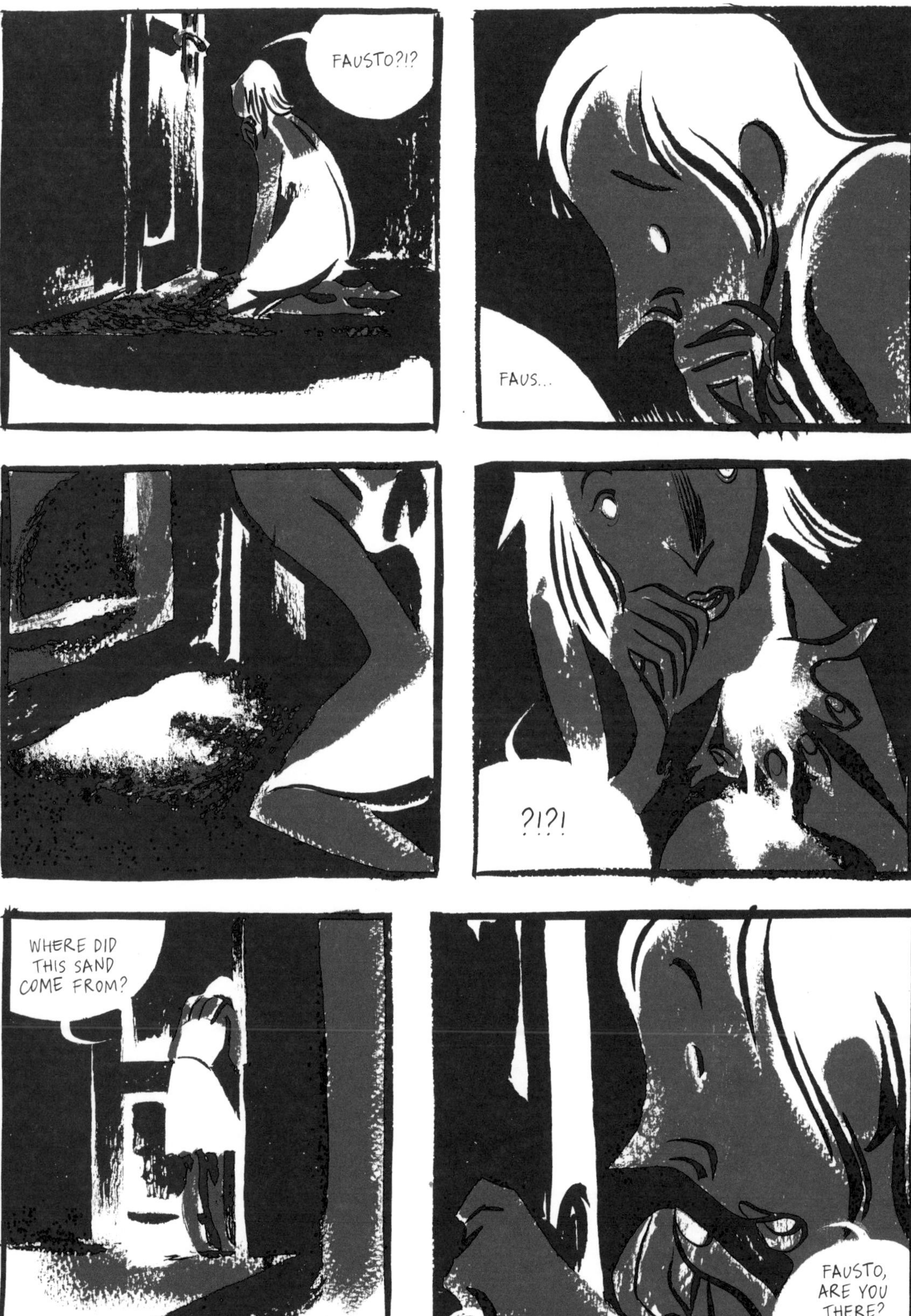
FAUSTO?!?
FAUS...
?!?!
WHERE DID THIS SAND COME FROM?
FAUSTO, ARE YOU THERE?

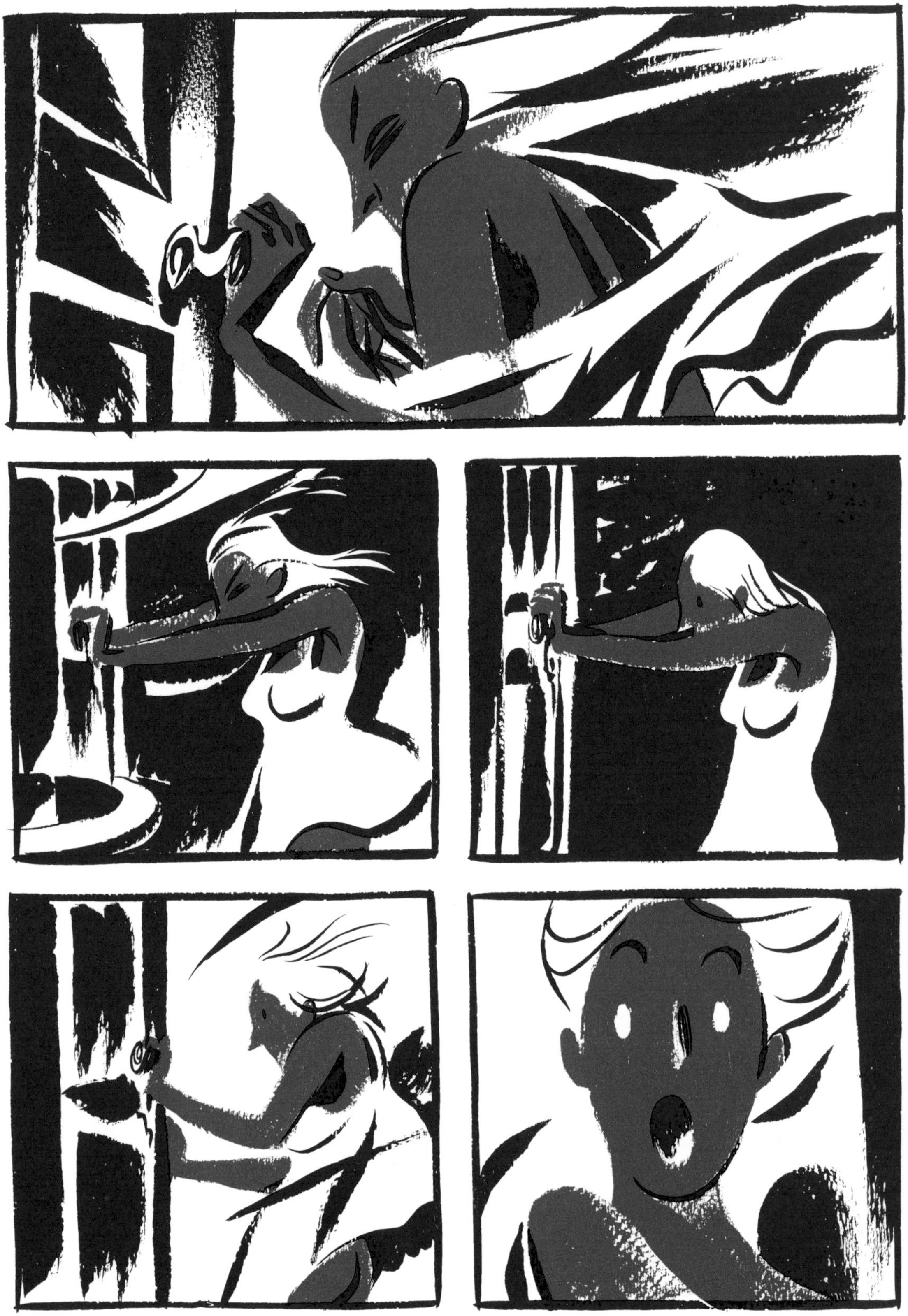

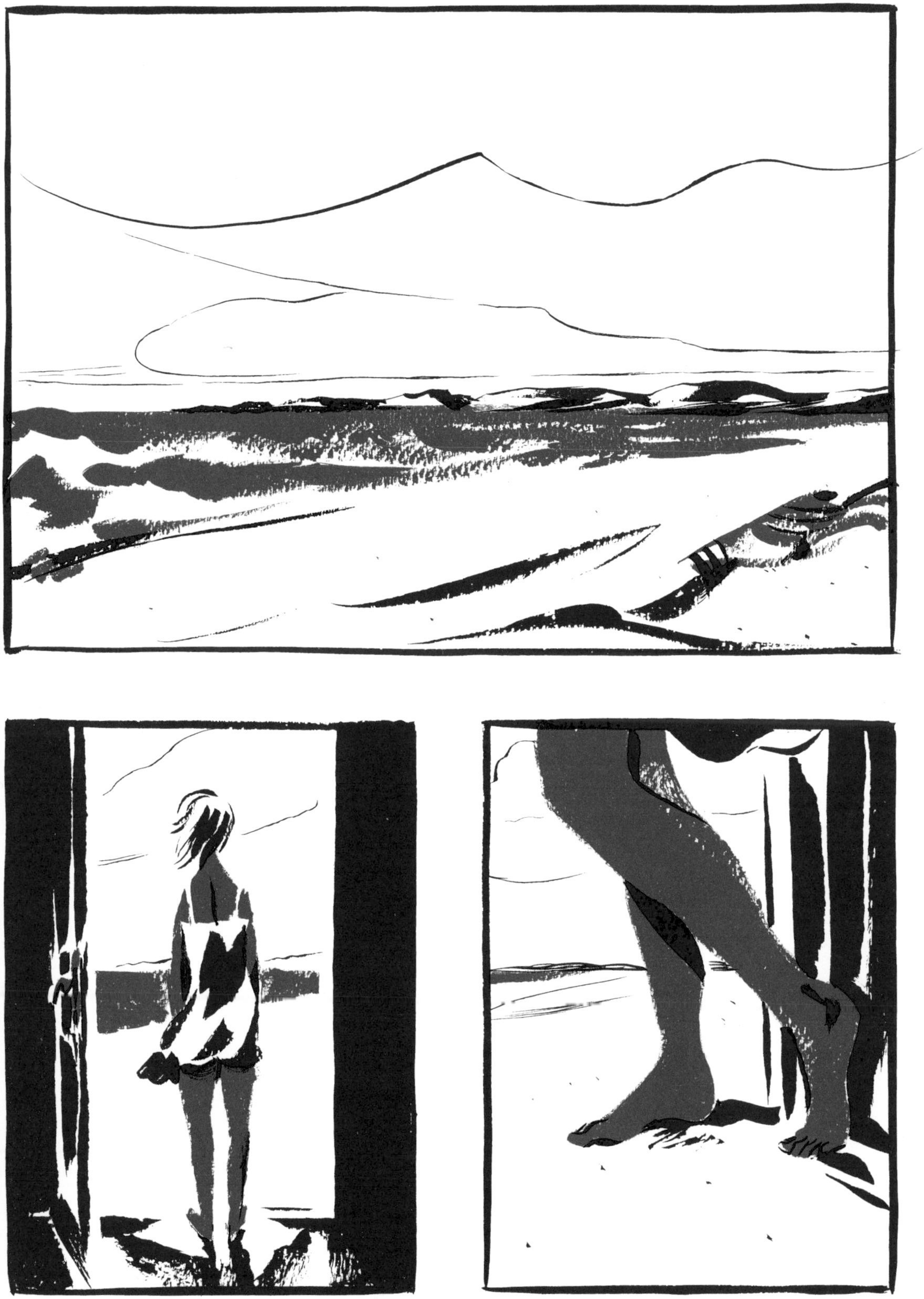

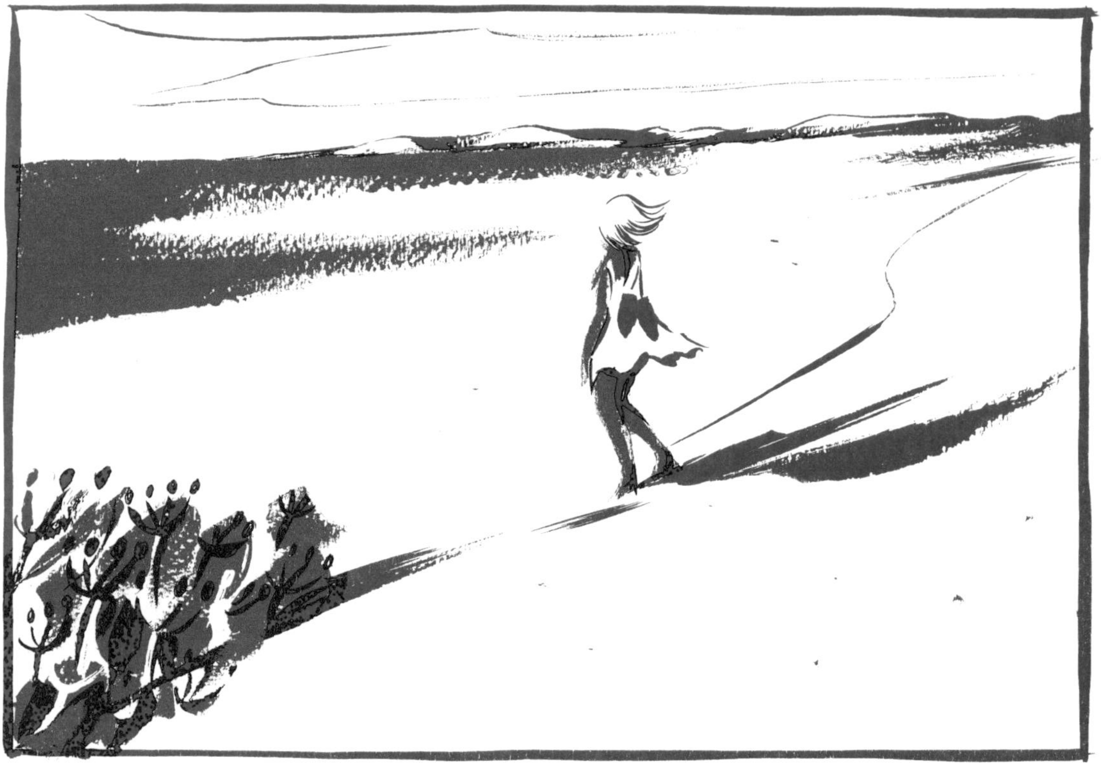

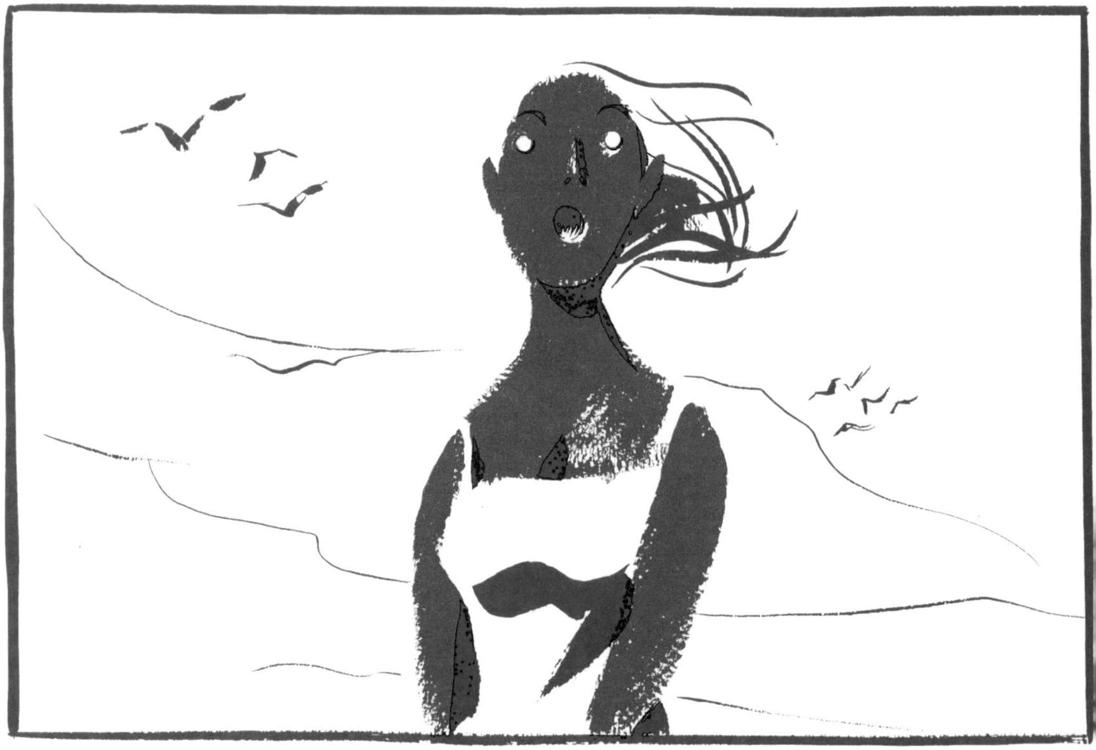

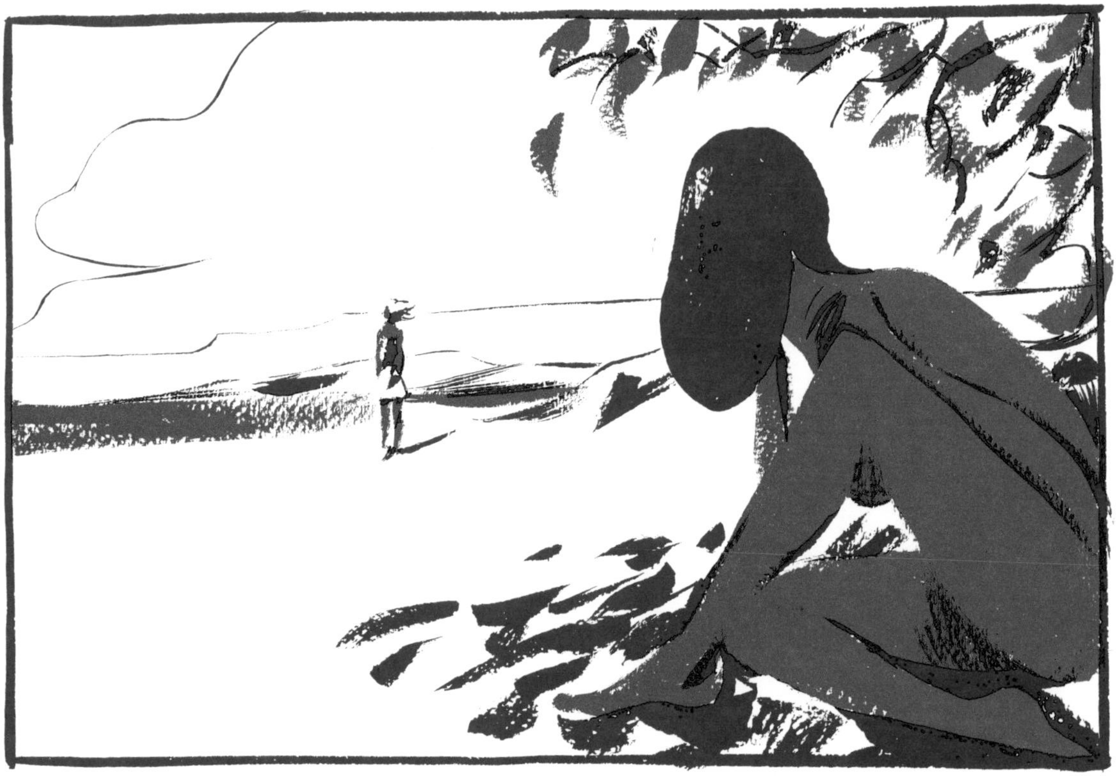

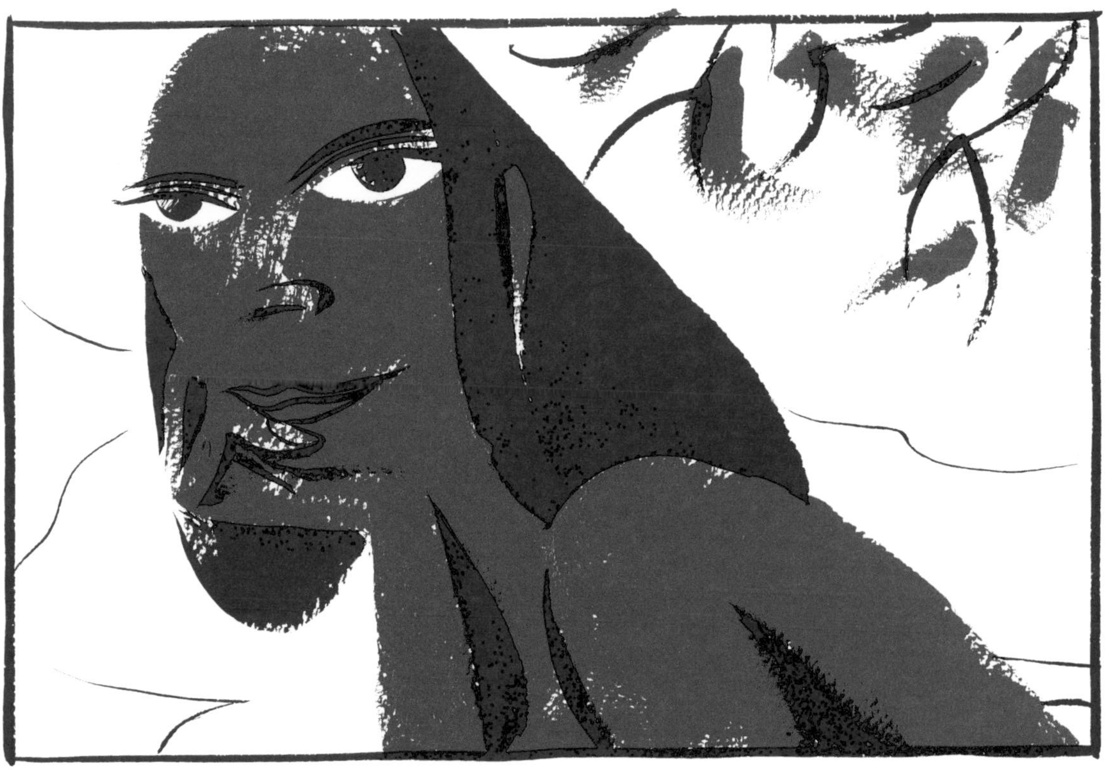

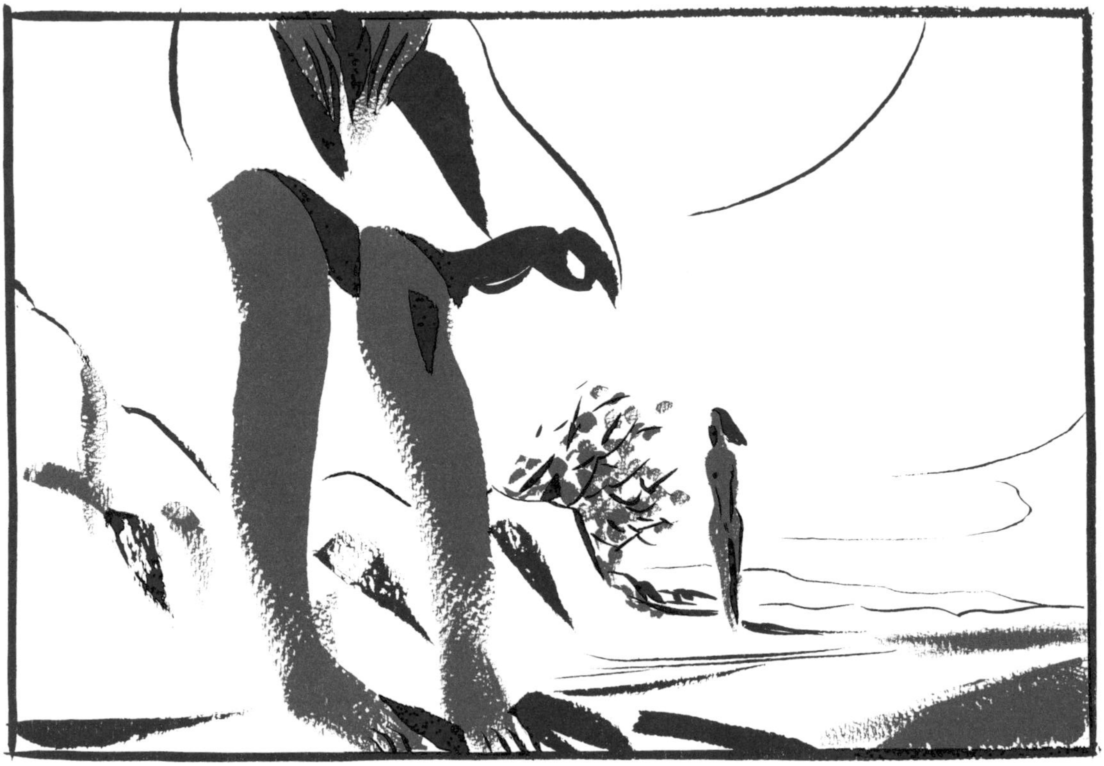

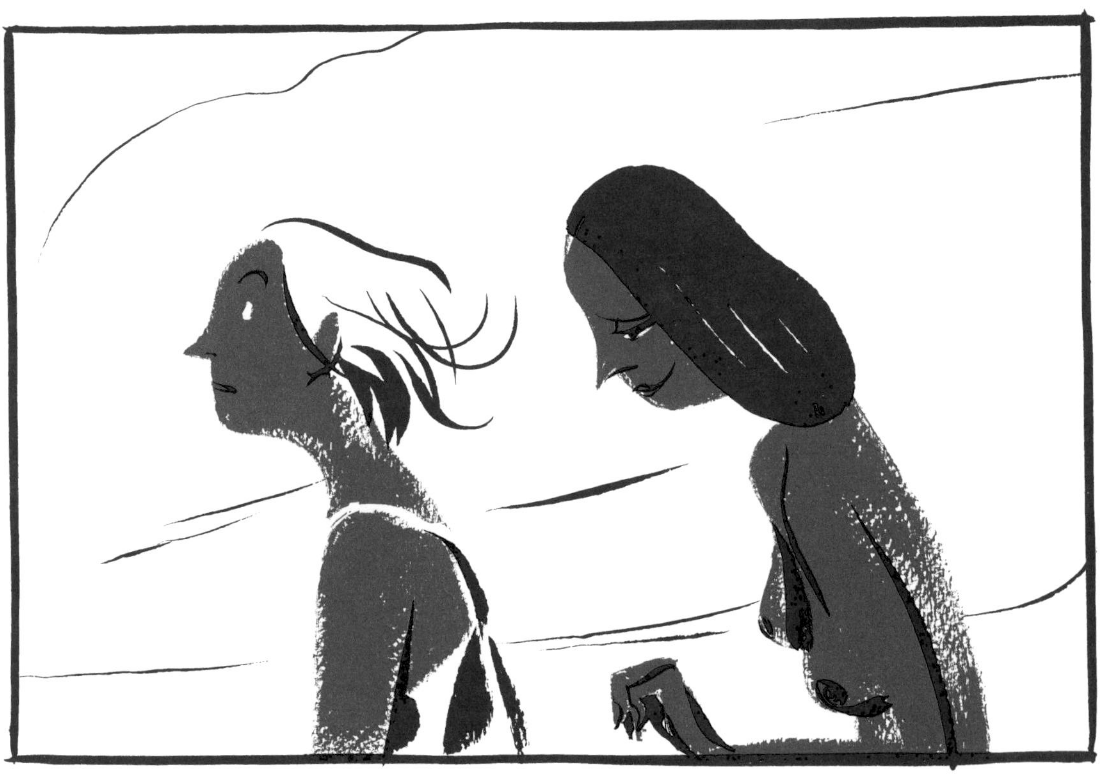

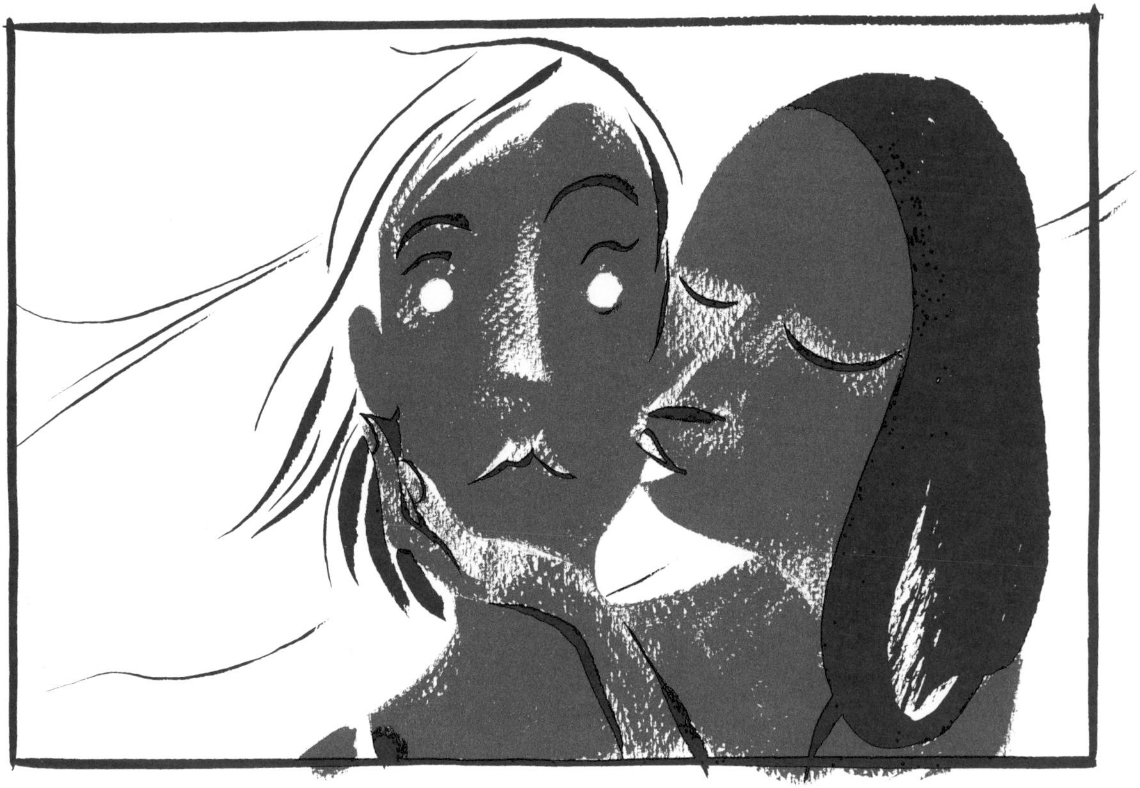

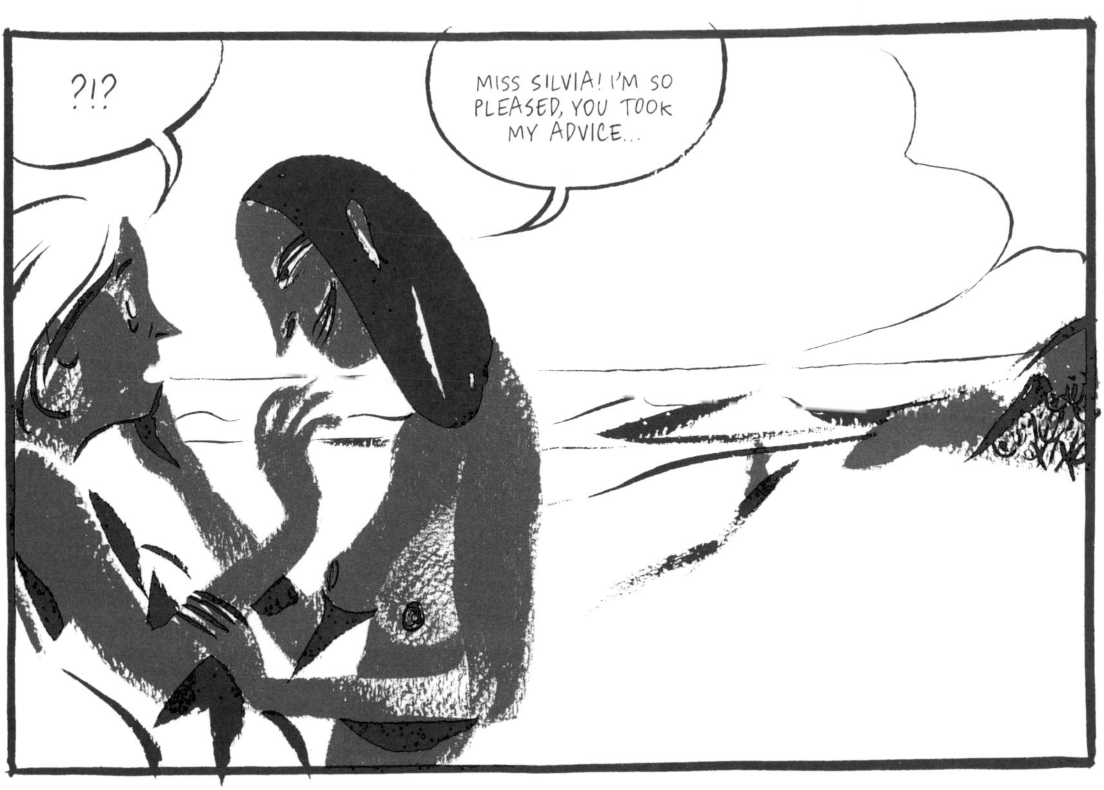
?!?
MISS SILVIA! I'M SO PLEASED, YOU TOOK MY ADVICE...

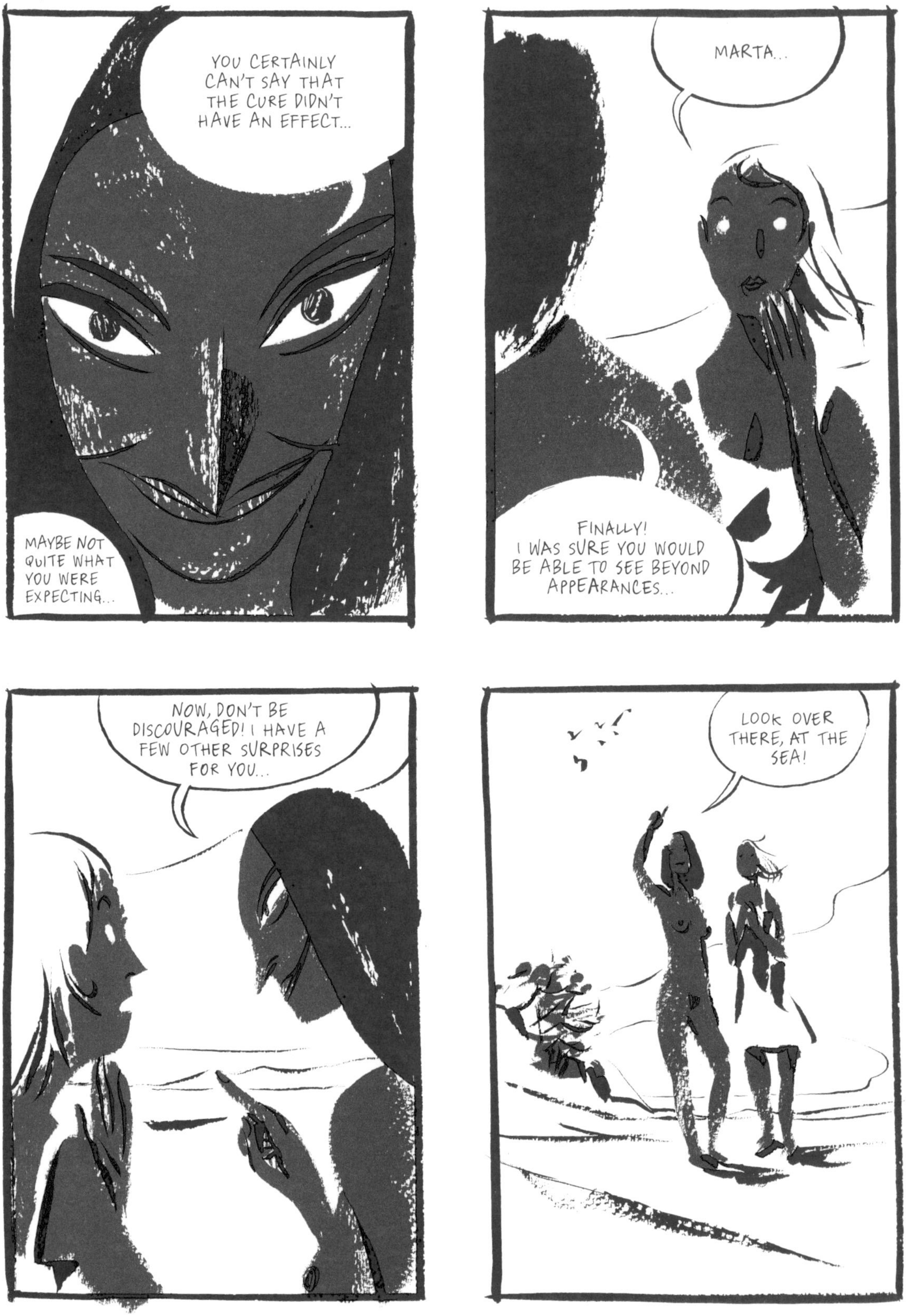
YOU CERTAINLY CAN'T SAY THAT THE CURE DIDN'T HAVE AN EFFECT...
MAYBE NOT QUITE WHAT YOU WERE EXPECTING...
MARTA...
FINALLY! I WAS SURE YOU WOULD BE ABLE TO SEE BEYOND APPEARANCES...
NOW, DON'T BE DISCOURAGED! I HAVE A FEW OTHER SURPRISES FOR YOU...
LOOK OVER THERE, AT THE SEA!

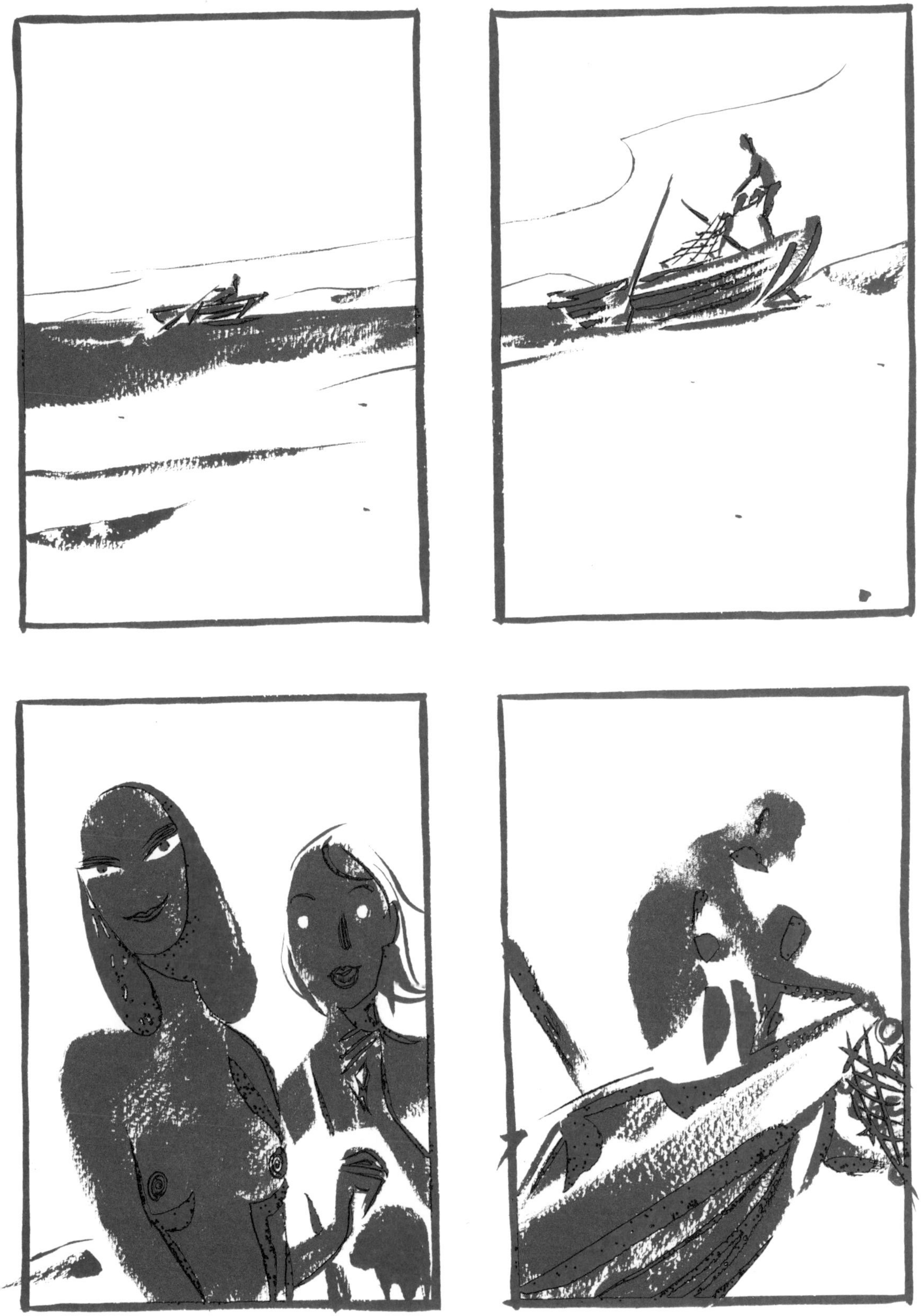

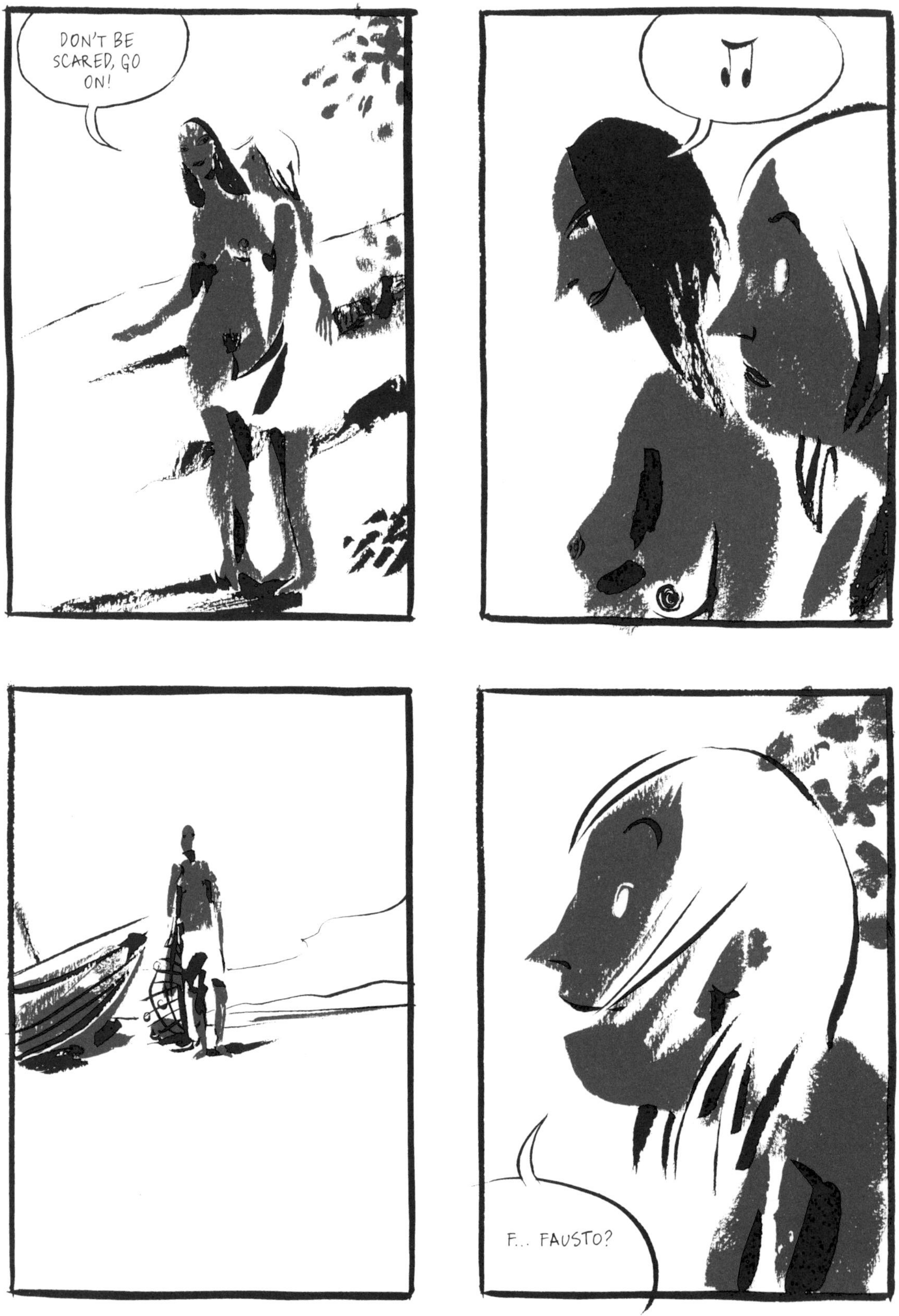
DON’T BE SCARED, GO ON!
F... FAUSTO?

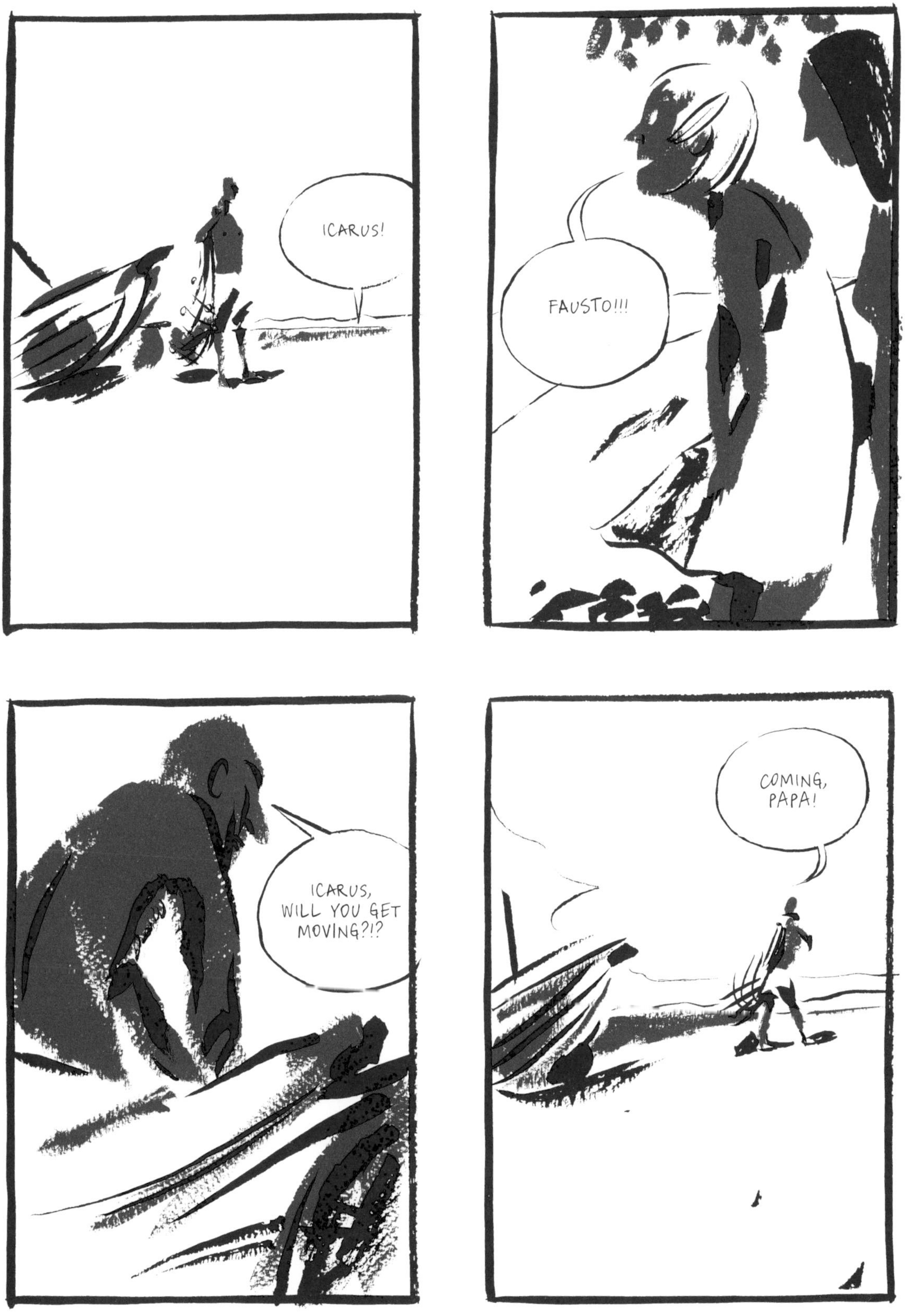
ICARUS!
FAUSTO!!!
ICARUS, WILL YOU GET MOVING?!?
COMING, PAPA!

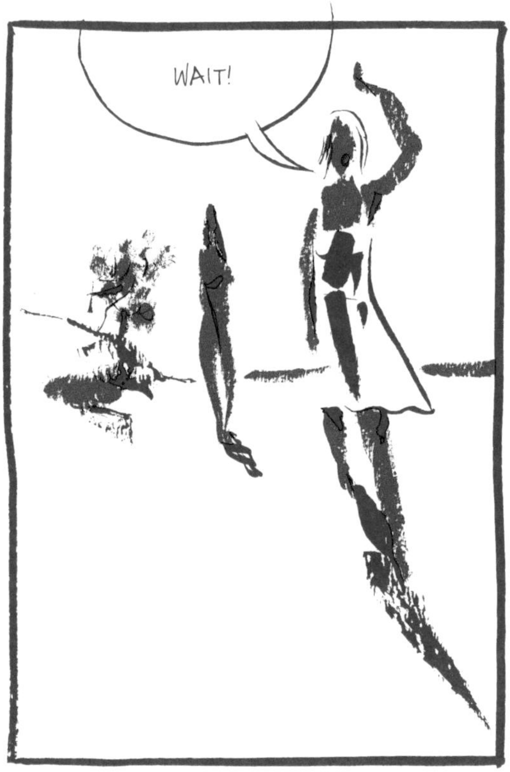
WAIT!

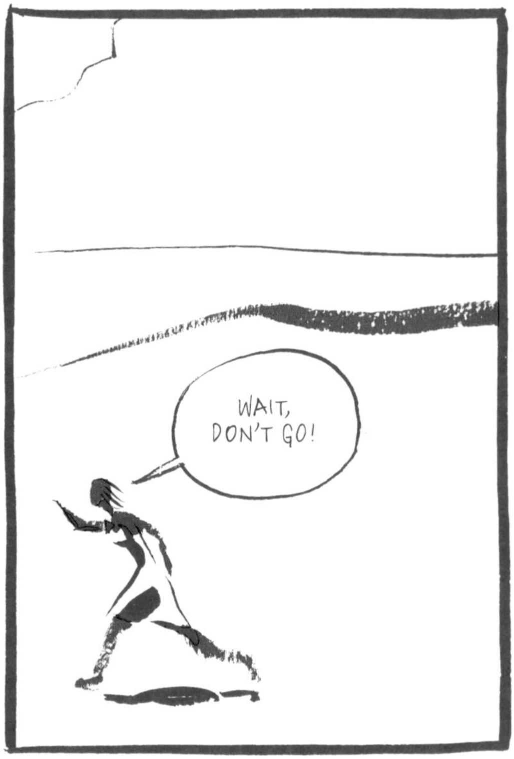
WAIT,
DON'T GO!

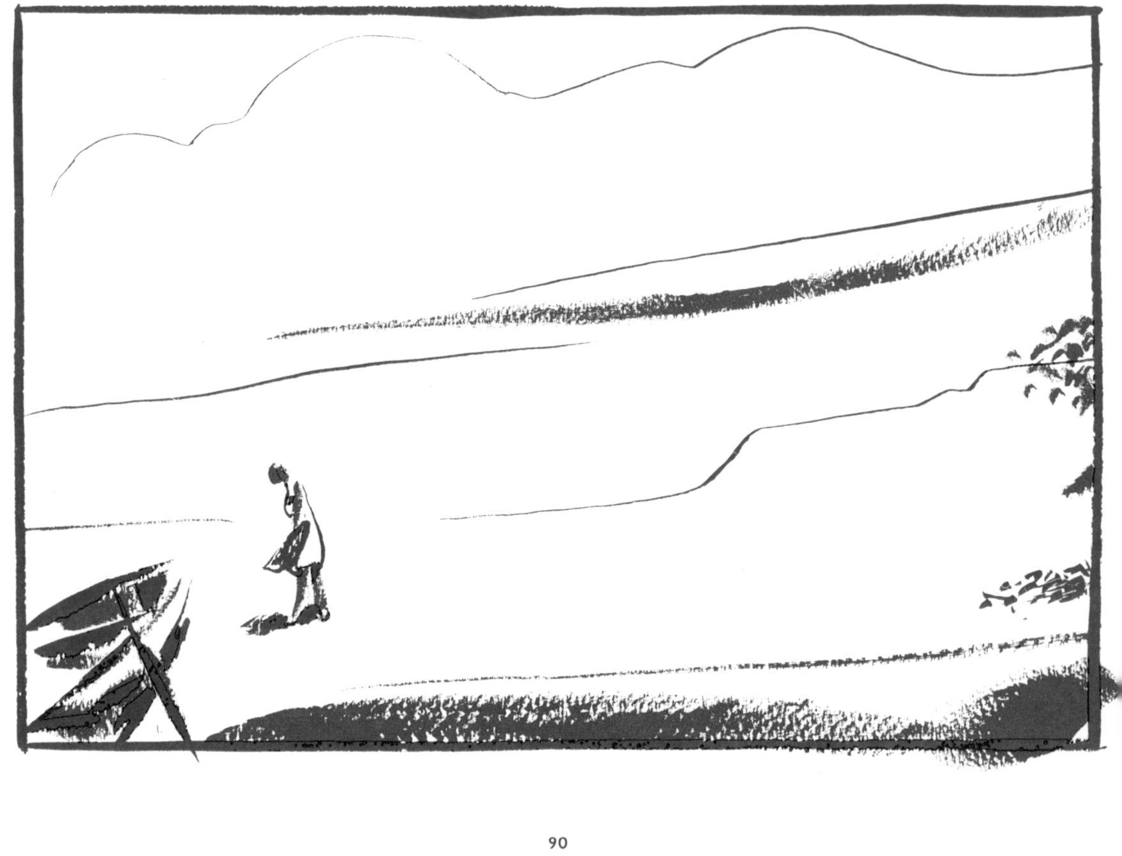

6.

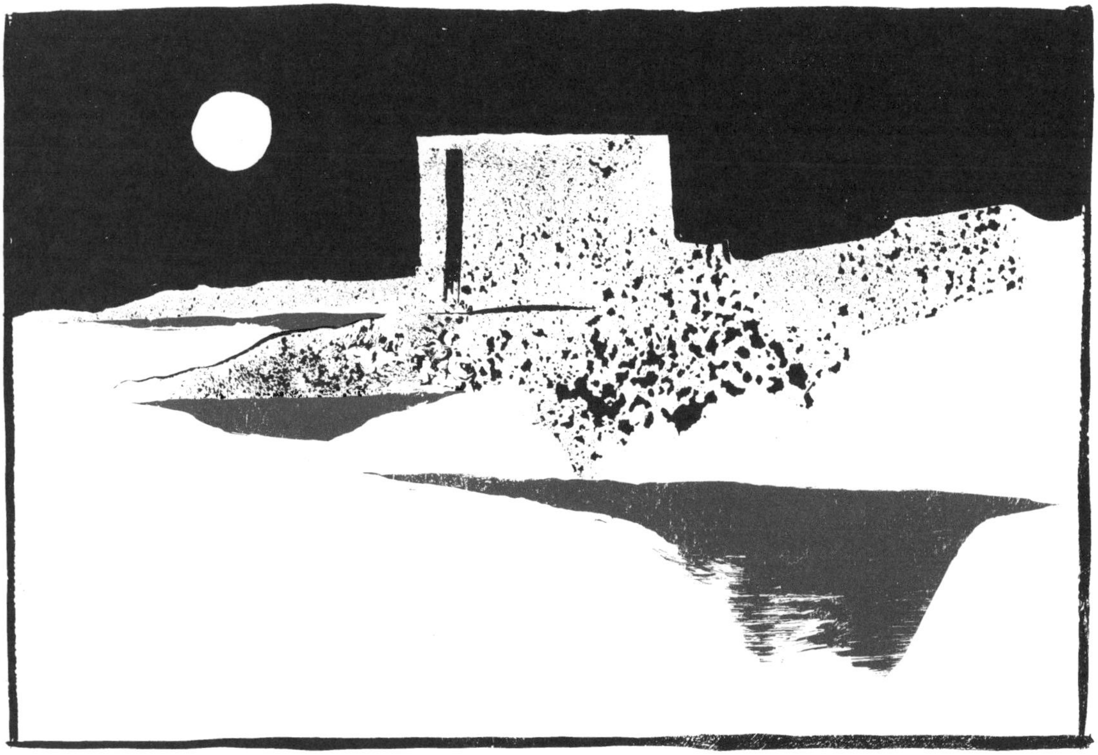

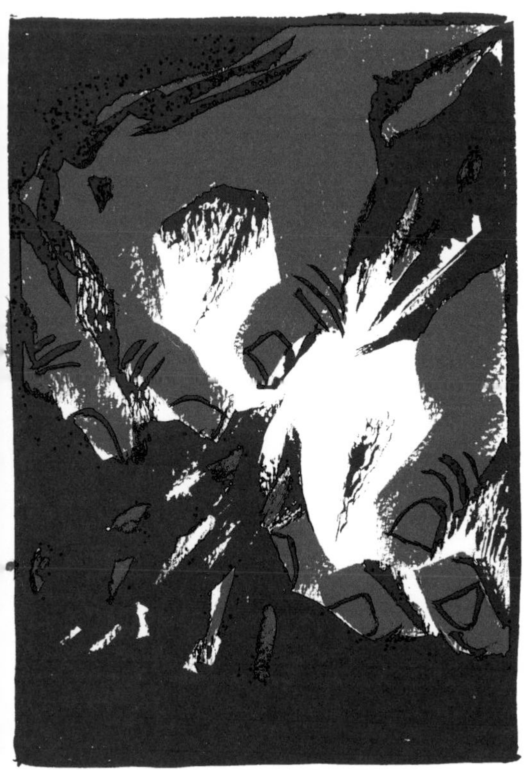

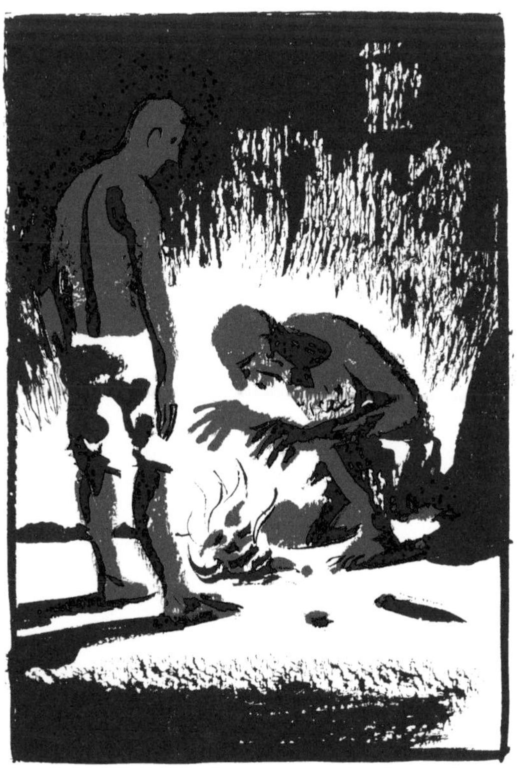

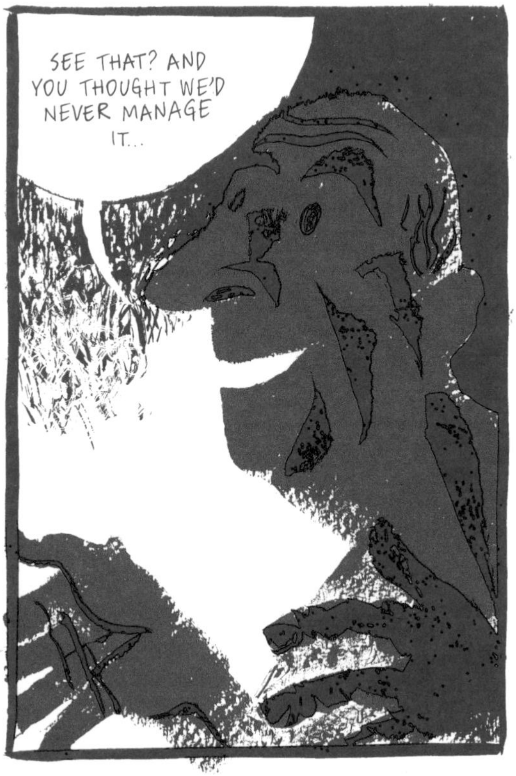
SEE THAT? AND YOU THOUGHT WE'D NEVER MANAGE IT...

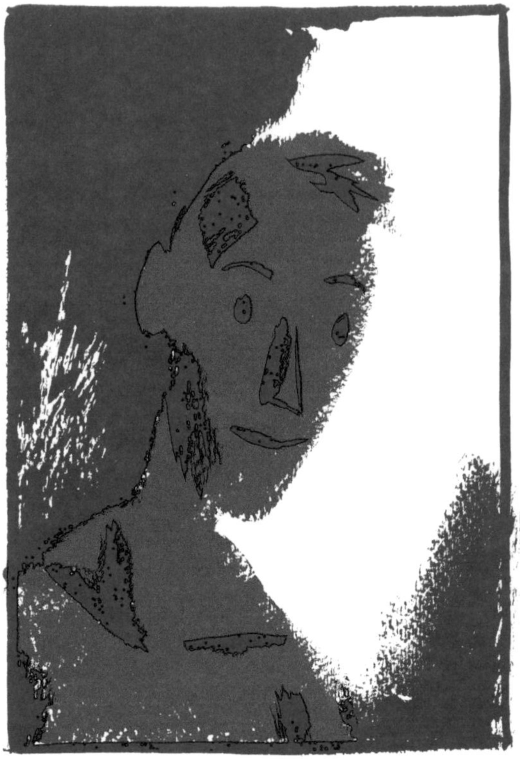

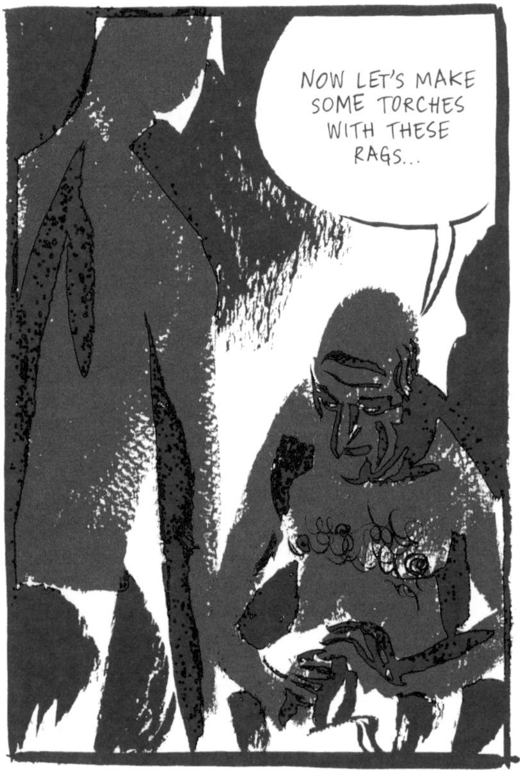
NOW LET'S MAKE SOME TORCHES WITH THESE RAGS...

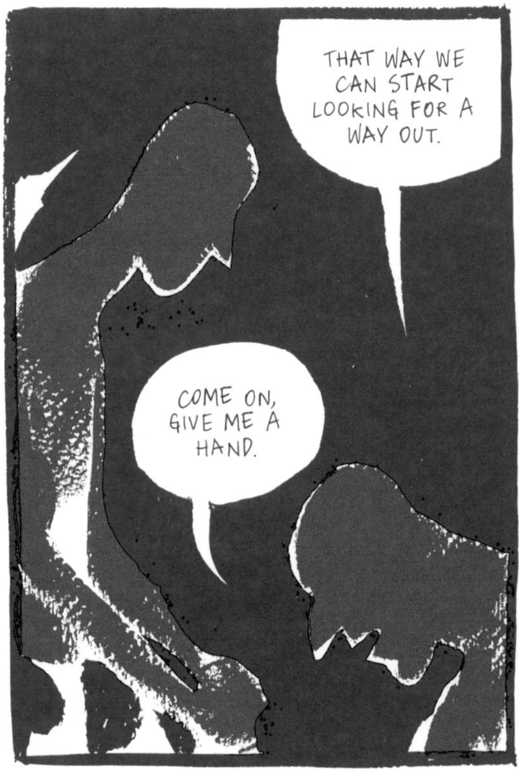
THAT WAY WE CAN START LOOKING FOR A WAY OUT.
COME ON, GIVE ME A HAND.

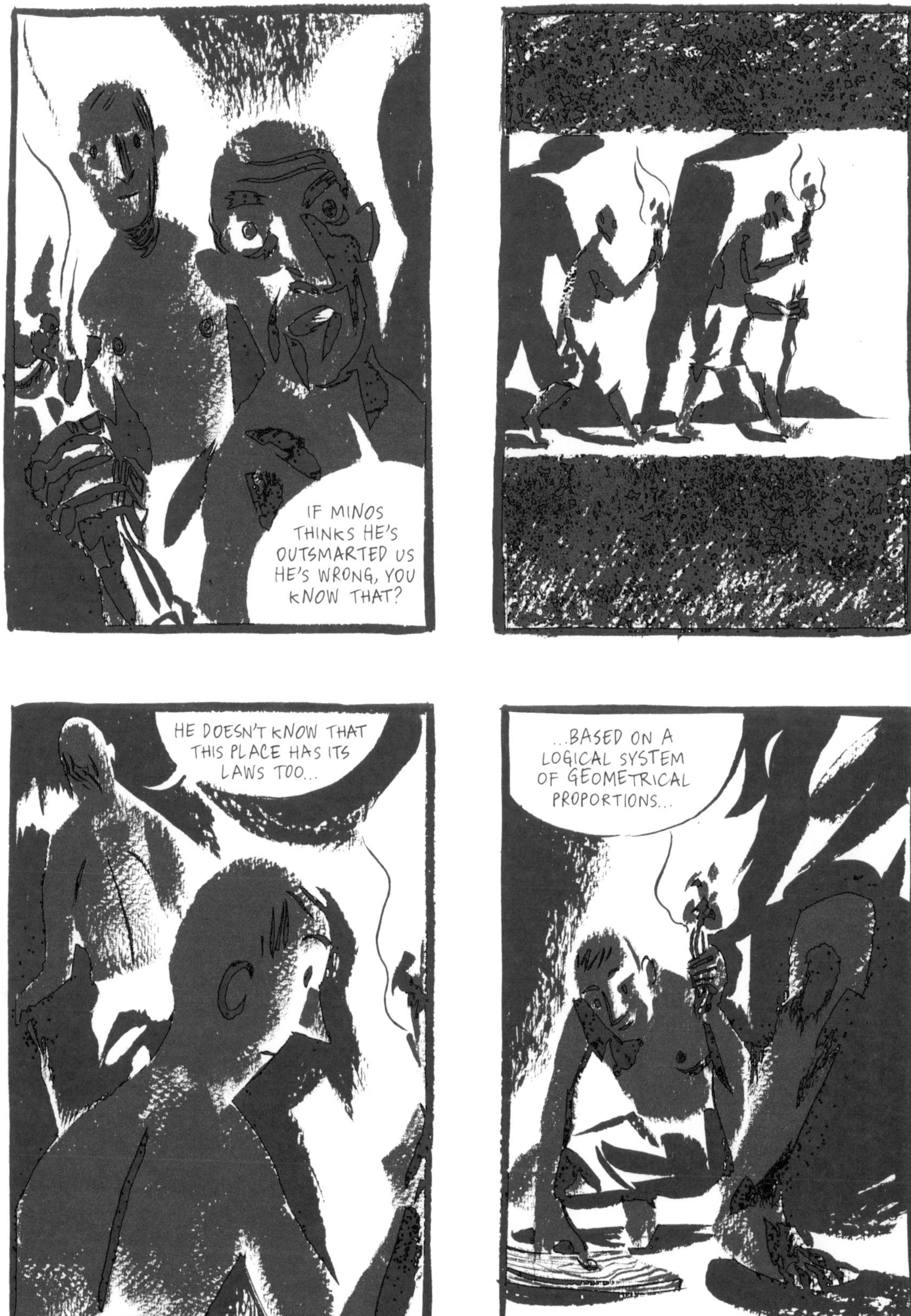
IF MINOS THINKS HE'S OUTSMARTED US HE'S WRONG, YOU KNOW THAT?
HE DOESN'T KNOW THAT THIS PLACE HAS ITS LAWS TOO...
...BASED ON A LOGICAL SYSTEM OF GEOMETRICAL PROPORTIONS...

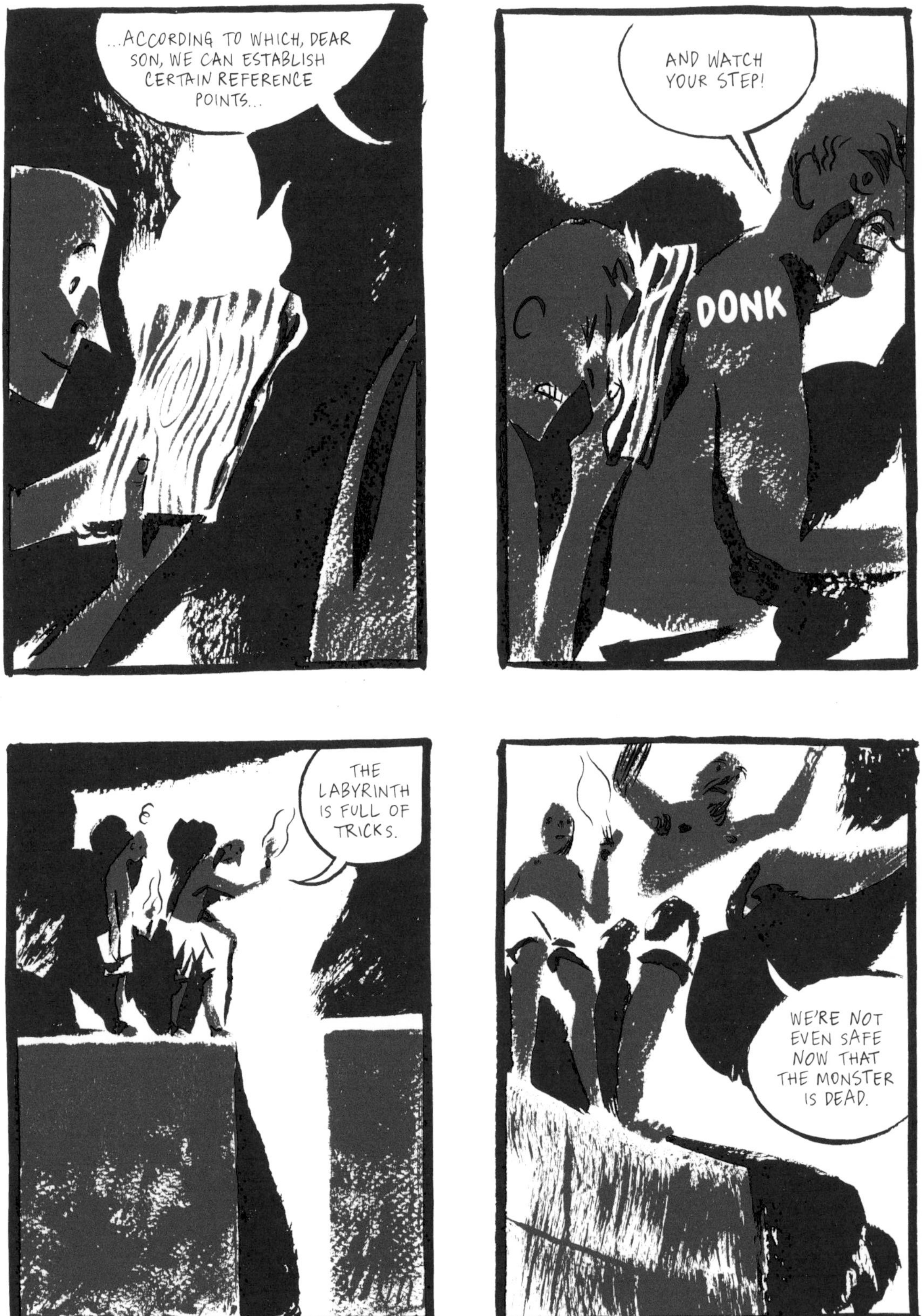
...ACCORDING TO WHICH, DEAR SON, WE CAN ESTABLISH CERTAIN REFERENCE POINTS...
AND WATCH YOUR STEP!
DONK
THE LABYRINTH IS FULL OF TRICKS.
WE'RE NOT EVEN SAFE NOW THAT THE MONSTER IS DEAD.

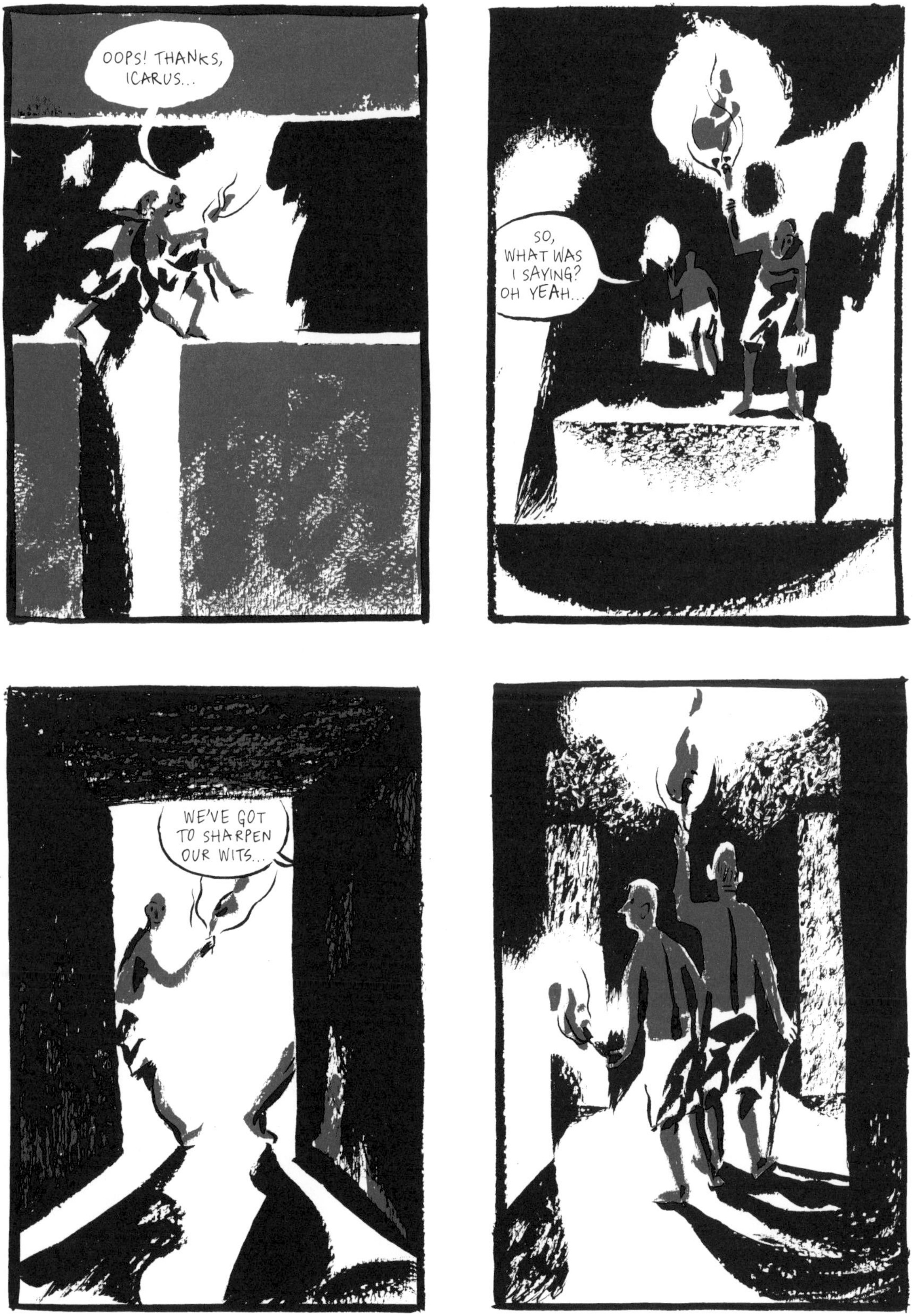
OOPS! THANKS, ICARUS...
SO, WHAT WAS I SAYING? OH YEAH...
WE'VE GOT TO SHARPEN OUR WITS...

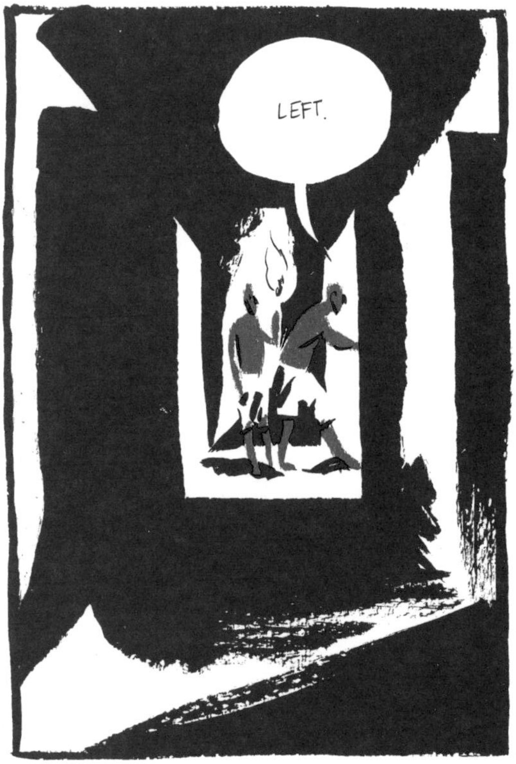
LEFT.

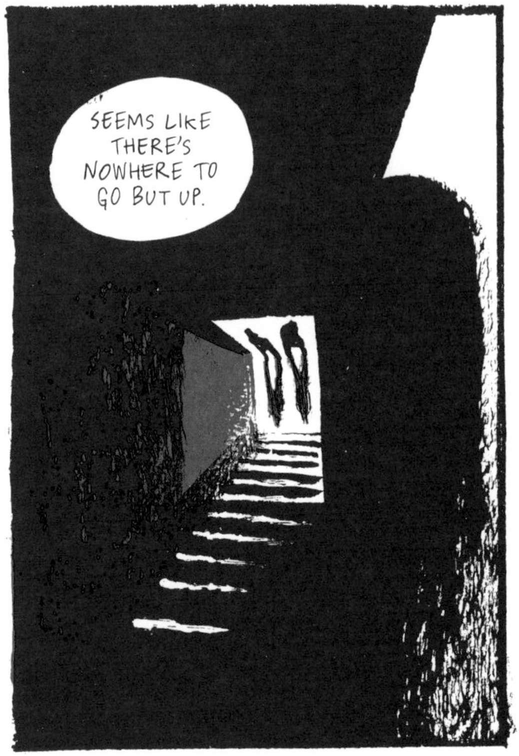
SEEMS LIKE THERE'S NOWHERE TO GO BUT UP.

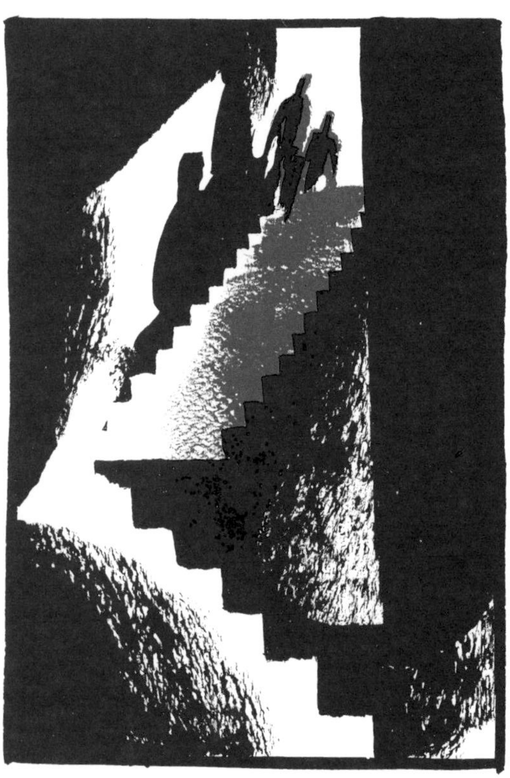

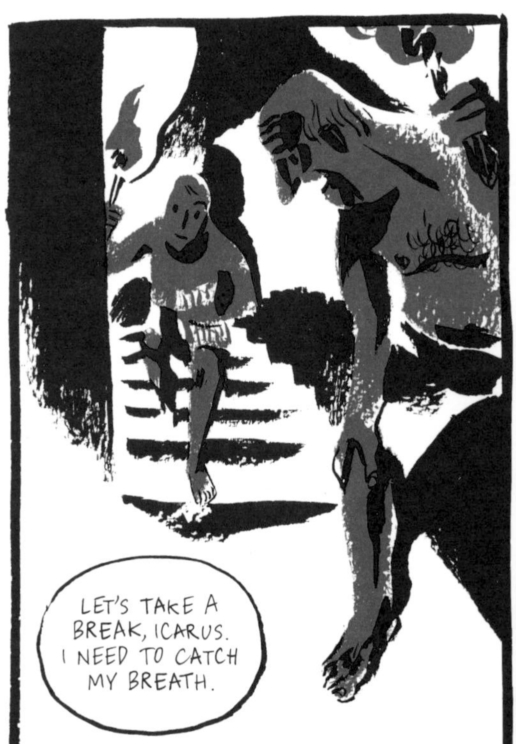
LET'S TAKE A BREAK, ICARUS. I NEED TO CATCH MY BREATH.

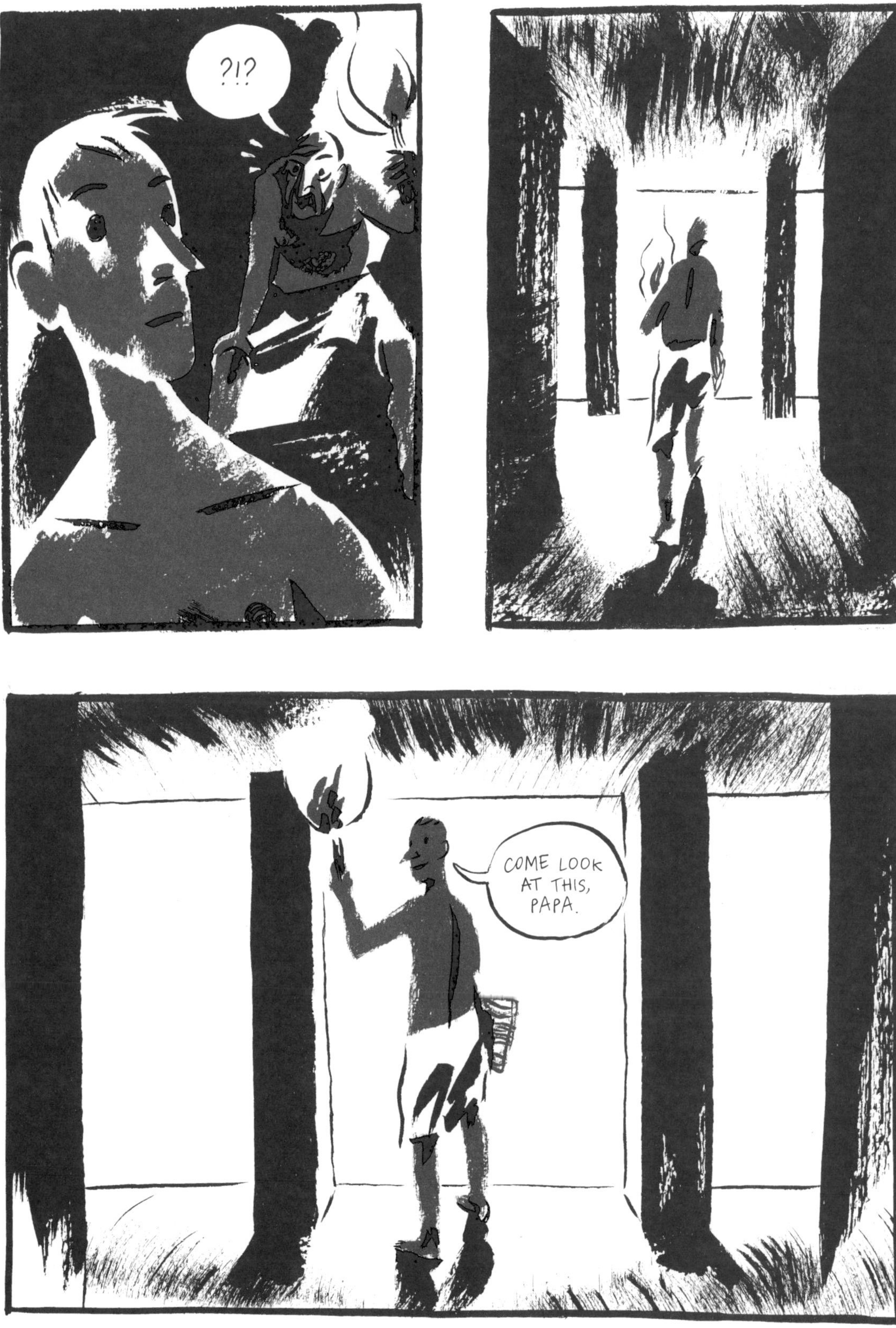
?!?
COME LOOK AT THIS, PAPA.

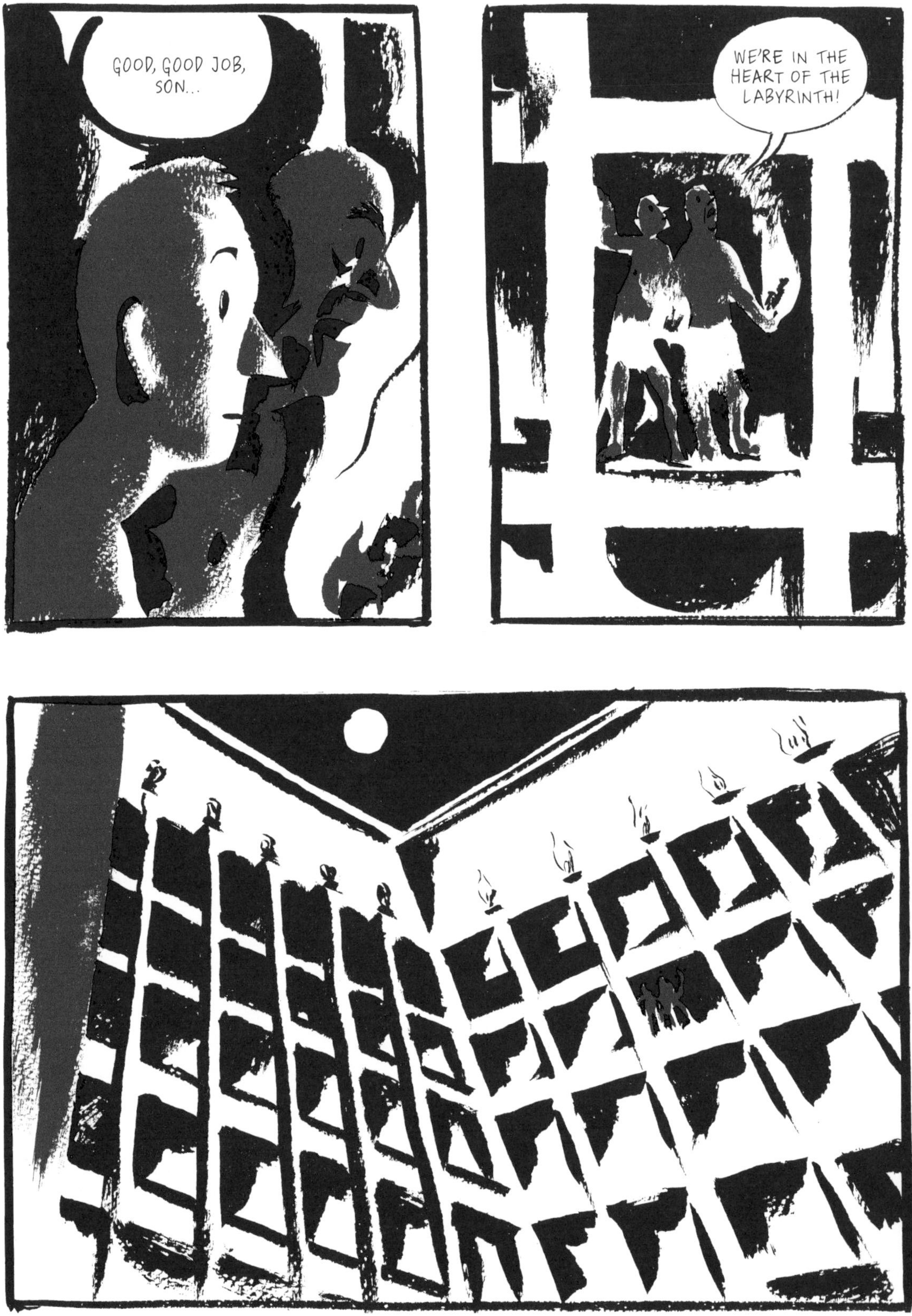
GOOD, GOOD JOB, SON...
WE'RE IN THE HEART OF THE LABYRINTH!

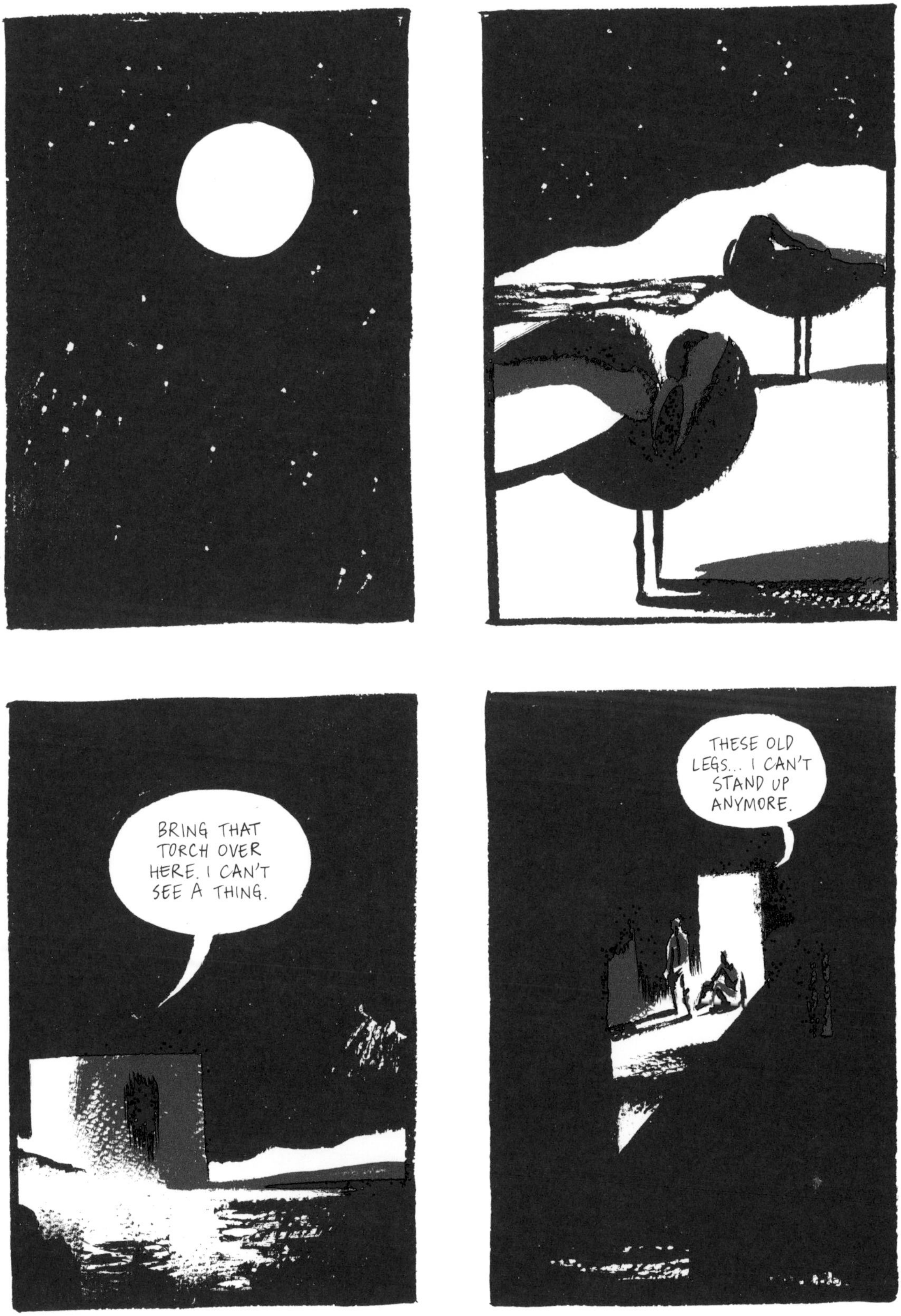
BRING THAT TORCH OVER HERE. I CAN'T SEE A THING.
THESE OLD LEGS... I CAN'T STAND UP ANYMORE.

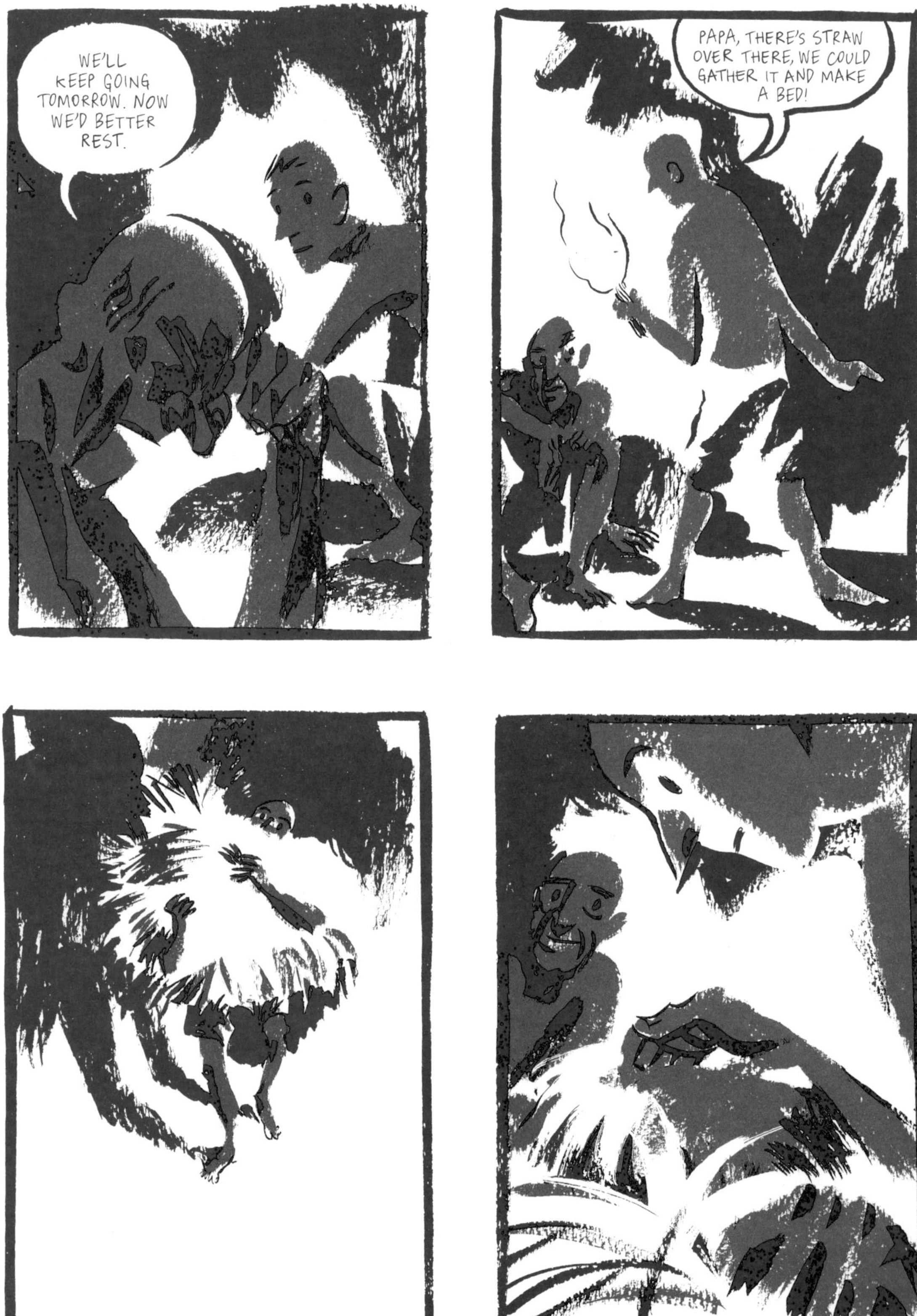
WE'LL KEEP GOING TOMORROW. NOW WE'D BETTER REST.
PAPA, THERE'S STRAW OVER THERE, WE COULD GATHER IT AND MAKE A BED!

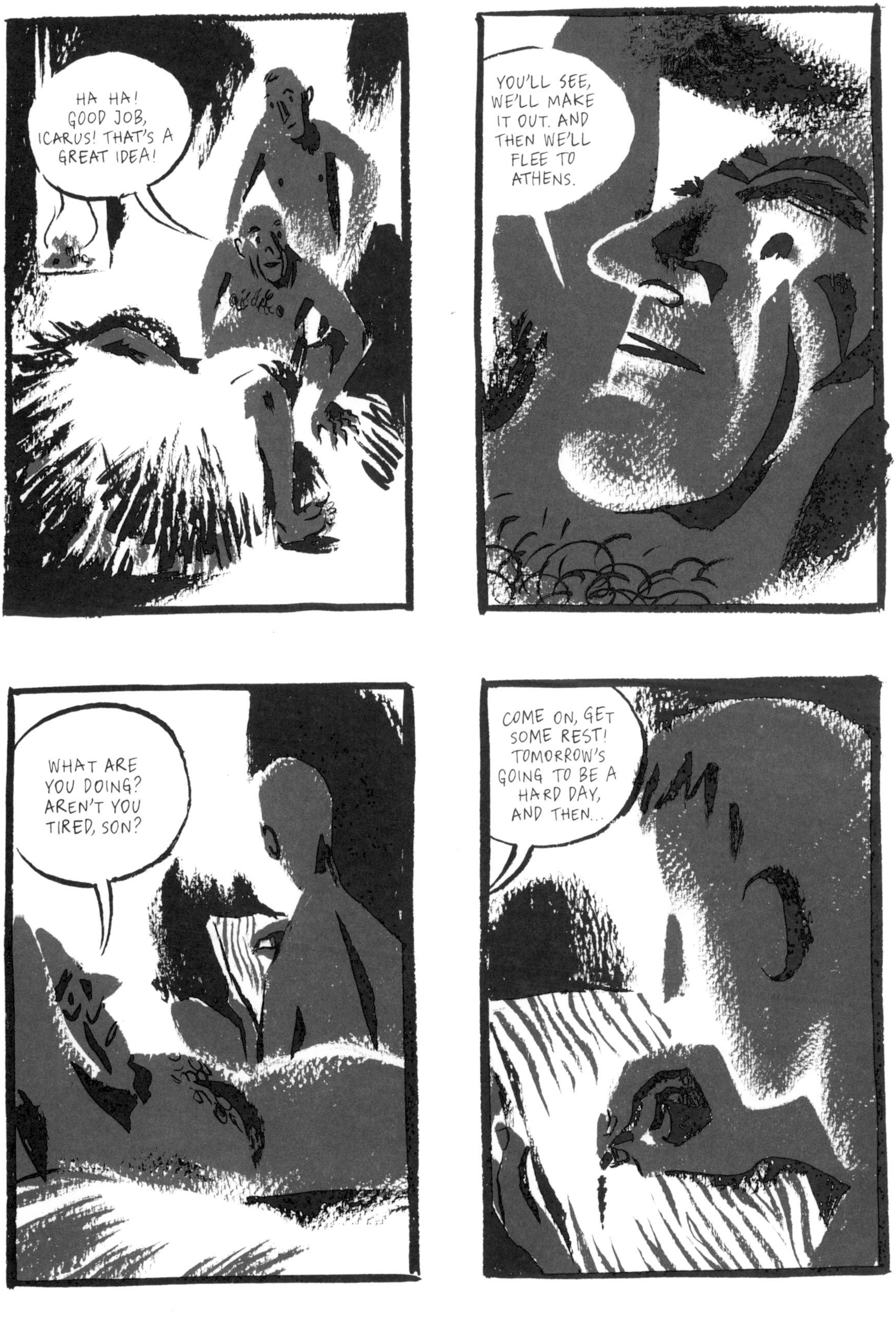
HA HA! GOOD JOB, ICARUS! THAT'S A GREAT IDEA!
YOU'LL SEE, WE'LL MAKE IT OUT. AND THEN WE'LL FLEE TO ATHENS.
WHAT ARE YOU DOING? AREN'T YOU TIRED, SON?
COME ON, GET SOME REST! TOMORROW'S GOING TO BE A HARD DAY, AND THEN...

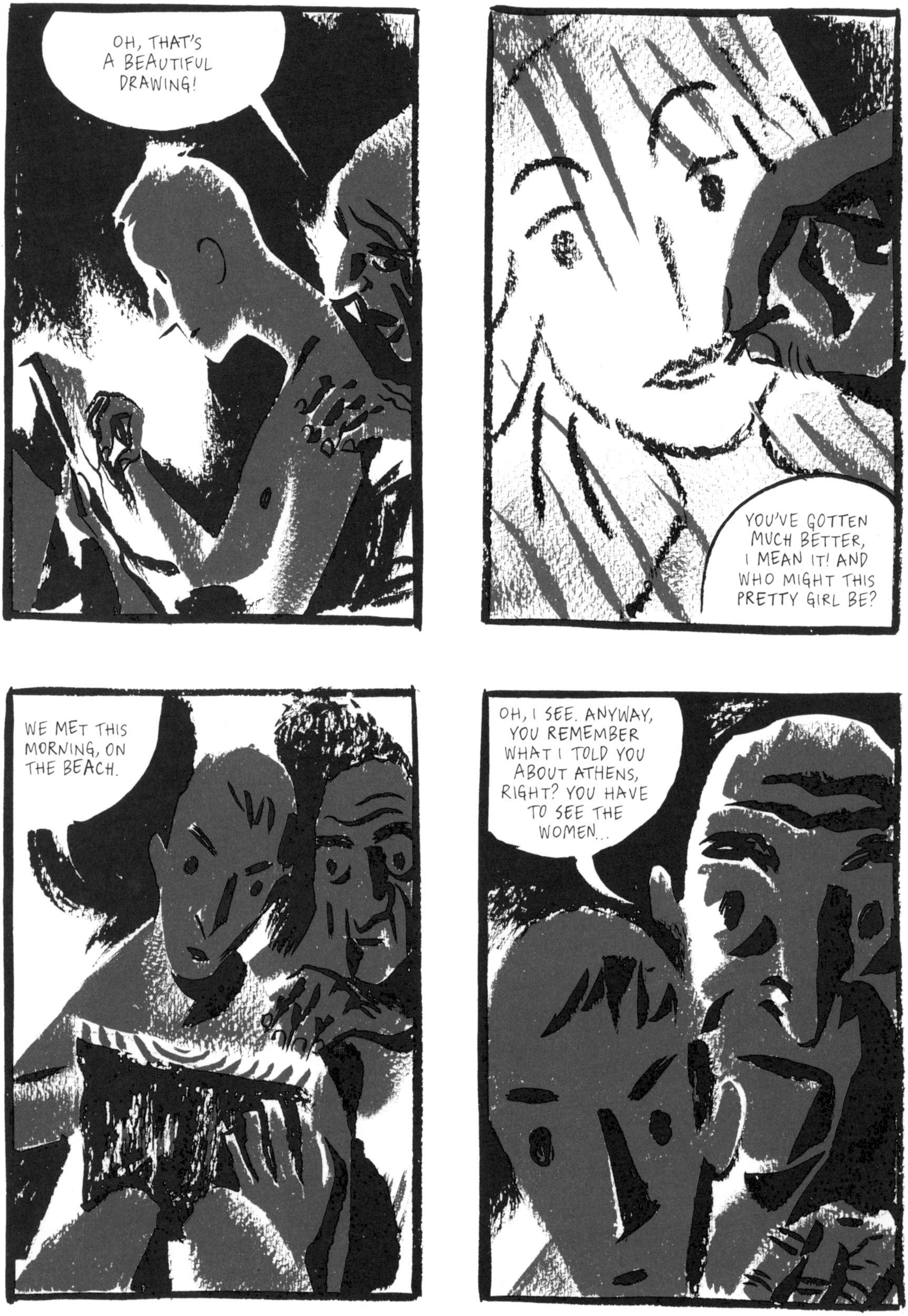
OH, THAT'S A BEAUTIFUL DRAWING!
YOU'VE GOTTEN MUCH BETTER, I MEAN IT! AND WHO MIGHT THIS PRETTY GIRL BE?
WE MET THIS MORNING, ON THE BEACH.
OH, I SEE. ANYWAY, YOU REMEMBER WHAT I TOLD YOU ABOUT ATHENS, RIGHT? YOU HAVE TO SEE THE WOMEN...

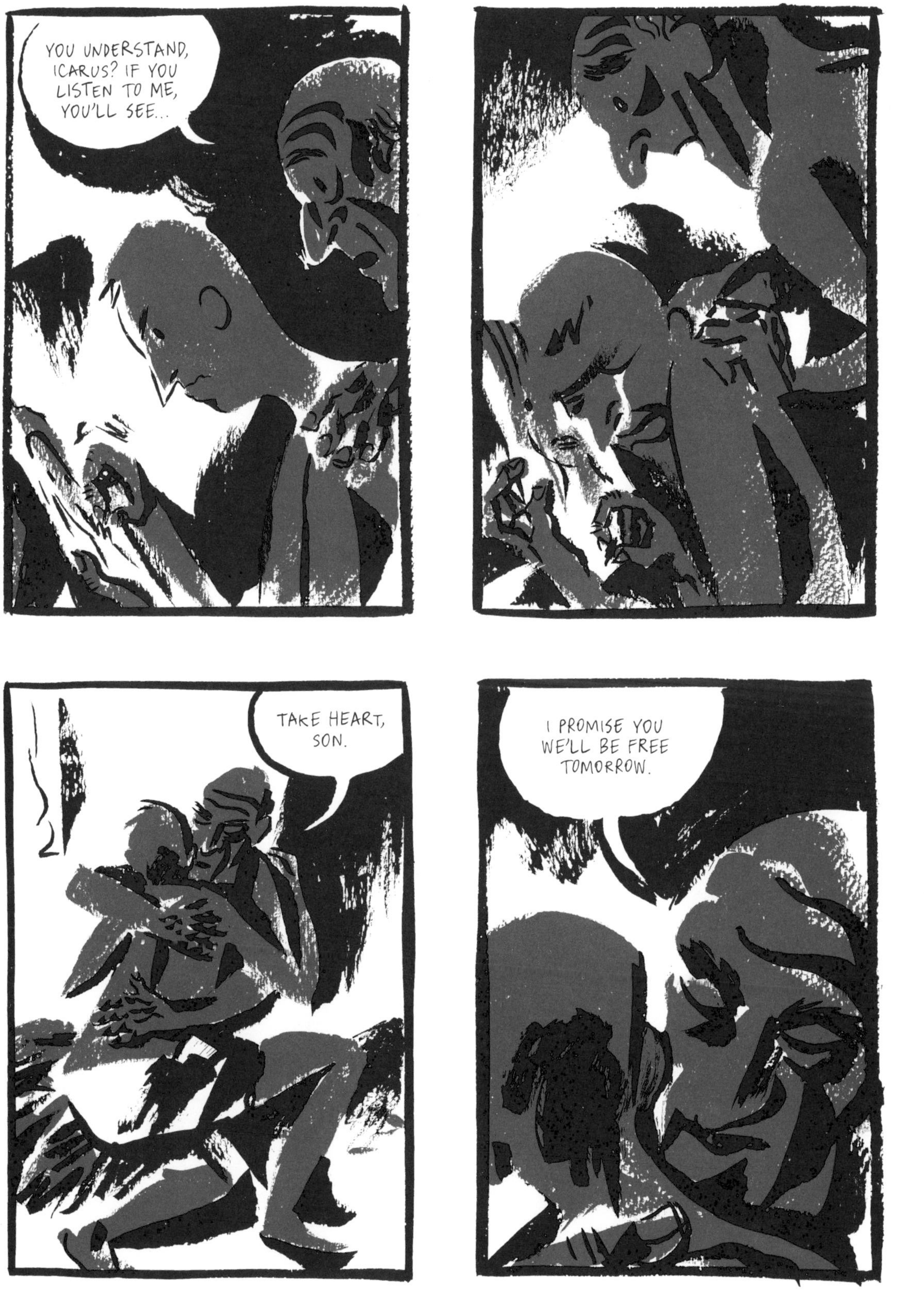
YOU UNDERSTAND, ICARUS? IF YOU LISTEN TO ME, YOU'LL SEE...
TAKE HEART, SON.
I PROMISE YOU WE'LL BE FREE TOMORROW.

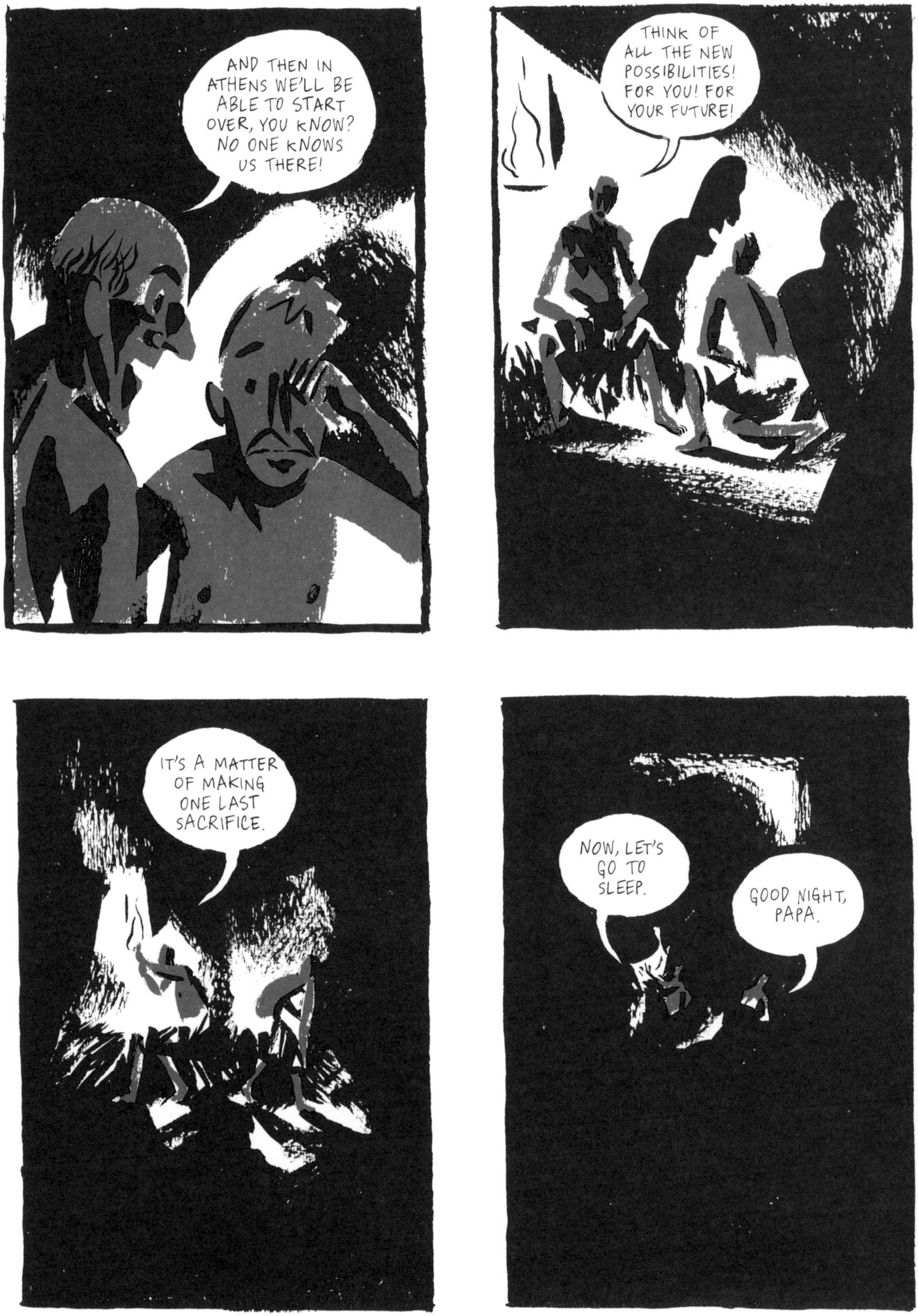
AND THEN IN ATHENS WE'LL BE ABLE TO START OVER, YOU KNOW? NO ONE KNOWS US THERE!
THINK OF ALL THE NEW POSSIBILITIES! FOR YOU! FOR YOUR FUTURE!
IT'S A MATTER OF MAKING ONE LAST SACRIFICE.
NOW, LET'S GO TO SLEEP.
GOOD NIGHT, PAPA.

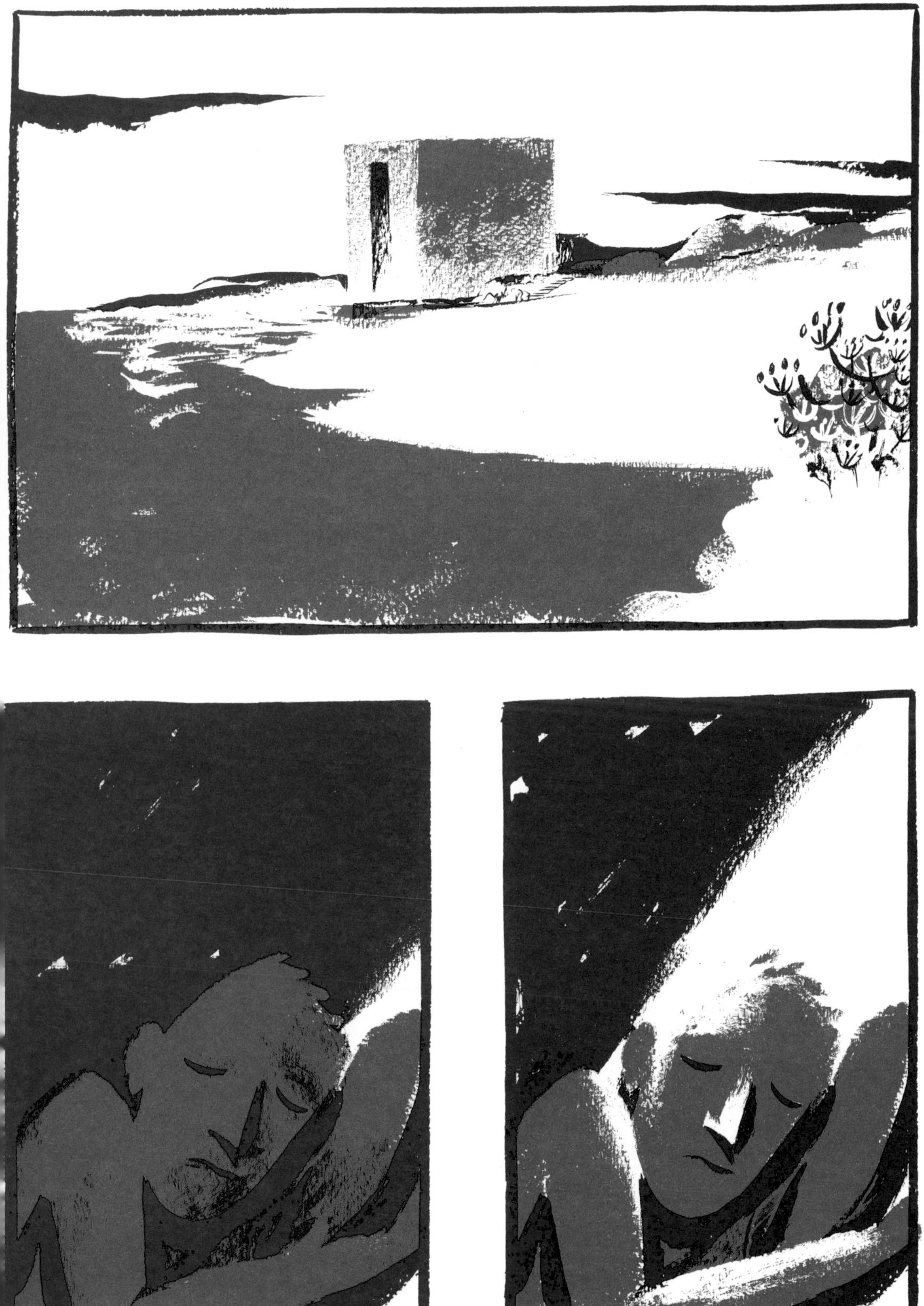

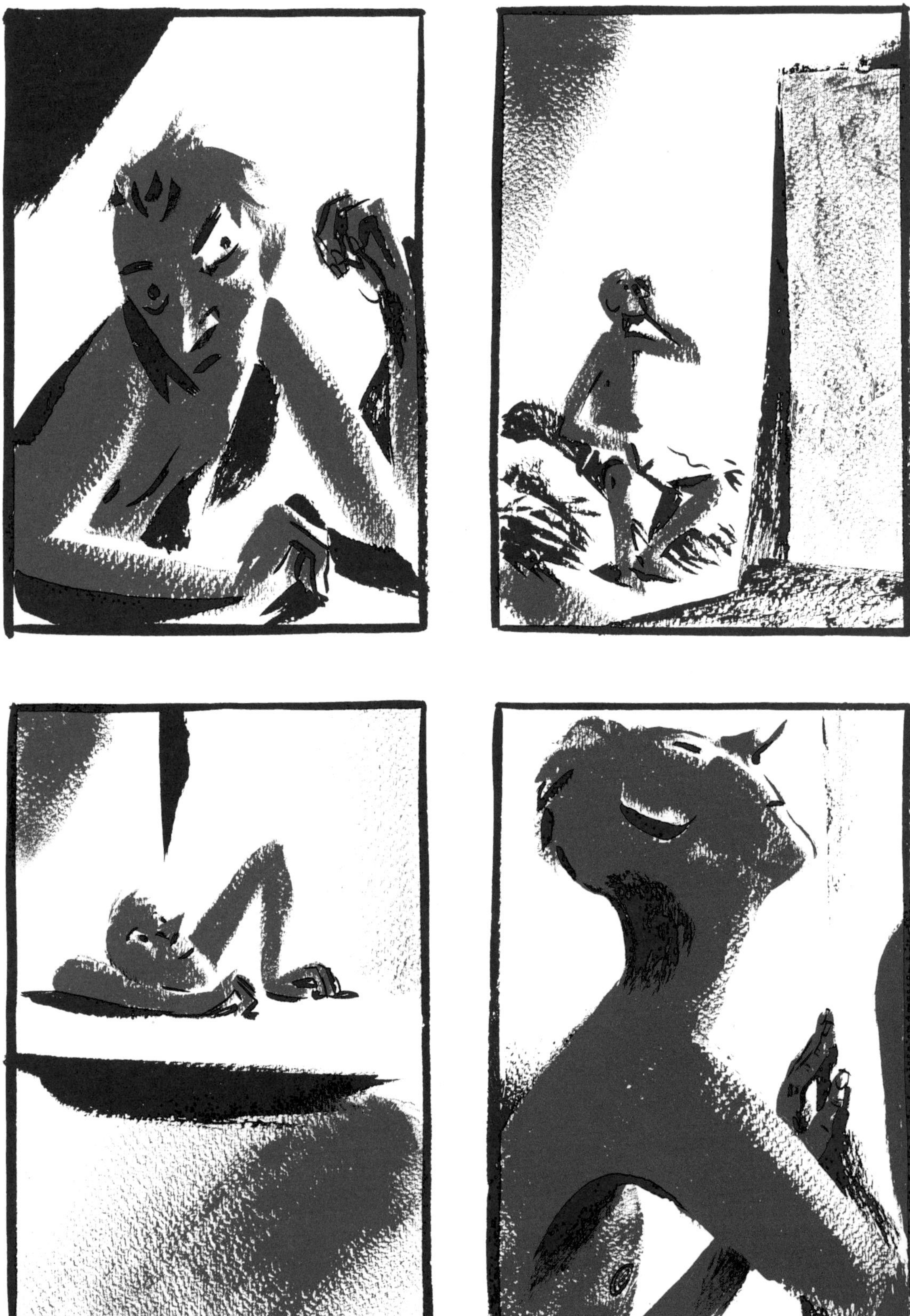

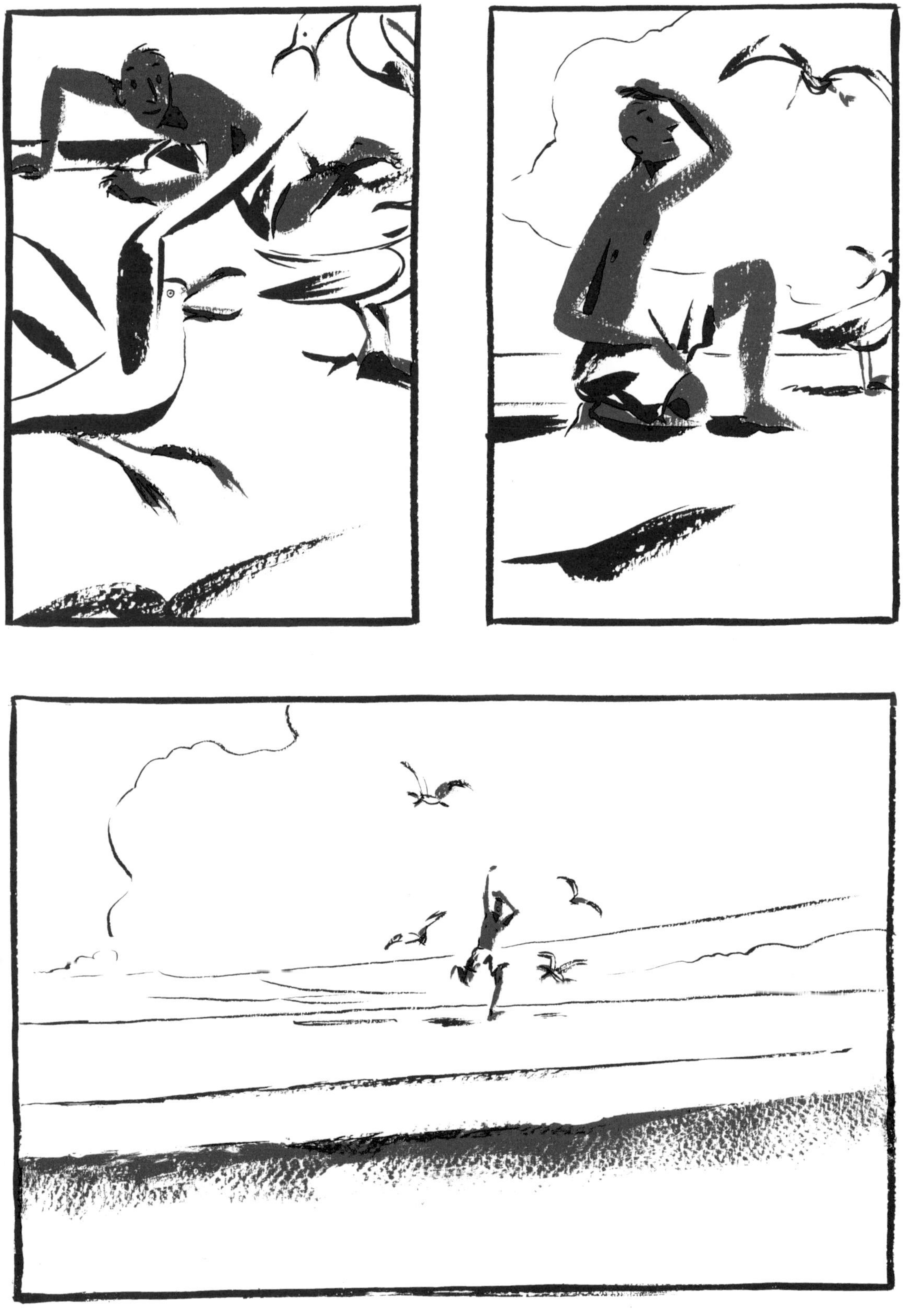

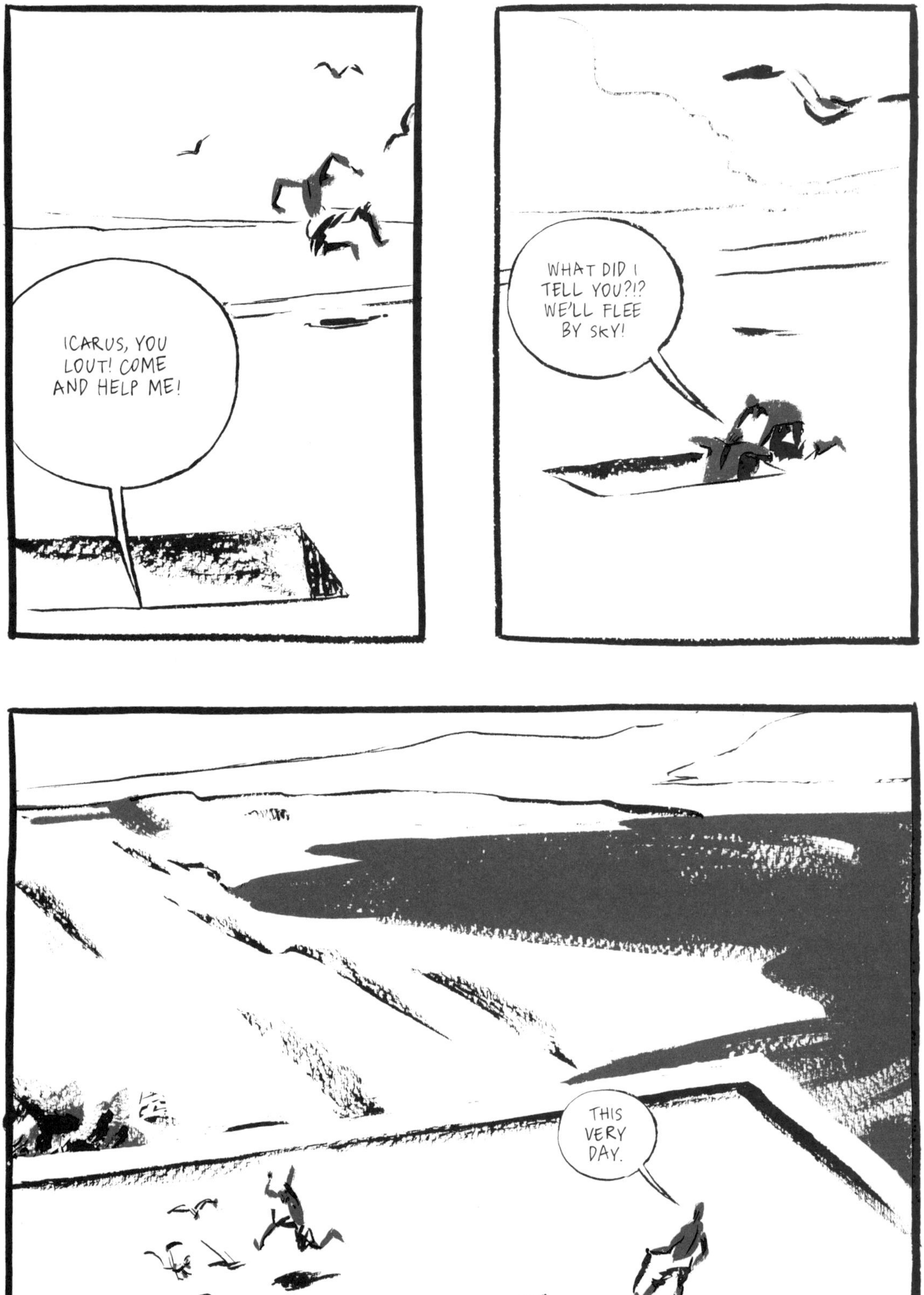
ICARUS, YOU LOUT! COME AND HELP ME!
WHAT DID I TELL YOU?!? WE'LL FLEE BY SKY!
THIS VERY DAY.

7.

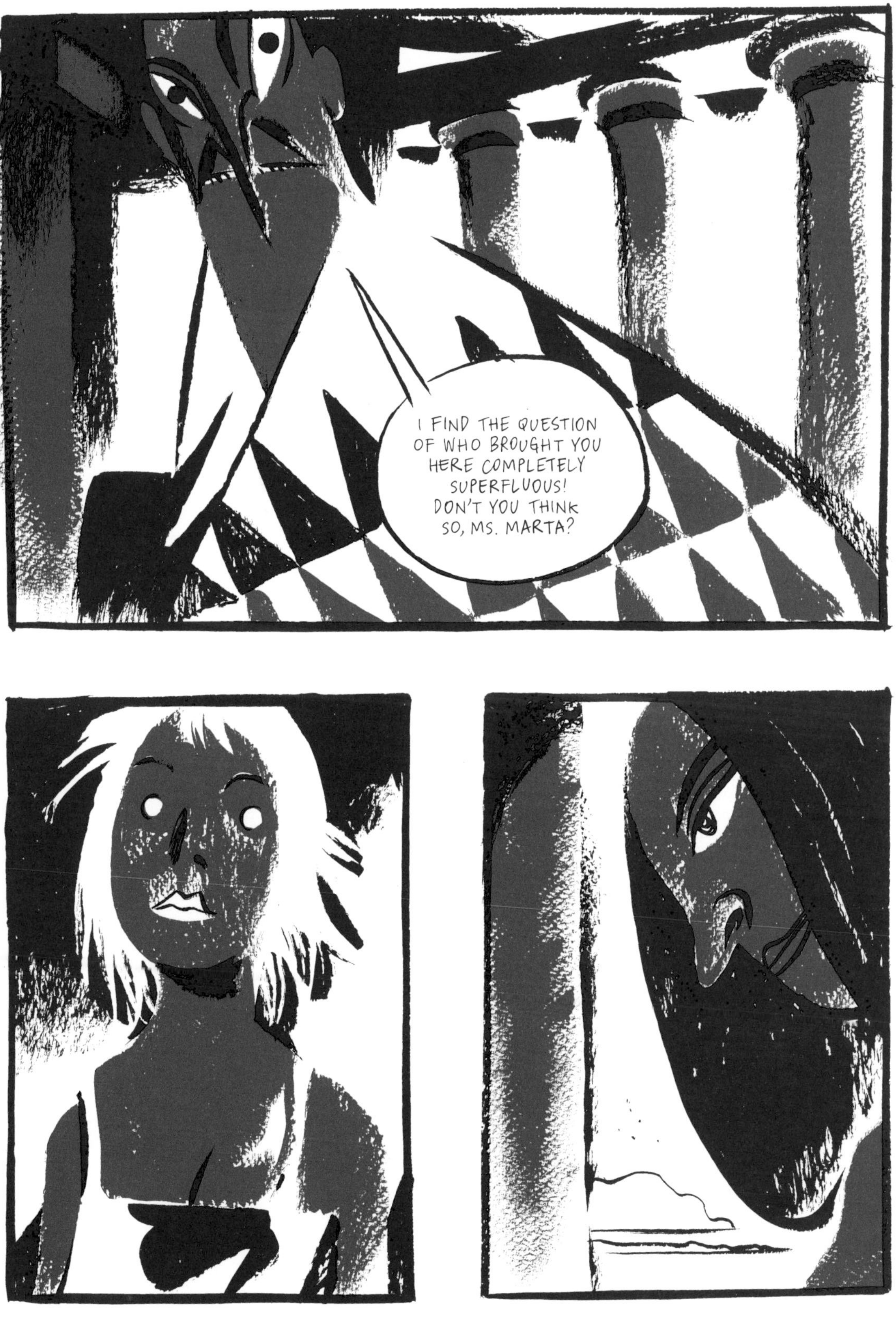
I FIND THE QUESTION OF WHO BROUGHT YOU HERE COMPLETELY SUPERFLUOUS! DON'T YOU THINK SO, MS. MARTA?

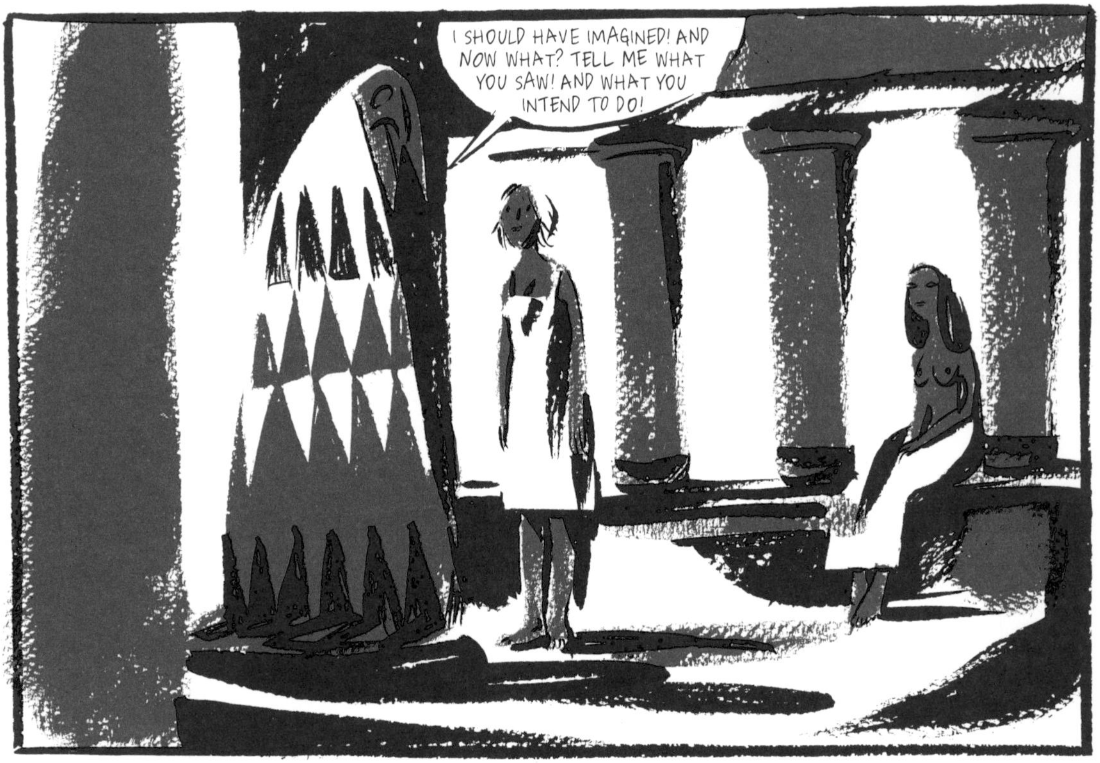
I SHOULD HAVE IMAGINED! AND NOW WHAT? TELL ME WHAT YOU SAW! AND WHAT YOU INTEND TO DO!

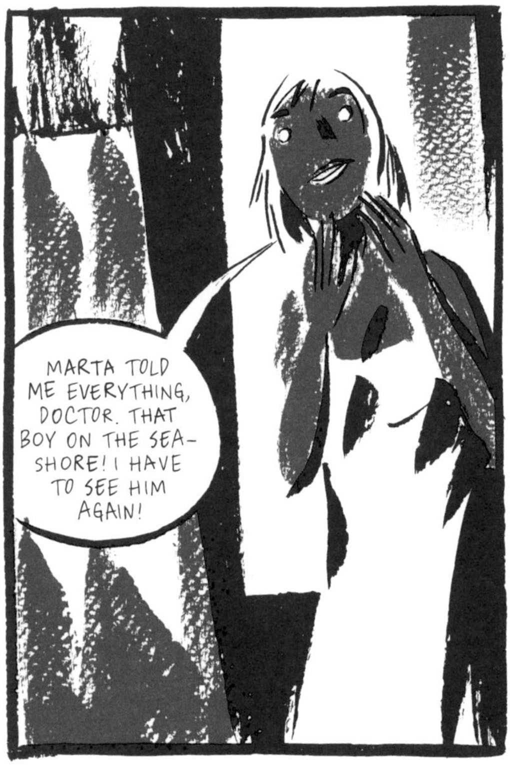
MARTA TOLD ME EVERYTHING, DOCTOR. THAT BOY ON THE SEA-SHORE! I HAVE TO SEE HIM AGAIN!

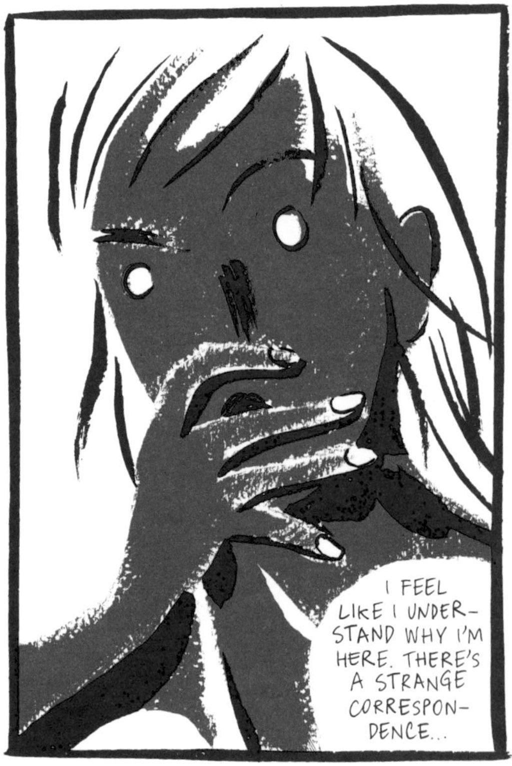
I FEEL LIKE I UNDER-STAND WHY I'M HERE. THERE'S A STRANGE CORRESPON-DENCE...

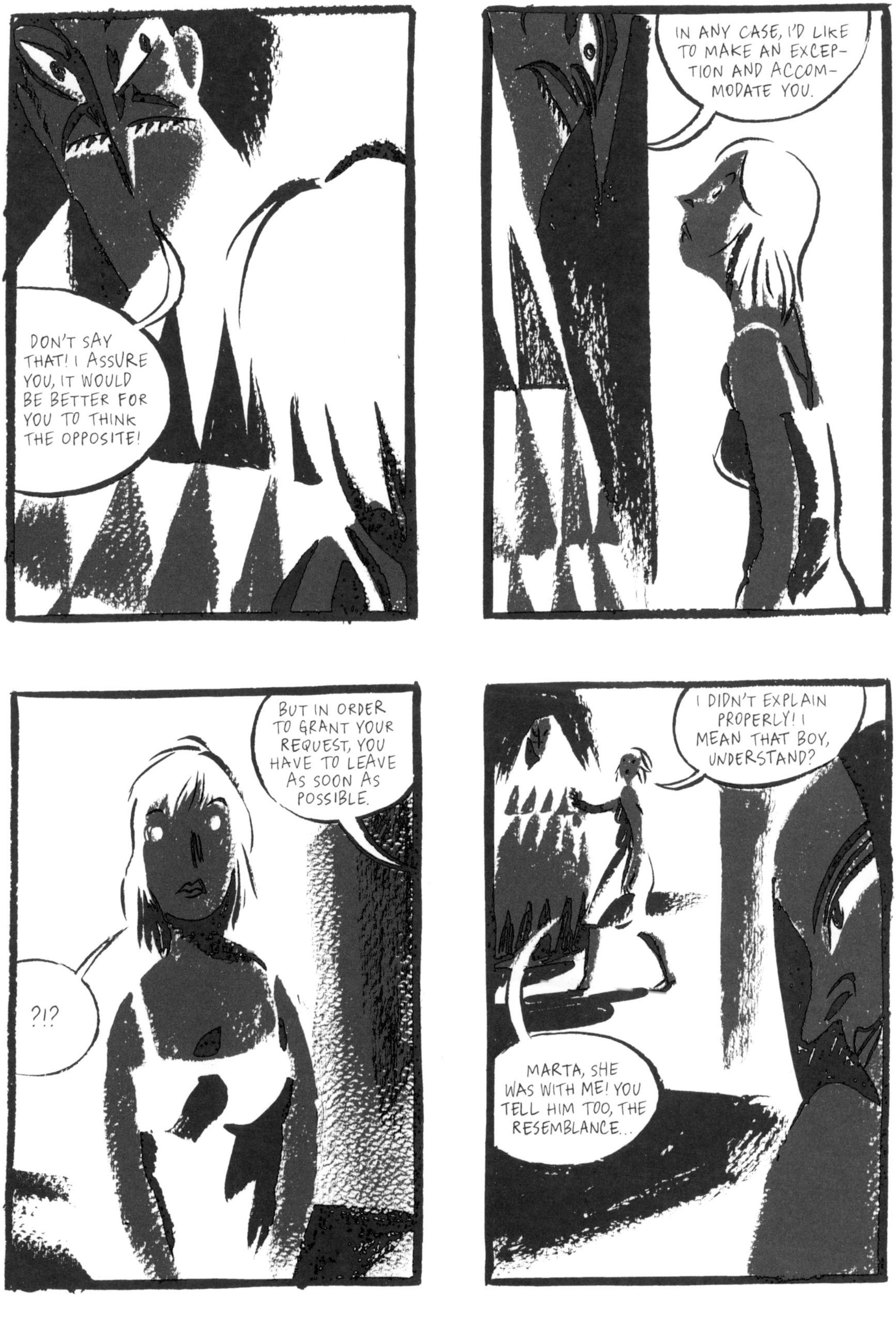
DON'T SAY THAT! I ASSURE YOU, IT WOULD BE BETTER FOR YOU TO THINK THE OPPOSITE!
IN ANY CASE, I'D LIKE TO MAKE AN EXCEPTION AND ACCOMMODATE YOU.
BUT IN ORDER TO GRANT YOUR REQUEST, YOU HAVE TO LEAVE AS SOON AS POSSIBLE.
?!?
I DIDN'T EXPLAIN PROPERLY! I MEAN THAT BOY, UNDERSTAND?
MARTA, SHE WAS WITH ME! YOU TELL HIM TOO, THE RESEMBLANCE...

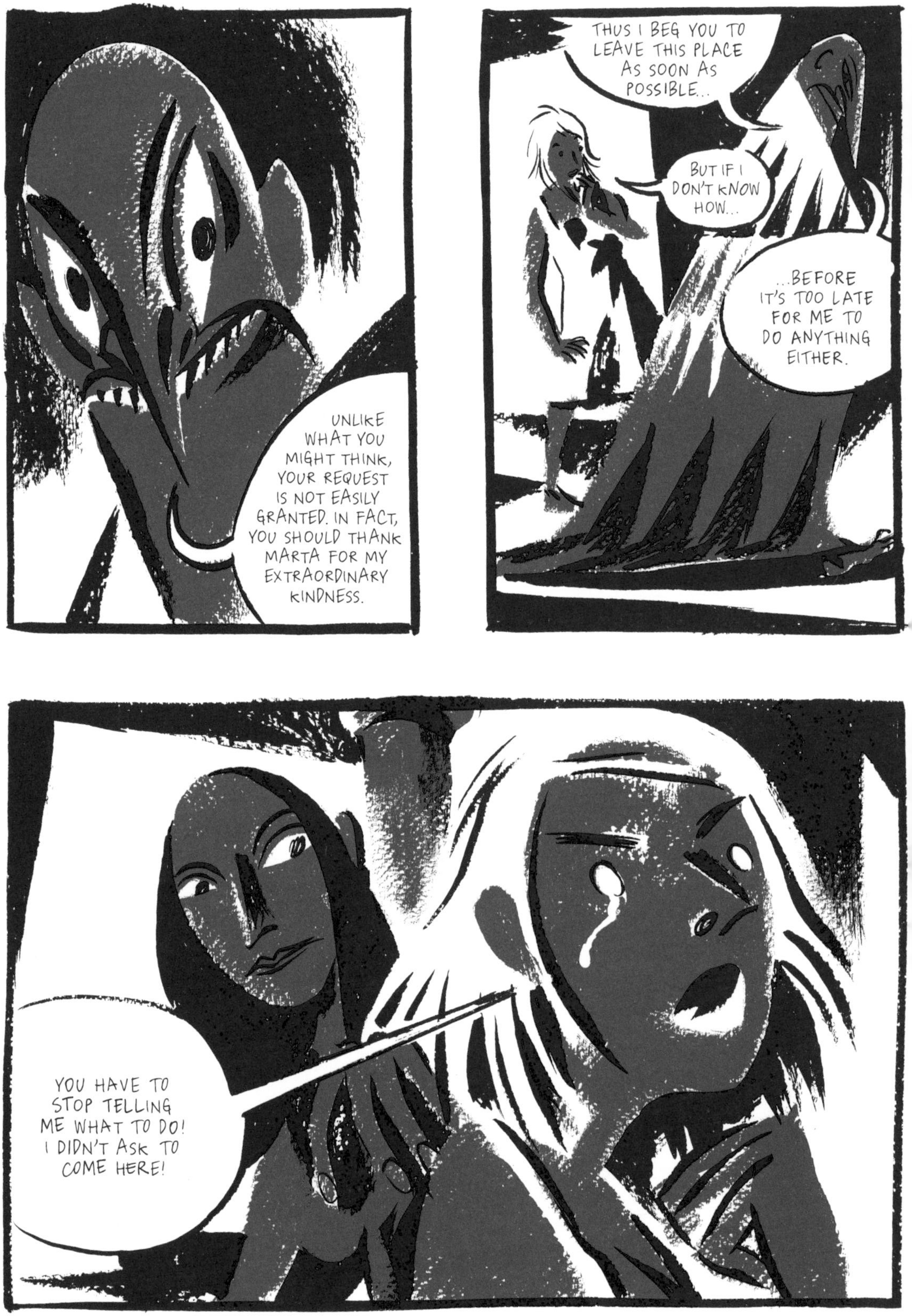

UNLIKE WHAT YOU MIGHT THINK, YOUR REQUEST IS NOT EASILY GRANTED. IN FACT, YOU SHOULD THANK MARTA FOR MY EXTRAORDINARY KINDNESS.
THUS I BEG YOU TO LEAVE THIS PLACE AS SOON AS POSSIBLE...
BUT IF I DON'T KNOW HOW...
...BEFORE IT'S TOO LATE FOR ME TO DO ANYTHING EITHER.
YOU HAVE TO STOP TELLING ME WHAT TO DO! I DIDN'T ASK TO COME HERE!

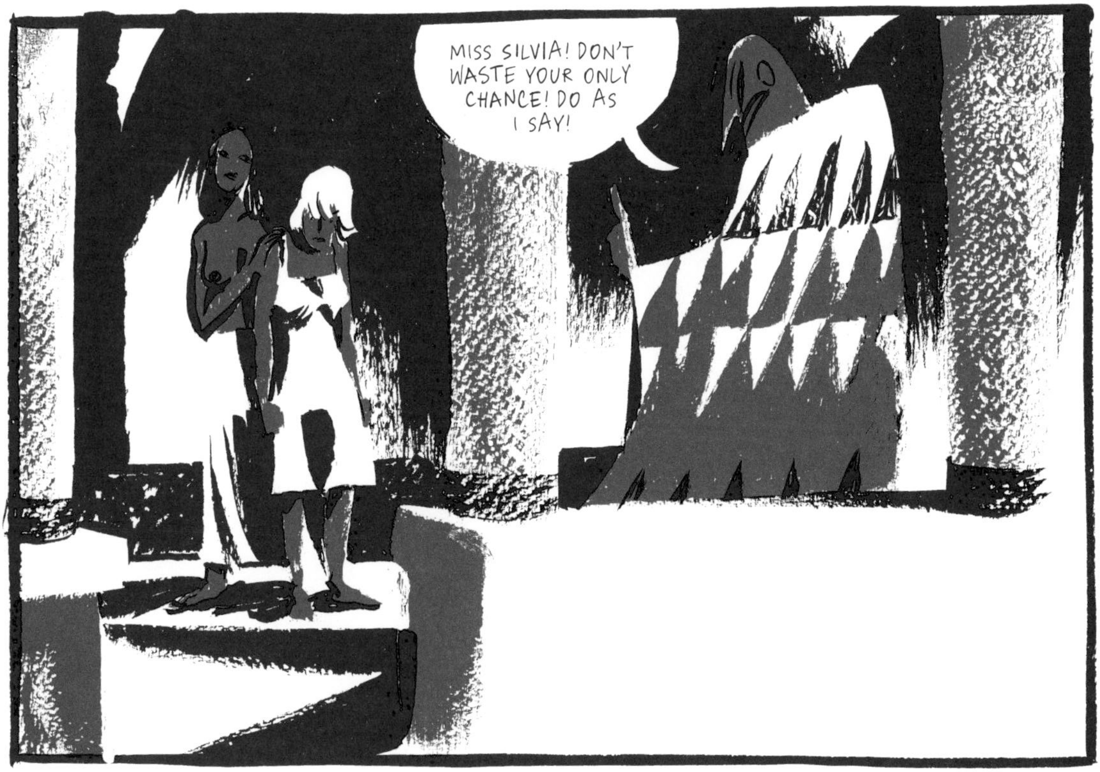
MISS SILVIA! DON'T WASTE YOUR ONLY CHANCE! DO AS I SAY!

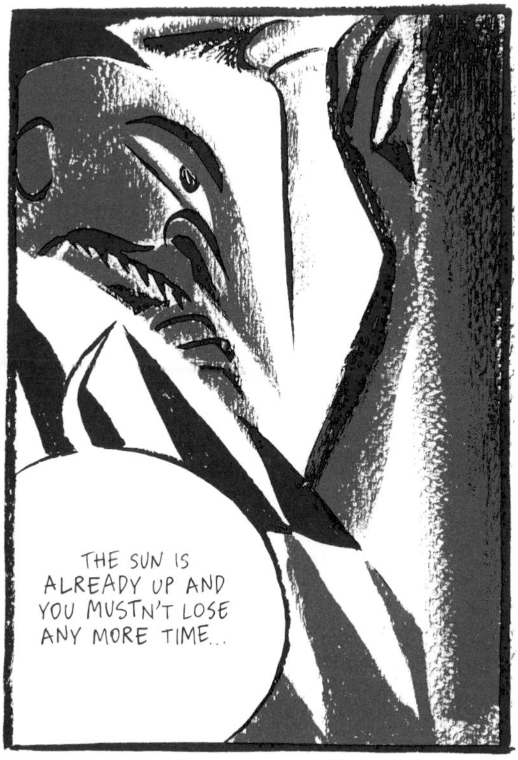
THE SUN IS ALREADY UP AND YOU MUSTN'T LOSE ANY MORE TIME...

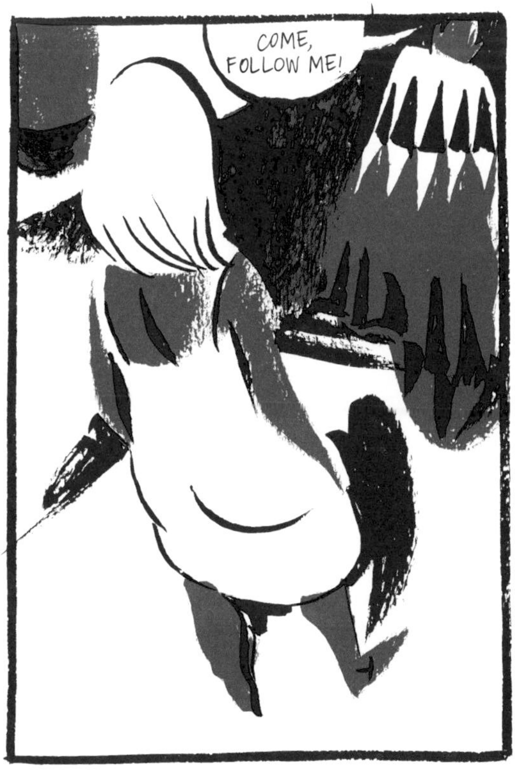
COME, FOLLOW ME!

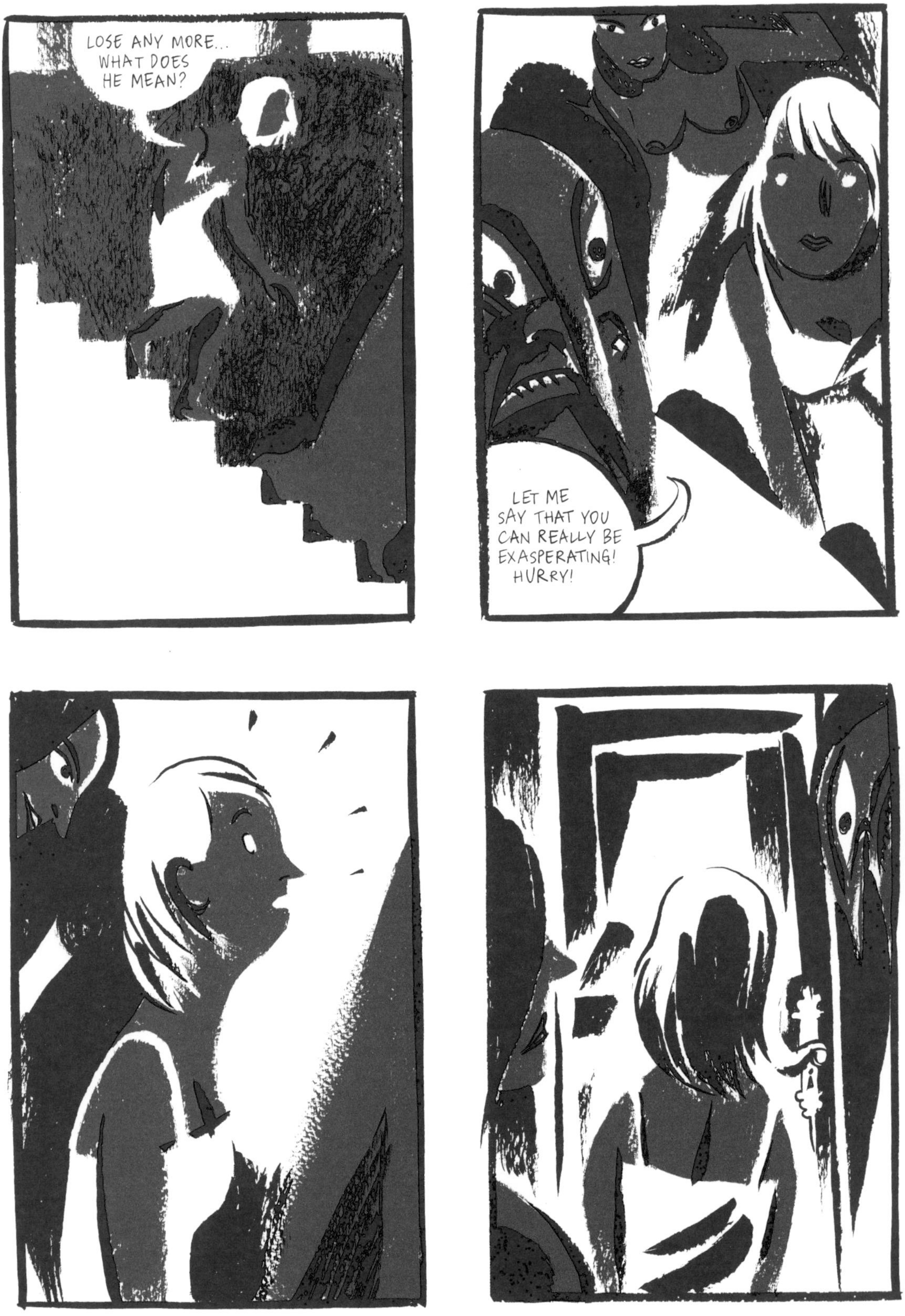
LOSE ANY MORE... WHAT DOES HE MEAN?
LET ME SAY THAT YOU CAN REALLY BE EXASPERATING! HURRY!

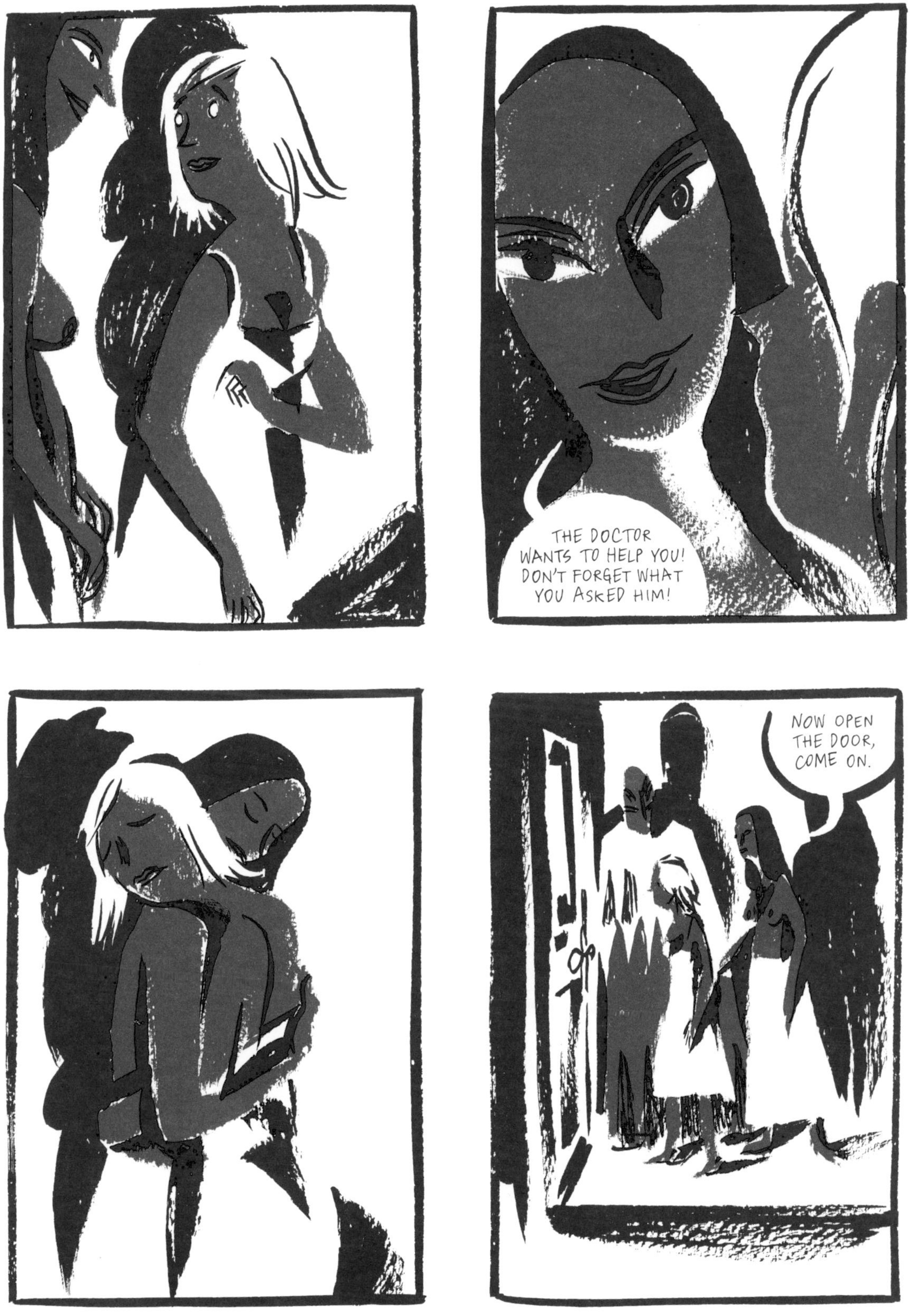
THE DOCTOR WANTS TO HELP YOU! DON'T FORGET WHAT YOU ASKED HIM!
NOW OPEN THE DOOR, COME ON.

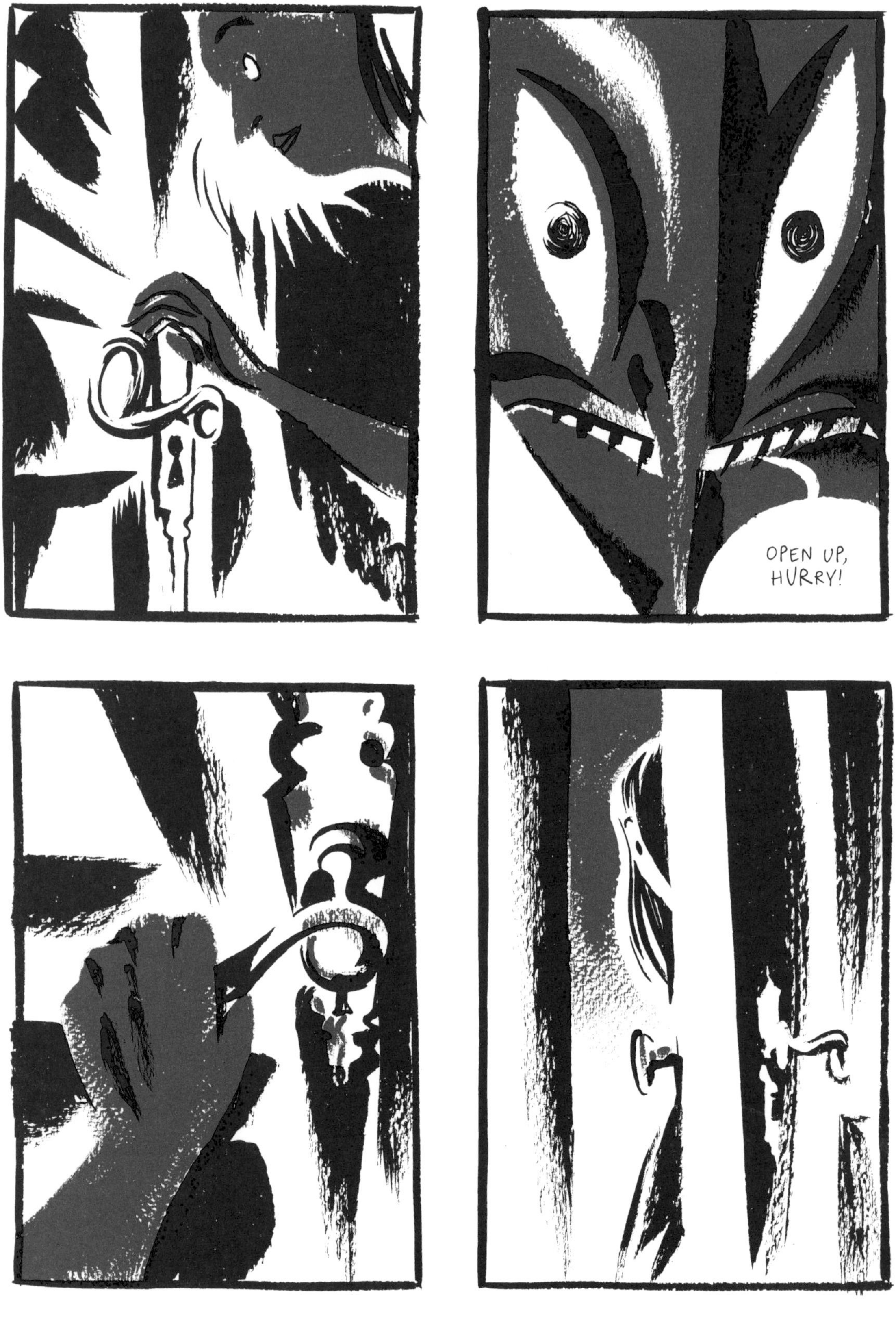
OPEN UP, HURRY!

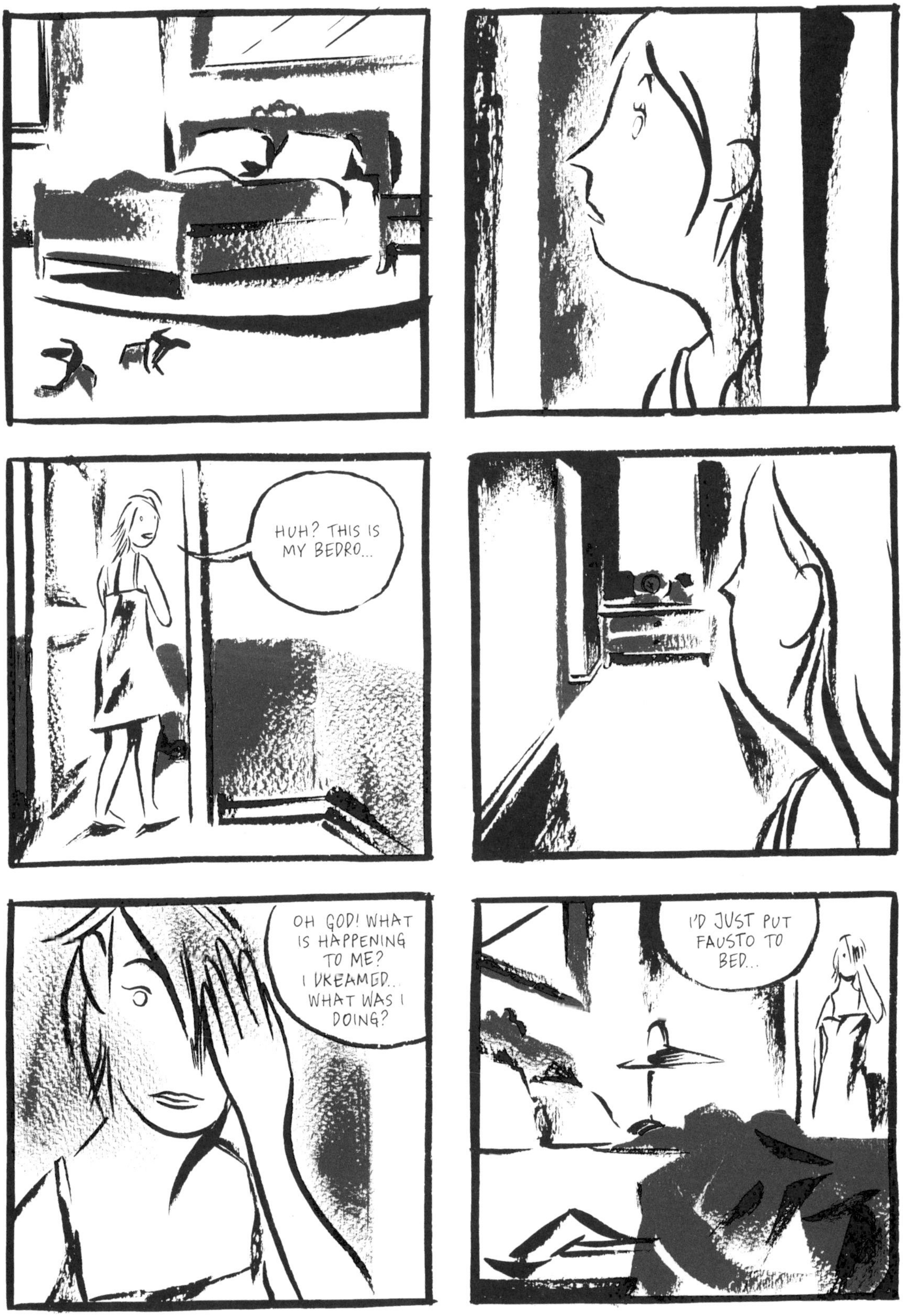
HUH? THIS IS MY BEDRO...
OH GOD! WHAT IS HAPPENING TO ME? I DREAMED... WHAT WAS I DOING?
I'D JUST PUT FAUSTO TO BED...

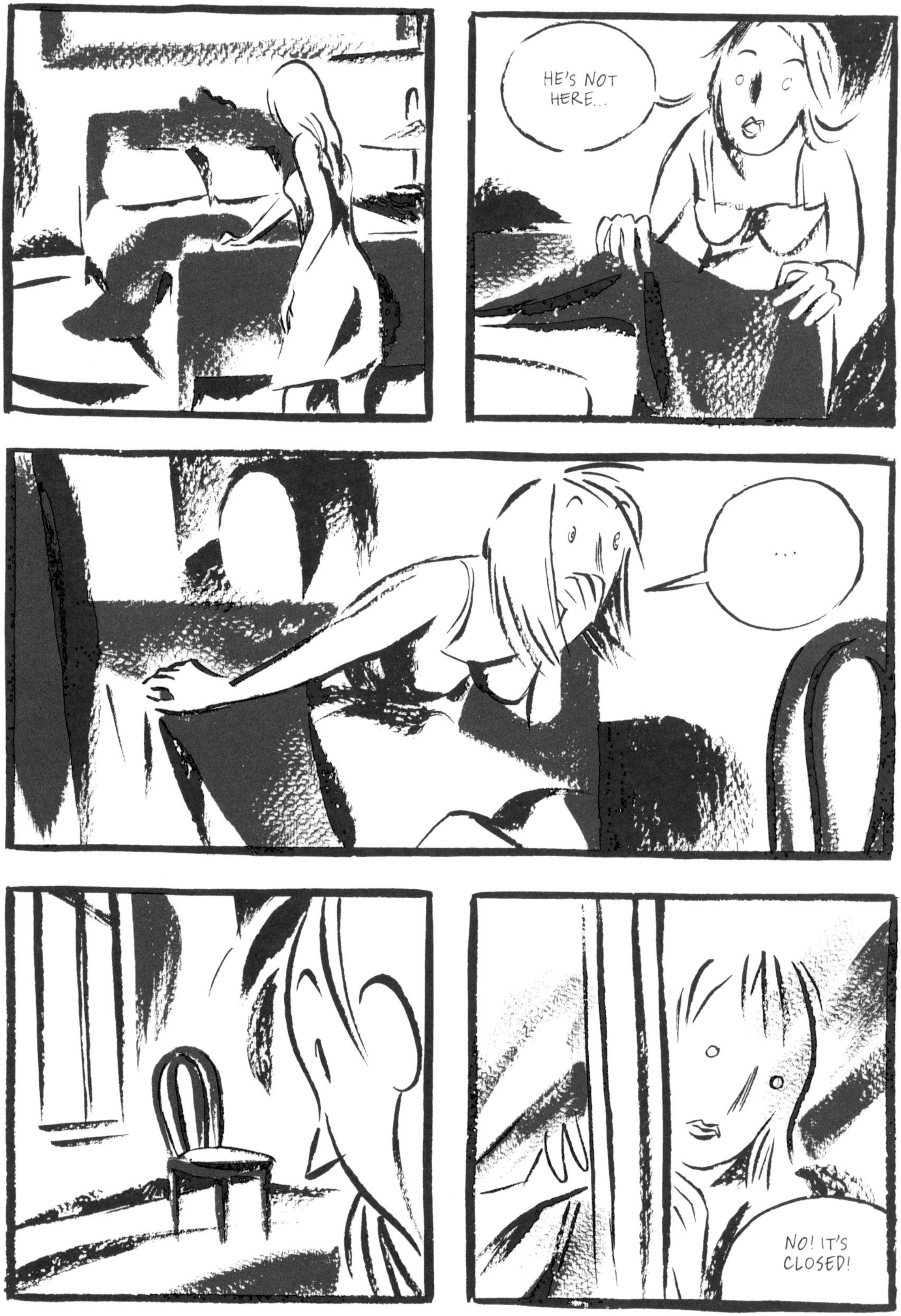
HE'S NOT HERE...
...
NO! IT'S CLOSED!

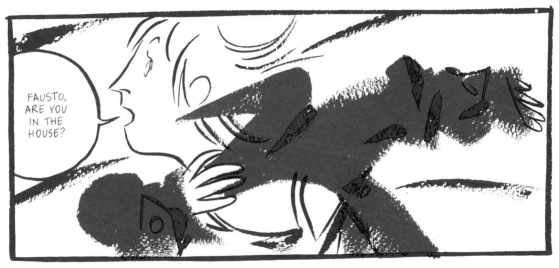

FAUSTO, ARE YOU IN THE HOUSE?

FAUSTO!

ANSWER ME!

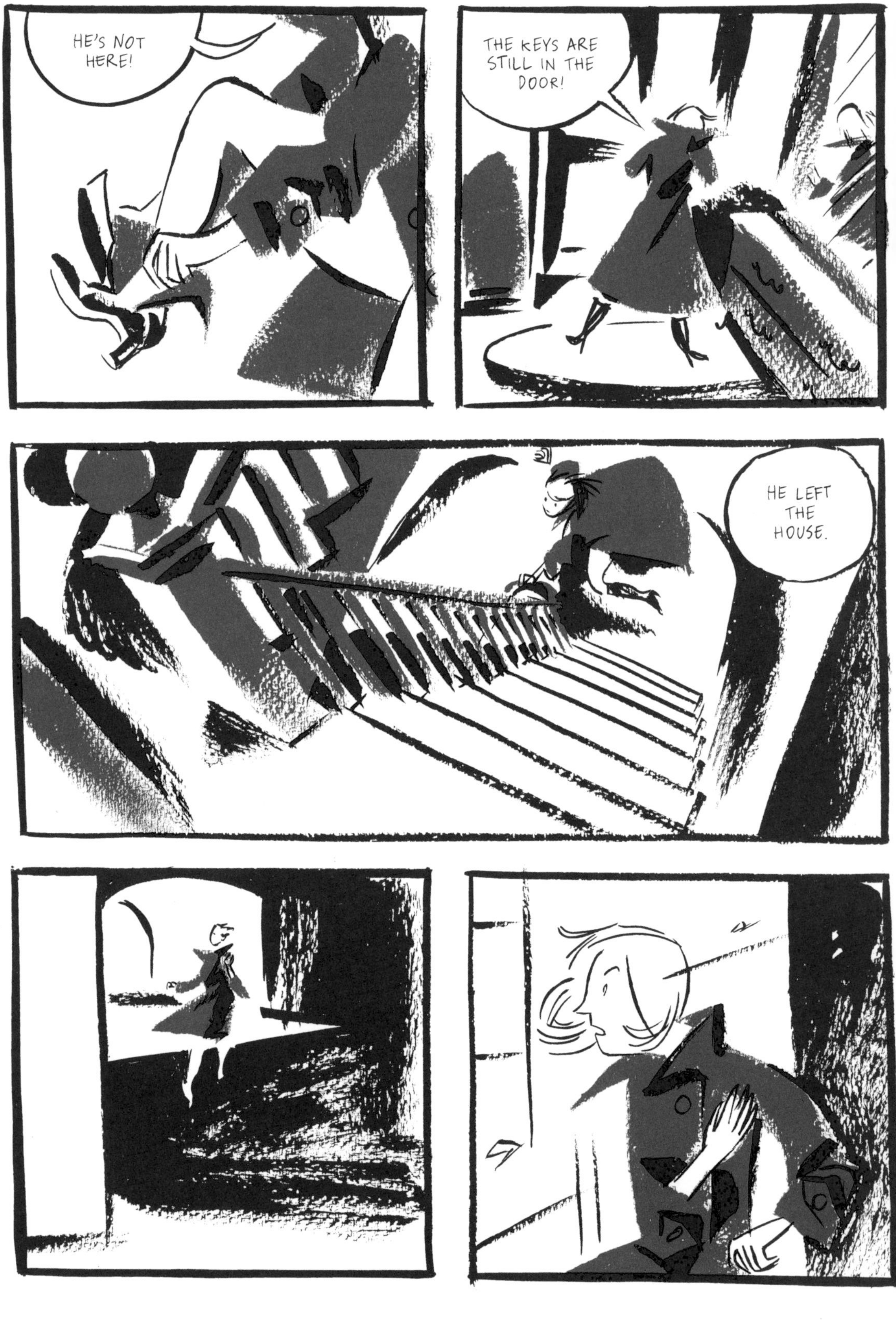
HE'S NOT HERE!
THE KEYS ARE STILL IN THE DOOR!
HE LEFT THE HOUSE.

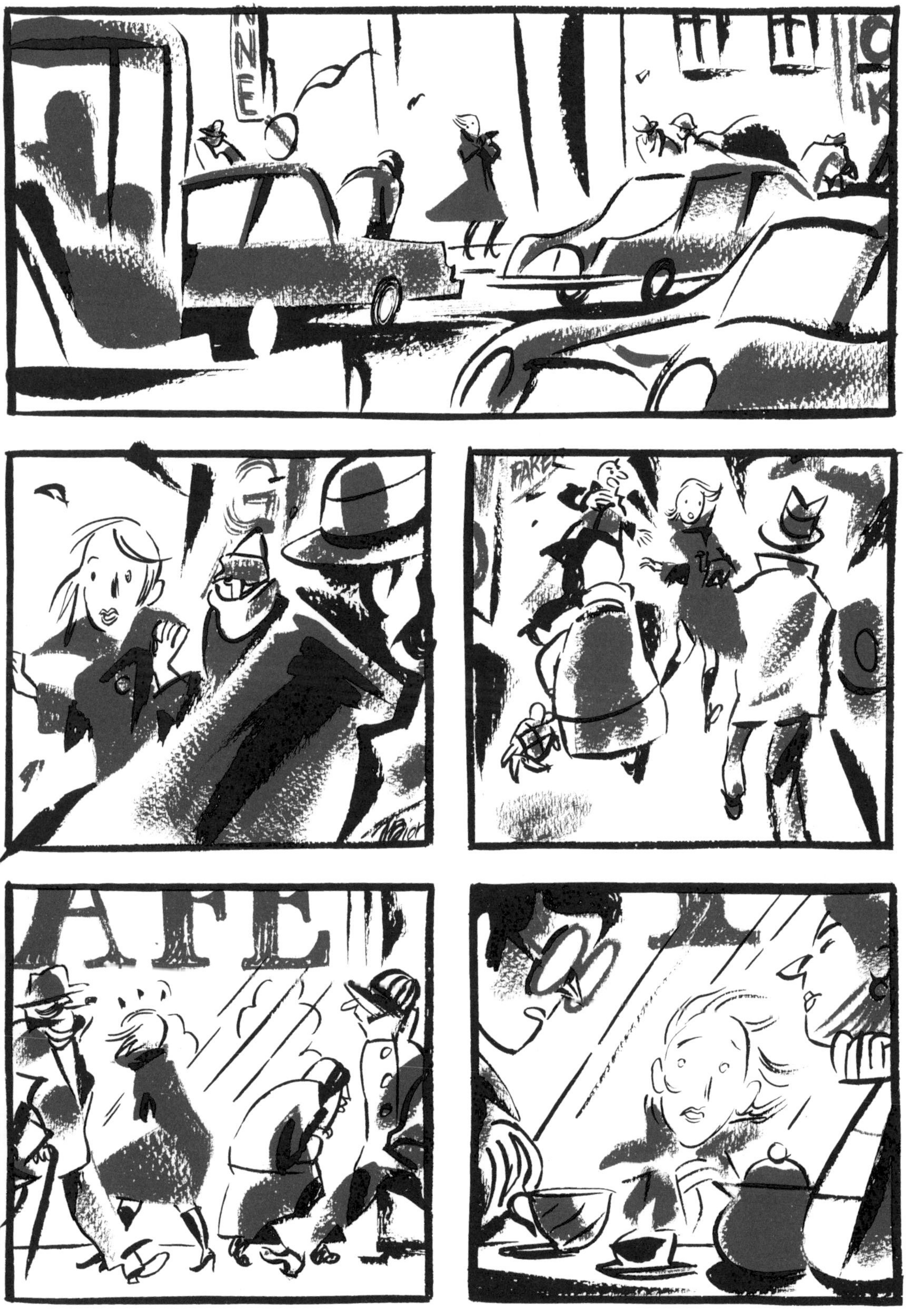
NNE
OK
AFE

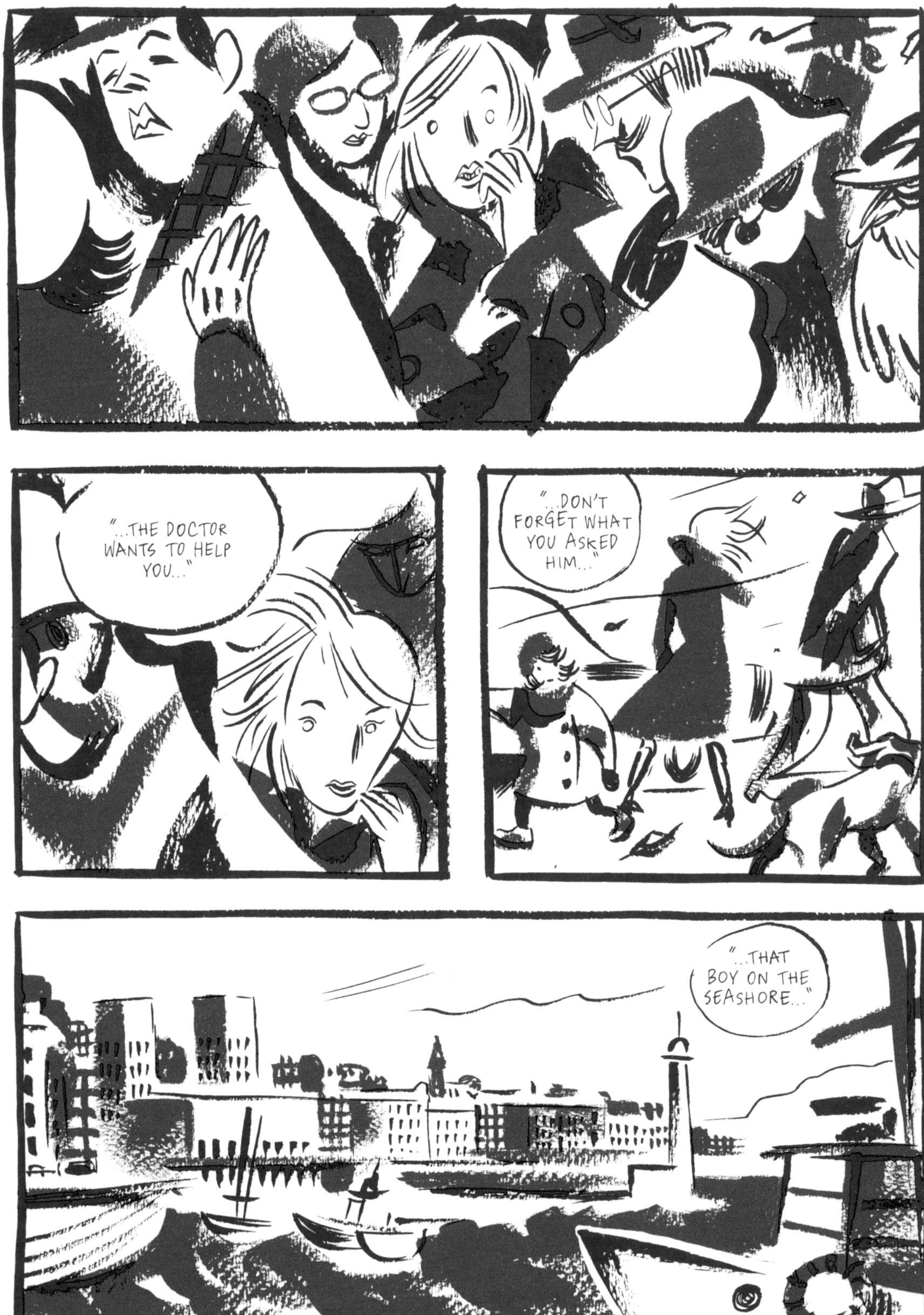
"...THE DOCTOR WANTS TO HELP YOU..."
"...DON'T FORGET WHAT YOU ASKED HIM..."
"...THAT BOY ON THE SEASHORE..."

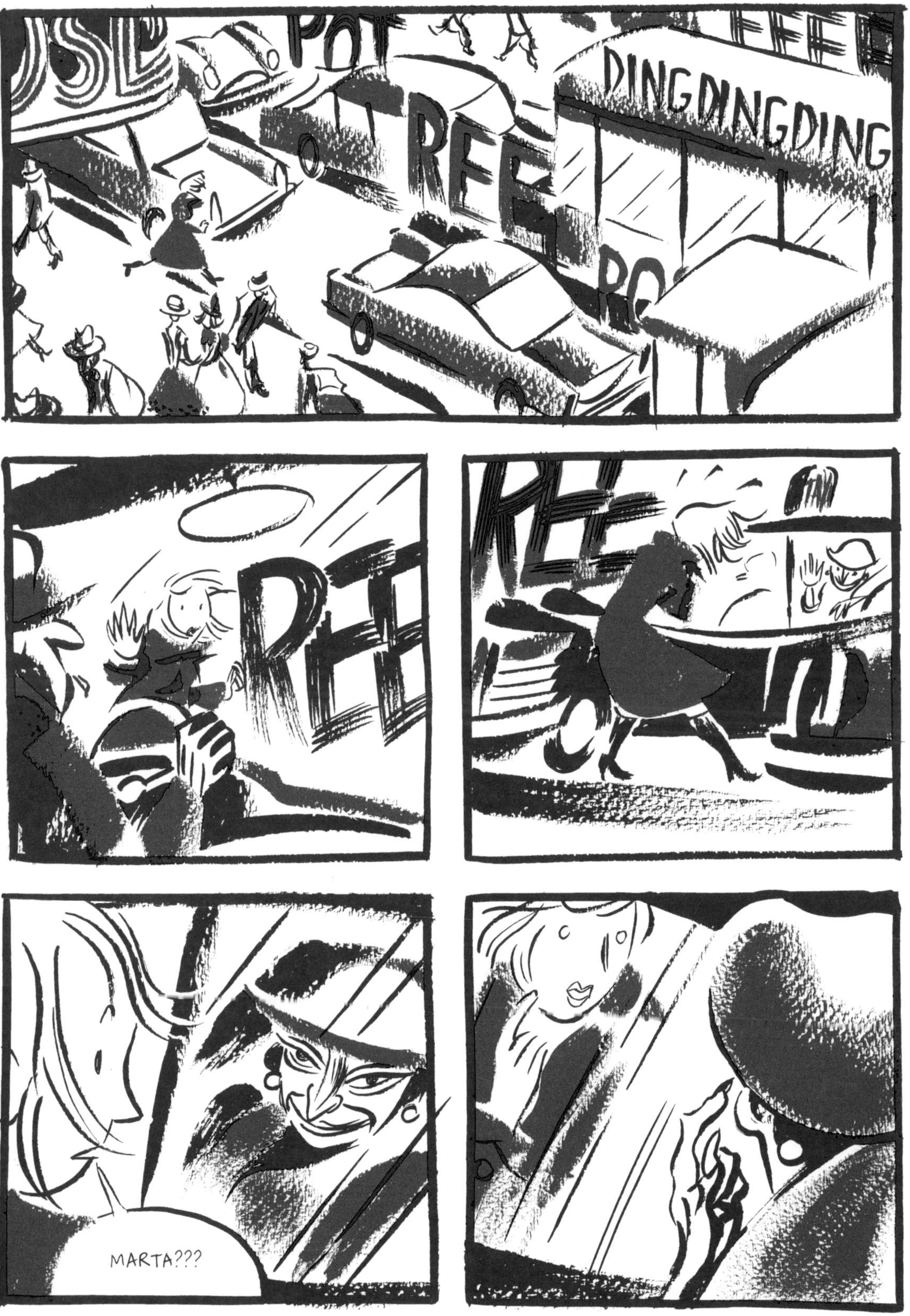
POT
REE
DINGDINGDINGDING
PO
REE
REE
MARTA???

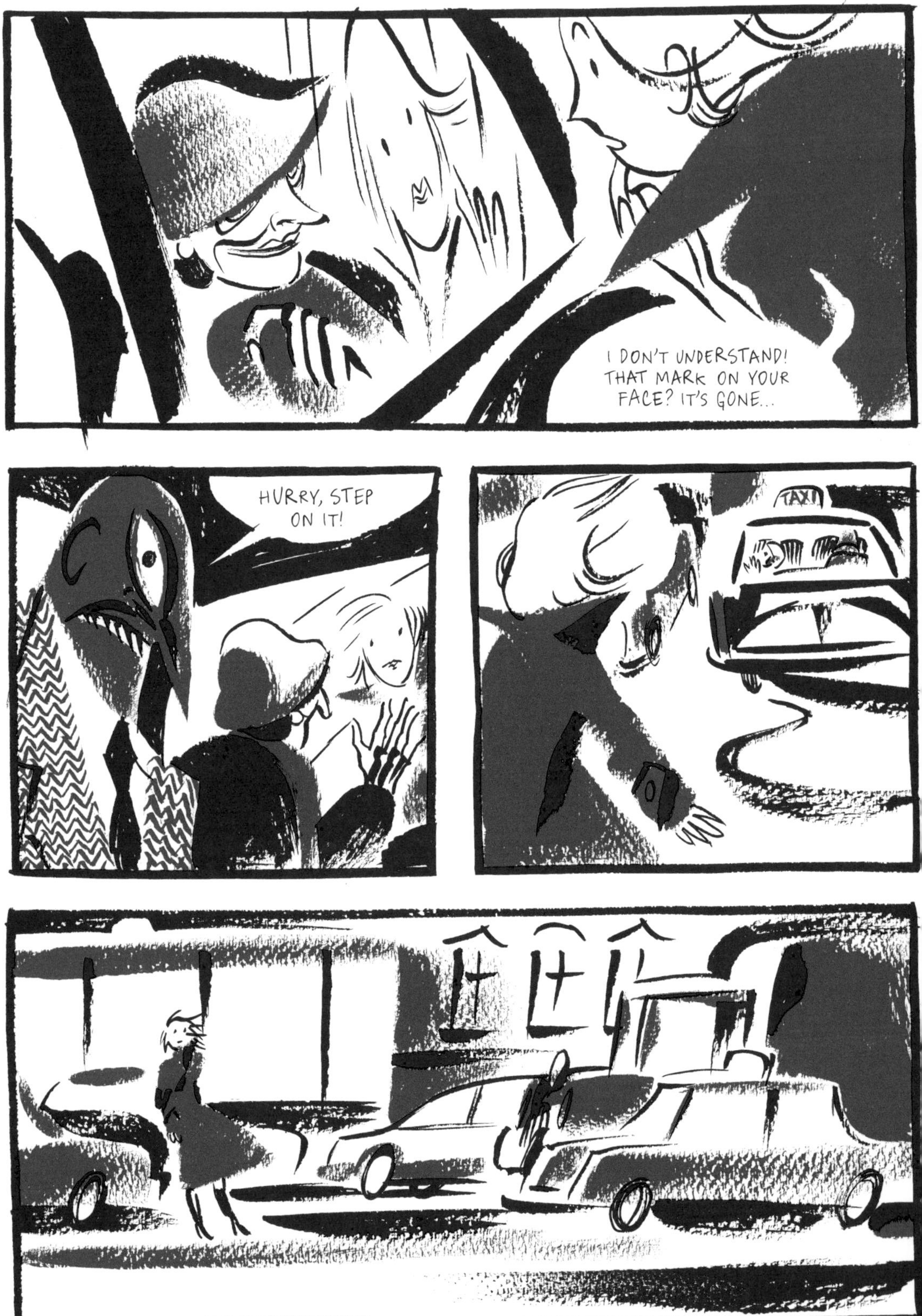
I DON'T UNDERSTAND! THAT MARK ON YOUR FACE? IT'S GONE...
HURRY, STEP ON IT!
TAXI

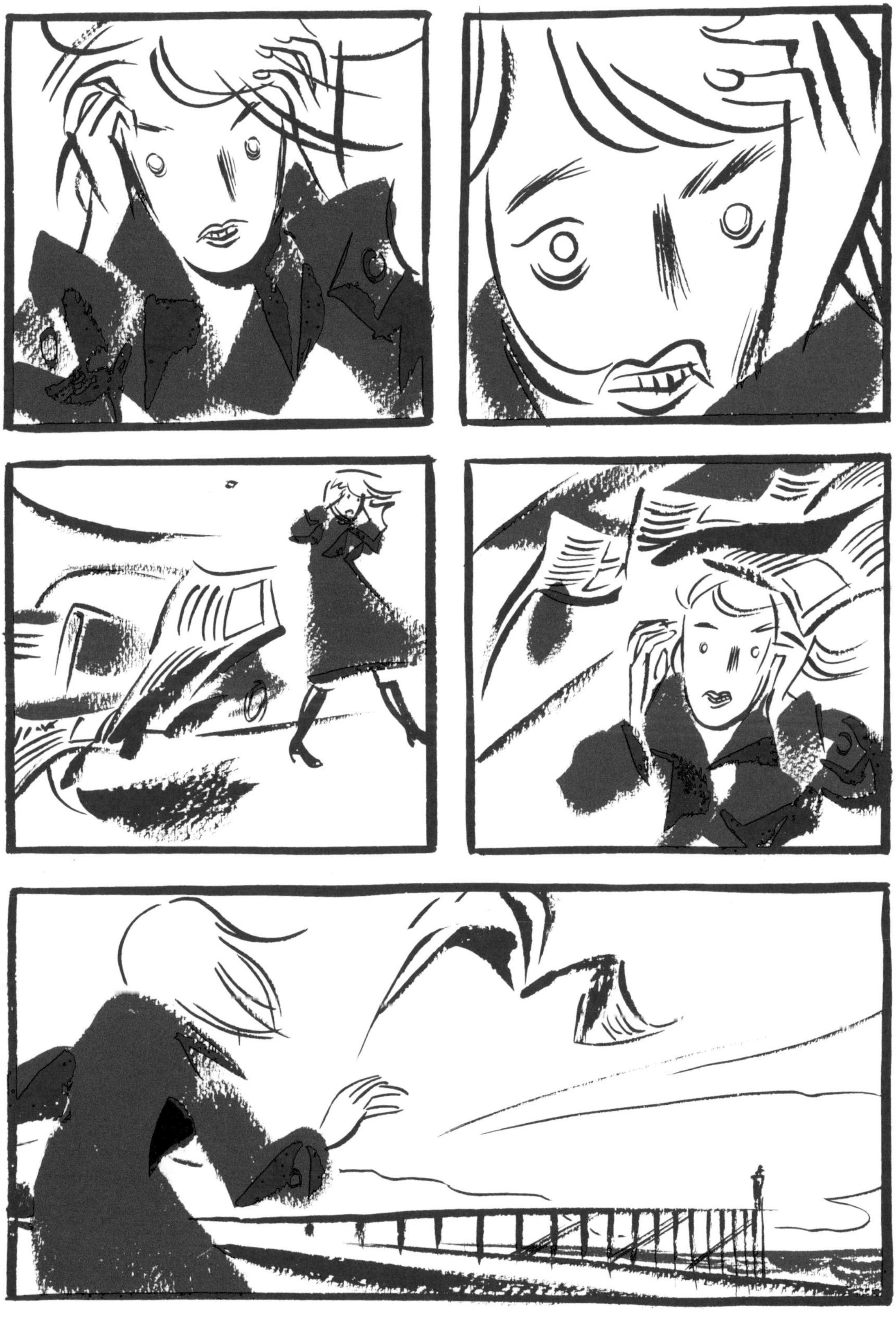

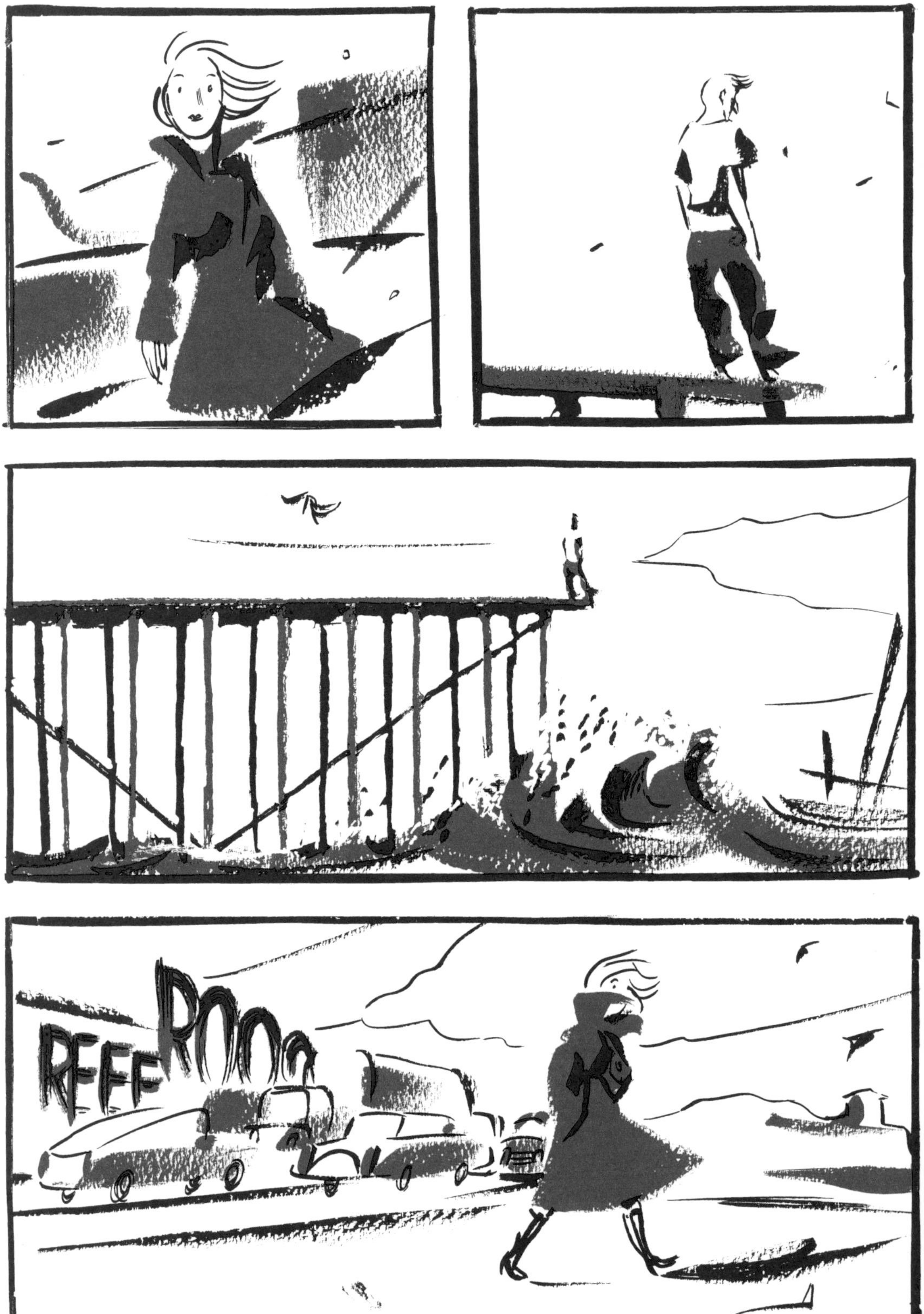
REFF RRRR

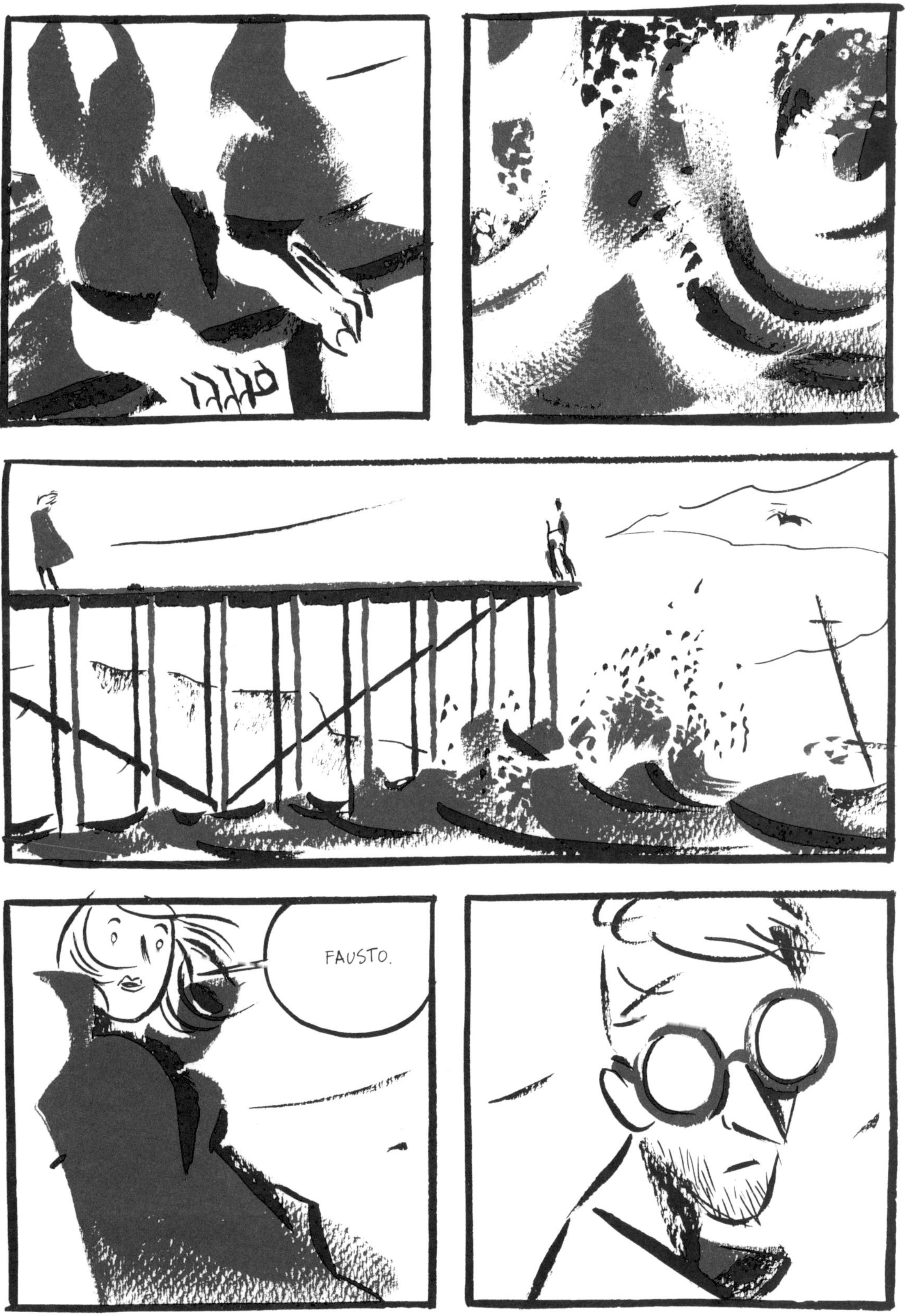
FAUSTO.

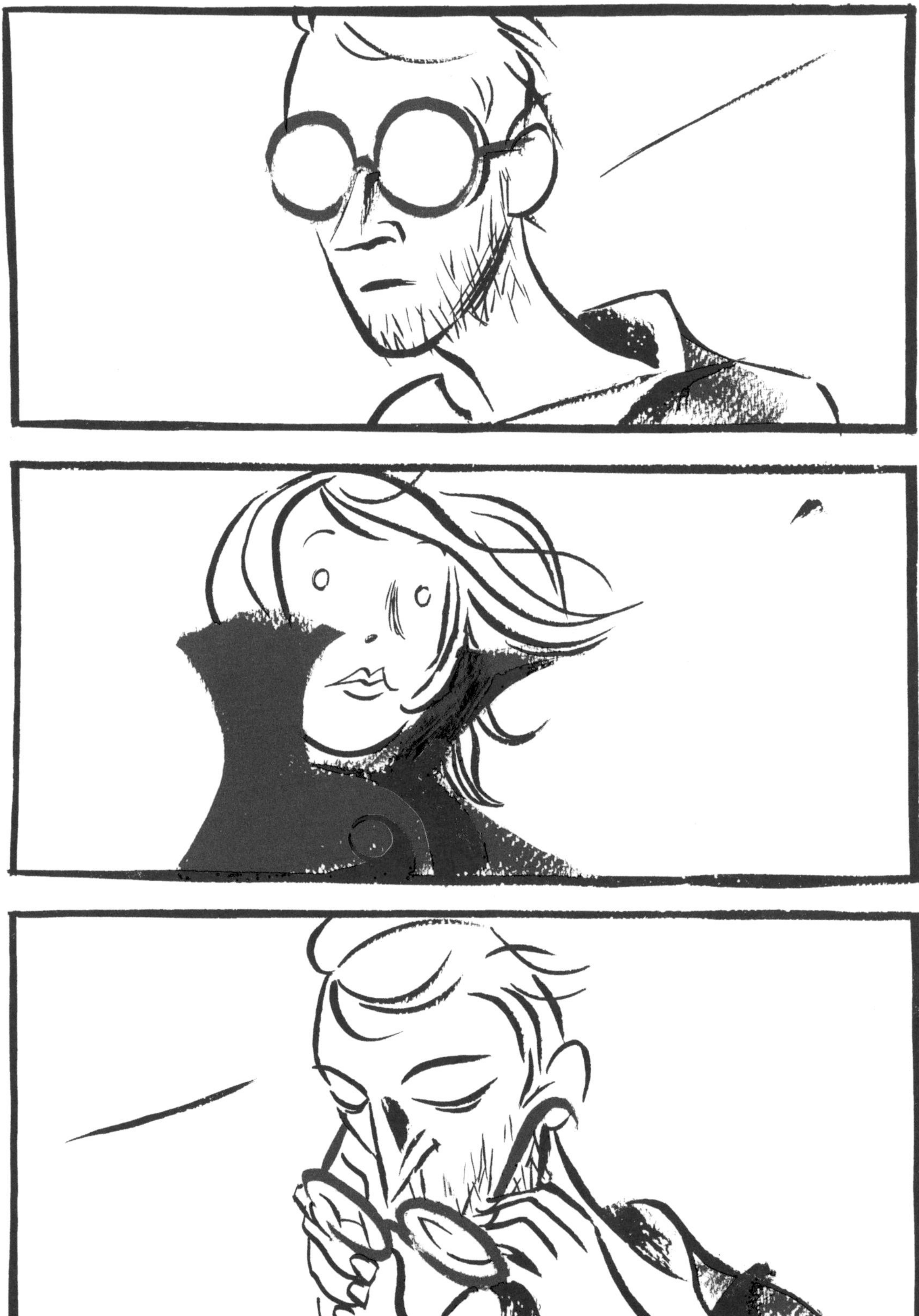

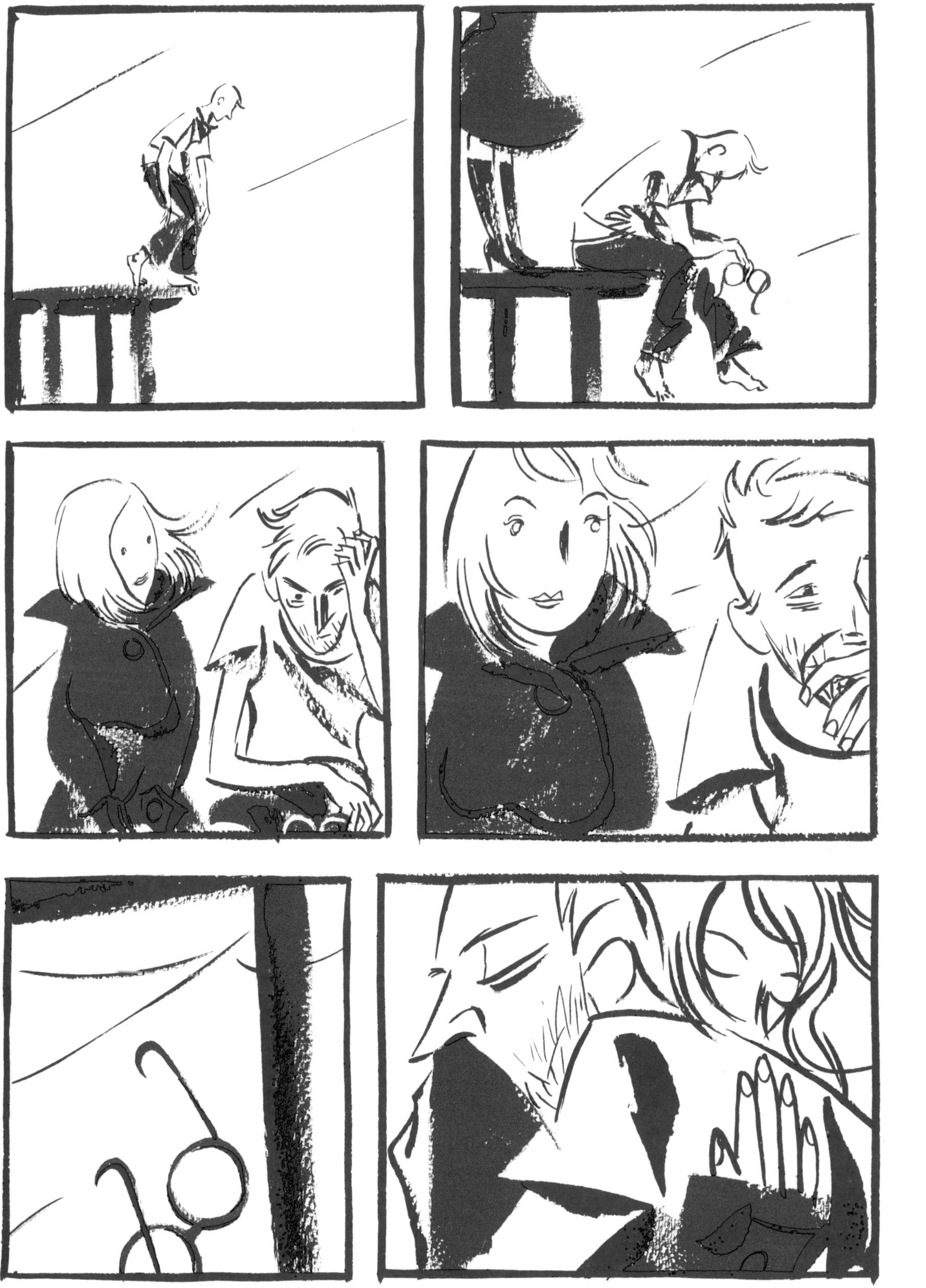

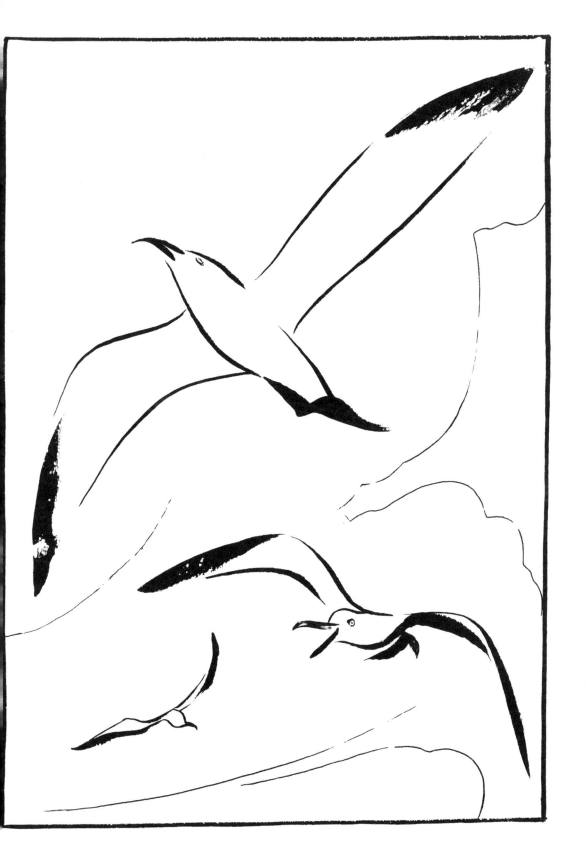

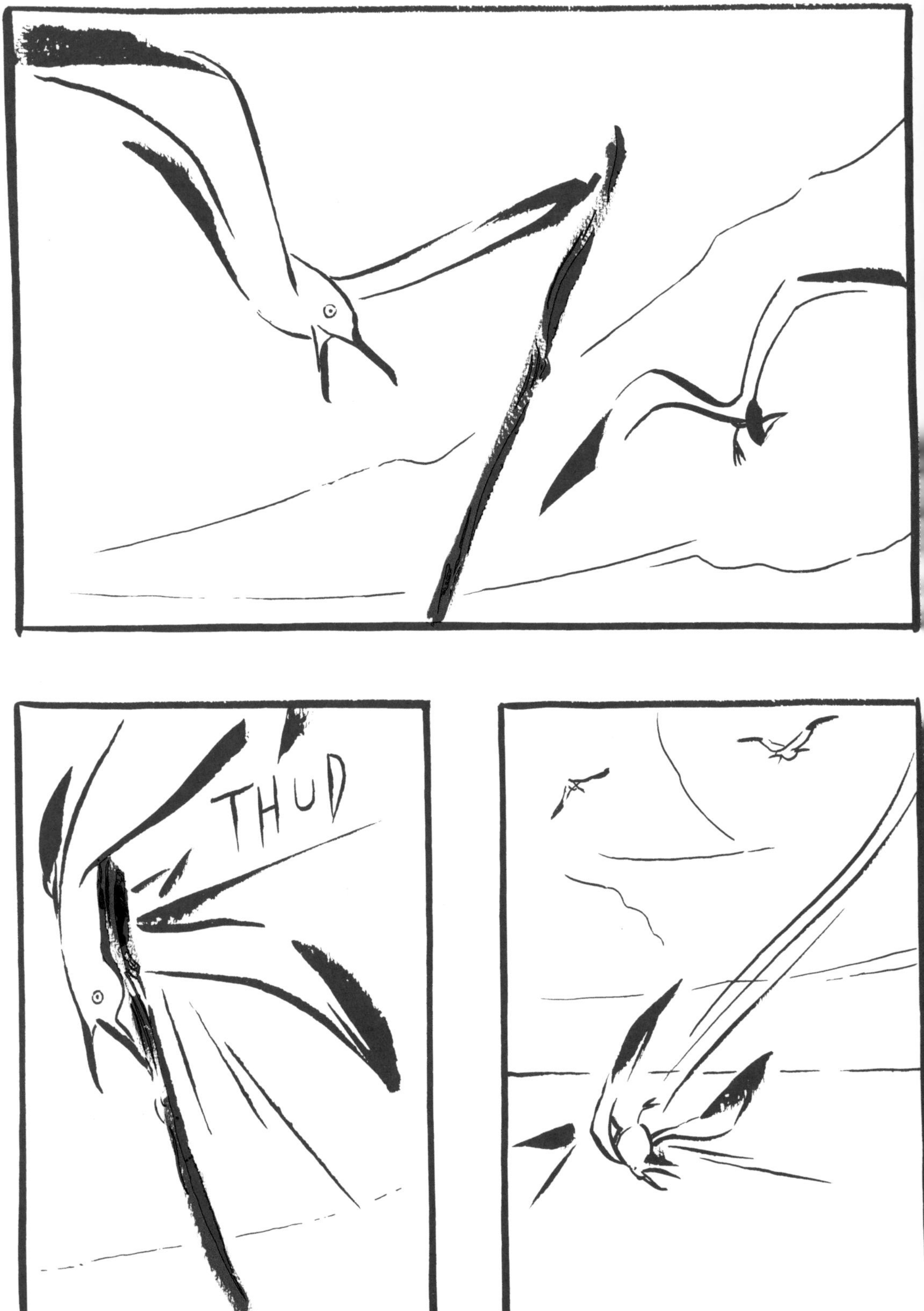
THUD

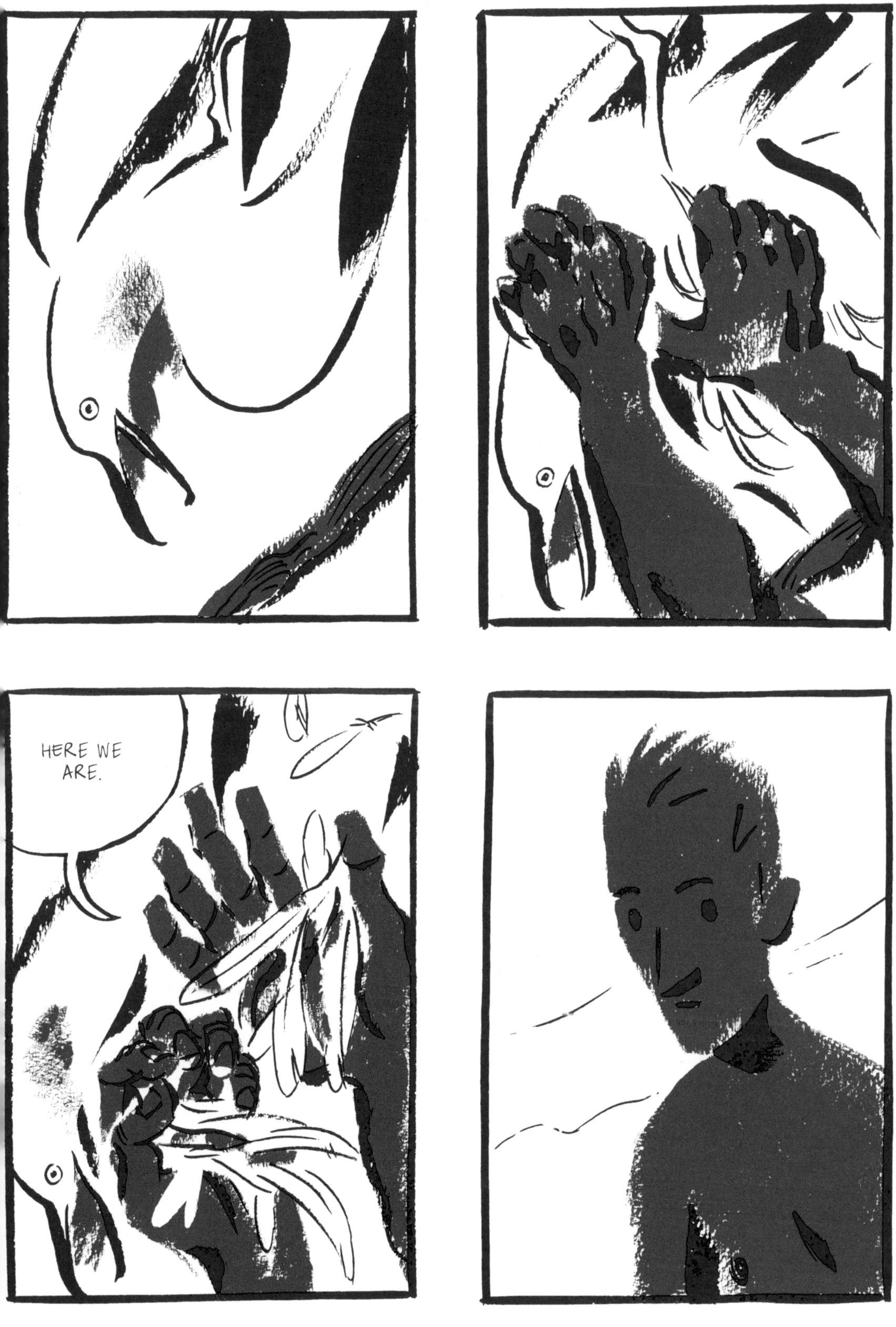
HERE WE ARE.

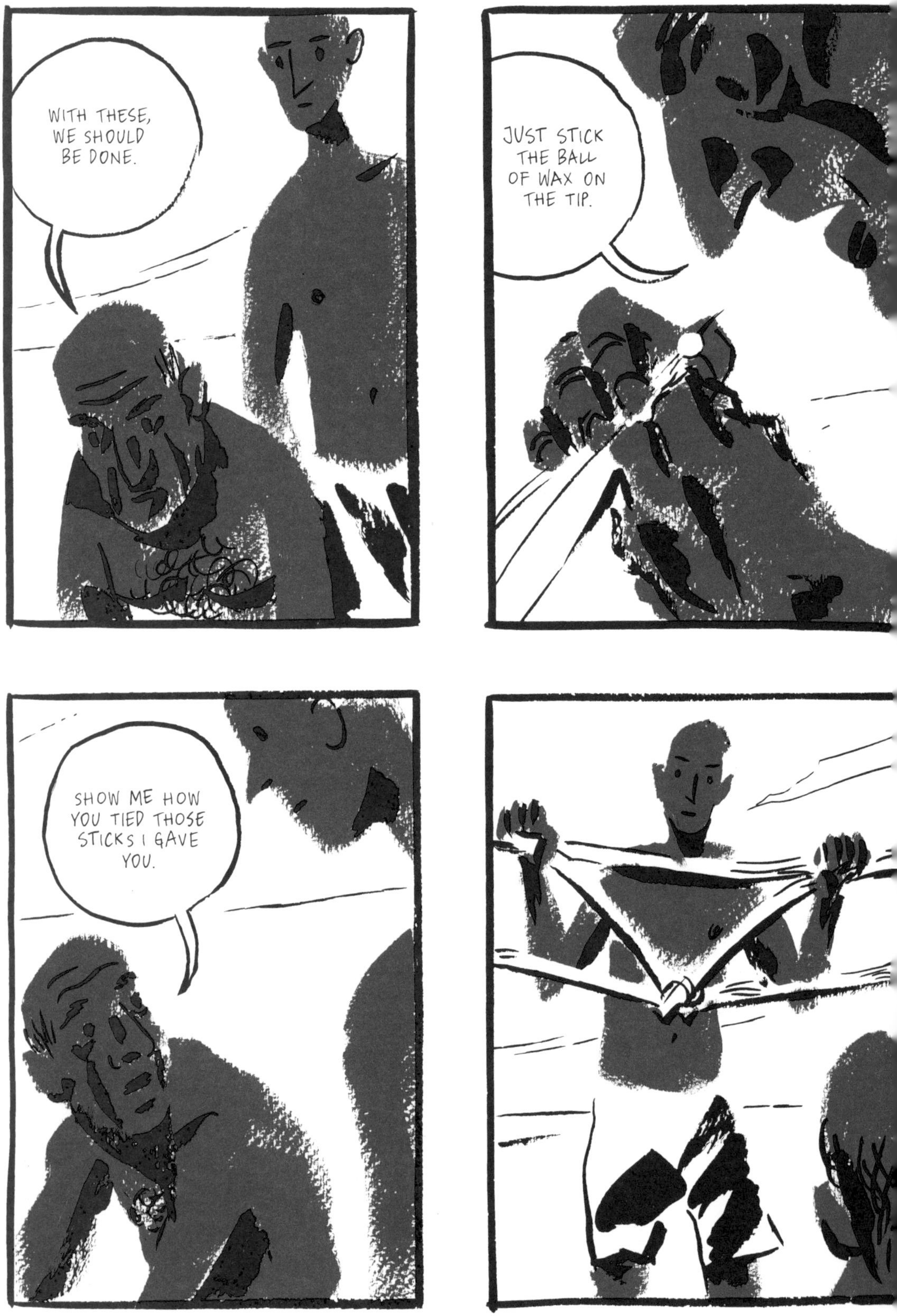
WITH THESE, WE SHOULD BE DONE.
JUST STICK THE BALL OF WAX ON THE TIP.
SHOW ME HOW YOU TIED THOSE STICKS I GAVE YOU.

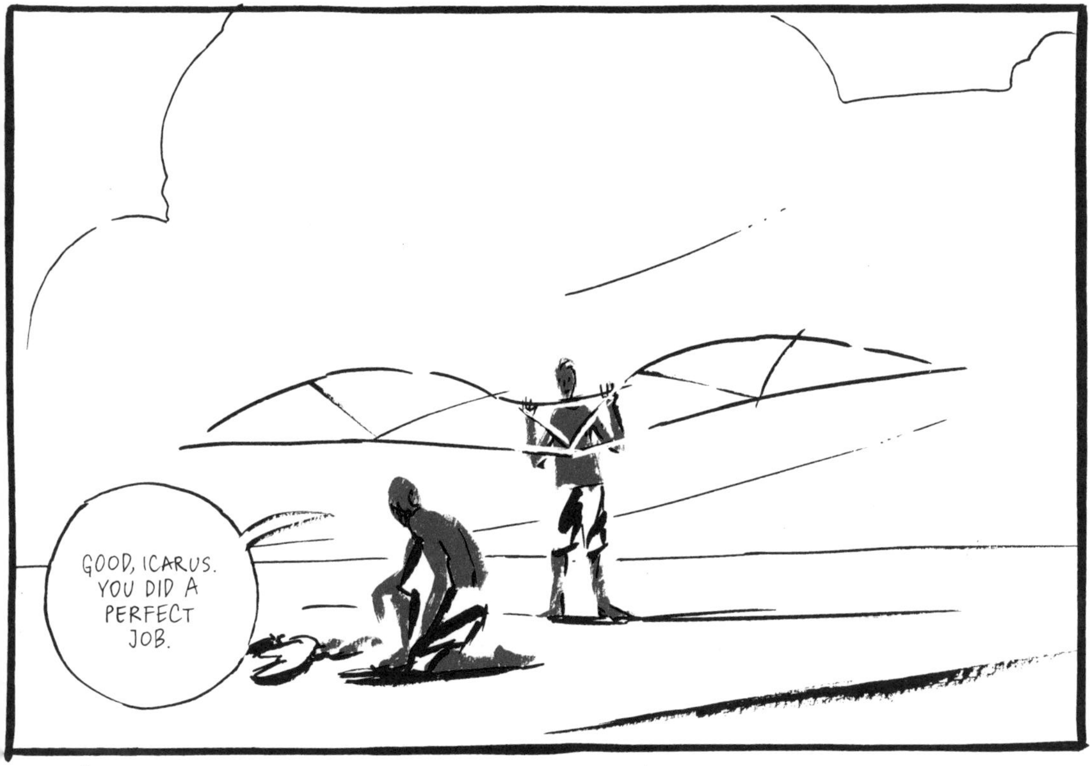
GOOD, ICARUS. YOU DID A PERFECT JOB.

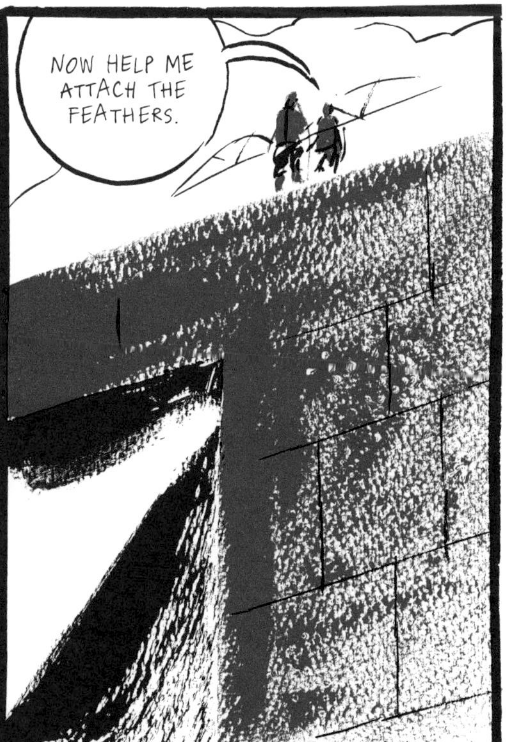
NOW HELP ME ATTACH THE FEATHERS.

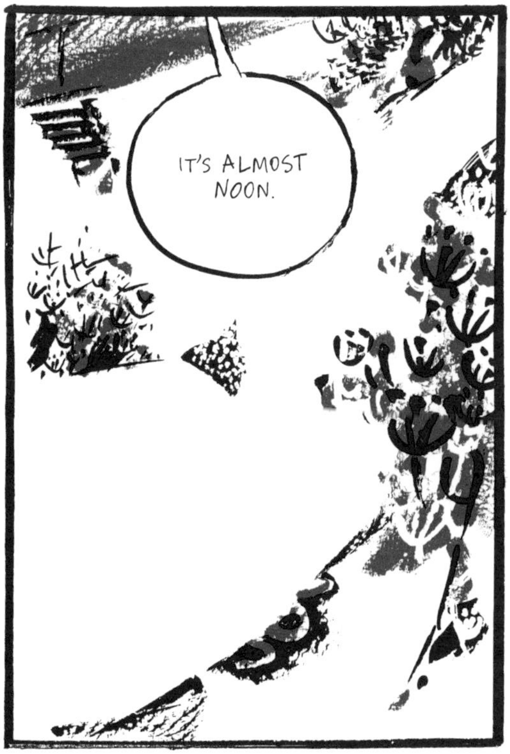
IT'S ALMOST NOON.

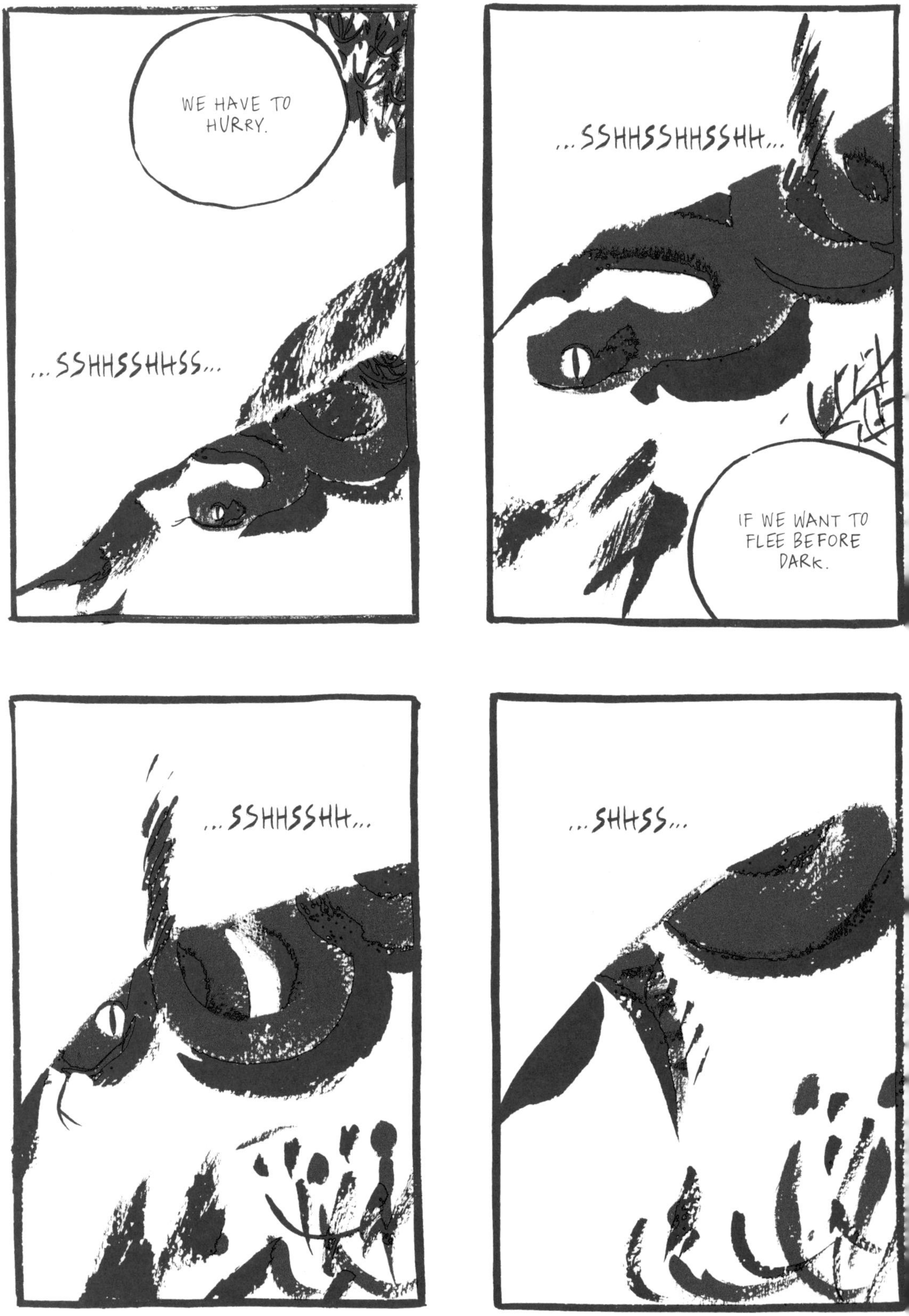
WE HAVE TO HURRY.
...SSHHSSHHSS...
...SSHHSSHHSSHH...
IF WE WANT TO FLEE BEFORE DARK.
...SSHHSSHH...
...SHHSS...

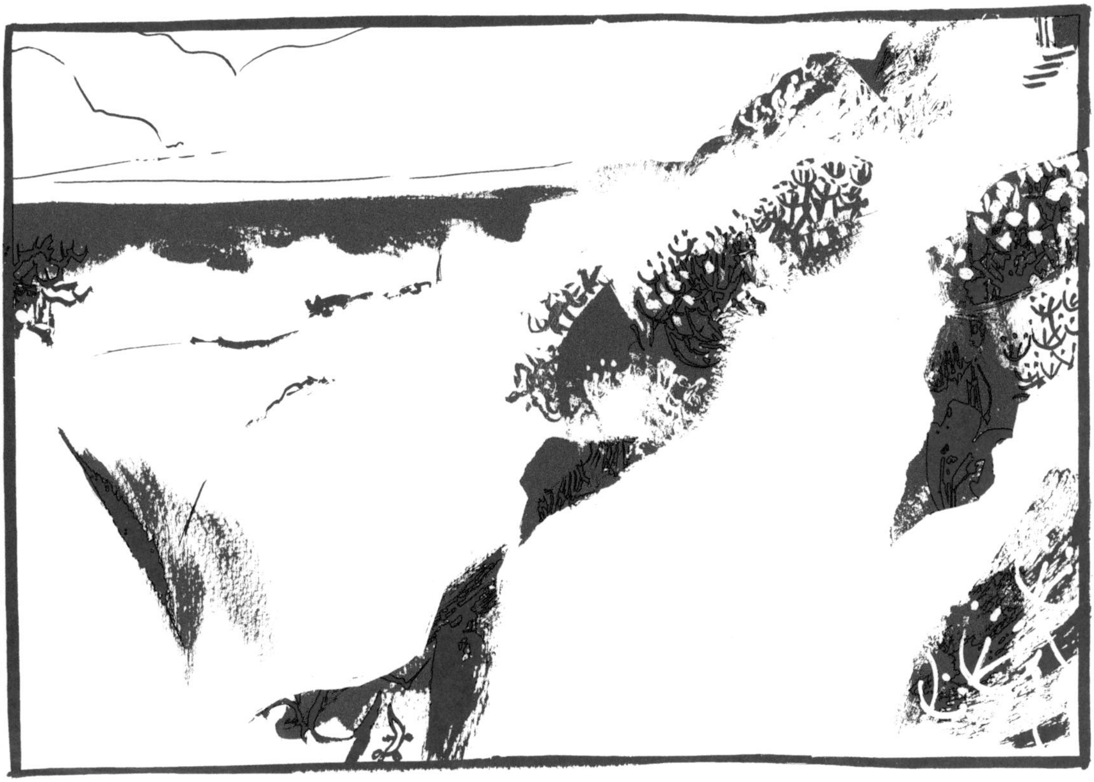

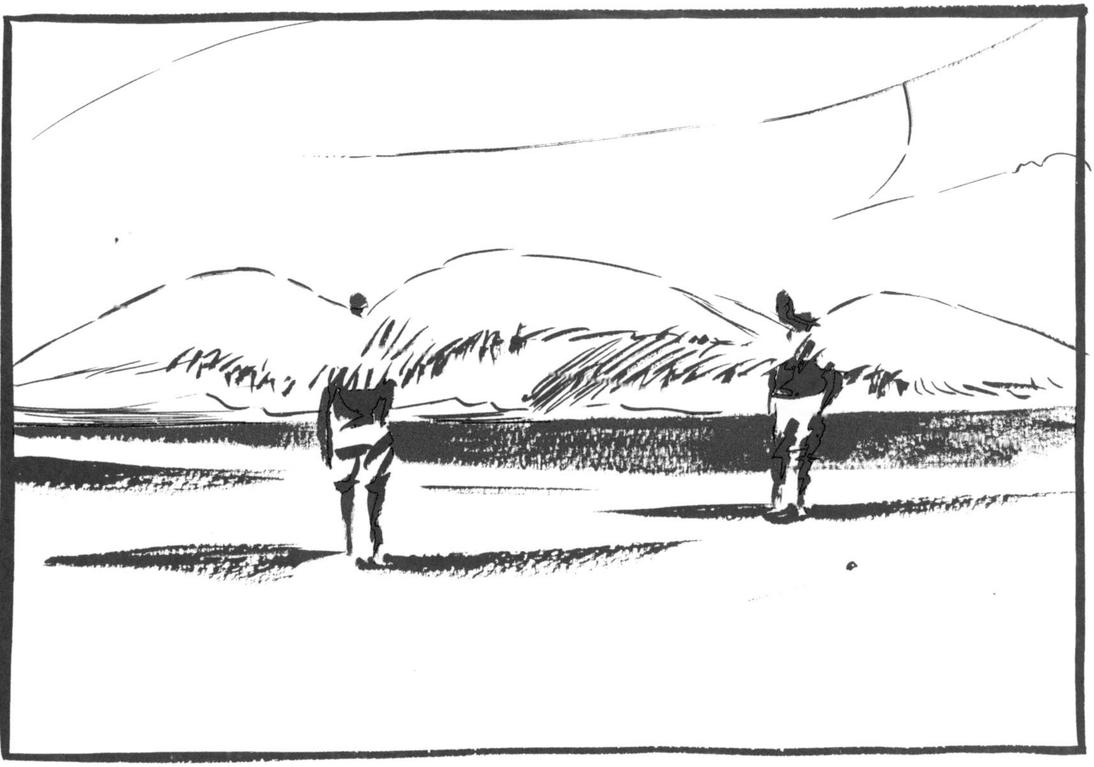

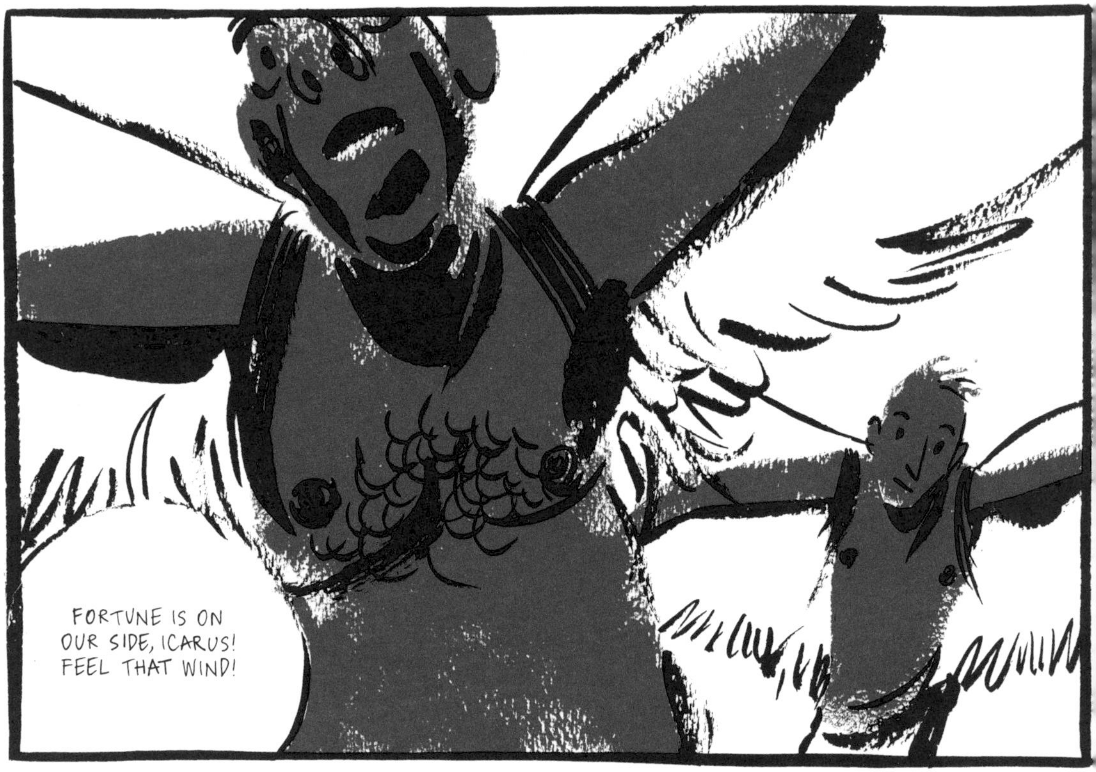
FORTUNE IS ON OUR SIDE, ICARUS! FEEL THAT WIND!

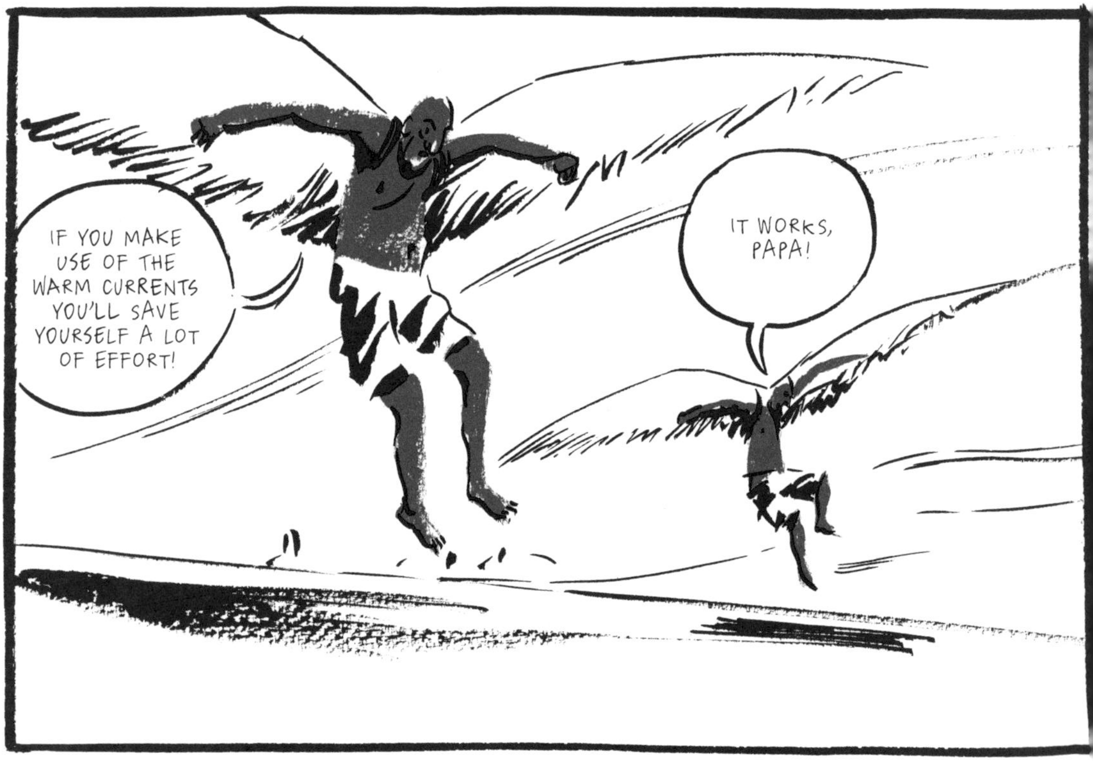
IF YOU MAKE USE OF THE WARM CURRENTS YOU'LL SAVE YOURSELF A LOT OF EFFORT!
IT WORKS, PAPA!

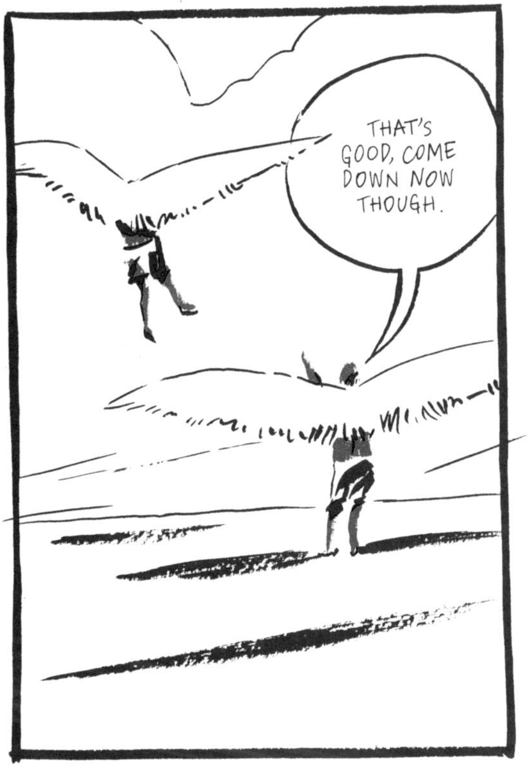
THAT'S GOOD, COME DOWN NOW THOUGH.

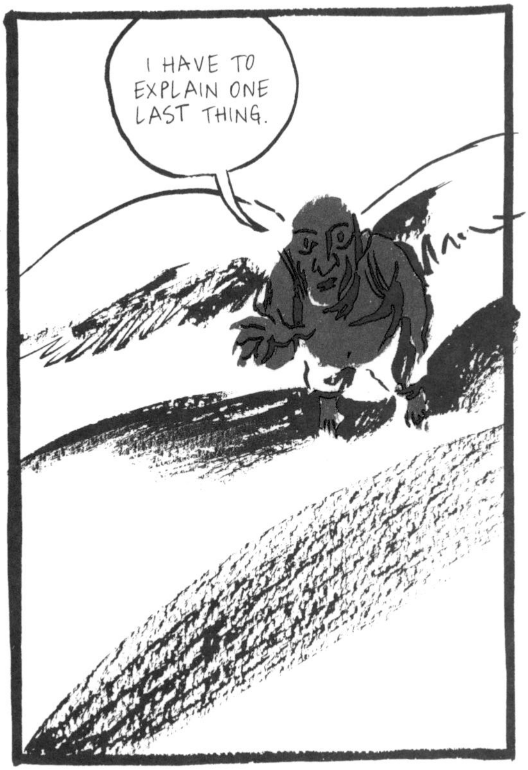
I HAVE TO EXPLAIN ONE LAST THING.

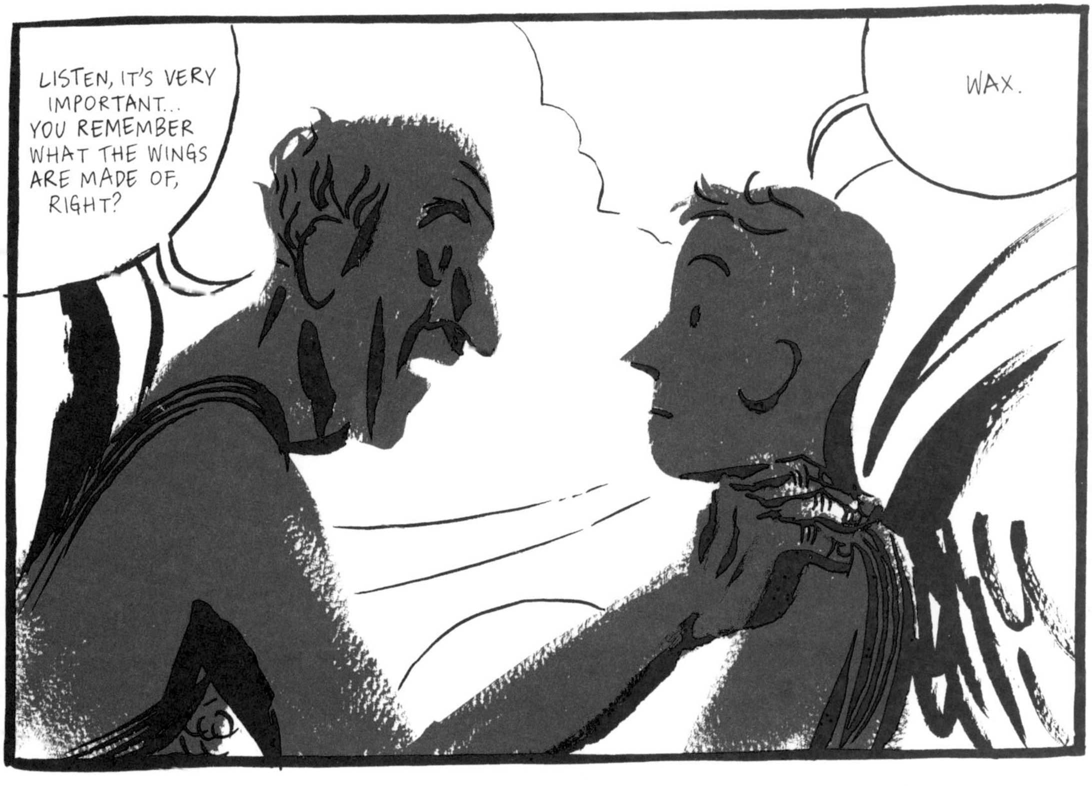
LISTEN, IT'S VERY IMPORTANT... YOU REMEMBER WHAT THE WINGS ARE MADE OF, RIGHT?
WAX.

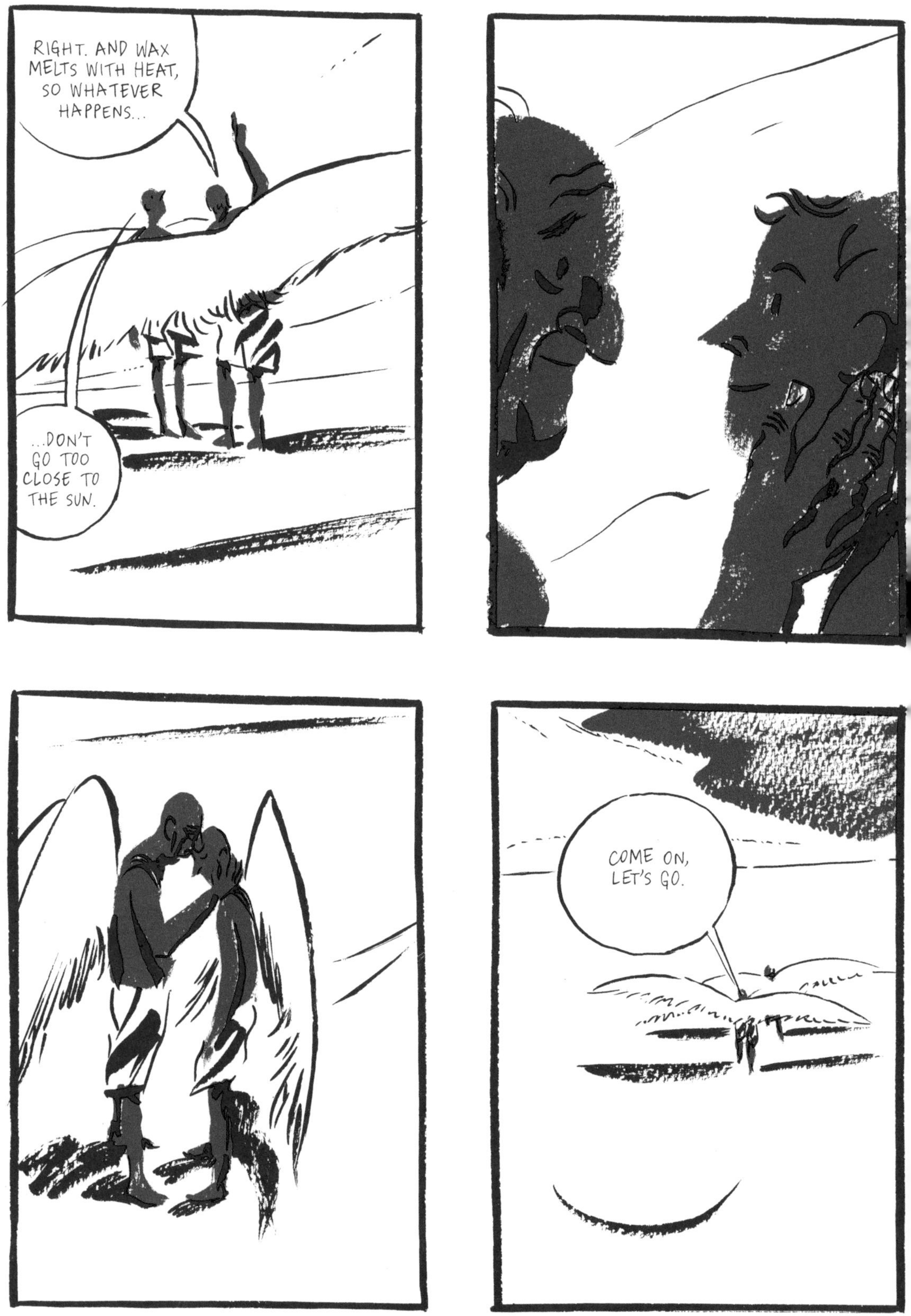
RIGHT. AND WAX MELTS WITH HEAT, SO WHATEVER HAPPENS...
...DON'T GO TOO CLOSE TO THE SUN.
COME ON, LET'S GO.

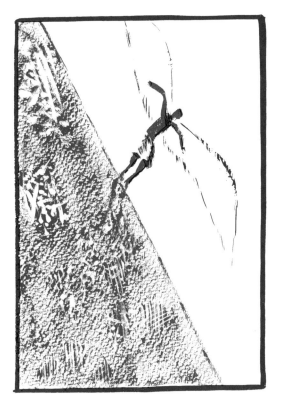

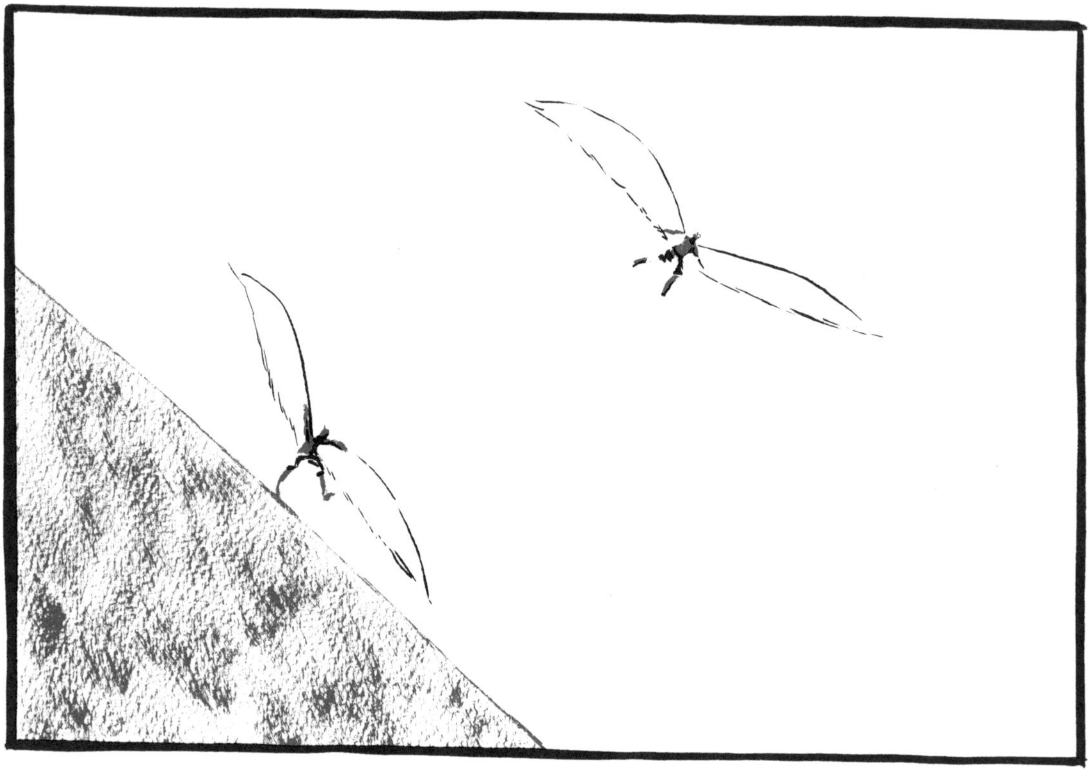

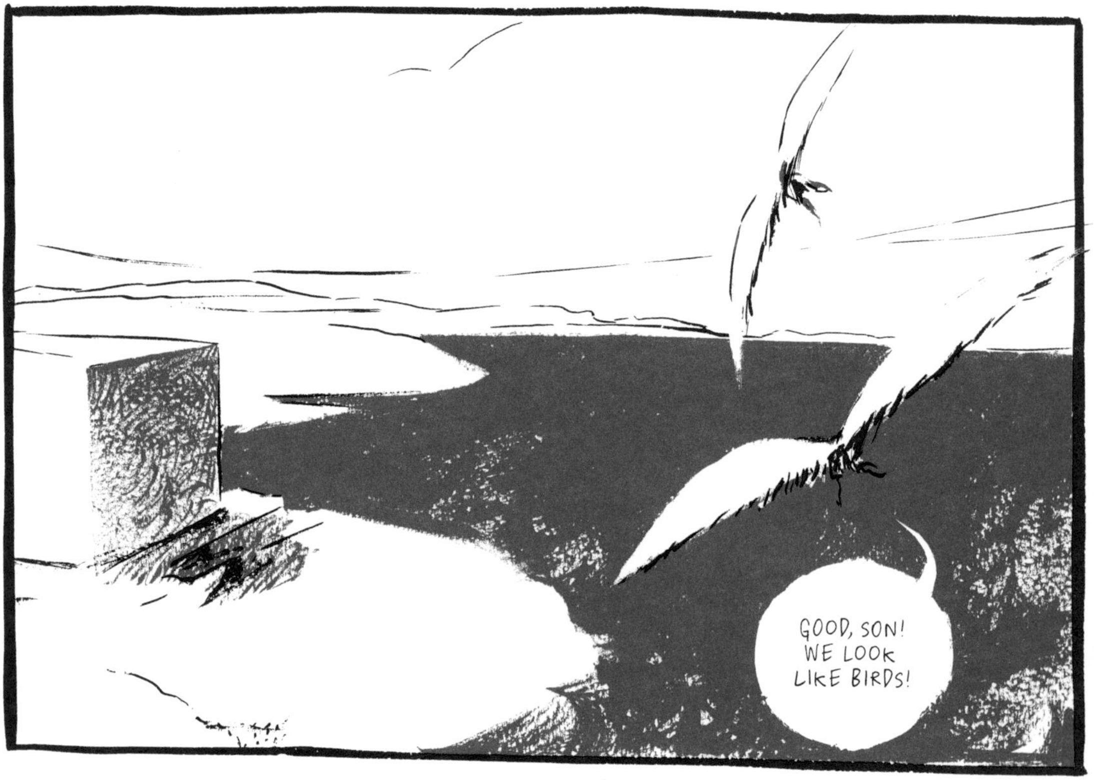
GOOD, SON! WE LOOK LIKE BIRDS!

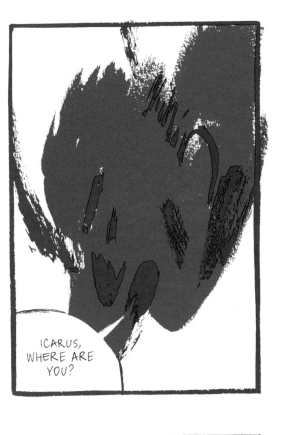

ICARUS,
WHERE ARE
YOU?

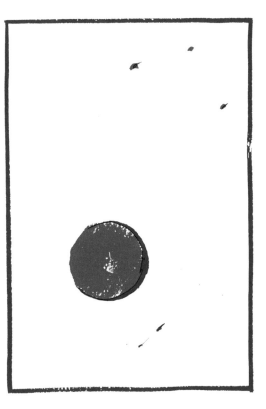

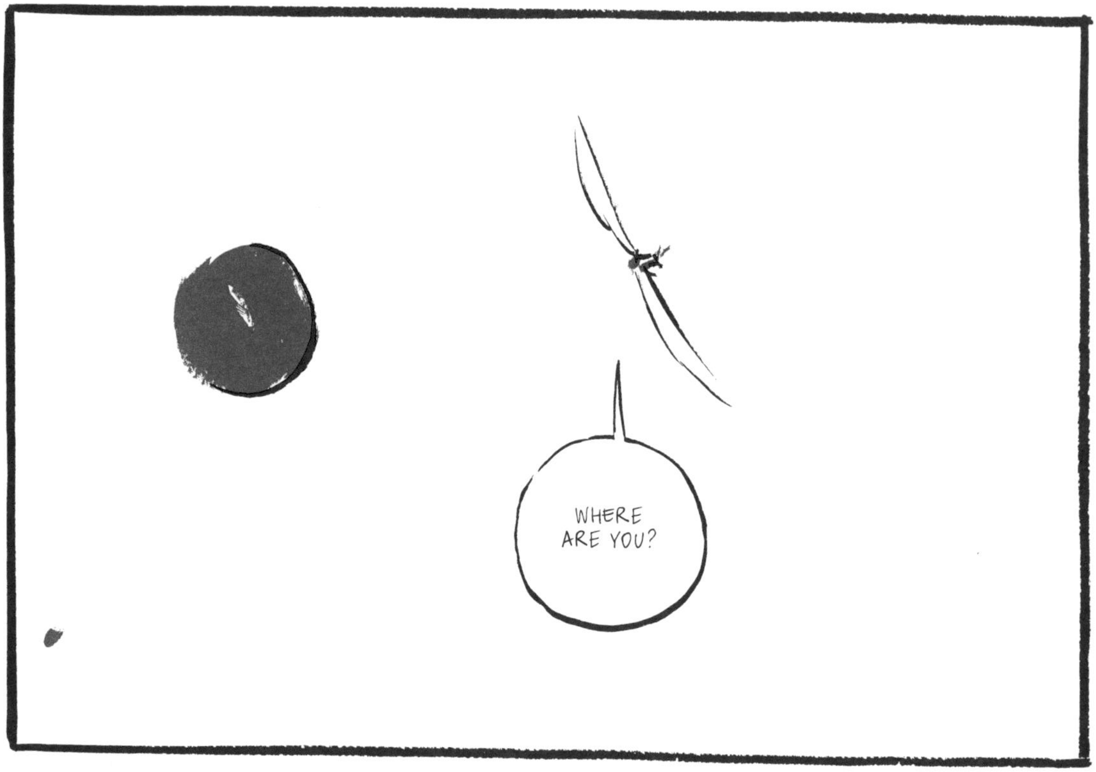
WHERE ARE YOU?

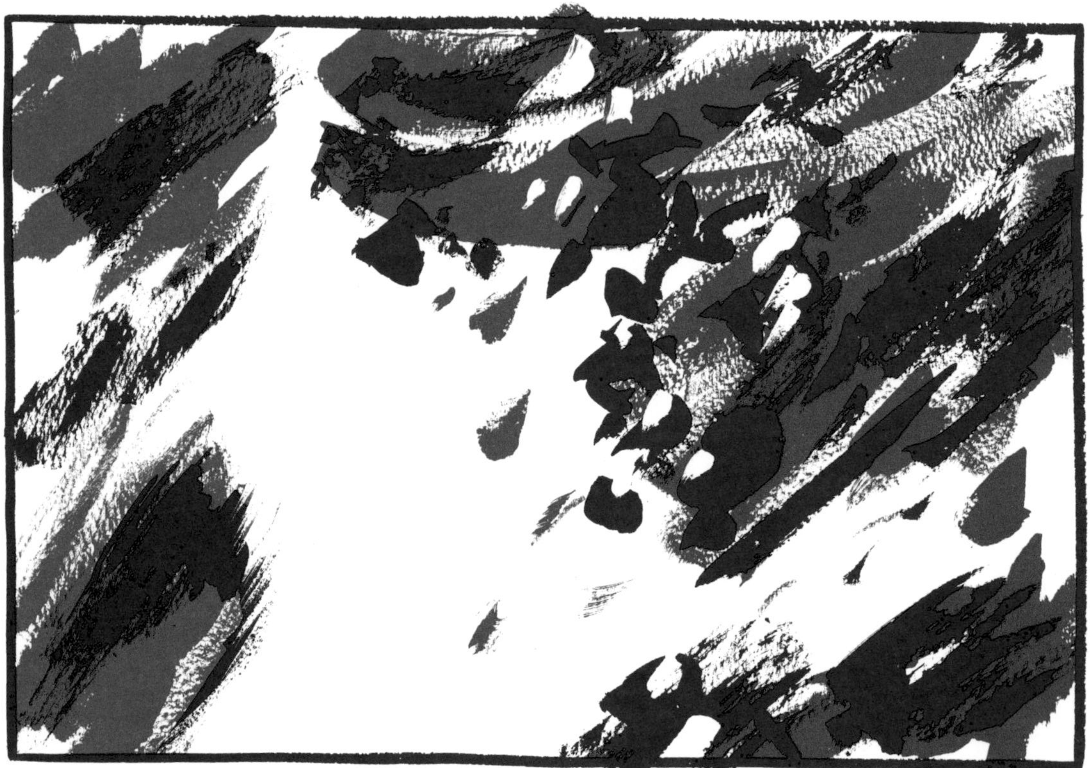

FINE

BERLIN OSLO 04-0
MANUELE FIOR

Thanks to Mom and Dad, Dani and Delica, Martin Gussone, Paola Bristot, and the Modalsli and Kalsnes families. A heartfelt thanks to Anne for inspiration and everything else. — M.F.

Other books by Manuele Fior:
5,000 km Per Second
The Interview
Blackbird Days

FANTAGRAPHICS BOOKS INC.
7563 Lake City Way NE
Seattle, WA 98115
www.fantagraphics.com

Translated from Italian by Jamie Richards
Editor and Associate Publisher: Eric Reynolds
Book Design: Keeli McCarthy
Production: Paul Baresh
Production and editorial assistance: RJ Casey
Publisher: Gary Groth

ISBN 978-1-68396-188-8
Library of Congress Control Number: 2018949683

First printing: April 2019
Printed in China